delicious

A Rumour Mill Novel–Book 1

erica hutchings

Paper Rabbit Books
607 E. Blanco Road, Boerne, TX 78006
Paper Rabbit Books and its logo are registered trademarks.
The publisher is not responsible for websites (or their content) that are not owned by the publisher.

Hutchings, Erica
Delicious/ A Rumour Mill Novel - Anniversary Edition//3rd Revision
ISBN-13: 978-0692401682
ISBN-10: 0692401687
EBook ISBN: 978-0692465882

Editor-Sabrina Scanlan
Cover Image-Shutterstock
Cover Art-Paper Rabbit Books Design

delicious

A Rumour Mill Novel-Book One

erica hutchings

one

uy accelerated on the petrol pedal. His black Range Rover tires squealed on the gravel driveway. He was on a mission to find a wedding cake. With the afternoon sun perched low on the western horizon for its evening sunset he was pressed for time. He had to find a cake and he needed to find it fast.

His best friend, Darren Dowling was getting married in four days time and Darren completely and utterly screwed it up. Even in a serious relationship such as an engagement, Darren couldn't keep his cock in his pants for a rest. And what difference did it make that he was getting married to uber famous glamour model, Tamzin Smythe, in the U.K.'s wedding of the century? The wedding price tag rivalled that of W.A.G.'s (wives and girlfriends of footballers) Coleen Rooney and Victoria Beckham.

Tamzin made sure that she had the best of the best, from her Jimmy Choo shoes, Mercedes Benz SLK and now a rich, famous, hot footballer, husband to boot. Darren was at the top of the English Premier League and the most wanted, valuable player of the League. It didn't matter whether he cheated on her or not. Come hell or high water, she was determined that they both walk the aisle for better or for worse.

And in keeping with their celebrity status and desire to reign as queen of the W.A.G's, Tamzin reserved Worthington Hall on the outskirts of a small village called Ivy-upon-Wye located on the border of England and Wales. It was to be a week of wedding celebration and debauchery that didn't typically come with ordinary wedding celebrations. Although they were pleased with the grounds and accommodations, Tamzin wasn't satisfied with the halls personal chef.

Rather, Tamzin hired renowned celebrity chef Trevor Hare to create and prepare elaborate menus for the week and day of the wedding. As for their wedding cake Tamzin had procured celebrity baker, Libby Blackwell. Libby devised cakes that made every young girl dream about for their own special day. Tamzin was an exception to the rule. The cake she commissioned was to be a gaudy, six tiers, masterpiece that cost over £50,000, which only they could afford.

Five days prior to their big day, the cake was delivered to Worthington Hall. When Chef Hare called Tamzin down to the large culinary kitchen to inspect the elaborate confectionary, she was fevered like a child on Christmas morning. Upon the grand reveal, her excitement diminished faster than a jet going down in flames. The cake presented wasn't the six tier masterpiece she had bought for her wedding. Instead it was a grotesque, white royal iced cake in the shape of a penis which read 'Darren you're a Wanker!' in bold red frosting.

Infuriated, she discovered a note enclosed within the cake box exposing a sordid truth about Darren's affair with the baker. He had ended their affair a little over a week before the wedding and much to the baker's dismay. Libby was under the impression that Darren wasn't going marry Tamzin. But Darren was following through and he couldn't continue the distasteful tryst.

Abashed, she didn't want any of his affairs leaked to the paparazzi, especially Rumour Mill. She stepped out to the south lawn and called Darren and Guy in from playing a friendly game of football with other wedding guests. She smiled sweetly as she coaxed them to the kitchen. There she drew the largest knife available from the butchers block and stabbed the cake in front of them in a feral rage.

"Why did you do this to me?!" she screamed like a wild banshee. *"Out of all the people in the world, you decide to fuck the baker! The world's best baker at that! Why didn't you fuck my best hen instead?"*

Guy didn't hide his disgust. He didn't understand why he had been called into the kitchen to observe another of their barneys. Unfortunately for him, he had been a witness to many of their heated arguments, in which he was forced to pick a side.

Tamzin would endlessly interrogate him, *"Who is Darren shagging besides me?" "Is she better looking than me?" "Is Darren leaving me for her?"* He would nod or answer in short sweet words, yes or no. When Darren finally had enough of Tamzin's questioning Guy, he'd threaten to leave her. It would force her to recoil to her corner and stand by him like a faithful leech.

Many times, Guy had considered ending their friendship and never speaking to him again. But, it was impossible. They played on the same English Premier League, the London Lions and they were also half-brothers, a secret no one knew about. And in typical fashion, Darren never apologised to Guy about his behaviour.

Yet days later after witnessing another battle between the lovebirds, a courier would arrive at Guy's flat with an envelope or package filled with a luxurious trip to Belize, a new set of golf clubs or lifetime VIP package at the gentlemen's club, The Spearmint Rhino. It was always followed by a simple handwritten note, *Thanks mate!*

Guy had hoped that Darren's engagement would have put an end to his playboy ways and finally keep Tamzin happy. Instead the spectacle continued. His stomach did a somersault when he thought of Tamzin as his sister-in-law. He was grateful that his family as a whole weren't close. Slowly and quietly he tried to retreat out of the kitchen, but Tamzin turned to him angrily.

"Stop right there! You're his best mate and you should've known about this matter!" she snapped. She laid it on thick and interrogated him as if he was a terrorist. He thought to himself that he would rather go through SAS rendition than deal with her. "You're going to find me a wedding cake, Guy and you're going to find one fast. Here's a blank cheque and if you don't return with one, I'll have my father rip your bollocks off!" she threatened with heat in her voice.

She wasn't leaving anything to chance. It was her wedding planner who had suggested Libby and persuaded to hire her for the wedding. *After that disaster the only person capable enough to handle the task of procuring a wedding cake is Guy Rowling!*

The brothers looked at each other. They both knew full well that her father was the notorious London gangster, William Smythe. William did anything for his precious princess especially ripping off said bollocks of the men who crossed Tamzin.

He ran his fingers through his jet black hair and sighed. She held out a cream colour envelope to him. He snatched it quickly in hopes of leaving a stinging paper cut on the palm of her hand and stormed out of the kitchen.

I can't wait for this to be over with. As soon as a I head back to London I'm going to have to cut ties some way, he thought bitterly as he drove down the winding roads towards Hereford.

♥

At The Savoury Plum the last customers lingered behind to settle their bills and take final sips of their cappuccinos.

Catherine 'Cat' Fielding smiled at the customers whilst wiping down dirty tables with her tea towel. She placed empty chairs on top of vacant tables. Her twin sister, Corinne 'Corrie' Fielding, was behind the counter laughing with a customer. She was advising them on the best antique shops to visit whilst they spent their weekend in Ivy-upon-Wye.

Through out the valley, it was a glorious fall evening and it wasn't in season for The Savoury Plum to be open so late. The upcoming wedding of celebrities, Darren Dowling and Tamzin Smythe at the nearby hall had brought an influx of customers which spent their weekends in the Cotswolds or the Lake District.

Ivy-upon-Wye sat on a lush green mountainside, above the sparkling river. The village consisted of centuries old stone built homes, thatched cottages and a castle ruin. The small idyllic hamlet was known for its fine art and literary summer festival that drew in a different type of crowd. It was the type that was interested in antique shops, scenic trails or paddling the river. Now the quiet village was overrun by media, celebrities and fans of the famous couple.

Cat and Corrie learned that these new customers were only interested in drinking, partying, fashion and football. It gave the village folk something to chin-wag about. Cat thought they all looked silly wearing woolly sweaters and tweed as they tried to fit in with the locals. Regardless of their looks and attitudes, the twins were grateful for their business. It had brought in profits that they normally accounted for only in the summer months.

The Savoury Plum was known for its aptly-named dishes and sweet delectables. It garnered a cult following in the village and was regarded as '*the*' place to eat brunch and followed by dessert. Customers cooed and awed over the food, especially the pies and cakes. Everyone insisted that whoever baked the treats, should move to London and open a shop.

Corrie would thank all the customers for their glowing compliments and proudly boasted that it was their niece, Grace, who devised the sugary concoctions. Tonight was no different. As Grace walked up the kitchen stairs, she overheard her aunts' conversation.

"Here she is! Our star, Grace!" cried Corrie, opening her arms wide to embrace Grace.

Grace wiped her floured hands on her apron. She gave a shy smile as she hugged Corrie.

"Your bread pudding is heavenly!" complimented a BBC reporter.

"Thank you. I'm glad you liked it." Grace replied, walking around the counter to escort the remaining customers out.

"Have a lovely evening miss. I look forward to the scones tomorrow that your aunt told me about." said the reporter.

"Goodnight, sir. I look forward to seeing you." Grace replied as she closed the door behind him. She flipped over the open/close sign to close and placed her back against the cool glass pane of the door.

"What a day!" Grace sighed heavily, "I've got carrot cakes cooling. There are three chocolate pies sitting in the fridge."

"That's great! All the sausage rolls been made?" asked Cat wiping down the last table, before placing a tray of dirty dishes on the service counter.

"Yes." Grace replied, tucking a piece of long caramel brown hair behind her ear. It fell from her tousled bun. "I wonder if it'll ever be this busy when I open my own shop." she wondered out loud.

Corrie and Cat rolled their eyes. The idea of Grace leaving them frightened the women. They had raised her since she was a little girl and thought of her as the daughter they would've had if they had only gotten married. Neither of the twins had settled down or married, and mostly because they didn't want to. The twins were quite content with their small family.

It was Jane, their younger sister and Grace's mother, who was to be the one to leave Ivy. Jane and her twin sisters, Corrie and

Cat were born in Ivy-upon-Wye, and they were raised in a three bedroom flat above the shop. The three-hundred year old bakery had been passed down from generation to generation. When Jane left for London to attend the London Culinary Academy, their parents retired from the bakery. They handed it over to the twins in Jane's absence.

During her education in London, Jane met and fell in love with her teacher, Gordon Knowles. Gordon was a handsome chap with short-blonde hair, cornflower blue eyes, and a wide grin. Besides teaching, he was a well-known London chef. In the 70's, Gordon worked in various hotels and in the early 80's, he made a big splash with Asian fusion in London.

Gordon opened a restaurant called Blue Monday in Covent Garden. He hired Jane for his dessert station. She quickly became known for her chocolate wontons filled with strawberry crème mousse.

It was in the small confines of the gourmet kitchen, the flirting between Gordon and Jane intensified. Under his tutelage and constant attention, Jane quickly became infatuated with him.

Within a year they started dating, fell in love, got married and bought a house together in Tooting Bec Common, a London suburb. Gordon had determined it was a great place to raise a family and convenient to travel to the restaurant by tube. On their days off, Gordon and Jane played tennis, swam in the Lido, and went horseback riding. They vacationed on the Devon coast and visited family during the holidays. One hot summer day in 1985, Gordon and Jane welcomed a plump, rosy, baby girl. They lovingly named their daughter, Grace Ann Knowles, and proudly introduced her to their family.

When she was three years old, a horrible tragedy struck their small family. Alistair Knowles, Gordon's younger brother, babysat Grace whilst her parents attended a dinner function in Kensington. On their way back home, their car was hit head on by a drunk driver. The couple died instantly. All that was left was an unrecognisable mangled mess of steel and blood.

Immediately upon hearing the news, Corrie and Cat drove to Tooting Bec Common to bury Jane and Gordon and collect Grace. Assigned as Graces' legal guardians they packed her belongings for her long journey back to Ivy-upon-Wye. Grace never stepped foot in London again.

Grace had inherited a substantial amount of wealth from her parents', including their Victorian home and the building where Blue Monday occupied the ground floor. At the time of their death, she was too young to manage her finances and so Alistair moved into the Knowles former home. Blue Monday had closed and the commercial front was leased to a fashion chain. The flats above the shuttered restaurant were converted and leased as commercial office space. All the money procured from the leases was placed in interest bearing accounts for Grace.

In the beginning and during the holidays Alistair frequently visited Grace and the twins. He wanted to ensure that he didn't miss any moment of his niece growing up. But by the time Grace became a teen the dynamics had changed. His visits were infrequent, but he continued to write to her and call often. When Grace felt her aunts' were being unreasonable, she would gladly talk to Alistair about it. He would listen like a friend and advise like one as well. He insisted that Grace called him Alistair and never, ever, an Uncle.

Years went by. As Grace grew older, taller and beautiful, the twins grew into two, overprotective hens. They didn't view her as a niece but as a daughter. It made life very difficult and awkward for her.

Although the twins had dated men here and there, they never dared to bring a man home, out of respect for Grace and for one another. They thought it was unladylike to do so. But Grace often felt that they had prudish, antiquated views on love, romance and sex. She daydreamt of having a boyfriend, falling in love and getting married. Yet Cat and Corrie insisted that she focus on her career as a pastry chef with the hope of one day running The Savoury Plum.

Since she was a baby, Grace always had a wooden spoon in her hand. Whether it was making mud pies in the garden with her father or learning how to bake the simplest of chocolate fairy cakes with her aunts, Grace had the love and genetics of a pastry chef. She often wondered if her parents would've been proud. Every night, before Grace went to bed, she would look longingly at a silver picture frame on the nightstand. Encased in the frame was black and white wedding picture of her parents.

When she graduated Upper school, Grace feared that she was leaving home too soon. Instead of continuing her education, she chose to work down in the kitchen alongside Corrie. Over the years, she honed her skills and soon her pastries were gaining attention from customers and critics alike. On several occasions small newspaper food critics visited The Savoury Plum and gave favourable reviews in decor, service, and food.

But it was a well-known *Guardian* food-critic who put The Savoury Plum on the map. The critic wrote a glowing review about Grace's strawberry cheesecake made from organic cow's milk and hand-plucked strawberries. The national publicity drew in tourists from miles and miles away all looking to sample her famous cheesecake. It was a popular summer item and would sell out frequently.

As the compliments and business increased, so too did Cat and Corrie's dependence on Grace. All the constant praise began to bother Grace, who now at twenty-five years old, felt as though she'd never leave The Savoury Plum. She felt she was destined to be a spinster and tied to her aunts' stove. This wasn't the destiny she had dreamt of and she wasn't sure if it was what her parents wanted for her either.

The feeling of leaving spun like a mixing bowl paddle. It started slowly and gradually increased in speed as time went by. A myriad of ideas in full spin tempted her to go off on her own and start a life without her aunts.

During her free time Grace developed a business plan and got her finances in order. She decided that this was to be her last winter in Ivy-upon-Wye. She was finally going to branch out and move to London. There, she was planning on opening her own bakery-cafe called *Delicious*.

"Again with ideas of your own place? Your home is here." Corrie commented dryly. She turned off the lights in the window.

Corrie pulled bread baskets from the window display and looked at Grace fiddling with some crookedly hung artwork on a nearby wall.

"I'll do it, you know. You can't keep me in Ivy forever," she sighed.

"I know, Grace. But we always hoped that you would inherit The Savoury Plum and stay with us. What's out there for you?" Cat asked.

"An adventurous life. All my life, I've lived in this village. The farthest I've ventured is to Hereford or on the odd chance a shopping spree in Cardiff. I always go to the same pub with Olivia and see the same people. I want to go to London and experience life like my mother." Grace straightened the corner of the frame; the glass reflected the twinge of sadness in her eyes.

The twins folded their pudgy arms under their bosoms in response. They reminded Grace of the fairy godmothers in Disney movies such as *Sleeping Beauty*. They had wispy silver hair, soft white round faces and plump bodies. They wore their daily uniform, black trousers and white cotton t-shirts with purple lettering of the business.

A loud bang on the glass panes of the door, made them all jump in fright. Corrie, Cat and Grace turned to see a shadowy figure peering through the panes.

"Bloody hell! Who's there?" barked Cat. She armed herself with a broom and marched over to the door.

"Who is it, Cat?" asked Corrie worried.

Cat looked out to see the face of a handsome young man staring back at her.

"Please...Please let me in!" a young man begged. He looked no more than in his late twenties. Cat thought it was a patron from the pub across the road, looking for trouble.

"We're closed. If you need a phone, you can go back to the pub across the road." Cat snapped loudly.

"I don't need a phone! I need a bloody wedding cake! I was told you're the best there is! " he growled loudly.

Grace walked up behind Cat. She saw the frustration on the man's face and pulled on Cat's arm.

"Let him in auntie. Let's hear him out."

Reluctantly, Cat opened the door. As the young man took a step in, Grace thought for a split second God must have heard her prayers. *Phwoar! He's a male model who must have fallen from the sky!*

Guy thanked Cat profusely as he entered, exhausted from his search. As soon as he saw Grace he at a loss for words. Guy tried thinking of something to say but he was stunned by the beauty. The gorgeous young woman standing before him was in between the two elderly women looking like Staffordshire terriers on the attack.

He noticed how pretty the colour of her eyes were, a cool aquamarine reminding him of the waters of Turks and Caico. Her skin looked naturally sun-kissed and flushed, which was unusual for fair English rose girls. Most of the girls he knew had airbrush tans to achieve the sun-kissed look. He loved the look of her hair, pinned up in a messy bun, and tendrils caressing her glowing face. It was as if she had woken up from a night of in between the sheets. He wouldn't have mind twirling his fingers in her tousled tendrils of caramel hair. Guy noticed a small spray of freckles on the bridge of her nose and pretty smile. She wasn't skinny. She had an hourglass shape which he desired in his women. *Perfect curves! Something to wrap my hands around as we make love,* he thought.

He shook his head in disbelief. He couldn't believe he was standing there and thinking about having illicit sex with this girl. He barely knew her and he needed to get his mind back on track. *No wonder Darren got into trouble. If Libby was this gorgeous, I would've shagged her too!* She spoke, breaking her bewitching spell on him.

"What can we do for you, sir?" she asked pointedly.

"I need a wedding cake for the Dowling-Smythe wedding." Guy answered hurriedly. "And I need it fast."

The aunts' mouths dropped open and Grace was rendered speechless.

♥

two

ou need a cake for the wedding?" Grace questioned. She didn't believe Guy. It sounded like it a bad prank. "You're pulling my leg and wasting our time. Everyone knows that Tamzin Smythe hired the famous Libby Blackwell to bake her wedding cake. It's all over the tabloids especially Rumour Mill. And just who might you be sir? *The Prince of Wales?*" She didn't hide her growing annoyance. The jolt from his loud knock and her prior conversation with her aunts' placed her in a bad mood.

Guy swiped his hand over his brows. *This is my last resort.* He had driven all the way to nearest, small city of Hereford, only to discover all the bakeries were closed. The nearest big city was Cardiff and he was reluctant to drive all the way there only to make the same discovery. He was fortunate that a stranger had recognised him and asked him for a picture and an autograph. He had obliged only on the condition of a favour. It sent him straight to the doorstep of The Savoury Plum.

"I'm sorry. I should've introduced myself. My name is Guy Rowling. I am a striker for the London Lions football team. I play alongside Darren Dowling and I'm his best man in his wedding." he replied with assurance. "There's a problem with the Blackwell cake. It didn't turn out as promised. Here's an envelope with a blank cheque from Tamzin Smythe." He held out the envelope to Grace, gesturing its contents. "She'll pay any price for the cake, even double that of the Blackwell cake, as long as you follow the instructions or provide something similar." he added, his eyes encouraging Grace to take the envelope.

Earlier on their tea break, Cat had read a two-page spread in Rumour Mill about Tamzin Smythe's cake. It was rumoured to have cost £50,000. It was to be a massive, six-tier-sponge cake with edible gold fondant. Each layer was to be decorated with handcrafted grape leaves, flowers, nymphs and faeries. On the top there was to be a handcrafted glass cake topper in the image of a Greek god and goddess resembling the couple. The women had joked that it wasn't something to be eaten.

"Tell us the truth. What are you playing at? We're closed for the evening and tired!" Corrie snapped.

After the restaurant closed for the evening the ladies would retire upstairs to their flat for a hot shower and tea. They loved to settle in front of the telly and watch *EastEnders*. Grace would have shower, eat a late dinner, and sometimes watch telly with them. As of late though, she'd retreat to her bedroom to email solicitors and accountants. Sometimes, if she was up to it, Grace would go out with Olivia, a young employee of theirs.

Grace saw that he was anxious. His face was red, and he had beads of sweat on his brow. He seemed to be telling the truth. Slowly her resolved softened as she watched him shift on his feet still gingerly holding out the envelope as a plea. She felt that there was more to the story than he was letting on and with her aunts on the assault it didn't help the situation. She was willing to listen to Guy, especially as handsome as he was.

Her mind meandered. She wondered what it'd be like to run her fingers through his thick windswept jet black hair. She loved his deep cocoa eyes which brightened against his tanned skin. Her imagination went wild with wonder on how Guy looked underneath his fitted shirt. She hoped he was muscular for a footballer. She imagined Guy pressing his big body against hers, pulling at her hair and devouring her succulent lips. It made her weak in the knees and she let out a small gasp of excitement. She prayed no one noticed.

"Aunties', why don't you go upstairs? I'll deal with him." she insisted.

"I'm not leaving you alone with him." Cat said narrowing her steely grey eyes at Guy. She wasn't leaving Grace alone with this sexy stud-muffin of a football player. She couldn't remember when men during her youth had looked this handsome. *If they did look this hot on the pitch, I'd watch football faithfully,* Cat thought in stony silence.

"I'll be fine. It's obvious he isn't lying. He needs a wedding cake. Let me discuss this with him. I won't be long. I promise." Grace implored. She pleaded with her eyes for her aunts' to let her be and handle it.

They stepped away and stalked off to the door that led up to the flat. They turned around a final time and Grace waved off. They closed the door, leaving it slightly ajar to eavesdrop whilst they perched on the stairs.

When she thought they were finally gone, Grace turned her full undivided attention to him. She went around the store counter.

"Would you like a drink?" she offered. Guy nodded. She took some elderflower presses from an under counter fridge. She twisted the bottle caps off setting one bottle down in front of him. He stood at the counter watching her, grateful. He hadn't stopped for a drink since he left Worthington Hall.

"Thanks!" he replied after taking a long swig from the cool green bottle. The cool liquid was refreshing just as she was appealing to the eyes.

"Please, tell me why you're here." she said throwing out the bottle caps in a wastebasket behind her.

Guy noticed a small, heart shaped birthmark on her neck as Grace turned her head. He wanted to reach out and touch it, but was startled when he realised she was now staring directly at him.

"Please, don't tell the paparazzi what I am about to tell you," he said. "I'm sure it'll be leaked at some point, but I'd rather that happen later." She nodded. He took her nod as acceptance. She had no interest in talking to the paparazzi.

"Long story short, Darren shagged the baker. It seems they were having an affair throughout his engagement to Tamzin. Libby Blackwell thought that he was going to leave Tamzin for her. When that didn't happen she finished the cake for Tamzin. Only it turns out that it wasn't *exactly* what Tamzin ordered. It was a giant prick–cake with some choice words for Darren on it." He felt relieved by the confession. *It's good to get it out in the open. And admitting it to a natural beauty is even better. This wedding is driving me up the wall. All I want to do is to get away from them, all of them!*

Thinking back on it, Guy was grateful that as a family, they *never* got together for the holidays and Sunday roast dinners. Their relationships were unconventional and dreary. They were certainly not normal and if the beauty before him knew the truth he was certain that she wouldn't be interested in him. Tamzin and the public had always assumed Guy and Darren were just best mates. And Darren and Guy preferred to keep it that way for the sake of keeping their family secrets just that, *secrets*.

Grace's eyes went wide in amazement. *A cake in the shape of a penis! How vile and vulgar! How embarrassing for the bride! How come Tamzin didn't cancel the wedding?*

He saw the million pound question was lingering in on the tip of her tongue. "They'd never leave each other." he answered noticing the puzzled expression on her face. "As a couple, they're worth millions of pounds together. She turns a blind eye to Darren's cheating ways just as long as she's kept minted in the finest of clothes, cars and trips. The public love and adore them. They're this generations' Beckham."

Grace understood it. Darren Dowling and Tamzin Smythe were always on the front cover of Rumour Mill. Every day the tabloids were filled with everything and anything about the celebrity couple and their wedding. There was even a special on the Rumour Mill channel called *Tamzin to the Altar*. It was even rumoured that the couple had sold their wedding pictures to Rumour Mill for more than what Hollywood's biggest movie stars were paid for. As the U.K.'s and Europe's number one best selling tabloid and with competition for other tabloids in international circulation, it was the best way to get worldwide recognition.

"So, now they need a wedding cake." she quipped. "Can I see the instructions?"

He slid the envelope to her. As she opened it he noticed the length of her fingers. They were long and her nails were cut short and shaped round. They weren't shellacked or the length of talons painted in an array of colours, a look coveted by W.A.G's.

She carefully read through the instructions and looked over the sketch. She frowned. There were similarities to the Blackwell cake, but it was virtually impossible to make given the time frame and space. *There's no way I can pull this off.*

"Where does she expect me to pull this from? A magician's hat? She's asking for things that are out of season like coconut filling. Coconut's out of season. Four days isn't enough time. We already lost today and besides I don't have the kitchen space or help." she concluded biting her lip in deep thought.

He noticed her biting. He wanted to lean over and grab her right then and to pull her over the counter to suck, bite and kiss her scarlet lips. He shook his head. He tried to focus at the problem looming before him. *She's my only option. I'm not leaving The Savoury Plum unless I have a cake and her, too.*

"Look, can you please put something, anything together?! It doesn't need to be exact. I can take you anywhere you need to go to get supplies. She needs it desperately." he begged.

"It's Tuesday night. I could try to pull something together by Saturday, but the problem is kitchen space and staff. I'm truly sorry. I can't help you."

She was sincere in her response. As much as Grace wanted to do this so she'd get a foot in the door among London's upper crust it was impossible. She didn't have the capability of creating such a cake in such a small space in such a short amount of time.

Guy looked at her with his sad, cocoa eyes. He was laying it on thick, trying to convince her. She pulled her shoulders back. He saw remorse in her eyes. A light bulb went on in his head.

"What if you stayed at Worthington Hall? I can get you a room and you can work directly with Chef Trevor Hare's staff. I'm sure he'd be willing to help. Trevor knows Tamzin's temper. He doesn't have the staff to create such an intricate cake whilst he is preparing a million of other dishes, but I'm sure he'd be willing to loan a junior chef. He's a bit miffed Tamzin didn't hire his pastry chef in the first place. Hare's pastry chef went to Paris to attend a conference instead."

Guy considered himself a genius for offering a promising solution and she thought hard about it. *It's an opportunity to do something for myself and the future of my business.* She'd hob-knob with

Chef Hare and he would give her advice on opening her own cafe. *He's very famous after all. Trevor started from humble beginnings. From busboy to his own restaurant the Rabbit & Hare and his telly show...* she believed that Trevor would understand her.

It was a brilliant idea and Grace quickly warmed up to it whilst mulling it over. She knew that taking the job would also give her the chance to get to know Guy. The more they talked about the wedding cake and possible solutions, the more Grace wanted to spend time with this raven haired stud. *God only knows there aren't many men in Ivy that are as good-looking and young! Even if it amounts to nothing, just to be away from Cat and Corrie is incentive enough,* her mind insisted.

"I'll do it." she finally announced.

He was visibly relieved, then excited.

"On two conditions," she continued. He raised his eyebrows. "I want the cheque written out for £65,000 to me exclusively and I want media recognition for the cake." She had wanted to add "and you." to the list, but felt it was cheeky to do so.

"And to whom do I make this cheque out to?" Guy asked. He realised that not once he asked for her name.

"Grace Ann Knowles." she replied smiling.

He scribbled her name and the amount requested on the cheque that Tamzin already signed. He gave her the cheque, looking at Grace like the cat that got the cream. Although she'd be working,

Guy couldn't wait to get her back to the hall to get to know her better.

"I've got to get a few of my belongings together. You can meet me at The Bird in Hand Pub. It's across the road. Is it fine by you?" she asked.

"It's more than fine. I'll see you in a bit then."

Grace walked around the counter to let Guy out the door. She held the door open allowing him to walk out. But before he stepped out, he turned his body to her and surprisingly, kissed her softly on the cheek. She turned a rosy blush from the impromptu kiss.

"A million thanks, Grace. I'll see you soon." he expressed.

Grace barely could breathe or utter a response. Somehow she managed to reply breathlessly "See you soon." and she closed the door behind him. She pulled down the shade and turned to walk to the flat only to see two very cross women standing right behind her.

♥

"I can't believe it! You've taken the bloody job without consulting one of us and it's such a huge task!" said Cat, not disguising her anger. She didn't like this one bit.

"I took it. I'm doing it for me, not the Plum. I'm going to start my own business and what's better way to start it than with a celebrity wedding?" she stated, annoyed by their reaction. They all stormed up the stairs like a herd of angry cattle.

"You're going to Worthington Hall by yourself and staying there? Why couldn't you bake the cake here?" Corrie implored.

"He'll rape you." Cat warned. "I read about them football lads. They have cocaine fuelled orgies on stag-dos and major celebratory wins. No good will come of this." she predicted as they entered the flat.

Graces' mouth went agape. She felt the colour draining from her face. *What did they know about drugs, orgies and men? They read way too many gossip rags and tabloids. I'm going to have to speak to Mrs. Penny at the Spar to cancel their subscription.*

"It's true! They'll probably grab you whilst you're putting the cake in the bloody oven and bend you over a butcher block..." Corrie cried.

In revulsion Corrie put her hands on her hot cheeks. Grace recoiled at their terrible remarks. The old women's hearts were palpitating hard. Cat thought she'd go into cardiac arrest at the thought of her niece being harmed.

"*Stop it! Stop it now! There will be no butcher block orgies. It's simply business!*" Grace shouted back at them. "I know you're trying to protect me, but I'm twenty-five years old. When I return, we'll have a long chat about my future."

Before sulking off to the kitchen they looked at her with teary eyes. Unable to deal with their overreaction, she rolled her eyes and huffed off to her bedroom to pack.

As the twins made their tea and moved about the kitchen, they whispered of all the worse possibilities that could happen to Grace. In their mind they were only concerned for their niece whom they had raised as *their* daughter.

♥

three

race looked at her bedroom. The pale pink walls were covered in old posters of boy-bands like *Boy-Zone* and *Take-That*. Her bedroom needed major updating, but exhaustion from working made it impossible. She was glad to be gone for four days. There were times when she lain in her bed feeling suffocated by her life.

It was a fluke that Guy arrived on her doorstep. *Maybe, it's God's way of telling me to get off my arse and do something with my life.* It seemed like such an unusual message but she felt it was true. Grace knew that she needed to stop living for her family and start living for herself. She had allowed them to coddle and treat her like a child all this time without so much of a rebellion.

It should've ended many years ago, she thought rushing around her room, packing her belongings into a dusty pink travel bag. She hoped Guy wouldn't think of it as childish as it was the only one she had tucked in her closet.

When Grace finished packing, she emerged with her travel bag. Her aunts waited by her bedroom door ready to hound her further with terrible tales. Corrie grabbed her and hugged her tight.

"Remember be cautious. Any problems, call on the mobile and we'll be right there." Corrie said. Grace stifled a laugh.

"Yes, we will be there. If this man tries to make a move on you, we'll sort him out!" Cat said stern.

"It's only a wedding!" she retorted.

The older she aged, her aunts' dramatization increased by tenfold. Grace recalled her first and last boyfriend, Ian Heeley. They had met in History class at Upper School. After weeks of dating, Ian had wanted to take Grace to the Glastonbury music festival. He decided to meet with the twins and ask for their permission for Grace to go. Instead the meeting had turned into a nightmare for Grace and a teenage cry fest for weeks on end.

Unbeknownst to her, Cat had managed to borrow a rifle from a farmer she was dating. Ian arrived at the Knowles flat and sat down on the couch for a cup of tea with Corrie and Grace. Cat emerged from her bedroom with rifle in tow and demanded to know about Ian's intentions with their sweet, innocent, Grace.

Grace had never seen such a sight. Ian bolted from the couch like startled deer and never saw him again. He changed schools and avoided her calls. She thought she would never forgive them. As time went by, she slowly did.

Since then Grace didn't date anyone. She decided it best to wait to make male friends. To keep her mind occupied, she read romance novels, and envisioned a day when she would fall in love, make passionate love and get married. She imagined it would be with a man like Guy, but she knew the reality was most likely different. But tonight the reality was far better than the fantasy she had imagined.

They said their goodbyes and walked Grace downstairs to back door. Her aunts' waved as they watched her walk across the road to The Bird in Hand Pub.

Grace entered the pub. She immediately noticed a crowd of blokes surrounding a table. They were roaring with laughter. Finally, a bloke moved to retrieve another pint revealing Guy to her.

Guy sat at a long rectangle table, entertaining the crowd with football stories, antics, autographs and pictures like a king holding court. The pub landlady gave her fizzy lemonade with a slice of lemon. She thanked the landlady and walked over to the table to join Guy. Her eyes twinkled as she observed him in his element. *He truly is a lad's lad.*

Smiling, Guy looked up to Grace. He patted the seat beside him. He was glad to see her. She had taken her time packing and he was beginning to wonder if Grace ran off with cheque. Before she could sit down one of the lads' stopped her.

"Can you please take a picture of all of us love?" asked the bloke handing his iPhone over to her.

She nodded. The blokes went behind Guy to pose for the picture. She snapped the shot. The lads' thanked her for the picture and thanked Guy for their complimentary drinks. They dispersed, leaving Grace to take her seat next to him.

"Do you have everything?" he asked, noticing the travel bag.

"Yes. I think I have what I need."

"Would you like to have dinner?" His stomach growled in hunger. Grace raised her eyebrows in amusement. She noticed his eyes studying the chalkboard menu above the bar.

"It's late. The kitchen here is closed. The cook won't make a meal, not even for a popular footballer like you," she revealed. His stomach made another loud rumble. "I know of another place for great pizza."

"Pizza sounds good. Ready to go?" he asked, drinking the last of his pint.

"I'm ready." Grace said getting up.

Guy jumped to his feet and picked up her travel bag. He waved off the staff and the crowd. They both said goodnight to the pub landlady.

"I parked over there." He pointed out as they stepped out into the cool, crisp night air. She followed him to the black Range Rover. He turned off the alarm and tossed her bag in the boot. He held the passenger door for her. *It's rare nowadays for a man to be chivalrous,* she thought.

"After you my lady. Your chariot waits." he joked bending forward with his arm cupped underneath. She laughed and climbed into the passenger seat. He went around the vehicle and got into the driver's seat.

He followed her instructions to the Three Trees. The restaurant was tucked in front of the Ivy-upon-Wye stone bridge crossing. The bridge was one of the three entrances and exit to Ivy-upon-Wye. When they stopped, Guy went in the restaurant to place his order. Grace sat patiently in the vehicle waiting for his return. A few minutes later he came out to sit with her and wait for his food.

"How long have you lived in Ivy?" asked Guy. He flicked on his iPod to play some tunes through the speaker.

"I lived here my entire life." Grace replied. As she sat, she watched couples entering and leaving The Three Trees.

"Have you travelled elsewhere?" he inquired.

She turned to see him staring directly at her. She felt the intensity of his dark and sultry gaze. She swore there was deep, sexual desire and intent behind them. Cat's words came back to haunt her. She shook it off. *Just because he's handsome doesn't mean he's nice.* He noticed.

"Are you OK?" he asked. *She's flustered and out of sorts. Why is she shy around me now?* It was on the tip of his tongue to ask, but he decided best to leave it short and simple.

"I'm fine. No. I haven't travelled outside of Ivy. The only exception is Hereford and Cardiff." she replied with a smile.

He focused on his iPod and scrolled through his music inventory. He put on Sean Tyas. Grace shivered. He assumed she felt cold and twisted the knob for heat. The blast of the warm air from the vents wafted the scent of his Jean Paul Gaultier, Le Male cologne.

She recognised the scent. She loved the cologne's aroma of mint, lavender and vanilla. It made her want to straddle him like a proper loved-up school girl. She wanted to kiss him whilst gyrating herself against his stiffened cock. She dreamt of Guy tugging gently on her caramel hair, allowing his lips to nibble all over her neck. The laughter of nearby patrons broke the revere bringing Grace back down to earth. She had to restrain herself. She didn't know if he felt the same.

Grace wasn't aware that Guy thought she was an angel that fell in his palms or that he wasn't leaving without her mobile number regardless of circumstances. Even if she couldn't make a wedding cake or if those bullish women tried stopping him, he was hell bent on getting her number.

During the drive to Three Trees, he imagined veering off course and parking in a secluded area along the river. He wanted to take her in the back seat. *There's plenty of room back there to kiss her.* He would pull off her top and jeans, in hopes of finding pretty white knickers underneath. He shifted in his seat, trying to focus his attention on hunger and not on a heated dalliance with Grace. He didn't want her to see his pronounced arousal.

"Do you plan on staying in Ivy for the rest of your life?" he asked. He looked around to see if they were bringing his meal.

"No. This winter I plan on moving to London. I'm opening a bakery called Delicious. The restaurant my father owned closed down and it was turned into a fashion shop. The lease is nearing renewal and the owners aren't interested in renewing." she replied confidently. Her response surprised him.

She isn't like any girl. Most of the girls I had dated were only interested in drinking, partying, and fashion. She's different and has goals. The determination in her voice made him believe that she would achieve her goals. *She's the classic girl next door and a rare, natural beauty. She's intelligent with great looks.*

If it wasn't for the fact that she was in his Range Rover for a wedding cake Guy would've asked her out on a proper date to some five star restaurant in London. He wanted to hear her talk about her life and get to know every little detail about her. Sadly, he couldn't say the same as he was forced to keep his secrets.

As Grace continued talking, he noticed how she smelled of warm cinnamon and sweet vanilla. *She'll taste delicious when I finally kiss her in all of her forbidden places,* he smirked wickedly. He prayed for the pizza to be ready soon. He wanted to hurry back to the hall without ravishing her.

"Where are your parents? Who were those two protective women?" he asked.

"They're my aunts. They've raised me since I was a little girl. My parents had died when I was three years old. They were killed in a car accident." she murmured softly.

Guy inhaled sharp. He hadn't expected such an answer, and felt sorry for her. *Such a pity. Poor girl.* All the dirty images swimming in his mind completely vanished.

"I'm sorry. I shouldn't be asking you personal questions."

Grace saw he was genuine. She placed her soft hands on his arm to assure him it was okay. He felt the hairs on his arm rise. The touch felt natural. It was as if there was an unspoken connection between them. *Maybe getting a cake for the bitch wasn't entirely that bad*, he thought. *After all, I'm sitting here next to this gorgeous girl.*

"No worries. It was a long time ago. I don't remember my parents. My aunts created dozens of scrapbooks for me to look at and think of them." She smiled and he relaxed.

There was a knock on the drivers' side of the window. It was a staff member with a piping hot pizza box. Guy rolled the window down to take the pizza and paid the staff member.

"Let's go to Worthington Hall. I hope you're prepared." he crooned.

She felt butterflies flutter in her stomach. She shook her head laughing nervously as Guy started the Range Rover to drive off.

♥

Worthington Hall was a monumental Georgian manor named for the late Lord Worthington and his family. Many years ago the manor had been converted to a hotel and function hall. The family struggled to afford the hall's expensive maintenance of the grounds and manor. They agreed to turning the property into a business as profits would suffice its' upkeep costs.

As they waited for the automatic gates to open the hall loomed before them in all its glory. The perimeter of its long gravel driveway was lit up with large candle lanterns. All of the landscaping lights faced the tall oak trees, English gardens and rose bushes. Landscaping lights shone on their limestone walls and highlighted English Ivy that seemed to take over a part of the manor. Late as it was there were people running across lush emerald green lawns. They were taking pictures, drinking, laughing, and overall having a great time. It was a festival-like atmosphere at the hall. Grace gasped when she saw her favourite *EastEnders* actress run in front of the Range Rover.

Guy followed the driveway to the back of the hall instead of the main entrance. He thought it was best to introduce Grace to Chef Hare immediately. The Range Rover came to a full stop and they got out. Guy went to the service entrance door with Grace. She was nervous and whispered a small prayer under her breath. As soon as his finger lifted off of the door bell, the door swung open. Grace's mouth dropped open in shock.

Here, in front of her very eyes stood the tall, brilliantly talented, Chef Trevor Hare, a culinary hybrid of Gordon Ramsey and Jamie Oliver in looks and talent. Now that she was standing in front of the world class chef and one that she respected, she couldn't manage a hello.

"Where the hell have you been? Tamzin's been looking all over for you. She's been in and out of the kitchen bothering all of us. Finally, I've got five minutes of peace to come out to have a smoke. She's driving us mad." Trevor growled. "Who the fuck is this?" he added waving his hand towards Grace.

"Mr. Hare, my apologies. I found a baker. Let me introduce you to Grace Ann Knowles. She works for The Savoury Plum in Ivy-upon-Wye." Guy introduced.

Trevor gave her the once over. He looked Grace up and down. *She's a pretty little thing and if I wasn't in such a foul mood...* Trevor bit his lip and sneered with disgust as he popped his cigarette between his lips.

"Are you serious? Is that the best you can do? A short-order cook from some pub?" he grumbled in annoyance, lighting his cigarette. Grace's blood began to boil and she snapped. She wasn't having any of it. She knew how hard Guy had searched for a baker. Now Trevor was insulting her.

"Chef Hare, with all due respect, I'm not some short-order cook! I come from a long line of culinary blood. My father was Chef Gordon Knowles and a teacher at the London Culinary Academy before opening his own restaurant in Covent Garden. I've worked hard to gain excellent reviews on my desserts and pastries. I was born to be a pastry chef!" She was short, snappy, and cross by his reaction.

Trevor took a step back. He was blown by Grace's sassy reply, and stunned by her lineage. *She's a bit more interesting,* he thought exhaling smoke.

"Come in then." he sneered. He held the door open to let them in whilst he flicked his half smoked cigarette to the ground.

They walked up a few steps into the grand kitchen. It was a hive of activity. There were busboys running to and fro, chefs cooking meals, whilst others made appetizers for wedding day. People shouted orders to one another which went along with the sounds of sizzling, cracking and stirring in pots. Piquant smells permeated through the kitchen.

"This is the hub. Here you'll concoct the wedding cake of the century. You'll have my full attention and the help of my staff. I hope you can pull this off within the time constraint." Trevor said, extending his arms out.

Grace felt overwhelmed. For a brief second, she felt like backing out. Guy noticed. He took her hand and squeezed softly for reassurance. It wasn't expected, but it was warm and inviting. *When was the last time a man held my hand?* Grace knew the sad answer to that and she also didn't consider Ian to be a man.

"You'll be fine," Guy whispered. He was close to her ear and she could feel his warm breath along her neck. It sent shivers up and down her spine.

"Mr. Hare, I'll leave Grace with you. I've got to get her a suite for the next few days. I hope she's in good hands." he said turning to Trevor.

Trevor nodded, waving him away as if Guy was dismissed. Grace felt his hand leave hers. *It's cold and empty.* She wanted it back. Guy gave her a friendly smile.

"I'll be back," he promised. She watched him walk away and wondered, *what has he gotten me into?*

♥

Guy walked across the foyer to the reception area. He heard the familiar sounds of stiletto heels clicking and clacking against the Italian marble floors. The sound approached him from behind. A thin bony hand touched his shoulder. Guy turned. He came face to face with Tamzin.

Tamzin was dressed to the nines. She was wearing a low-cut silver, Dolce and Gabbana, mini-dress. Her long platinum blonde hair was straight as a pin and styled in a side ponytail. Recently she had her fake-bake tan applied. He thought she resembled a heavily made-up Satsuma. Her icy grey eyes focused on him as she smiled wickedly.

Standing next to her was Gemma Wharton, another W.A.G. wannabe. Of late it was reported that Gemma had broken up with a rival Tottenham Heat football player, Darius Bishop. Now she had her eyes set on her next male prey, Guy. Tamzin had privately assured her that Guy was a perfect match.

Gemma didn't impress him. She was a tall, waif thin model with fake breasts that resembled Christmas baubles. She never wore a bra underneath her clothes, forever showing off her permanent, erect nipples. She was a protégé of Tamzin. She had the same long blonde hair that was predominantly extensions. Gemma's skin too was covered in the same Satsuma orange tan. She had unnaturally white veneers covering her crooked jagged teeth. Guy didn't like her long pointy nose and small beady blue eyes. She always looked hungry forlorn and bored. He thought Gemma needed a good meal and to lighten up a bit..

"Have you come back with a cake?" Tamzin asked straight to the point.

"No, Tam. I've come back with something better. A pastry chef will be working with Chef Hare on your cake." he replied, continuing his walk towards the reception desk. Tamzin and Gemma each took an arm and walked with him in between them.

"A pastry chef? That's what you call the best you can do? I asked for a cake, not a Chef! As you recall Darren shagged the last one!" she hissed. Guy turned to her. He threw her a fiery look and pulled himself out of their arms.

"I know full well what happened. To be frank this is your bloody job Tamzin not mine! I'm not your fucking lap dog. I only did it as a friend." he snapped harshly. He was irate and wanted to hurry back to Grace so that they could have dinner together.

As Tamzin spoke with Guy, Gemma stared down at her French manicure nails. Tamzin wasn't impressed and Gemma was bored by wedding details.

"That's what friends do, Guy. Small favours for each other. You're Darren's best friend, his constant alibi and his partner in crime. So, I *do* expect you to do anything he can't do or isn't willing to do." she retorted. "Matters aside, have you met my friend Gemma Wharton?"

Tamzin pulled Gemma close to her. Gemma extended her hand to him which he politely shook. As a matter of fact it wasn't the first time that they had met. They met several times in various nightclubs that they both had frequented. Each time they were introduced Gemma was high, drunk or just aloof.

"Gemma's mending a broken heart after that cruel Darius cheated on her with *that* slag. I said to Gemma that you'd be a perfect gentleman. Maybe you can go out on a date. I think you two will make a great couple." Tamzin mewled.

"After the party in the library, I'm available." Gemma said. Her voice was barely above a whisper. Guy struggled to hear her.

"Tamzin, I've got to attend to business. I'll see you later." he replied. The reception manager emerged from the back office.

"See you soon." Tamzin said over his voice whilst he inquired to the manager about an available suite.

She snapped her long hair over her shoulder, tugging Gemma along with her as they made their way to the library for cigars and a drink with other guests.

♥

Guy reserved a private guest cottage at the bottom of the north lawn of the hall. It was the last one remaining. He couldn't get her a suite within the hall as it was fully booked. He paid for the expensive cottage with his black Amex. He didn't need the headache of Tamzin or Darren complaining about cost.

As he signed the documents to settle the reservation, Darren appeared alongside him. He was dressed in a smoking jacket with a cigar hanging from his lips and clutching two shot glasses in his hand.

"Where the hell you've been all day? Are you coming to the library mate?" Darren questioned, putting the glasses down onto the reception desk, pulling the cigar out of his mouth.

"I was dealing with your business." Guy answered curtly. *It still amazes me that we are from the same gene pool.*

Unlike Guy, Darren suffered from an arrogance complex. It was made worse when he was voted World's Sexiest Footballer in 2012. He was a cocky, arrogant and reckless playboy. Although slightly shorter than Guy, Darren was a hot, metro sexual, male who had all of the girls throwing themselves at him. He wore his natural blonde locks in a short, shaved and nearly bald haircut. He was always clean cut, with his nails manicured and clothing crisp and pressed. He pulled off a confident persona to make up for his terrible social skills and generally rude nature.

On the pitch, Darren was *the* best player. At the very least, his skills matched Rooney or Beckham and he often went above and beyond those skills. Although he was a great player, Darren had his vices. He couldn't wait for the game to be over with, to shower, change and hit the nightclubs in search of the next big thing. He loved hanging with models, drink and party until the wee hours of the morning. More often than not, his antics were front-page fodder for Rumour Mill.

"Ah, come on mate! Let's have some fun! Fuck the cake! You know how Tam is and I got something special to make up for it." Darren joked as he wrapped one arm around Guy's shoulder. He handed a shot glass filled with Sambuca to Guy.

Accompanying Darren were London Lion team members. They laughed at Guys' expense. They knew Tamzin Smythe well, all too well perhaps. Before she sank her teeth in Darren, Tamzin had slept with most of the London Lions or provided some of them with the occasional blow-job. Guy was aware of her tricks and therefore kept a far distance. He swallowed the liquorice flavoured alcohol. The warm sting filled his belly and Guy shook it off.

"Meet us in the library in fifteen minutes. Come on, lads!" Darren roared. He gave Guy a final pat on his back. Guy shrugged his shoulders in disgust.

Guy watched his team leave as he placed his shot glass on the counter. With a frown, the manager took the glass shaking his head with disgust. He felt the same way. He knew his team and Darren were up to no good. Key in hand, he headed back to the kitchen with no intentions of going to the library afterward.

♥

When he entered the kitchen, Guy saw Grace engaged in a deep conversation with Trevor. Not wanting to interrupt, he politely asked a sous-chef if he could reheat the pizza and whip them up a salad to share. The sous-chef obliged and took the pizza box that was sitting on a nearby stainless steel counter.

He sat on a stool, watching Grace move her hands about like two flitting birds. She made animated expressions regarding the height of the cake and as she did this, Guy wondered how her hands would feel like brushing against his bare chest. He wanted them to explore every inch of him and travel further down, past his navel into his trousers.

Trevor nodded in agreement at something that she said. Guy continued watching her with intense scrutiny. She was contrary to all the girls that he knew including Tamzin, the tyrant and Gemma, the flake. He loved the fact that Grace didn't fawn over him like every other girl chasing a rich footballer husband-to-be with million pounds and the lifestyle it would afford them. As advertisers approached Guy, asking him to promote their sports drinks, clothing lines and what not, he decided it was high-time to steer away from *those* women. She seemed not to care and Guy knew that she didn't have a clue about his celebrity status.

Finally, Grace finished her conversation with Trevor. Out of the corner of her eye she saw Guy waiting patiently. Grace walked over to join him for dinner, sitting down in the stool across from his. The hot pizza, a salad, and a bottle of chilled Chardonnay were placed in front of them. Guy poured her a glass of wine.

"Is he satisfied with you?" he asked. He needed to know as he really didn't want to go out searching for another baker.

"I pray so. He said that I know what I'm talking about but he has his concerns about pulling it off."

Grace took a bite of her pizza and sip of wine. She realised that she was starving and feeling a bit ravenous so she took a large bite of her slice. Throughout the meal they discussed the wedding in more detail and gorged on mouth watering artichokes, aubergines, parmesan cheese, and fresh basil all on a thin crust.

She explained that Trevor gave her two of his junior chefs who were interested in pastry and desserts. She was truly grateful for his help. She admitted that she was excited that Trevor promised to lend her a hand.

"I reserved a private cottage for you. I thought you might want to be away from the hall and Tamzin. She's trouble, and you should concentrate on the cake." he interjected.

Grace yawned and gave a small smile at the thought. Belly full and exhausted after a long work day, she was desperate for the comfort of a warm soft bed. Guy noticed.

"I'm sorry. Thank you for the cottage." she apologised.

"It's OK. Let me take you there now." he replied with a soft chuckle.

They finished up their meal and said their goodbyes to the staff. On her way out, Grace said goodbye to Trevor, promising him that she'd see him in the early morning hours. Outside, Guy helped her in the Range Rover.

When they arrived at the cottage, Grace had fallen asleep in the passenger seat. Guy got out, unlocked the cottage door with the key, and turned on some lights to find his way through the cottage. He retrieved Grace from her seat and brought her into the bedroom. There he rested her down on the bed as softly as possible. She stirred a little, but not enough to be woken.

She's a beauty! He thought smiling. He pushed some of her caramel hair from her forehead. He turned off the nightstand light and retreated to the kitchen. There he wrote a note: *See you tomorrow for lunch!* He also left a makeshift map of the trails leading to the hall kitchen along with a torch. Before he left, Guy turned the lights off in the kitchen and the living area. He closed the cottage door softly behind him.

When Guy returned to the hall he was equally as tired. He needed a hot shower and he wanted to watch Sky Sports before he nodded off. He waited for the lift that would take him to his floor. When the lift opened, Gemma was standing inside.

"There you are! I've been looking all over for you." Gemma purred. Not thinking properly he entered the lift. He quickly pressed the button to his floor. The doors closed.

"I was attending to some business."

He wasn't interested in chatting with her. On further thought he wished he had walked away to wait for another lift. Swiftly and surprisingly she came around to him and wrapped her arms around his waist. It was a tight squeeze like a large squid catching its prey. Shocked by her tactic he pushed his hands down to remove her arms from around him.

"Don't fight it. I know you're attracted to me. Tamzin told me so." she mewled in a seductive tone.

"No, I'm not. Tamzin's got it all wrong. She lied to you. You're definitely better off with someone else!" he snarled.

Gemma brought her lips down to his neck. She kissed him, leaving a bright ruby red lipstick stain on his collar. He eyed the lift's monitor as he pried his way out of her claws. She pawed at him like an eager puppy with a new toy. Finally the lift bell rang and the doors opened. She released him. He pushed Gemma aside to pass.

"As the days go by, I hope to see you Guy." she sing-songed, trailing behind him, down the hallway towards his room.

He nearly blurted, *Gemma you're appealing as a mosquito,* but kept quiet.

"Gemma, I said it once before and I'll say it again, I'm not interested in *you!*" he angrily retorted, reaching his suite door and unlocking it.

As he was about to let the door slam behind him she wedged her Dune high heel between the threshold and the door.

"Come on, Guy. I can give you a blow-job if you like. I bet it'll be the best you ever had," she moaned in a Liverpool accent. He had heard enough from her. He kicked Gemma's heel out the door and looked directly into her eyes.

"Not interested! Goodnight!" Guy growled and not giving her another opportunity. He slammed the door shut.

When Guy thought she was gone, he took off his clothing, had a hot shower and climbed into bed, naked. He tried to watch telly, but his mind was on other things. All he could think about was Grace. *God, she really is beautiful. Those eyes of hers and her hands! Where has she been all my life?* Thoughts of Grace aroused him. As Guy wished that Grace was right there lying next to him, his cock stiffened. *It's been one of those days.* He needed release.

He reached for lotion that he kept on the nightstand by his bed. Slowly, he stroked his arousal with his palm, easing its way up and down his lengthy shaft. He imagined the creamy wetness to be Grace and her sweet tender mouth. He wanted her naked and on top. He imagined his head nuzzling her round, soft breasts. There he'd suck and taste every square inch of her bosom. Guy wanted her floured hands all over him and licking dark chocolate off of his steel hard abs. The more he dreamt about Grace the harder he'd squeezed his cock and the faster he stroked.

"Grace," he hissed, fantasising about her bouncing up and down his cock. He wanted his hand on Grace's shoulders with her caramel hair cascading on her back. Her head was thrown back as she moaned loudly above him, massaging her clit as she rode her hips onto his. He was desperate to come, he needed to come. His thumb grazed the head of his cock. He could feel his pre-cum wetness.

"Bloody hell, Grace! I need you." he muttered.

Finally his orgasm took hold. Guy ruptured hot sticky cum down his steely rigid cock onto his hand. His body trembled at his climax. *No one has ever done that to me before, not even in fantasy.* It was true. No one turned him on like Grace did. He was going to make it *his* point to get to know her better before the week was over.

♥

$$four$$

t four A.M promptly, Grace awoke startled. She was still groggy and unaware of her surroundings. She sat up in the bed, thinking that she was in her bedroom and she must have dreamt it all. When she reached for the bedside lamp and switched it on, she discovered it wasn't a dream.

She rose from her bed, showered and changed into her work clothing before walking to the kitchen for breakfast. There she found the note Guy had left, along with a map to the manor and a torch for which she was grateful. She blissfully smiled at the thought of Guy's promise of meeting her for afternoon tea.

Grace continued to explore the kitchen. She found it to be fully stocked. It enabled her to make a light breakfast of porridge and tea. As she ate and drank, she read the note he wrote over and over again.

He's so handsome! What does he want with a girl like me? He'll forget about me by tea time. There are so many famous, beautiful guests staying at the hall; why would he want me?

With breakfast done, Grace walked the path that took her across the Hall grounds to the kitchen. It was dark. The sky was overcast with no moon or star light to guide the way. She held the torch tightly in her hand, thinking she needed to thank Guy for it. She heard an owl hooting loudly on a nearby branch. The wind blew softly through the trees. Leaves fell tenderly from the towering oaks lined the path. Grace shivered. She was glad to be wearing her Top Shop parka because it was cold. The first frost covered ground. It was silent until Grace reached the service entrance.

At the service entrance fresh deliveries arrived one after another from the milk to the meat man. Trevor stood aside barking orders to the chefs and busboys lending a hand.

"Good morning Grace." he gruffed, handing her a box of fresh vegetables. "I called a few favours last night. Your deliveries shall all be here by noon."

"Thank you Chef." Grace replied excitedly.

"Good luck. And remember we work as a team." Trevor added as he signed off on some more deliveries.

She walked up the stairs and put the vegetable box in its' respective area. She took off her parka and hung it in the cloak room. As she returned to her station to place on her chef's apron she felt her nerves tingle. *Today's the beginning of the rest of my life. Please don't let me screw this up.*

♥

Loud chatter from London Lion teammates outside his suite door woke a slumbering Guy. The lads banged their fists on his door. Grumpily, Guy got out of bed and opened the door allowing his teammates to pour in like a tidal wave.

"Come on! We didn't see you yesterday! What happened? Did you shag one of the hens?" Darren joked.

He groaned and ignored the comment as he didn't want to get in an argument. He went to the loo to change as the lad's carried on their conversation of last night's wicked debacle.

As Guy brushed his teeth he listened to their exploits and was glad he didn't partake in any of it. *Yes settling in for the night with Rosie palm was a better option. Especially with that fantasy about Grace!* Guy needed to see her and he was desperate for tea time.

When he was dressed, Guy followed his team out of his suite. They went down to the dining hall where a breakfast buffet was set.

He helped himself to a cup of coffee and a full English breakfast. It consisted of bacon rashers, fried eggs, beans, black pudding, tomatoes, mushrooms and fried toast. He took a chair next to Darren. Laughing about a strip club incident with his other team-mates, Darren looked to Guy and nudged him in the ribs with his elbow.

"We missed you last night!" piped Johnny. Johnny was a scrawny tall lad and good mates with Guy.

"I was out buying the wedding cake." he replied, tugging his knife across fried toast. Darren noticed and gave a wry grin.

"Give the cake a rest, mate." Darren said. "Tonight's going to be a wild wicked night filled with naked willing gorgeous women. We're going out to Cherries in Manchester. Tamzin's going with the hens for a night out in Hereford! The Hummer limo's collecting us around seven." he added eagerly.

Guy groaned knowingly. He gave his brother the look whilst he drank his coffee. He knew that Darren's future father-in-law owned Cherries. It was one of the many strip-clubs owned by William and it bode for a terrible night. He rather spend his night with Grace than play babysitter to Darren.

"Are you sure you want to party at Cherries? There are a million other strip clubs in Manchester that aren't owned by your father-in-law. Do you want problems?" he questioned. *He's my brother after all. I can't let him do this. Darren is going to fuck up the rest of his life if he does what he normally does at strip-clubs.*

The lads chuckled. They knew Darren was notorious with the ladies.

"No worries here. Besides it's a free night out. All bought and paid for by her old man. Who could ask for more? As my best man you were obligated to make arrangements, and you didn't do your duty." Darren replied with a grin.

"This is your marriage we are talking about, Darren. If you fuck around you'll suffer severe consequences that I can't save you from." he admonished.

Darren didn't like Guy's tone or reaction. Guy had treated him like a child in front of the team and if there was one thing Darren hated, it was being reprimanded.

"Marriage isn't going to tie me down. Nor do I need you to be telling me what to do." The lads bellowed out in another round of laughter.

Guy vowed he was not going to play a knight to Darren's damsel in distress act when the time came. He ate his meal in silence whilst others around him continued on with breakfast and chatter.

"Let's go shooting lads!" Darren ordered to the group as soon as breakfast was complete. They got up from their chairs to follow Darren out to the lawn as Guy sat in his seat finishing the last of his coffee.

Tamzin and Gemma sat at a nearby table, finishing their breakfast with the other hens. Tamzin kept her eye on Guy as the lads went off to shoot. Seeing him alone, she decided to take her chance and approach him about his rude behaviour towards Gemma. Gemma followed her to his table.

"Gemma told me that you rejected her advances. Why?" Tamzin questioned heatedly, placing her palms down on the table. Her steely grey eyes looked like two small bullets ready to fire from her skull.

"Tam, how's this your business?" he asked. *She needs to give up on the idea of Gemma and me.*

"It's my business Guy when you turn my best hen away." she snapped, bringing her hands back on her hips.

"Gemma, if you felt the need to speak about your feelings of rejection, you should've spoken to me. I didn't realise you need Tamzin as your mouth piece." he lashed.

Guy looked directly at Gemma's eyes as he got up to leave the table. Gemma maintained her deadpan expression.

"I have better things to do with my time than waste it with you two." he added disdainfully.

"I felt you could've tried harder. We would be so perfect together." Gemma moaned woefully.

"And I told you I'm not interested." He was trying hard to be civil, but his patience was waning, and he didn't know how long he was going to hold out. Without speaking another word, Guy left a fiery Tamzin, and emotionally void Gemma.

"Come back here!" Tamzin shrieked.

He didn't look back at them. *Let them lick their wounds.* His mind was on Grace, but he had to get through clay shooting first.

♥

The sound of gunshots firing and plates shattering startled the kitchen staff. Grace looked up from her work. She was cooling six red velvet cakes along with some faerie cake samples for Trevor to taste. *Flipping Nora! When will it end?* She silently thought. It was distracting for everyone around including her.

Trevor came over to inspect her work. He approved of the new cake instead of the original version. They both had agreed red velvet would surely win the wedding guests over since it was a flavour most Brits didn't find in the U.K. After many years of catering for celebrities Trevor knew they'd love it.

As another perfect shot echoed it marked the arrival of another person in the kitchen. It was Tamzin. The staff briefly looked up from their stations and quickly diverted their eyes away from her in case she demanded a change in the menu. In a heartbeat Tamzin could destroy countless hours of work if one person only said hello to her.

Instead she bypassed them all. She marched straight over to Grace's work station. She was curious in meeting the pastry chef and to see if Grace was up to the challenge. She ran her long talons along the stainless steel countertop. They made a horrible scraping sound.

Grace looked up to see one of the U.K.'s top glamour models standing before her; yet she looked nothing like her pictures. She wasn't as pretty as portrayed on the glossy print covers and Rumour Mill pages. Tamzin's face was covered in old acne pock marks. Her make-up, fake tan and airbrushing hid the scars terribly.

"Hi. I'm Tamzin Smythe, the bride. Guy told me that you'll be the one creating my wedding cake." Tamzin introduced. Grace offered her hand to Tamzin for a hand shake, but it was rejected. She pulled her hand back quickly.

"Hello. I'm glad to finally meet you. I'm Grace Knowles of *Delicious* Bakery." she replied with a warm smile.

"I've never heard of your business, Delicious. Is it here or elsewhere?" Tamzin questioned, eyeing her to see if she was another *distraction* for Darren.

"Oh. I haven't opened yet. We're located in Covent Garden. We're in the process of refurbishment." she fibbed.

It's a small white lie. More of a half truth, reasoned Grace. She hoped Tamzin didn't think she wasn't experienced in cake making.

Tamzin gave a weak smile, noticing Grace and her beauty. *She's got a curvaceous body and innocent charm,* she thought sourly. It's a charm that she knew drew men like a moth to flame. She pursed her lips in dismay. She prayed Darren wouldn't come into the kitchen to inspect *this* wedding cake.

"Tell me about the cake." Tamzin said, rubbing her bottom lip with a finger.

Grace went into great detail about the wedding cake. She gave Tamzin a faery cake for her to sample. Whilst Tamzin looked over the sketches she devoured it greedily allowing crumbs to fall haplessly everywhere like a slob.

Even though Tamzin had concerns she adored the sample. It was tasty. She didn't know of anyone who'd ordered red velvet for a wedding cake. She'd be the only one in her social circle to have it for her wedding. It was original, unique and Tamzin knew her guest would bowl over it.

"I approve. Make it six layers and smashing! I want this cake to be the talk of the town." Tamzin concluded.

Abruptly Tamzin turned to walk away. She didn't bother saying goodbye. It was her way of letting Grace know that she'd been dismissed.

♥

"Well done, Guy!" Jonny said, watching as Guy hit another clay plate in a perfect shot.

Guy pulled off his ear protectors. He handed Jonny the rifle before giving him a high-five. "Thanks! Let's see you have a go at it." he said.

He walked over to the ice-buckets that were filled with a variety of imported beer. He took out a Red Stripe and opened it. A few other London Lion teammates patted Guy on the back, but the jovial mood was interrupted by the sudden appearance of Tamzin. She came face to face with Guy, snatching his beer from his hand. She quickly took a drink and grimaced.

"You didn't tell me she was so pretty!" Tamzin snapped. He could see she was cross.

"What are you on about now?" he asked, his patience stretching on thin and his mood increasing in anger.

He didn't care what Tamzin was rambling on about. All he was interested in was meeting with Grace for lunch. He ordered a picnic basket from one of the in-house chefs and was planning on take her on a riverside picnic. He thought she would enjoy a well-needed break from the kitchen.

"The chef, *what's her face?!*" Tamzin snarled.

The lads scurried away from them like frightened mice. They left Guy to fight his own battle.

"She'd better not sleep with Darren before my day." she huffed thrusting the beer bottle back into Guy's hand.

"Tamzin, I'm done with you. I did you a favour. You should be grateful instead of being a bitter, arrogant, slag..." Guy angrily spat, but his sentence was cut off by Tamzin's father's approach.

"What's the problem, princess?" William asked. He peered through his thick eye glasses at Guy. *He's trying to intimidate me*, but Guy held steadfast. *No man will break me.*

William Smythe was a hulking and broody elderly man who exuded dominance. Feared up and down the U.K., he was known to make someone disappear due business ventures going sour, gambling debts or overall, if he didn't like you. There was never a dead body to recover. After a few months of heat from the police, the case would turn cold or would never be discussed in the media again.

"Nothing, nothing at all Daddy." Tamzin cooed syrupy. She placed a hand on his shoulder and kissed him softly on his cheek whilst keeping an eye on Guy.

William smiled and hugged his princess tight. He blinked his eyes and Guy thought they looked like eyes of a large-eyed goldfish. Darren came up behind Guy to see what was going on.

"I'll see you tonight." William coughed. He nodded in Guy's direction. "Let's go darling. Your mother wants a word regarding the flower arrangements."

Tamzin threw Guy an icy glare as she sauntered off on her father's arm.

"Darren, you need to deal with your wife." Guy snapped as he turned to his brother. Darren's eyes went wide.

"What's it now? When will you give this matter a rest?" Darren replied.

"When you grow up and learn to keep your cock in your pants. Let me be and deal with Tamzin on your own or I'll head back to London tonight." he threatened forcefully. Darren knew Guy meant it.

"Don't go. Just ignore her." Darren replied sheepishly. Guy stormed off.

♥

Glad to get away from the insanity, Guy walked to the kitchen to see if Grace was available for lunch. He thought about the way she looked when he had first laid eyes on her. He swore there was an instant spark. *She surely makes my heart skip a beat. It has been a long time since I felt this way about any women. It feels real good.*

When he approached her station, she was putting away a few mixing bowls. She looked up to see him before her. Her cheeks went hot and blushed. His dark eyes had a devilish glint to them and she knew he was up to something. *Phwoar! He looks hot in his dark denim jeans and St. Georges' t-shirt!*

"How's your day so far?" he asked politely.

He moved beside her the thin gap between them shrinking. Grace could smell his cologne. It made her giddy and weak in the knees.

"It's going well. The cakes are cooling, the fondant is made and we're working on some intricate flowers. There's so much to do, but Chef Hare has provided a lot of help. I'm beginning to think I can do this. Thanks for giving me this opportunity."

Guy placed his palm on the small of Grace's back, tugging her apron strings to remove it. She felt a nervous flutter in her stomach.

"Grace, I was wondering...would you join me for lunch? I had a lovely picnic basket made especially for us. I thought you might like a bit of fresh air and good company."

Bashful, she brought her eyes up to his. *I want this...I want him...*

"Yes. I'd love to. I'm done for the day." she replied softly. There was a quiver in her voice. He chalked it up to nerves.

"Good. Now we have plenty of time to get to know each other. Are you ready?" he asked.

Returning from his cigarette break, Trevor noticed them together. *He's standing to close to her. Her body is turned to him and she's enjoying whatever the hell he is telling her.*

He wasn't going to let Guy piss all over his new bird. *She's mine. Not his!* After last night's meeting, and having spent most of the day with her, Trevor decided that he had found a new conquest.

"Everything alright here?" Trevor interrupted.

"Yes. Everything's fine. I'm done for today. I'll be back tomorrow morning. Is it fine by you?" she replied.

Trevor didn't want her leaving with Guy. He hovered over her like a swarm of bees over the finest flower. He wanted more time. Grace had the talent that some of his junior chefs' lacked and he liked her spirit. *She isn't afraid to speak her mind.* He stared cold-heartedly at Guy. Trevor wondered what he wanted with Grace. He knew of footballers and their infamous actions. *I don't want him tainting my Grace,* he thought bitterly.

"It's fine with me." he replied with a heavy sigh. "Have fun. Enjoy the rest of your afternoon." He was eying the picnic basket an in-house chef had brought to Guy.

They said goodbye to Trevor and hotfooted out the kitchen and to the parking lot. Grace insisted on going back to the cottage to change her clothing, but Guy told her not to. "It's only a picnic." he insisted. Time with her was precious and not to be wasted.

Guy promised to have her back early to shower, change and relax. Grace sat patiently in the passenger seat as he placed the picnic basket in the boot.

Soon they were off. They drove along the winding narrow Welsh roads peppered with large trees in all their autumn glory. Their delicate leaves were in various fall colours of bronze, copper, and citrine. They floated gracefully onto the road. Grace directed Guy to a narrow road leading down to the bank of the river Wye.

"Its' beautiful here." he commented parking his vehicle.

"It's one of my favourite places. After a hard day of work, I like to come here to relax or to swim." she said climbing out.

It was a gorgeous Indian summer day. Grace felt the warm sun against her face and exposed skin. It was a little too warm and she wished he had let her change in a more comfortable outfit.

She watched him as he lay out a London Lions blanket for the picnic area. Once he was done, she sat down on the blanket and opened the basket. She set out the plates and napkins. She pulled out some of the delicious fresh fruits such as grapes, strawberries and apples. There were ham and brie sandwiches on ciabatta bread, slices of dark chocolate cake and some bottles of sparkling water. It was a feast to behold.

"Wow! When did you do this? she asked bemused.

"I had some of the staff put it together. You deserved it. You really helped me out." he gladly explained. She handed him a plate filled with fruits and a sandwich.

"Thank you so much. I'm starving."

For the first few minutes they ate their meal in awkward silence. After a few bites he decided it was time to get to know her better. *I hope she doesn't think this is an interrogation.*

"Grace, tell me; what's life like for you?"

Grace bit into her sandwich, chewing in thought. *How am I to tell him that I'm just a boring, inexperienced girl unlike him?*

"There really is nothing to tell. I'm just a girl who grew up in Ivy and I'm looking to get out." she replied.

Even though she liked the fact that Guy wanted to get to know her better, she was curious about him. "Now I have a question for you; what does a famous footballer like you want with a girl like me?"

Guy raised his eyebrow at her question. *She's a spitfire.* It was forward, but it showed her determination in getting to know him. She wanted an honest answer and what a better way to get an answer by asking a direct question.

Grace felt the doubt stirring that he might only be interested in her sex. *There's a possibility I'll be a notch on his bedpost. I don't want that...*she concluded in her mind.

"So what if I'm footballer?" Guy answered, starting to defend his career and explain himself... "Does it mean that I have to go with girls who only chase footballers? As a child, I wanted to be a fire-fighter, but my father didn't want it for me. He said he didn't want a commoner's job for his sons. For many years, my father was a coal miner. Then an accident rendered him disabled.

We grew up in a gritty grim area of Yorkshire. Our home was a small two up and two down row house. Whilst my dad stayed home with us children my mum went to work in a chip-shop. With the few quid mum earned and dole money from dad, my father placed us into football.

My brother, Gareth, didn't want to be a footballer. Gareth had learned that our father had an affair with a neighbour. It resulted in Darren's birth. His mum had put down Dowling as Darren's surname on his birth certificate because she wanted a combination of her surname and my dad's.

The relationship between Gareth and my father changed for the worse. Gareth quit football, and he started to sell drugs. His only interest were in making quick money, stealing, partying and getting high.

It wasn't until Darren had fallen ill that we learned of the truth. Darren's mum knocked on our door. She demanded to see our father. She told our mum the truth about their affair. Gareth was angry. Shortly after his eighteenth birthday, he died of a drug overdose.

Darren, on the other hand, was well-taken care by dad and by his mum. At school we played on the same football team even after we graduated and moved into the leagues."

She was struck by Guy's honesty. She hadn't expected him to be forthcoming with his past, but he reassured her that it was okay by touching her cheek lovingly. Grace felt her head move in his palm and she was tempted to kiss it, but thought better of it.

He felt by telling her the story of his home-life prior to the glitz, glamour and money that the football fame brought; she would feel more comfortable around him.

"I'm telling you this because I've never told anyone about my family life. Our history is dark, bleak and grim. There's a lot that the media isn't aware of, but I trust you. From the moment we met, Grace, I knew you weren't just any girl. You're the girl I want to know more about and possibly go forth from here." he said. His voice never wavered and it was stern. He sounded like a man who wasn't willing to give up on what he wanted. He leaned into her body by scooting close. It excited her to no end.

Guy wants me...

After a moment of silence, he slowly pushed her caramel hair away from her face and tucked it behind her ear. He looked at her. *She seems so shy and innocent, not like many young women today.* Her innocence struck a chord with him.

"I want to get to know who you are Grace. I want to know *everything* there is to know about you." he whispered with his forehead pressed against her. His mouth was just inches away from hers.

Her heart pounded furiously beneath her breast. She thought she might faint from over excitement. They were close to the point of kissing, her first real kiss since Ian. *I have to stop this now, this is madness. We barely know each other.* She pulled back and shied away from his hands. She turned her head so that he couldn't see her blush. When the heat from her cheeks had gone, she returned her attention to him.

"I grew up with my two aunts, Cat and Corrie who've kept me under lock and key since I was a little girl. Due to my parents' accident, the loss of my mother, their sister, they're afraid that I'll suffer the same fate if they let me go. At times, I feel stifled by their love, but I know it runs deep. This winter is my last winter here, though. My bakery, Delicious, will be fitted out and I'll be moving to London to start my own life. Would you believe that a twenty-five year old woman has never been to London?" she said with a nervous laugh.

"London, there's no city in the world like it. I think you'll love it. I can show you around when you move. Would you like that?" he asked. She loved the idea of them meeting again.

"Yes I'd like that." she replied shakily.

"Why are you nervous?" he asked drinking the last drop of his sparkling water and holding his gaze on her.

Looking down away from his eyes, she tried to hide her shame and then she replied "I've never been around a man like you."

It was a sad, dreary fact about her. Grace didn't want Guy to see that she was inexperienced. Flattered and assuming that she meant his celebrity status, he laughed heartedly. A part of him didn't believe her naivety. He was under the premise it was nothing but nerves. He stood on his feet and grabbed her hand.

"Come up." Guy said as he helped her to her feet. She was quickly in his arms. They wrapped around her waist. He grinned down at her. She felt so small in his arms.

He's so much taller than me! His body overwhelms mine. If it wasn't for the fact that he was a footballer, she would have guess he played rugby.

She let her hands roamed over his taut biceps. *They're strong, sturdy and ever so muscular.* She looked at his supple lips. They weren't too big nor were they the size of rubber bands. *They're perfect.* She trembled, thinking of him kissing her with his lips.

He moved away from her. *If I don't bloody move now, I'll end up taking Grace right here on this blanket.* He needed to hold back. He wanted her trust and friendship. He didn't want her to think he was only chasing her knickers.

"Let's walk together."

She agreed. Guy held his hand out to her. She clasped her hands around his and held it. They held hands whilst walking along the bank. She loved his rough fingers clutching hers. She tried not to show disappointment when he let go. He explained he wanted to take a closer look of the river, but didn't realise the moss covered rocks under his feet were too slippery. Before long, he felt his body skid down the rocks into the river.

"Bloody hell! Are you ok?!" Grace shouted as she brought her hands to her mouth.

It wasn't his intention to fall. He stood up, waist deep in the river, soaked from head to toe. *There's no way I can get back in the car without ruining my seat.* Usually he kept an extra set of clothing in the back of his SUV, but this time there weren't any.

Grace started laughing hysterically. To see him in demise was priceless. It was the funniest thing she'd seen in a long time. He scowled, but laughed too. *I'm an idiot for thinking that the rocks were good to walk on.* She went down to help him out.

"Ta." he smirked.

"You can't get in your car wet." she advised.

"I know. I hope you don't mind driving back with a half-naked man. You'll drive us back and I'll give you the keys to my suite where you can grab some of my clothes. I'll shower in your cottage. I don't want to walk across the reception area naked."

She nodded. They walked back to the site. He walked to the boot to strip off his wet clothing, whilst she collected the picnic basket. Lucky for him there was a London Lions towel in the boot.

She went to the boot of the Range Rover to put the basket away and gasped in awe. Her eyes couldn't believe what they saw. Here in front of her was a hunk of a half-naked Guy Rowling. He had faultless, washboard abs that Grace wanted to run her fingers along. He wasn't hairy, but buff and tan. His pecs were taught and perfect.

Her legs felt like wobbly gelatine. Guy looked at her as he wrapped the London Lions towel around his waist. He flashed his brilliant smile at Grace. *I'm glad she is getting a sample of things to come. Judging by her reaction, she likes what she sees.* Stunned she dropped the basket at his feet. She turned around, rushing back to the driver's seat of the Range Rover.

On the drive back to the hall the sexual tension between them crackled like static electricity. Unspoken words highlighted their thoughts of one another. She kept her eyes firmly on the road, trying not to think about what she just saw. When they arrived at the hall, she dropped Guy off at the cottage and drove to the manor. She followed his instructions to suite and entered his room.

Grace sought out his clothing, unaware that someone else was in his suite. She stuffed a fresh pair of clothes in Guy's Prada backpack and left. A Rumour Mill spy was hiding behind the bathroom door and exhaled loudly in relief as soon as the door closed behind Grace.

Stealthily the spy emerged from behind the door to look around. *The mobile phone's gone! Who's this new girl and what's she doing in Guy's room?* the spy thought. The spy checked the hallway to see if it was empty and quickly left Guy's suite to rush down the hall to see Gemma.

Breathless and nervous she returned to the cottage. As she stepped inside she heard running water from the shower. She gulped hard. *He's naked in my shower!*

Quietly Grace walked in her bedroom, gently placing his backpack on the bed. As she turned to walk out of the bedroom, she noticed that the loo door ajar. Curiosity besieged her and Grace walked over to the door to take a peek. The shower curtain was pulled back to the point that she could see Guy fully naked. His back was turned to her.

In admiration for him, her eyes went large and wide whilst she watched soapy water wash down his rippled back and over his arse. She fantasised about digging her nails in his shoulders whilst wrapping her legs around his buttocks as he pounded madly into her in the shower.

Sensing a pair of eyes, he knew she was watching from the door. Slowly he cocked his head up to the shower to rinse the lather off. When he did this, they locked eyes. He pretended not to notice and went back to washing off the soap.

"Grace, are you there?" he called out.

She stumbled backwards, trying to escape from the room. *I've been caught!* She felt her face turn scarlet from mortification. *Oh bollocks! He's going to think I'm a pervert!* She rushed to her bedroom door, pretending to close and open it as if she had just arrived.

"I'm back! I've got your belongings. Would you like a cup of tea?" she fretted.

"That'll be great." he replied, turning off the shower. He chuckled under his breath shaking his head.

She smacked her palm against her forehead. *I'm such an arse! Guy knows that I was watching him!* She left the room before making a further fool of herself. In the kitchen, she rushed around. She put the kettle on the hob and searched for digestives. She found a box of Worthington Hall biscuits to put on a dish.

Ten minutes had passed when a fully dressed Guy padded out of her bedroom into the lounge area. She had two steamy cups of milky tea and a dish of biscuits on the coffee table. She looked up to see a freshly showered Guy dressed in a new pair of dark wash denim and a crisp white buttoned down Gucci shirt. His dark hair was still damp. He picked his cup of tea, taking his seat next to her on the couch.

"Thanks for getting my clothing. I appreciate it." he said before taking a sip of his tea.

"You're welcome."

"I wonder if tonight I can stop in for a nightcap."

He looked at her. Biscuit crumbs settled on the bottom of her lips. He wanted to lick them away. He placed his mug on the coffee table and made his move. He reached out touching her lips with his thumb. He wiped away chocolate crumbs. As he pulled back, he licked his thumb. She felt faint. *What's this man doing to me? I want his thumb in my mouth.*

"I'd like that very much..." she whispered breathlessly.

She felt as though room was being stripped of air supply. He sat so close to her that their knees touched. It sent shivers all over her body.

Guy finished his tea. He reached into his pocket to pull out his iPhone. It was late. He needed to leave for his excursion with the lads. He turned his body to Grace to say goodbye. *I'm not leaving without a kiss,* he thought wickedly. He cupped her face, drawing her body up into his. He pushed her soft, silky, hair back from her face and drew her chin to him.

"I know you saw me." he murmured huskily.

She felt her heart stop. He plied her lips with sweet, soft kisses. They felt like creamy butter melting in summer sun. She responded to his kisses by allowing Guy to run his tongue against her lips to pry open for a deeper kiss. *She tastes deliciously sweet.* In agreement his cock hardened.

Their kissing intensified in passion. She raised her arms up wrapping them around the back of his neck. Guy brought his heavier body into her, pressing his chest against her bosom. The action caused them to fall back on the cushions forcing his body on top of hers. As they kissed, his cock strained in his jeans, begging for sexual release. Instinctively his hips moved against her aching mound. On a sultry high, she moved her hips against his. She felt her knickers getting wet, and very hot down there.

He trailed his lips to her earlobes. *Cinnamon sugar!* Guy thought. He nibbled and growled from sweet taste. She moaned softly in his ear. She kept her eyes close as he continued kissing along her ear and neck. She wanted him to go further with his exploration.

His iPhone unexpectedly rang. Her eyes flew open and reality sunk in. Rapidly, he got up to pull together. He looked at his mobile to see Darren's name on the screen. He decided to let Darren's call go straight to voicemail. Grace sat up and straightened her clothing.

"I've got to go. It's Darren. I promise I'll be back later." he said.

"Ok." she mumbled rising to her feet. She walked him to the door. She didn't want him to leave.

Guy felt the same way. *I'd rather spend my evening with her instead of a strip-club.* She opened the door and he turned to her. He noticed that her lips were ruby-red and swollen from their kissing. She bashfully looked away from him. *She's something else.* He took her chin in her hand and gave her one final tender kiss.

"I'll see you later." he whispered.

She bowed her head and watched as he walked away. Once he was gone, she fell with her back against the door panting heavily and thinking about what she done.

♥

five

illiam waited for the lads to arrive at his strip-club, Cherries. The club catered to high-end clientele like footballers. Rarely did he visit his dodgy businesses. But tonight there was a reason. He wanted perfection.

He thought of himself as a prowling lion stalking a herd of gazelle as it pranced over the range. In his line of sight was the biggest gazelle of them all, his soon to be son-in-law, Darren. William wanted to make sure that his plan, a year in the making, took off without a hitch.

He checked the liquor stock behind the bar. It was stocked to the hilt with the finest, most expensive liquor money could buy. He knew what rich gluttonous men liked; after all he was one of them. William knew they loved to spend copious amounts of money on booze, beautiful women and toys. Tamzin made sure her father knew of all Darren's indulgences. Darren was no exception to the rule.

From his son-in-law's taste in women to booze, William's princess, Tamzin left no small detail out. He knew Darren was going to be an easy target. *I'm going to blackmail the shite into anything I want including fixing matches so the bookies will pay out. It's a great plan.*

Tamzin ensured her father that if he kept her in jewels and fashionable clothes; she'd go along with it. And when she was ready for divorce, she knew that her father's connections would allow her to walk away with a large hefty settlement. Alana, a tall dark African beauty, sashayed over to the bar to greet William.

"Alana! It's good to see you. I like your choice of bikini!" William exclaimed peering at her through his thick bottle lenses. "Remember what I told you about tonight. Your job is to pleasure the groom. No one, but Darren. Understood?" he added, briskly as he checked the ice buckets.

Alana looked every inch of a mouth watering vixen to him. *Tonight, I'll have a go at her,* he thought, his mouth salivating. She wore a tiny gold bikini, specifically bought for this occasion. Her ebony skin was shimmering in glitter passion-fruit lotion. A pair of large gold hoop earrings swung from her ear lobes and her long, straight, coffee-coloured hair, cascaded down her back.

"Yes boss. I'll do as you ask." she smirked. William came around the counter and playfully spanked her bottom.

"Good girl. Afterwards, come see me." he whispered in her ear.

She planted a gooey, lip-gloss kiss on William's cheek; her lips grazed his cheek stubble. Alana gave William a cheeky wink before sauntering off in her plastic clear stiletto heels clicking on the tiles, to check on the champagne room.

♥

The strip-club was packed with tons of men, other players from various teams, all of the London Lions football club, and friends of the groom. The music blared loud hip-hop and rap music. Half to fully naked girls danced against stainless steel poles set on stages in front of lavish red velvet couches and chairs. Money was thrown and champagne flowed liberally. Darren was in his element. The DJ yelled out "Welcome to Darren Dowling's stag-do!"

Guy bought a round of Sambuca shots. He gave them to his mates and Darren before taking his seat at a reserved table for the groom. Men were hooting, whistling and cat-calling women. Guy shook his head. His head ached from the loud music and noise. He needed fresh air.

A few strippers came over to offer private lap dances, but Guy politely declined. His only interest was in Grace, not some dirty night with a stranger. His decline garnered snickers around the table from the lads. Most of them had gone off to their own private lap dances whilst others stayed enjoying the view.

Tray in hand and aware of her mark, Alana seductively strutted her way over to the table. Resting on the silver platter was Darren's favourite whiskey and his favourite Cuban cigars. She slowly bent over Darren's knees, placing it on his table.

"I have a drink and cigar for the groom." she purred.

Licking his lips in surprise, Darren watched Alana pouring the drink before handing over the glass. In a bent position, she managed to do it all.

"Thank you." Darren huffed.

She's a beauty, Darren thought to himself. He wanted her to stay.

"Please, take a seat." he said opening his arms for Alana to sit on his lap. She took the invitation and eased into his lap.

Alana grabbed a cigar and placed it into her mouth. She lit it up, puffing on the cigar before handing to Darren. He was impressed by her drag as she placed the cigar in his mouth.

"I like a girl who knows to suck a cigar," he teased.

Alana's smile went wide. *He's taking the bait!*

Guy watched them. *I know where this is going and it isn't good,* he thought to himself. He didn't want any part of it.

"I'm an expert. Come with me to the champagne room so I may further indulge you with my expertise." she cooed with the smile still stuck in the same position.

Darren placed his drink down on the table and his cigar onto the ashtray. With his fingertips, he caressed her silky legs, drawing them up and down her thighs.

"I can't love. You see that man over there?" he said loudly, pointing his chin in Guy's direction. "He's my best mate and best man. He's watching out for me and this is my future father-in-laws place. I'm sure you know that."

Alana knew his words were for show. His cock was saying otherwise as she moved her bottom against him. Darren found it hard to resist sexual temptation. The way she moved against him made Darren want to push her bikini aside and shove his cock inside. Guy rolled his eyes.

"Don't let me stop you." Guy gruffed. He stood on his feet and drank the last of his Stella Artois pint.

"Where you're going?" Darren asked.

Not paying attention, Alana continued gyrating hips and bottom against Darren steel hard cock. He tugged on her hair in excited pleasure. He was desperate to fuck her, but Darren knew Tamzin took out the condom from his wallet.

"Out for air." Guy replied. He was leaving the club with no intention of returning. He was going back to be with Grace. He prayed for his sake it wasn't too late.

"Your sitter left you alone. Come with me. I promise your daddy-in-law won't see or know a thing." she whispered briskly, watching Guy leave the club.

Darren nodded and took the liberty of dipping his fingers inside her gold bikini bottom. He rubbed her wet clit fiercely, deciding then and there he was going to join her. Darren needed a good fuck with a complete stranger before he walked down the aisle to *that* ball and chain.

He followed Alana into the champagne room. It was a room decorated in long flimsy white drapes, a round gloss white table, a leopard print couch, with wall to ceiling mirrors. On a table there was a large ice bucket. Divulging in Darren's taste for uber-luxurious, William had an ice bucket filled with Heidsieck champagne. It was flown in from Russia, chilled.

Alana uncorked the champagne bottle pouring its golden liquid into crystal flutes. She handed a flute to Darren. He quickly drank his before placing it on a side table. Alana got up onto a small stage before him and began to do a seductive dance.

"You're wasting time." he growled.

He wasn't interested in a strip-tease. Darren got up from the couch and pulled Alana down into his lap. He kissed her hard against her lips. He pulled down her bikini top exposing her taut chocolate-drop nipples. Hungrily, he suckled at the sweet drops. Alana moaned loudly. She was enjoying this.

"I want to fuck you." Darren breathed against her ear.

"Do you have a condom?" Alana asked.

"No, but a girl like you won't mind being fucked bareback by a footballer like me." he chortled.

"I can't." she said trying to get up. He grabbed her by the wrist and brought her back to the couch.

"You must and you will fuck me. You can't start something and expect it to stop because there's no condom. I'm sure you've allowed other punter's to fuck you without one, especially for the right price." he growled.

Alana knew his point, but she had to play coy as William had planned. She couldn't go in for the kill. She didn't say another word. She allowed him to rip off the bottom half of her bikini as he pushed her down on the couch. He spread her ebony legs before him. He wasn't going to let a two-bit whore tease him merciless. Her heart was pounding. She prayed he wasn't going to be too rough with her, but it was part of William's plan after all.

♥

"About time you called! We were worried about you!" Cat said, walking around the kitchen making tea. They waited all day and night with baited breath for Grace to call.

She dutifully informed them that there were no orgies of any kind going on. They were grateful to hear that her time was spent baking alongside Chef Hare. On Sunday afternoons, they enjoyed watching Chef Hare's show, What Hare Eats.

"Please get an autograph! Or better yet get him to come to us for a small bite to eat." Corrie cried out in the background.

"I must go. I'll speak to you soon." she replied laughing. Grace was on the hall patio, having dinner. She wanted to finish it before it went cold and before Guy's arrival.

"Good night Grace. We'll speak soon." Cat said.

"Good night." she chirped as she ended the call.

Trevor emerged on the patio for a cigarette break. Staff told him that she had returned for dinner, alone. Ever since they had met, Trevor was interested in her sexually. *I want her in my bed and I'm going to get it!* She appealed to him because he knew her father very well. She was unaware that her father had instructed Trevor in a few cooking classes. *Gordon was cocky and arrogant twat. Now he's dead,* he laughed inward at the thought of Gordon rolling in his grave when he finally had Grace naked.

Earlier, when Trevor spoke to her, he told Grace that her father served as an inspiration for his chicken pomegranate. She was flattered by the memory. Trevor knew that he had found his way to her body.

"Everything alright?" he asked pulling seat in front of her. She hadn't expected to see him or for him to take a seat.

"Yes. Everything's fine. I'm finishing this lovely meal, and I just finished conversing with my family." she replied warmly, swirling her glass of water with lemon. "My family invited you to The Savoury Plum for tea."

"Thanks. After the Dowling wedding, I'll be sure to visit The Savoury Plum." Trevor said laughing.

She had spoken highly about her family to him. Trevor knew they had a crush on him, but he didn't care. His focus was Grace.

"Grace, I was wondering...when you move to London, if you would like me to help you with your business? I'd be more than happy to assist you. I know London is a large, challenging, and daunting city. You need all the friends that can help. It'll make things much easier and better off for you. I'd hate to see the daughter of my former teacher starting off badly." he offered.

Trevor took a puff from his cigarette, flicking his ashes on the stone floor. To Grace, he sounded sincere in his advice.

She was unaware that Trevor only wanted her away from two overprotective aunts. *Grace is young with a hot body. I need her badly. I bet she's a nice tight thing.* Judging by her expression of genuine content , he knew she was hooked.

I can't believe it! Here's the world's most recognised chef willing to help me with Delicious!, her mind screamed.

"Thanks, Chef Hare! I really appreciate it!"she squealed. She wanted to throw her arms around his neck in delight. She thought of raining kisses on his cheeks, but held back. She didn't want him to get the wrong impression.

"Tomorrow let's have dinner at my cottage." he invited, exhaling smoke from the corner of his mouth.

"That's great! I would love that!" she replied. She sounded like a young fan smitten by her favourite boy-band singer.

"Good! Tomorrow night it is. I've got to get back." Trevor said. "Good night." he added, rising to his feet and pushing the chair back underneath the table.

"Good night, Chef Hare." Grace called out after him.

She looked at her Blackberry to see the time. *It's late.* She didn't want to miss Guy. Once she finished with her dinner, she sped walk back to the cottage feeling as if she was on cloud nine. She couldn't believe her luck, first Guy and now Chef Hare. Grace hoped her luck wouldn't change before the wedding day.

♥

Guy paid a mini-cab driver a large sum of money to get him back to Worthington Hall. He knew it was late and he hoped Grace was still interested in seeing him. He didn't mind leaving the party. After all Guy didn't want to witness his half-brother screw up the rest of his life.

The mini-cab pulled in front of the cottage. Guy thanked the driver for the ride. The driver asked for a picture with Guy and happily took one. He even autographed the driver's iPhone as a keepsake. He exited the cab and waved at the driver before knocking on the cottage door.

Grace looked at the clock sitting on the nightstand. *It's midnight.* She heard the knock as she was retiring to bed. She had given up hope that Guy was coming to see her. But now, her heart skipped endless beats and her stomach was performing somersaults as she grabbed her robe and went to open the door.

She smiled at the sight of Guy. His sooty hair was ruffled and his cocoa eyes glinted with mischief. The two top buttons of his shirt were open, exposing some of his skin. The wide smile on his face showed her that he was glad to see her. The grin on her face showed that she was pleased to see him.

She opened the heavy door further allowing him inside. Guy noticed the terry cloth robe she wore hid her curves and a hint of fabric peek-a-booed out from the robe. It told him that she was wearing a pale, pink, polka-dot nightgown.

"Come in," she welcomed. "Would you like a drink?"

"A glass of wine, please."

Grace took out a bottle of Chardonnay from the fridge. She poured two glasses of wine and walked over to the lounge. Guy sat on the couch. She handed him a wineglass.

"How was your evening?"she asked as she tucked her bare feet beneath her bottom.

"Not too good. I'm sure it'll all be in tomorrow's paper. Darren's walking a fine line." Guy groaned loudly, "To be honest, I've had enough of him and his wild, crazy antics. How was the rest of your day?" His tone of voice told Grace that it was a sore subject to him.

"Fine. I'm doing very well, even with the constraints." she replied.

He thought for a minute. He wondered if Grace wouldn't mind answering some personal questions. He had to know the truth about her, whether or not she was seeing someone else. He didn't want to take things further if he knew that he was encroaching on another man's bird.

"Grace, are you in a relationship with another man?" Guy asked. She balked at his suggestion.

"No. I'm not. There's no one in the cards. My life's about work. Many moons ago I had a boyfriend, but it didn't work out." she replied. Before continuing with his questioning, he drank some more wine.

"Did you love him?"

"No. It wasn't anything like that. It was a small romance. Nothing spectacular or special about him. It was young love."

She really wanted to tell Guy about her big secret. Her mind debated back and forth like a ping-pong game on whether the timing was right. Against her better judgment, she decided against it. *What if this encounter is nothing? What if he wants to be friends?*, her mind snapped. *Would he have kissed me the way he did?*

Absent-mindedly he placed his hand on her naked knee. She leaned in, drinking her wine, whilst his fingers circled her knee. It caught her off-guard making goose pimples erupt along her arms and thighs.

"What about you?" she asked, turning the tables on him.

"I had a girlfriend once. Her only interest was in becoming a WAG. At one point in our relationship I was serious about her. But she was wrapped up in fashion and having her name in the press. It really turned me off. She had no goals or aspirations. Most of all she didn't want children. I ended our relationship over a year ago. Since then I've been focusing on football and the pitch." he replied honestly.

She shook her head as if she understood what he had gone through. He softly continued to graze her knee with his finger tips.

"I don't want to keep you up too late. I know you've lots of work to do and wake early." he murmured, looking directly at her. She shied away from his gaze, turning her attention to the flickering flames in the fireplace as if they were amusing.

"Don't worry. All's taken care. I wouldn't have answered if I wanted to sleep." she replied eagerly.

She bit her lip, wishing she could take back her answer. He noticed the way she bit the supple pink flesh. He felt his cock twitch in arousal. He was pleased with her answer as he had no intentions on leaving even if she said otherwise. She leaned forward to place her wineglass down. He placed his hand on her lower back to stroke her through her plush robe. He ran his hand up to the base of her neck. There he brushed her hair aside to massage her neck and shoulders.

"Mmmmm." she moaned. *It feels oh so good, he's gentle with his hands.*

Her hand fell on his lap and he drew into her. He cupped her face, and planted a kiss on her lips. She willingly obliged. His sensual lips parted her own and felt his warm tongue swirling around hers. She moaned softly as he pulled away to kiss her neck. His hands were now tangled in her hair, tugging ever so gently to expose more of her neck.

Grace felt his hands untie her robe, pushing it open to pull it off. It was tossed to the floor. As he had guessed correctly, she was dressed in a sheer pink polka-dot nightgown. In the glow of the room he could see that she was half-naked underneath it. Her pert nipples were taut and straining against the fabric. For a flitting moment he considered pouring his wine over the fabric to lap at her succulent breasts. He sucked in his breath. *She's gorgeous!*

Her body glowed in passion. He pulled Grace into his arms to continue their kissing. Sexual electricity flowed between them as the kissing increased in eroticism. He brought his hands up to her shoulders, pulling the small, thin, pink straps down. Grace trembled with delight and moaned again.

"Guy..." she moaned breathlessly.

Grace wanted Guy to touch her and she was going to allow it. *He isn't some boy!*, her mind shouted. Her body and mind were desperate to feel what it would be like in the arms of a true man.

Teasingly, Guy brought his thumbs up to her nipples. He rubbed them softly through the fragile fabric. She gasped loudly. He took this opportunity to pull it down around her waist. He brought his lips to her bosom.

There he showered her breasts in kisses. He cupped her right breast and flicked his tongue over the rosy bud of a nipple. He suckled at her breast like a parched man in a desert dying of dehydration. His other hand covered her left breast. He playfully tugged at her pert nipple.

She felt her knickers moisten in excitement. Her clit felt as though butterfly wings were pressing against her. She placed her hands behind his neck bringing them both down onto the couch.

Guy came up for air before giving her another tense kiss. His rock hard steel cock strained in his jeans. It needed releasing, but first he wanted to satisfy her like she'd never been before. He pulled back on his knees. He gazed down as she wantonly spread herself for him. Her long caramel hair fanned around her face and her eyes half-shut in drunken seduction.

He ran his hands up her thighs, pushing fabric up around her waist. He came across her cotton white knickers. He was use to women wearing Agent Provocateur or La Perla, but the Marks and Spencer's knickers excited him to no end. It proved to him Grace didn't care about the highlife nor did she need to show off expensive goods in order to please a man.

His fingers hooked underneath the elastic waistband of her knickers. He drew them tenderly around her arse, down her thighs, and over her ankles before tossing them on the floor. He didn't expect to be stunned by Grace, but revealing her pussy did surprise him.

Once exposed, he noticed how bare she was. He was taken back that his English rose had a Brazilian wax. It turned him on. In anticipation of what was to come next, his stiff cock expressed sticky sweet goodness. He revelled at the sight of her sweet rosy lips and beautiful nub of her clit. It reminded him of a dark pink lotus flower. He ran his finger down her slit making her cry out loudly. *I think I'm going to die here!*, her mind swirled.

"Oh my! Bloody hell! Guy, please...please." she cried, whilst he rubbed her creamy clit. She had to stop him before he went further. She had to tell him her secret.

Guy ignored her pleas and cupped her arse in the palms of his hands. He brought his face down to her honey lips. He ran his tongue over it, forcing her to explode with orgasmic pleasure.

She brought her hips up to his face as his tongue ran ovals around her lips before dipping into the entrance of her pussy. He lapped every drop of sugary nectar she expelled. She screamed in pleasure. *Oh my god! This is a first! No one's ever done this to me.* She clenched her hands in his jet black hair as she rotated her sex against his mouth.

Finally she collapsed onto the cushion, panting heavily in satisfaction. Once she finished tugging at his hair, Guy pulled himself up. He looked down at her quivering in orgasmic defeat. Before she'd even catch her breath, he began to run his fingers down her sopping slit. He ran his fingers on the outer rim before stretching the entrance with the tip of his index finger. *I've got to stop him!*

Guy pushed one finger in. *She's tight, unusually tight.* He barely had a knuckle in when Grace contracted around his finger.

"Guy, no! Stop, please!" she screamed.

Baffled by her reaction, Guy shot up. Grace quickly sat up, recovering from their encounter. She fixed her gown, putting her robe on to cover herself. She placed her hair in a messy ponytail. He looked confused by her reaction.

"I thought we're having a good time. You're scrumptious. I never tasted anything like you." he growled huskily.

She turned around to see him sitting on the couch. His expression said it all. *He's confused and thinks he's done wrong. I can't have him believe that...it's not him.*

"Guy, I have to tell you something." she said with a heavy sigh.

"What is it? What's wrong?" he asked in fear.

Her words told him that something wasn't right. He felt his gut churning in horrifying anticipation.

"Guy...I'm a virgin." she blurted. She didn't hold back. The confession made her face turn crimson in embarrassment.

♥

For a brief second Guy thought he heard wrong. *A virgin!* He was shell shocked. *In this day and age finding a twenty-five year old virgin is like finding the Hope diamond all over again. A rarity!* He got up from the couch and paced the floor. He tried to soak it all in. It was on the tip of his tongue to say, *how the hell does one stay a virgin for so long?* But he kept mum.

"Guy, are you okay?" she asked twice, before he heard her on the third. He ran his hands through his hair. He nodded.

"Are you mad? I should've told you before we started. I'm sorry. I really want you, Guy, but I thought you should know that I've never had sex." she continued as she followed him into the kitchen. He poured another glass of wine. Instead he drank from the bottle.

"Are you saving your virginity for your wedding night?" he wondered aloud.

"No... I'm not saving my virginity. Marriage isn't relevant. I just never got around to it. It wasn't like I was ticking it off on a check list. All I want is to have sex with the right person. I want a man who loves me and cares about me, not a one night stand." she countered.

She felt the sting of his reaction. She was hurt. *I can't believe his only interest is in sex.* She scowled.

"Do you have a problem with it?"she spat ferociously.

She knew it was a strong possibility that it would've been a weekend tryst, but she had hoped that their unspoken connection made their bond stronger.

"No...No." he stammered. "I meant every word I said to you. I want to be with you, Grace. It's just that I'm afraid I might hurt you."

He took another swig from the wine bottle. He coaxed out the last drop of the wine before putting it down to drink the wine from the glass. Once he finished his drink he walked over to Grace and tried to put his arms around her. Instead she pulled away. She stood her distance and remained cool.

"Please Grace. Don't do this. I want to have sex with you, but not in these circumstances. I want it in better circumstances and on *your* terms." he pleaded.

"Five bloody minutes ago, you were keen to stick your cock in me. Now I tell you I'm a virgin and your response is, *'not under these circumstances.' Bloody hell, what's it mean?!*"she seethed.

"Grace if you're going to lose your chastity to me, I want it properly. I want the promises of a relationship and not a weekend tryst. I want us to get to know each other better and continue seeing each other. Is that too much to ask?" he replied.

She recoiled and she felt herself become horrified. *He has a good point!* Now, she was the fool. *We're just getting to know each other.*

Guy felt as the room beginning to spin. His stomach was bubbling from all the drinking. *I'm about to be sick.*

"I'm not feeling well." he groaned, running to the loo to throw up.

♥

six

he next morning Guy awoke with a terrible hangover. He was in his bed with no recollection on how he got back to his room. It was from all the booze from the Hummer limo, Cherries and the cottage, but he did recall his time with Grace and stunning confession. *Maybe it wasn't the booze; it was the shock of my life.*

He turned on his side, reaching for his glass of water, and two paracetamol tablets. A note leaned against the tumbler. He opened it.

Guy,

I'm sorry about last night. I should've been forthcoming, but I didn't know when would be the best time to tell you. I think you're right in saying that we are still getting to know one another. Maybe it's best we take it slow.

Truly, I do want you Guy. I can't deny it. I can't think of a better man to lose my virginity to even if it means I may never see you again. At least I know the pleasure was worth it.

- Grace

A grin broke across his lips. *She's not mad at me. Thank heavens for that!* He drank the tablets and water. He glanced at the clock. It was eleven. He had to meet the lads for rafting along the river. He rose from his bed. He took a hot shower, dressed and hurried downstairs to meet the team for their trip to the river.

In the reception area Guy saw deliveries arriving from florists to decorators. He took the liberty of plucking a few fresh flowers from a nearby vase. He wanted to see Grace before he left with the lads. When he turned the corner, he walked straight into Gemma.

"Allo, Guy. Where are you off to in such a rush? I've been looking all over this hotel for you. We haven't spent any time together!" Gemma crooned, reaching outing to fix his collar. She pressed her body into his, hoping that he'd kiss her. "What lovely flowers you've got there! Are they for me?" she purred.

She snatched the flowers from his hands and inhaled the fragrant scents of roses and lilies. She hoped that it made her look seductive and innocent all at once, but it didn't and instead she ignored Guys' foul frown.

"No, they're not for you Gemma." Guy replied non-plussed.

With her hands, Gemma pushed Guy up against the wall. She ignored his reply and decided to go in for the kill. She tried to pry his lips open for a kiss. He responded by pushing her back. It was a hard push and it wasn't expected. Gemma screamed as she fell on her arse, skidding across the cold marble floor.

"*Guy!*" she shrieked. "*You bloody twat! Why did you do this to me?! My dress ripped!*" The fall made the Versace dress to rip. He rushed to her aid to help her to her feet.

"I'm sorry. I didn't mean to push you. I wanted you stop kissing me." Guy apologised. She smacked his hand away.

"Stop kissing you?! You're some sort of *poof?*" she snarled as she rose to her feet. He didn't like the insult.

"Gemma, you're not the one. It's final!" he boomed.

Gemma crossed her arms beneath her bosom. The flowers he plucked were scattered on the floor. She stomped and crushed them with her heels.

"You're like a child throwing your toys out of the pram, Gemma!" he gestured wildly at the ruined flowers on the floor.

"You'll be mine!" she hissed, followed with an angry pout. Her eyes filled with daggers as she watched Guy storm away. "*You'll be mine...*" she repeated before stalking off angrily in the opposite direction.

Guy arrived at the kitchen only to be greeted by two surly security men dressed in black suits.

"What's going on here?" he asked eying the men.

"No one's allowed in the kitchen. You must be hotel or Chef Hares' staff." the first guard puffed. Recognising Guy, the second guard spoke.

"Last night, a paparazzo snuck in on the grounds by the cottages. He wanted to take a peek at the cake."

Guy understood completely. He put his arms up. It was only a matter of time before Rumour Mill knew about the cake incident.

"Okay. Thanks." Guy replied defeated.

As he walked away, the first guard shouted out to him. "Get us into the World Cup!"

Guy turned to the guards, flashing his charming smile and made two pistols. He pretended to shoot and blow smoke from his finger. The stony faced guards laughed. *I'm not letting Gemma, these guards or anybody else ruin my day*, Guy thought positively.

♥

Throughout the night, Grace tossed and turned in bed. A few times she kicked off her duvet and turned her pillow over to find a cool side. Visions of Guy hovering over her naked, drove her mind insane. He had left her body craving, aching, and screaming for more.

She didn't give a damn whether he took her now or later. She wanted to escape the invisible binding chains of her past; her family, her life in Ivy and death of her parents. She wanted him to do things to her that she was certain were forbidden in most parts of the world.

As she laid in her bed in dark silence she would see flashes of his face full of pleasure and desire.

At one point she kicked her feet wildly in anger for telling him about her virginity. She wished they had continued. Instead she regretted stopping him. *No man's ever touched me this way.*

Even though Guy had too much to drink he was coherent when he had asked questions regarding her virginity. He was sure of his promises, and she felt he wasn't feeding her a load of bollocks.

Grace had just fallen asleep when her body clock woke her at its morning hour. Sleepily she managed to shower, dress, and make herself a hot cup of coffee.

This morning's walk felt different to Grace. The sky was clear with a full moon. It was cold and brisk. It woke her right up. She looked at the stars shining radiantly in the sky. Their unexpected twinkling made her feel like it was a good omen.

She continued to think about their encounter. *What's the point in waiting? We can be together now even if it only turns out to be a dirty weekend. He's perfect in comparison to Ian,* her mind reasoned.

Suddenly, Grace heard the snap of a branch. She turned to see if anyone was behind her. She shone her torch down the path. *Silly me, it's just a fox or a badger.* Her mind wasn't as convincing as it was a few minutes ago.

There was another snap. It was followed by a loud crunch of leaves. An owl hooted. Her instincts told her not to look back, but she needed to see who was coming up behind her. She saw a tall shadowy figure emerging from the trees onto the path.

"Who's there?" she called out. The figure ran towards her. She let out a blood curdling scream, one that surely would wake other guests. She dropped her mug, clutching her chest. Her feet were frozen to the ground. Grace couldn't run. Fear gripped her.

"Shhh! It's okay! Shhh...Ma'm, I didn't mean to startle you. I'm from Rumour Mill. I'm trying to get the story on Libby Blackwell and the wedding cake," the man coughed in need of air and holding his knees. Grace thought that her aunts' warnings had heeded true.

"*Grace! Grace!*" shouted a familiar voice.

In between the break of trees she saw torches flashing. *Trevor must've heard me scream.* Trevor knew she walked alone to the kitchen. The reporter saw the flashes of light. He ran in down the path in the opposite direction, leaving her bewildered.

"Are you alright?" Trevor asked. He came up behind her.

Trevor saw her. *Her skin's white as a ghost! Her body is shaking like leaves in wind.* He pulled her into his arms. The staff shone their torches down the path and into the trees.

"I'm fine. It was the bloody paparazzi from Rumour Mill." she sighed. There were tears in the corner of her eyes. She was visibly shaken. "They're trying to get the story on the cake."

"Which way did he go?" asked a staff member.

She pointed down the path. The others ran after him in hot pursuit. They left Grace and Trevor alone on the path.

"You're safe now. Don't fret. We'll get it sorted. We've got much to do today so let's get back to the kitchen. I'll make you a cuppa." Trevor said. He cradled her in his arms. It made her feel uneasy.

"Thank you, Chef Hare." she muttered. She shrugged her way out of his arms.

"No worries. We've got to look out for one another. I know how it feels under the spotlight. But you, you're just starting out. You're just a babe. I should've warned you." he said with concern.

"Thank you. I appreciate your help." Grace replied softly. She didn't know how to react to Trevor's kindness. *In the kitchen, he's a mad man barking orders and making the others cry. Here, he's like a gentle father figure? It's strange to see him in such light.*

Staff members returned to them waiting on the path. They didn't catch the perp. On their cautious walk back to the manor, Trevor grabbed her hand.

"Grace, think of me as a friend. For future reference you don't have to call me Chef Hare." he said with a warm smile.

She didn't know how to reply to his sincere gesture. *This is all a bit overwhelming. It's like he wants something from me.* She searched his eyes for a hint. She could tell he was keen on her.

"Okay." she mumbled. She tried to wiggle her fingers out of his tight clutch, but he held on tight as they continued their walk back. When they reached entrance of the manor, he let her hand go. His demeanour returned to that of Chef Hare, the man she knew from telly.

♥

Like a queen on her throne, Tamzin was perched in her chair being primped and preened for tonight's family dinner. In the parlour of her suite, there was a flurry of activity.

Her mother overlooked every detail on Tamzin's three bridal gowns provided by Vivienne Westwood, Christian LaCroix and Vera Wang. Her bridesmaids gossiped on a nearby settee. Tamzin's personal assistant hovered nearby, talking with a reporter on her iPhone. Word had gotten out about the Blackwell incident, and they were trying to maintain damage control over Libby's tell all interview.

William roughly knocked on the door before entering the room with a few of his henchmen trailing behind him. Everyone paused for a moment to watch him enter, and quickly resumed to their business. He pulled a Louis XIV chair in front of Tamzin and sat down. She was busy blowing on her French manicured nails whilst her hairdresser ran the blow dryer over her rollers.

"This morning, I read Rumour Mill's front page. How come you didn't tell me Darren shagged the baker?" William croaked like a frog. He drew out his twenty-four carat gold cigarette case from his jacket to retrieve a cigarette. He tapped his Embassy cigarette on his case before putting it in his mouth and lighting it.

"Daddy, I can take care of it. It's all sorted out. It gives me that kind of leverage I'll need when I divorce him. Think of all the money I'll collect when all of the U.K. sees me as the betrayed and scorned wife. And even if I decide not to divorce him, a wife who stands by her man, through thick and thin, always comes out trumps. For now, things are fine. He promised me he would stop his cheating ways when we are married." Tamzin said without batting an eyelash. Her father exhaled smoke out of the corner of his mouth and gave a hearty laugh.

"You really think so? That pig will never change. This is why I have this." William snorted. He pulled out a USB memory stick from the inner pocket of his bespoke Henry Poole suit. "It's an insurance policy, princess. This is our money.'

Tamzin reached out to grab the stick. He pulled his hand back and returned the stick to its pocket for safe keeping.

"What's on it?" she asked.

"It's nothing to worry about, especially now. As I said, it's our insurance policy, princess." he said rising from his seat.

William flicked his stub onto the expensive Persian rug before snuffing it with his shoe. He kissed his princess on her forehead and gave a cordial wave to his wife. William ignored his younger daughter sitting on the settee with some bridesmaids.

Tamzin looked down at her nails, deep in thought.

What has Darren done now?

♥

seven

ews and tabloid helicopters increased their presence over the manor's air space. The scandal regarding the wedding cake fuelled public curiosity to a fever pitch. Grace tried having lunch on the patio, but the constant sounds of helicopter blades disturbed her meal. She collected her plate and entered the restaurant. A few busboys and maids were having their tea.

During lunch, her Blackberry notified her that there were unread messages. Some messages were from her aunts. They were complaining about how busy The Savoury Plum was due to the wedding melee. Another was from Olivia, pleading for Grace to return as her aunts were driving poor Olivia crazy. Grace was about to ring her aunts when a text message from Guy came through.

I've been thinking about you. I'm sorry for last night's reaction. I'd love to make it up to you. I tried to stop in the kitchen, but security detail is tight. Can I see you tonight before the family dinner? XX Guy

Quickly, she replied with a text.

I'll be busy tonight. I promised Chef Hare I'd help him with desserts. Can I see you beforehand? I have a few hours. XX Grace

Guy responded shortly after he received the message.

I don't care how long I have to wait. I'm going rafting with the lads right now. I don't know when I'll be back. I'll contact you after. XX Guy

She felt her stomach flip. She did want to see him tonight, but she knew she was going to be knackered. After her call to her aunts Grace went back to the cottage for a quick kip. She needed her rest before returning to help with dessert service. The next two days were going to be full on. *It's going to be difficult seeing Guy. I hope we can spare all the time we have together.* At the hall, Guy thought the same thing. *I've got to make time for her.* He decided he was going to do something about it.

♥

Darren rented kayaks and canoes for the lads from Up the River. Some relatives of the Dowling-Smythe family decided to join in on the fun. The journey down the River Wye was five miles long and took approximately two hours to reach the Boat Inn at Whitney.

"Oi! Guy!" Jonny shouted. He went over to Guy's aide as Guy was trying to lift a canoe. They lifted a canoe down to the river bank. "Can I canoe with you? I'm not a great swimmer. I'd rather paddle with you than the others." Jonny asked as they walked down the gravel slip.

They placed the canoe down at the edge of the river. Guy looked back at the group. He knew they weren't interested in safety. They roughhoused and played around with one another. Darren was busy chatting with William.

"No worries mate. You can paddle with me." Guy replied.

"Ta!" Jonny said. Jonny retrieved his rafting gear, whilst Guy strapped on his life vest.

Soon, they were all off down the river. Although the river was fairly calm, it worried Guy that Jonny wasn't wearing a life jacket.

Even in the calm natural surroundings Darren made a point to be loud and rambunctious as possible. They sang songs at tops of their lungs about women's private parts, flatulence and Rolling Stone. They smoked cannabis and drank beer. The noise startled the nearby grazing sheep that looked up in disgust or so Guy thought.

Darren decided to play a game he coined bumper canoes. The objective was to have those paddling drunk hit the other canoes and attempt to throw the other party into the river. If successful the hitter would say to the wet party "Sorry mate, have a drink on me." Then the wet party would get back into their canoe or kayak and have a proper drink.

The first few times everyone laughed and joked about it. They thought it was good fun. Owen Collins, the team captain, was tossed over first. Darren was next and a cousin of his who Guy didn't know. As the river rapids turned swift and rough, he thought Darren would stop the silly and dangerous game. It was tough to navigate through, but Guy managed to lead the canoe.

"I should've worn a life vest." Jonny muttered. He paddled hard following Guy's lead.

"Take it easy mate. Don't worry. We'll get to that small island there and rest. I'll give you my jacket." Guy assured Jonny.

"That's a plan!" Jonny replied. He was grateful in having chosen Guy to paddle with instead of someone else.

As they came out of the rapids, Darren rammed his canoe into the side of Guy's. The brunt of the hit was strong. It tipped the canoe on its side causing Guy and Jonny to fall out. In this part of the river, Guy noticed that the murky water was at least twenty feet deep. He immediately surfaced for air.

"Sorry mate! Have a drink on me!" Darren shrilled.

"You fucking idiot! Jonny can't swim!" Guy screamed. He saw Jonny floundering and swam in his direction. He struggled against the current. His life jacket was making it difficult for him to swim towards Jonny.

Quick-thinking and a strong swimmer, William took off his own life jacket and jumped in the river. He reached Jonny before Guy and pulled him up the muddy river bank. The lads pulled their canoes and kayaks to shore. Guy ran to his side. William placed Jonny on his side to expel water from his lungs.

"Are you fine, mate?" Guy asked.

"Yes." Jonny managed to say through fits of coughing.

"Jon! *I'm sorry!* I didn't know mate!" Darren cried. His hands were on his head in panic.

William picked himself off of the ground. He wiped mud off of his jeans and shirt that he had recently purchased from Harrods. Soaking wet, William was clearly annoyed with his son-in-law to be. It was rare to see the 'softer' side of a mob boss, but William hatred ran deep for arseholes like Darren.

"You're always sorry!" Guy barked.

"What the *fuck* is your problem?! I apologised! What do you want from me?! *Blood?!*" Darren snapped.

"My problem is *you*! You never act responsible. You never grew out of your upper school ways. Everything's a game to you, but everything has its price!" Guy retorted with heat in his tone.

Guy was irate. Darren didn't like his reaction and caught William sneering in disgust. Guy's attack in front of his father-in-law made his blood boil.

"I said *sorry!* I'm not giving blood over it. It seems you're the one with a problem, Guy. *Perhaps a touch of envy?!* I'm getting all the attention whilst you cry your sad, lonely, heart out. You should have stayed at Cherries and bought yourself shag. *Then again, I can't fathom who'd want an arsehole like you!*" Darren attacked angrily.

It was the straw that broke the camel's back. Guy lunged forward. His fist hit Darren squarely on the bridge of his nose. Blood spewed and splattered everywhere.

"Fuck!" Darren screamed. He clutched his nose to stop the bleeding. Darren gained his balance to throw a punch right back at Guy.

The lads jumped back, out of the way, Guy and Darren locked in fist fighting. London Lion teammates tried breaking the two, but it was like trying to break up two wildebeest. It was a battle of pent up anger and issues. Guy wanted more than blood from Darren. *I want respect!*

A single shot fired from a gun echoed through the valley. Troubled birds flew out from nearby trees. William stood on the bank with his Glock. He rarely fired it. At his age, there was no intention of breaking up a fight between two strapping lads. His henchmen typically did all his dirty work for him.

"All of you get the fuck back in your canoes! Get your arses moving before I make all of you disappear! Now!" William snarled. His voice strong, solemn and icy.

The men quickly parted. Without another word, the group walked back to their canoes and kayaks. When William spoke, it was as if God spoke. They were all familiar with his history. He had the ability to make his enemies vanish like a Las Vegas magician making an African elephant disappear.

Guy and Darren pulled away. They wiped blood off of their hands and face. Darren took off his shirt to stop his bloody nose. Jonny got up onto his feet. He thanked William again for the rescue.

As Darren walked back to his canoe he gave Guy a chilling glare. Guy shook it off. He returned to his canoe with Jonny trying not to give it another thought.

The remainder of the river Wye was uneventful and quiet. When the group arrived at the Boat Inn, a string of paparazzi were waiting patiently. Darren bypassed them. He stormed off to the inn. William grabbed Guy by the collar.

"It's none of my business on what goes on between you and my son-in-law, but Mr. Rowling I must say you're a good man. If you ever need a favour, please feel free to contact me." William said as he smoked on a cigarette.

Perplexed by William's offer, Guy had no words. *Why's he telling me this?* He shook his head.

"I must go. My driver's here. He has a set of dry clothes for me."

William left Guy in stupefaction. Guy headed into the pub for a pint. With his throat parched, Guy felt a cool pint would do the trick. Paparazzi shouted at him with questions about the cake and Grace. *How the hell do they know that? I haven't told anyone about*

Grace, but they're screaming questions. Guy flipped them two fingers and ignored their calls.

He went over to the bar and ordered a pint of Stella. As he waited for his drink, Darren approached him. Darren had a tea towel filled with ice resting on his nose to ease the swelling.

"I don't know what's gotten into you, Guy. We use to be best mates. We're brothers and now you're acting like you're too good. What the hell's happened to us?" he asked.

"You've changed for worse, Darren. The guy I use to know doesn't exist. All you care about is booze, money and women. You don't even care about the game or give a damn about who you marry." Guy retorted.

Guy didn't want another scrape with Darren. He wanted to drink his pint in peace. Instead, Darren was desperate for answers. He continued on with his questions.

"Judging by your reaction, I'm assuming you've heard the news. Guy, you're upset that I signed the trade contract to the Tottenham Heat for £45 million pounds. You're jealous because I'll be making *more* than you." Darren gloated.

Guy knew nothing of Darren's trade. Football trades were always splashed on the front-page of every paper. *How did he keep that a secret? Darren loves the spotlight!* He shook his head. *There's something dodgy here.* He drank the last of his pint and placed the glass on the bar.

"You're wrong, Darren. That's not it, at all. You've got your head so far up your arse, you can't see the daylight. Nor do you give a *fuck*." Guy gritted through clenched teeth. The words cemented the end of friendship and loyalty as brothers. Guy left the pub feeling liberated.

♥

Mercedes Maybachs, Aston Martins, Rolls Royce and Bentley's lined Worthington Hall's driveway all waiting for valet parking. As the sun began to set in the west, lanterns were turned on and landscape lighting changed to pink for tonight's occasion. It was to be a family dinner, but Darren and Guy's true family weren't in attendance.

Grace finished the last of the treacle pudding. She turned to Trevor to see if he needed any help.

"No, Grace. We're done. My staff will take care of the rest. I've prepared a wonderful dinner for us and I'm looking forward to sharing it with you." Trevor said as he wiped down a counter.

At first, Grace was flattered by the initial invitation, but all day in the kitchen she had seen Trevor's true colours. He barked orders at the staff, he made some cry and he often swore loudly.

Yet when he was around her, Trevor acted sweet and kind. He hovered about Grace extending a hand here or there and giving unsolicited advice. It was as though he was Dr. Jekyll and Mr. Hyde.

The other members of staff noticed Chef Hare's peculiar behaviour around Grace, and began to distance themselves from her.

She didn't like it. Grace wanted to be liked among her peers. Whilst she appreciated his help, it wasn't her intention to ride on the coattails of his success. Trevor had noticed her hesitation.

"I'm sure it will be lovely." she finally said. "I'm going to dress for dinner. Is it okay with you?" Grace asked, collecting her handbag.

"It's fine. I'll see you at eight." he replied. She said good-bye and hurried off to prepare for dinner.

As he watched her walk away, Trevor couldn't help but think, *Finally I'm getting the time I deserve with her!* He relished in the fantasy of getting her in bed when dinner was over with. His cock stirred at the thought of giving her a long, hard, and violent fuck. *I'm going to leave that naive, innocent, doe-eyed girl bowlegged and whimpering in the morning.*

Trevor knew that she was a lot like the other girls he pursued. They were all innocent, even the whores. They looked up to him because he was a celebrity, only to realise too late that he truly was a monster. *Grace is no exception. She looks at me like a protégé. And that's what I want...for her to worship me...not like her father who demeaned me.*

♥

Tamzin was seething. Darren had returned to their suite with a bloodied and bruised face. She wanted to march to Guy's suite and batter his face, but Darren told her that he was handling it.

Tamzin contacted Clive Wallace, her personal consultant and make-up artist, and demanded that he fix Darren's face. Taking one look at Darren's face and nose, Clive assured them it was fixable. Tamzin shook her head.

Shortly after Clive had applied some finishing touches to Darren, Gemma arrived at the suite. She had heard from other girls that there was a fight on the river. She had to confirm it from Tamzin before snitching to the Rumour Mill spy. Curious, Gemma wondered about the severity of the fight and hoped she still had chance with Guy.

"I don't believe it! Bloody hell! Oh my!" Gemma cried.

She looked at Darren's nose. Clive had managed to do his best to conceal Darren's damage.

Tamzin twisted and pinched Gemma's arm as she pulled her to the bedroom. She flung Gemma into the room. She turned her back to close the door. Then she came forward.

Tamzin wore an ice-blue, taffeta, Oscar De La Renta evening gown. As she made her way towards Gemma, her gown made a swishing sound. Her long blonde extensions were piled high in a towering bun. Tamzin dripped in expensive Asprey diamonds and wore a tiara on her crown. Gemma thought she resembled an ice queen.

"You need to give Guy a good fuck! I don't understand why you haven't had sex with him yet! He's ruining my wedding!"

Tamzin howled. She grabbed Gemma's arms, twisting the skin to cause burns. Gemma winced in pain.

"He's not interested in me!" she moaned. "Trust me, I've tried!"

Although Guy believed Gemma couldn't take a hint, she knew from her sources he isn't interested. The Rumour Mill spy that Gemma shared a room with elaborated how she saw Guy getting in his Range Rover with the baker. It was up to Gemma to find out who this girl was and to get pictures for a story. But Gemma wanted the story to be about her and not about some other girl. Besides, Tamzin's threats weren't helping.

Tamzin let go of Gemma and looked in the mirror to check her make-up. In her rage, Tamzin was worried that she had let something slip out of place.

"Make Guy interested! Take his cock out! Give him a blow-job he won't forget. A great blow-job brings any man to his senses." Tamzin growled. She turned back to Gemma with her hands on her hips. She watched as Gemma picked up a piece of chocolate from a chocolate box, and greedily stuffed it in her mouth.

"You're my best hen and friend... Do your job. Keep Guy Rowling satisfied, and out of my way. Do you understand?" she mewled as she walked over to Gemma. She patted Gemma's hair like a mother would to a child before she smacked the next piece of chocolate out of Gemma's hand. Gemma snickered.

"Fine." Gemma relented. "I'll get him Tam." She wanted to add *Maybe if you weren't such a bitch Guy would look at me in a different light.* But Gemma couldn't bring herself to say it. Besides she knew how vengeful Tamzin could be.

"Good. Put a smile on your face. Make me proud." Tamzin cooed. She pinched at Gemma's hallowed cheeks as if they had any fat to pinch.

♥

As she stood in front of Trevor's cottage door, Grace hesitated to knock. She was ten minutes late. Earlier, when Grace returned to her cottage, she took a long hot bath. During her bath Grace's mind went wild in thought of Guy. Her hands ran along her soapy breasts and legs in arousal. She became excited thinking about Guy sucking, kissing and tasting her. It wasn't till the sound of a clock chime announcing it was seven-thirty Grace realised she had let the fantasy carry her away.

Grace got out of the tub and rushed about the cottage. She dressed in a floral button-down Top Shop dress, cream tights, and brown Dorothy Perkins penny loafers. She spritzed some Matthew Williamson perfume on the crook of her neck and wrist. With no time to do her hair, she quickly ran a brush through it and prayed it would dry in beach comb tresses. It wasn't her finest look, but tonight she felt it was appropriate. She didn't want Trevor to think she was interested in him in another manner. In her eyes he was a man to admire, not to get in a relationship with.

Grace gained the courage to knock on the door. As soon as her fist pulled away, Trevor opened the door as if he was waiting there all along. He stood before her. He was dressed in a white cotton button-down shirt that billowed out over a pair of chinos. His dirty blonde hair was wet and curled from the shower. Grace looked to his feet. They were bare and large and unattractive. He smiled.

"Come in. I thought you weren't coming as you're late." Trevor said inviting her with his arm. "Would you like some wine?" he asked.

Before she could decline, Trevor thrusted a glass of red wine in her hand. He had poured it before her arrival. He had wanted to make sure she didn't say no. Trevor ushered her to a small table set for dinner for two. He pulled out her chair and let her sit.

"It's the best red wine you'll ever taste. It came from my own Tuscany vineyard." he boasted. "Tonight's menu is pheasant with parsnip puree. I'm sure you'll love the meal." he continued.

During dinner, she barely got a word in edge wise. Trevor revelled in his accomplishments before, during and after dinner. He wasn't interested in her or her business. He rambled on about his fine restaurants and the celebrities who ate there. She felt it was a long evening and couldn't wait for it to end. *I rather would've spent the night reading my Grazia magazine than being entertained by this bore.*

Throughout dinner, she daydreamt of Guy. She wanted to be with him at the family dinner. She wanted to get to know him, his family, and his friends. The more she dreamt about him, the more Grace wanted out of this weekend. *A tryst is great and all, but is it possible to have more out of this fling? I barely know him, I want to get to know him better and be someone special to him.*

Trevor noticed that her eyes had a faraway look to them. *She's not thinking about me! She's thinking about him,* he scowled. His brows creased with worry. He had to get her attention. He took away the dinner plates, refilled her wine glass and served her a plum crumble for dessert. This time he queried her about life, The Savoury Plum and her business pursuit. As soon as she answered a question, he replied with his own anecdote.

Trevor told her about his life, attending and dropping out of Oxford much to his parent's dismay. He spoke of his time attending London Culinary Academy and moving to Paris. Whilst he divulged in his personal history, she found him to be draining and soul sucking. She wanted to return to the comfort of her bed and wait for Guy to continue where they had left. *Trevor's such a condescending man and a snob! I'm surprised that everyone loves him. He's so different than his telly persona. I wish he was different but this is who he really is.*

Grace looked at her watch. She saw it was that it was half past ten. She was desperate to make her way back to the cottage, just in case Guy was waiting for her.

"Thank you for dinner and dessert. It was lovely." Grace complimented. She rose to her feet anxiously.

Trevor looked at her. *Damn it! Why is she leaving? It's not over till I say it's over. This tart needs to learn.*

"Where are you going? It's early."

"Yes, but we have an early day tomorrow. The rehearsal dinner and the wedding cake final touches." Grace said, grabbing her parka off of the couch.

Trevor followed closely behind her. He placed his hands on her shoulder, forcing her to turn to face him. *You're not getting away so easily.* His cock ached to push inside Grace's trembling womb. He wanted her to feel his searing seed explode against her walls. Trevor knew how to make Grace stay.

"Come. Stay awhile. I want to hear all about your plans for Delicious." he insisted.

Briefly she considered staying for a little whilst longer. Trevor thought his words had affected her and he won. *She's falling for me,* he convinced himself. Trevor took her palms in his hands. The touch nerved her. It repulsed her. She pulled away to step backwards.

"Stay. A few minutes more. We're not done here." Trevor said firmly.

Trevor moved his body closer to her. He was invading her personal space. She felt like she was a small mouse backed into a corner by a hulking cat. He inched towards her and wrapped his arms tight around her waist. She felt the doorknob press into her bottom and his arousal press against her.

He knew he had her. He cupped her chin and pressed his lips against her lips. She squirmed. She tried to wrestle her way out of his tightening grip, but to no avail. Trevor, proving stronger than Grace, forced her lips apart with his tongue. The intrusion made her eyes go wide in horror. He released one of his hands which found its way to her breast. There, he fondled her roughly. Grace gathered all her strength and pushed him away. She brought her hands to her lips in shock.

"I'm sorry, Trevor. I've got to leave!" she snapped.

Trevor tried to regain his footing to grab her, but it was too late. She ran out of his cottage, leaving Trevor angrily sulking by the door.

Grace ran all the way back to her cottage. By the time she arrived she was out of breath and exhausted. *What did I do? Why did he touch me that way?* She felt confused and disoriented.

She locked the cottage door behind her. She prayed that he hadn't followed her back. When Grace felt he hadn't, she went to the loo. She undressed and slipped into the shower. *Something about the way he looked at me. The way he touched me. It felt so dirty.* The hot water washed over her skin. She needed to feel clean. *Trevor's nothing like Guy. Now I know...*

♥

It had been another long evening for Guy. The so-called family dinner turned into a loud party that really had nothing to do with the meeting of the families. It didn't matter anyway as only Darren's mother and her sister attended with a distant cousin. In comparison to the Smythe family, it was nothing. Guy knew that it was best to keep their family hidden away, instead of the truth being revealed.

Guy wasn't happy with the seating arrangements during the sit-down dinner. He was forced to sit next to Gemma. In an attempt to arouse him, Gemma tried to rub him through his trousers. She knew he would maintain a stiff upper lip.

Without breaking a sweat on his brow, Guy retaliated by smacking her hand away. In return, she would laugh obnoxiously garnering curious looks from the other guests at their table. He hissed in her ear to stop, or he would embarrass her. Gemma grinned, pretending not to listen or notice his anger. When dessert arrived, Guy decided it was time to excuse himself from the party.

Tamzin threw Gemma a red hot glare. Instinctively, Gemma knew Tamzin was ordering her to follow him. She saw Gemma's attempts at getting Guy's attention failing but she wasn't going to allow him to leave without knowing who, what, where and why. As soon as he left, Gemma quickly gathered herself and followed him out of the dining room.

Maintaining her distance, Gemma kept Guy in her sight. She followed him out of the hall, into the parking lot, where she saw him retrieve a bottle of champagne and a dozen of red roses from his SUV. Gemma knew his gifts weren't for her and she was frantic to know which WAG sunk their teeth into Guy. By now she should've heard through her gossip vine, but no one knew who the girl was. Her Rumour Mill source only had limited information. *Whoever it is knows how to keep their lips sealed!*, she thought sourly.

Unaware of his female shadow, Guy walked the winding path to the cottage. He was oblivious and in his own thoughts. He wondered if Grace would like the champagne and the flowers. *Did I make the right choice? I should've bought Cristal instead of Krug? Maybe she prefers pink instead of red roses?*

After the terrible trip down on the River Wye, Guy had a long think about Grace. Before dinner, he had settled on his bed cringing at his terrible reaction when she confessed about her virginity. The more he thought about it, the more he was grateful that she was untouched. He pondered the idea of waiting even though he was experienced and worldly. He loved the fact that he would be able to teach her things no other man had the pleasure of teaching her and showing her how special lovemaking can be.

When she moves to London I'll take Grace on many dates. I'll gain her trust and respect. I want us to fall in love with one another. When the time is right, I'll whisk her away to somewhere exotic like the Maldives so we can have all the time in the world to explore each other.

Thinking about it now, his chest puffed out in pride. *I'm a hopeless romantic. How the hell does one fall for a perfect, beautiful stranger in under three days? I wonder if she feels the same about me.*

He couldn't believe it. It was her unique and beautiful sweet persona that made him like this. Given she was working on a wedding cake and their time was limited, but the moment he laid eyes on her he just knew. *I have to have her.* Guy knocked on her door. When she didn't answer, he knocked again. He made sure his knock was louder than before.

In the darkness and cover of large trees, Gemma hid from him. She squinted her eyes as she tried to get a view of the door creeping open. She couldn't see the face in the doorway.

Grace jolted when she heard the louder second knock. She was towel drying her hair. She prayed it wasn't Trevor. She walked over to the door.

"Grace, it's me, Guy." he said through the door.

Cautious, she pulled the door open. She was relieved to see Guy standing before her. She ushered him in swiftly. Gemma didn't get a chance to see who opened the door.

She locked the door and turned to Guy holding a bottle of champagne and roses. He noticed her face was a ghastly white colour.

"Are you sick?" he asked worriedly.

She shook her head no. *How am I to tell him that Trevor kissed me?* The thought of his reaction frightened her. She didn't want to lose the opportunity to date Guy Rowling.

"These are for you. I thought we'd celebrate meeting and getting to know one another." he said. "I missed you dearly and today. All I thought about was you."

Grace felt as if her throat was closing in on her. Her words were choking in her throat as tears gathered in the wells of her eyes.

"Trevor kissed me." she admitted softly. "He wanted more, but I stopped him."

He sensed fear in her voice. Guy walked over to assure her that he wasn't going anywhere just because another man kissed her. He gave her a strong hug, and kissed her softly on her crown.

A loud clap of thunder shook the cottage. Gemma was now by the window. She peeked through the flimsy watching Guy hold Grace in his arms. *That's the cow who stole my bloke! This has to stop immediately!*

Thunder rumbled through the valley. Gemma needed to hurry back to the hall before the heavens opened up. She couldn't wait to tell Tamzin and the spy what she had witnessed.

♥

eight

In the Wye Valley a late night thunderstorm had rolled in bringing fierce winds and rain pellet rooftops. Guy lit a fire in the fireplace. Grace sat down opposite the fire and he sat next to her. He cuddled her in his arms as she told him the sordid details of dinner with Trevor.

Guy wasn't surprised. He politely explained that any man would want her. He convinced her that she was beautiful inside and out. Yet it didn't excuse the fact that she wasn't interested in Trevor. Guy tried being rational about it.

"Why didn't you tell Trevor that you're seeing someone?" he asked.

"I was afraid he'd ask me to leave the kitchen. We're one day away from the wedding. The cake is complete, but there are many final touches. I don't want to lose this opportunity." Grace looked up into Guy's eyes, worried.

"Look, I hired you. I'll have a word with him and sort it out. Trevor should have never laid a hand on you, especially without your permission. Do you think he's going to hurt you?" he questioned.

"No…I don't know." she said, shaking her head.

The whole scenario perplexed her. She felt it was her fault and maybe she was overreacting. A nagging feeling told her that Trevor had tried to take advantage of her.

"I'll deal with this myself. Just leave it." she insisted firmly.

Guy hugged her tightly in his arms. He decided to change the subject before his mind would no longer reason. *It'll result in me marching over to Trevor's to pummel the shite out of him.*

"You're not the only one in a mess." he assessed.

He told her about the incident on the river and the fight with Darren. Grace sat up astonished.

"Are you OK? Where does that leave you and Darren?" she asked. Her eyes were filled with concern.

"We're not speaking. If it wasn't for you being here, I would've left a long time ago." he replied bitterly.

Guy was angry that it came to blows. The last time they had gotten into a fight, was when they were in Upper school. They had learned that they were brothers and the anger besotted them. *We*

made up, moved on and promised to be there for one another. We promised
to keep our secrets and leave home for good.

Attempting to soothe him, Grace rubbed his back with the palm of her hand. *It's been a bad day.* The rain and wind seemed to project their feelings.

"Let's get our minds off of our problems." she chimed.

Grace saw the bottle of Krug sitting on the coffee table and wondered why he brought it. He noticed her eyeing the bottle.

"I bought champagne for us to celebrate. If it wasn't for this bloody wedding we would've never met." he said happily.

"I'll drink to that!" she chirped. She ran to the kitchen to grab some flute glasses whilst Guy popped the bottle open. The champagne overflowed and they laughed as he poured it into the crystal flute.

"Here's a toast to us and to our future. May we find happiness in each other's arms!" he bellowed. In merriment they clicked their flute glasses together. They drank the champagne.

The first sips of champagne went to straight to Grace's head. She felt lighter and happier since Guy had arrived. She loved the way he listened to her and how he held her in his arms. She wanted to stay in his arms forever. She wanted Guy to stroke her silky caramel hair and to whisper words of affection against her ear. After their third glass they locked eyes.

The look between them spoke a thousand and one words. Both of them thought whether they should or shouldn't continue last nights' sexual escapade.

"Shall we take this into the bedroom?" he asked. His voice was firm yet tender. He knew it was a forward question, one he hoped Grace will say yes to.

She felt her heart skip a beat. *I want this and this is who I want it with...I will do this.*

"Yes." she whispered.

Guy held out his hand to Grace, and she took it. Each step they took towards the bedroom confirmed that there was no going back.

He isn't Trevor. He's Guy, one of the sexiest footballer on the planet. What girl wouldn't want this with him? Olivia would think I'm stupid for not taking a chance on him, she managed to convince herself.

As soon as the bedroom door closed behind them, Guy spun Grace on her heel to him. He pressed her body against the door and kissed her with zeal like he had never done before. Amorously, she lifted her arms wrapping them around his neck. She kissed him with carnal desire. *I want him and I want him now!*

He moved away to untie her pink robe, dropping it to the floor. He looked at her longingly as she stood before him in her pink floral bra and knickers set from Debenhams. Her honey skin still had residual water beads from her hot shower and her damp hair was semi-dry in long beach-combed tresses. In excitement he held his breath. *She's stunning! God she's striking, my sweet pretty babe.* Unable to control his actions, he crushed his body into her. He nibbled at her earlobes, and kissed her neck.

In return, Grace did the same, if not, with more zest. She loved the feeling of his rough five o'clock stubble against her lips and the taste of his skin. The smell of his Prada aftershave with tones of woodsy scents drove her body into madness.

Guy continued his kisses further south. He slowly pulled at her bra straps and brought his lips to the top of her heaving bosom. Her bosom was blushed from arousal. He wanted to rip the bra off of her breasts, but he knew he had to be gentle. He knead her soft supple breasts through the brassiere fabric. Her hard thrilled peaks reached out to his touch and ached for his tongue to circle and swirl around them.

Grace brought her hands up to his necktie and shirt. She removed the tie and unbuttoned his shirt. As she pulled off Guy's shirt, she exposed his chest, taut abs, and muscular arms. Guy nuzzled his face into the top of her bosom. He planted soft kisses there as his hair caressed her skin in tantalising fashion making her arch her aching body towards his.

They returned to kissing passionately with their tongues touching, kissing and swirling around one another's. He brought his hands to the apples of her arse cheeks to lift her up, wrap her legs around his waist, and held her tight. She gasped as he took steps to the bed. There Guy softly placed her on the bed so they'd continue their exploration of one another.

Guy took his place beside her. He propped an elbow next to her as she laid still. He ran his index finger along her swollen scarlet lips. Succumbing to temptation, he brought his mouth crashing down on hers. He took the bottom lip between his teeth and tugged gently. It was a bite that Grace ravishingly enjoyed.

"Grace you're beautiful. You're more than beautiful. I've never met anyone like you. Every time I'm in your presence, I'm in awe of you. I've never been with a woman as gorgeous, driven and gracious as you. I need you." Guy crooned. He stared at her basking in every inch of her beauty.

Grace was stunned by his words and was at a loss. She felt a need to show appreciation by kissing him. He accepted her kiss, but pulled back.

"Grace, promise we'll see each other when you move to London. Promise that what happens tonight this will be more than a weekend encounter. I really want to see what happens between us." Guy pleaded softly.

His words made her body shudder happily. It was exactly what she wanted to hear and she felt it was sincere and from his heart.

"I want to see you become a success. I want to be by your side when you open Delicious. I want to be a fixture in your life. Promise me, Grace, promise me that it's possible." He searched her eyes for the answer.

"I promise." she murmured.

Guy's moved his body so that he was looming over her. This time he kissed her with no intention on stopping. Each kiss escalated to another thrilling level which included a chance at love. He returned to trailing his kisses to her bosom. He moved his hands to her back where his fingers swiftly unclasp her bra. Delicately, Guy pulled her brassiere off, the cool air causing her pink nipples to harden. He brought his mouth down on her plum breasts where he suckled on the sanguine peaks.

Around her rosy areola he swirled his tongue, blowing his hot breath across the skin, causing Grace to shiver. He applied the same affection to her left breast. She gasped loudly. In passion she felt her body shake. His undivided attention remained on her nipples as if they were aperitifs before a main course.

If he doesn't take me now, I'll surely die of madness! she screamed within as she twisted her head on the pillows.

Guy rose to remove the remainder of his clothing. As she watched him peel away his jeans, she trembled in anticipation. She recalled seeing him in the shower, but now she was going to get the opportunity to see him fully naked.

He smiled down at her. He decided it was best to leave his shorts on. He didn't want to give her a heart attack when he exposed his cock to her. As her eyes wandered down to his chest and abdomen, she couldn't help but notice the stiff, aubergine, head of his cock poking its way through the boxer flap. *Phwoar! He's aching and hard! I wonder if he'll let me touch it.*

She brought herself to her knees and faced him. He took a fist full of her ochre tresses, tugging back gently to expose the valley of her neck. There he devoured her, dragging his tongue over the dip of her shoulders down to her breasts again.

She ran her hands along the naked firm flesh of his chest and palms down to the top of his shorts. He brought his hands to her arse and he drew her close to his body so she could feel his hardness throb against her soaked knickers.

As they kissed and rubbed their bodies against each other, Grace moved her warm palm to the inside of his shorts. Her hand stroked his hard, silky cock. He let out a deep, guttural moan. *Fucking eh! Does she know what she's doing to me?*

Guy's knees went weak from her touching. He thought he would collapse on top of her. She stroked his meaty girth and long length. She flicked her palm over his bulbous head and rubbed its pre-cum secretion against the pad of her thumb.

She swooned. *How am I to take this all in? How is it to fit? He's too large, too thick. He'll rip me apart.*

Another ripple shook her body. Grace ached for his touch and her womb trembled. He noticed and let out a small laugh. He knew what she was thinking, and found it charming.

"Easy, girl. I haven't gone down on you yet. I want this moment between us to last." he whispered.

"I know I've got to be patient."

It was hard to pull her hand away, but he thought it best. He wanted to be in charge. He wanted to teach her.

"I want to do something to you." he said, whilst tugging her knickers down over her arse. He pushed her softly down on the bed. He drew her knickers down her tan thighs, over her knees to the base of her ankles. He threw them aside.

Her heart palpitated as though wild horses charged in her chest. He took off his shorts, bringing his body down next to hers. Fully naked against her, Guy brought his hand to her creamy wet slit. There, he stroked her rosebud as she held tightly to his wrist. Her clit felt as if it was on fire. Her wetness was like molten lava and her womb shrieked for his cock.

"Oh...god...."she moaned, arching her body to meet his fingers. "Please...Guy...Please."

She muffled her screams by biting on his shoulder. Guy didn't wince. He watched her face contort with pleasure. Her lips pursing and opening as she gasped for air.

"Come for me Grace." he roared in her ear.

The intensity of words and touching made Grace explode in feverish climax. She felt the room collapse around her and she was now in a sexual space from which there was no return.

Guy drew his fingers away and moved Grace's body up the bed. He pulled her in a sitting position and she hovered over his head.

"Hold onto the headboard." he ordered.

She did as she was told. Curious, she looked down at Guy. With his hands on her arse, Guy drew her sopping pussy onto his mouth. She cried out from the shock of it all.

In disbelief and pleasure, Grace felt her body move along Guy's tongue as he explored every nook and cranny of her pussy. His tongue swirled, licked and dipped in places she never knew a tongue would go. At one point she thought he licked her anus.

As if nature knew the carnal erotic pleasure that Guy was applying to Grace, lightning struck nearby and thunder clapped loudly. Every time he suckled at her, she felt electrical charges course through her body. It made her clit pucker forward and her nipples harden like marble.

Guy brought one of his palms up to her breasts. He rolled her plush skin in his hand whilst he continued to lap at her. Grace gripped the upholstered headboard for dear life. Her body felt as though it was on fire. From this moment onward she knew her previous life had melted away and disappeared.

All my innocence, my naivety is washed away with each lap of his tongue! She gasped and panted.

She tastes so sweet. The finest nectar I have the pleasure of tasting! I can do this all night. Guy thought as he watched her toss her head back and the tendrils of her hair cascade around her face.

"Oh my...I'm coming!" she cried.

Grace felt pressure building inside her body. Her womb contracted against his tongue. Guy kept his focus. Beads of sexual sweat formed all over her skin. She glistened and glowed. Each moan and movement of her body, Guy felt his own need constrict his testicles and tighten his cock.

Blood rushed and flowed in their ears. The sound of the storm was no longer audible to Grace or Guy. Her gasping and cries of mercy and pleasure filled the bedroom. Several times she called out his name in frenzy as her hips buried her pussy on his face. Guy held onto her tightly as he lapped up every last drop of her delicious orgasmic release.

Panting, Grace fell forward on the headboard. She rested against the cool wall. Faint and intoxicated by what just happen, Guy removed Grace from her position and pulled her down over his body.

"I enjoyed that." Grace murmured.

"I'm glad you did because I'm not through with you." he replied. Guy spooned her naked body. His solid rock hard cock pressed against Grace's bare arse. He pulled her dewy hair aside to kiss the back of her neck. Slowly, he drew his hand down her body, caressing gently, bringing it around to her belly. There he followed his hand down to her soaking pussy.

"Guy...please...I beg you take me now."

"No!"

He ran one of his fingers along her creamy clit. He found Grace's nub to tease it. She grounded her arse against Guy's cock in an attempt to persuade him to enter her. It took a great deal of restraint not to come all over her backside. Suddenly, he was at the warm tight entrance of her pussy.

"I'm not going to take you yet. I'm exploring a bit." he growled.

She nodded as he continued his kisses. Grace gyrated her arse against Guy's cock. She felt the roughness of his finger enter her dripping pussy. Her breathing was shallow as he bucked his hips against her arse. With only the tip of his finger in her, Guy felt her tightness. *Damn, she's too tight. I'll break her. I don't want to hurt her.*

"Guy...Guy..." she chanted deliriously.

The more he toyed with her, the wetter she was. Soon her pussy flooded against his palm all the way down to her arse giving Guy the slick friction his cock it needed.

I need him inside me. I need him now. This can't go on any longer! Grace thought to herself, but she didn't realise she said it out loud.

"Do you need me inside you Grace?" Guy questioned. His voice intense with heat. "Do you want me inside you?"

"Please...I beg of you! Take me now...take me tonight." she cried to him. He turned her body to him. He wanted to see if she was telling him the truth. There were tears in the corners of her eyes from the sexual torture he had given her through foreplay.

"Are you sure, Grace? Do you really want this? Look at me, tell me, Grace." he demanded roughly. He gripped her waist and pushed his hardness to her.

"*Yes! Yes!*" she shouted.

Grace kissed him in carnal joy. He flipped her on her back. His muscular body rose above hers. Guy spread her legs wide to look at her coral lips. They puckered creamily.

"Look at my cock, Grace. Feel it. Touch it." he growled.

Her eyes were glassy with ecstasy. She looked down at his bulging cock. It twitched before her like an angry serpent.

"I might hurt you, Grace and that's the last thing I want to do to you. Do you understand?" Grace nodded weakly.

"I want this with you and only you." she replied in a raspy voice.

"Grace, I don't have a condom, but I don't care if I get you pregnant. After tonight you're mine, mine alone." his voice was deep, guttural and sure of himself.

He pushed her thighs apart with his strong athletic legs. The move jolted her back into reality. *There's no going back. I've gone too far.*

He held the tip of his cock at the entrance of her quivering sex. Slowly, he pushed his cock into her tight entrance. He felt his cock tearing her apart.

Oh my god! The tip alone is bloody massive! His cock is huge! Grace bit her lip, wincing in pain. Inch by inch, he pushed his velvet hard cock within the scorching heat of her womb. He stretched her slowly, creeping along to reach the brink of her hymen. In protective reaction, she felt her body clench. She felt heat and tightness and knew he had to break her hymen.

"Grace, I'm going to enter you now. Brace yourself." Guy hissed. She yelped yes.

"Hold still."

With one long hard thrust Guy plunged deep into her. Her womb coated his cock with a gush of hot liquid juice. He roared.

"Oh god, Grace!"

Guy bent his head forward. He was beyond aroused. As he plunged into her again, they both felt the skin rip and tear. Grace cried in pain. She bit down on Guy's shoulder again. He grabbed her waist. He begged her to be still before he came. He wanted to enjoy it all. Grace clasped her hands onto his arse as Guy brought her legs up to wrap around his own. When he did this he caught sight of his cock. There was a slick ring of blood around it. *She's mine.* He had marked her. *No man will ever have her like the way I did.*

Guy pumped his cock in and out of her puffy and bruised sex. He groped at her breasts and sucked on her nipples whilst she clawed at his back. In unison they moved. The rhythmic movement lessened her pain. It made sex pleasurable.

Grace held on Guy like a person clinging to a life preserver lost at sea. She could feel his heart pulsing along the ridge of his cock. Each time he thrusted deep within her, Grace felt the head of him swell bigger and bigger. He ran his hand down between their bodies so he could rub her clit. Her cries of rapture were frequent, demanding and loud. She was hot, wet and raw begging for more of Guy's cock. Unable to hold back she cried out and released herself. Wave after wave orgasmic pleasure burst forth like a dam. Her pussy thrashed, quaked, and tightened around Guy's cock in attempts to milk him.

"Keep coming, Grace." he murmured in her ear.

Another squeeze of her womb was all it took. Guy gave in to the throes of orgasm. Enthralled, he ruptured sticky ribbons of hot white semen into her quivering womb, extracting every last drop. Every inch of her was covered in his seed. Guy fell over her body panting. He kissed her.

Bloody hell! That's quite powerful! He never encountered an orgasm like he the one he had tonight. What made it special was that it was the first, sexual orgasm in Grace's experience.

As Guy pulled his body off of Grace, the sights and sounds returned to normal. The thunderstorm moved away as they laid in bed. They listened to the slowing of the rain. After awhile, they began to talk about the sex. Grace assured Guy he hadn't hurt her and she enjoyed every minute of it. Soon focus shifted to food. They were starving. They got up from bed and went to the lounge to have the last of champagne, eat some pretzels and chocolates.

Once they were done eating and talking, Guy drew them a hot bubble bath. They sat in the tub, talking and laughing. Guy promised that he would continue to see Grace in London and that he couldn't wait for her to move. As he made promises of the future, Grace felt apprehension.

I hope he's telling the truth...I hope his promises are kept because I'm falling in love with him, she thought to herself.

♥

Not pleased by Grace's reaction, Trevor went to find his parka to chase her down. *She's run off before she's given me a chance!* He scowled. *Women like Grace usually fall into my bed with ease! What's gone wrong?*

Normally, Trevor would've forced Grace into his bed without her knickers on. His hand would wrap tightly around her delicate neck whilst she would squirm during the rough sex. He loved watching his women suffocate before he'd climax. His intentions were to never let a girl climax and to leave them sore and bruised.

It'd been ages since Trevor had sex with a girl like Grace. Trevor's schedule was hectic from filming shows, writing a cookbook and catering Tamzin's wedding. It all proved to be time consuming. *Tonight was to be the end of this drought!* But Grace's reaction had fanned the flames and he was determined to finish what he started by going to her cottage.

His anger boiled as he searched for his parka. When it was in his hands, he stormed to the front door and swung it open. There, in front of him stood Gemma, wiping off a fat droplet of rain that hit her head. Startled, he took a step back.

"Can I help you?" Trevor asked.

"I'm lost. I was trying to find my way back to the hall, but the rain started and the trees are dense with foliage. It makes it difficult to see the lights." she mumbled.

During Gemma's walk, the skies grew increasingly dark. The stars and moon covered by storm clouds. Although she saw some of the lights in the break of the trees, it was impossible to walk through them.

"Where we're you coming from?"

"The cottage further down the path." Gemma replied.

The wind howled and hard rain fell from the sky. Trevor engrossed in his thoughts didn't notice Gemma getting wet. *She came from Grace's cottage?*

"Can I come in please?" Gemma begged.

Trevor nodded, beckoning her in. He went to fetch a towel and Gemma took the liberty to sit on the couch.

"Is it ok to stay until the storm passes?" she asked. He handed her the towel and nodded yes.

"Did you come from my baker's cottage? Grace's cottage?" Trevor asked coming around the couch and taking a seat next to her.

"Yes! She's shagging my boyfriend, Guy, as we speak. Guy Rowling, the footballer. That dirty slapper!" Gemma sneered whilst rubbing the towel through her wet hair. "At dinner Guy left me alone. So I followed him to the cottage. I saw them shagging!"

Trevor smiled like a Cheshire cat. He clapped his hands as he got up from the couch.

"Would you like a cup of tea?"

"Yes, please." Gemma replied politely.

He placed the tea kettle on the hob. He couldn't help but think about Grace. *Grace isn't interested in me because she prefers dirty footballers. Ah, when one mouse gets away another comes through the garden door!* He knew girls like Gemma had horrible reputations. She was an opportunity not to be missed. *For now, Gemma will have to do.*

The kettle whistled as he poured brandy into the tea cup along with a sedative. *This one's not getting away so easily.*

♥

When lightning struck the hall, the stinging slap of Tamzin's palm on Darren's cheek made him feel he was struck by the same bolt.

"*What's bloody wrong with you?!*" Tamzin shrieked. "*First the baker and now my sister! Between your indiscretions, Guy's antics and these scandals, I wonder why get married!*"

My father's right. Darren will never change. I'll be damned if this marriage doesn't follow through. It's my career and money on the line, Tamzin thought, infuriated.

Darren shrugged. All he wanted was time to unwind with someone who wasn't high-strung like Tamzin. He chuckled at the thought. *High-strung. Much to be said about that!* He had finished off a bump of coke on her sister's Tara's tit and was about to stick his cock inside her, when the door swung open. Tamzin pulled him by his ear and dragged him back to the suite to argue.

"I need to unwind. The fight with Guy has me stressed. I need to be myself." he gruffed.

She twirled on her heel. She marched away from him. Darren knew where Tamzin was heading to her purse to find her mobile and call daddy.

"My father's going to cut your cock off!" she howled as she reached inside her Louis Vuitton bag to fish out her iPhone. He grabbed her arm and pulled her body close to his own.

"Come on, babe! Don't be a sourpuss. We both know lately you've been absorbed with wedding plans to satisfy my hunger." he claimed in a haughty manner.

It's true. I haven't been doing my duties as a loyal fiancée. He's right, she sulked.

He held her wrist and brought his lips crashing down onto hers. "Babes, please get on your hands and knees and suck my cock. Make me forget." he hissed.

Maybe a good fuck will do us both some good. And maybe Gemma's doing her job so we can get back on track. Tamzin pouted and he kissed it. Tamzin gleamed whilst slowly unzipping his trousers and got down on her knees.

♥

nine

awn broke along the horizon. For Grace, it was a new day and a beginning. The dew evaporated in the fields, sheep graze and baaed. Birds sang their morning song as they searched for worms. The sun shining through flimsy curtains or chirping from birds didn't wake them from their slumber. Instead it was the sound of her mobile ringing loudly that woke her. Grace looked at the clock on the nightstand. *It's eight thirty! I'm late! Bollocks! Trevor will be mad!*

Grace picked up her mobile and saw it was her aunts. She ignored the call, for it to only ring again. Briefly, she considered answering the call, but feared it would wake Guy. She ignored the call, but it rang again. This time she had to answer it.

"Allo." Grace whispered.

"Finally! Grace where are you? We haven't heard a word from you! You haven't responded to any of our texts or our messages!" Corrie cried.

"I'm fine. I've been busy." she murmured.

"Why are you whispering? Are you in the kitchen? I don't hear any background noise. Did you get fired? Where are you?" Corrie interrogated.

"I'm fine. I'm in the pantry. I've got to get back to work. I'll see you tomorrow afternoon." Grace lied. Next to her, Guy was stirring awake.

"Wait! Grace!" Corrie cried out. Corrie wanted to speak to Grace regarding an article she read in Rumour Mill, but it was too late. Grace ended the call and turned off her Blackberry.

"Good morning." Guy mumbled as he kissed her shoulder.

"Good morning." Grace replied, tugging the sheet over her naked breasts.

"You're getting all shy on me? You slept without your kit and told me how you wanted more." he teased.

"You're fibbing. I didn't say those things." denied Grace.

It's true, Grace slept with her kit off. But she didn't recall asking for more sex. *Maybe just once!*

Guy pulled her body close to his naked flesh. She felt his warmth. His cock stiff and hard pressed against her lush thigh.

"I've been dreaming about you. Come under the sheets. I want to show you what I want to do to you."

His fingertips caressed the skin on her thighs. They slowly brushed over her pussy. Grace shuddered. As enticing as it was, she knew she had to go to work. Guy brought his hand up to her right breast. He pinched her nipple to its diamond peak. Guy brought his other hand down between her legs. He pushed the hood of her pussy back to caress her clit with his thumb.

"Guy...maybe a quick one. I've got to get to work. I'm late." she moaned.

"I promise I'll be quick." *Little does she know I want an hour or more with her!*

He rubbed her clit the way she liked it. She quivered as his finger began to circle its wet entrance.

"Let's try something new." he murmured in her ear.

He pulled her body over on his. Her breasts pressed up against his hard pecs and her tummy lay against his own. Her soaking wet sex pushed against his solid cock. She felt his head trying to push its way in. They continued kissing. Grace brought her body into a sitting position. She was about to impale herself onto his long steel rod and ride him like a jockey at Ascot, when Grace heard a familiar voice shout out.

"Grace! Grace!"

She pulled herself off of Guy, wrapping a blanket around her naked body. Annoyed, he bolted up and out of the bed. He threw on his underwear.

"What the fuck!" he snapped.

"Grace?" It was followed by a knock on the bedroom door.

"I'll be right there!" she answered loudly.

She wrapped herself in a robe and put her hair up in a bun before opening the door. She emerged and walked to the lounge.

"What are you doing here?" she asked firmly. Her eyes saw red. She couldn't believe Trevor was standing in her lounge.

"You didn't show up for work. I was concerned for your well-being, so I walked here and found the cottage door open." Trevor replied. His eyes glanced over at the empty champagne bottle, the roses and crumpled packets of crisps, pretzels and chocolate wrappings resting on the coffee table. Guy stormed out of the bedroom, taking his place behind Grace. He brought his arm to her waist.

"Why are you here? How'd you get in?" Guy interrogated.

Trevor grimaced bitterly. *Gemma's telling the truth! The little slut! Grace pretends innocence yet she's shagging Guy! Slag! Whore!*

"I knocked. No one answered. I saw that the door was open, and I felt the need to check the premises. After yesterday's attack by a Rumour Mill pap on Grace, I thought she might be hurt." Trevor angrily retorted.

Guy looked at Grace puzzled. She hadn't mention it to him.

"Is that true?" Guy asked.

"No...Not entirely. He didn't attack me. He wanted to know about the wedding cake. He followed me to find out information." Grace replied confidently.

Trevor watched Guy placing his arms protectively around Grace. Guy caressed her hair and kissed her softly on the lips like a concerned lover. The action infuriated Trevor. He wanted to push Guy off of Grace and pummel him. He narrowed his steel, grey eyes on Guy. The look told Guy that he was in for a fight.

"Grace, I expect you in the kitchen shortly. Hurry along. Get dressed. If not, shall I search for another baker?" Trevor ordered. Before Grace could answer, Guy answered for her.

"On Tamzin's behalf, I found Grace. You didn't hire her, I did. You didn't pay for Grace's cottage, I did. I wrote the cheque. I paid for the cottage. *Not you.*" his voice boomed. Trevor ignored Guy's outburst. He directed his attention to Grace.

"I expect to see you soon, Grace." Trevor repeated bitterly.

"Yes Trevor." she replied meekly, whilst Trevor walked away. Trevor turned back to Grace.

"It's Chef Hare to you." he corrected, before slamming the cottage door.

Trevor walked away like an injured fox. *It's not over yet! Gemma provided to be resourceful. Grace isn't aware of Gemma's plans and it's going to stay that way. When Guy breaks her heart, she'll come crawling back to me. They always do.*

"What a pompous twat!" he growled.

Trevor's unannounced arrival left him in a foul mood. He wanted to punch the snotty chef in the face.

"I've got to get dressed. I've got work to do." Grace said padding back to her bedroom.

"Tonight's the rehearsal dinner. Beforehand we're to do a pub crawl, but I can miss it. Instead we can have lunch together."

Guy knew they had little precious time to share together. Tonight was the final night before the wedding, and then they would return to their lives. Grace walked into the loo. She peeled off her robe and turned the shower on. She stepped inside.

"I can't. I promised I would help with tonight's desserts. I'm late as it is. I'd love to have lunch, but I'll be busy." she replied sullen.

"We don't have much time together, Grace. Will you be my date for the wedding? I want you there, and I didn't come with a date." he asked. *I hope she says yes.*

"Are you sure you want me there? I don't have anything to wear." she replied whilst washing her hair.

"Yes I want you there. As for a dress, make-up and what not, I'll have Clive, a celebrity fashionista, prepare you. I'm sure he has plenty of dresses in his trunks that'll fit you." When she didn't answer, Guy continued his plea.

"Grace please don't turn me down. I want you by my side." She poked her head from behind the shower curtain.

"Yes. Yes, I'll be your date." she replied cheerfully, kissing him.

They said their goodbyes. Guy hurried to his suite to get ready for the day and find Clive.

♥

As she sat reading through her text messages, Clive rolled a hot curling tong in Tamzin's extensions.

"Tamzin, Rumour Mill is here. They want their exclusive shots of the wedding preparations. Also they want to hear your side of the scandal." her personal assistant interrupted.

"I thought you handled the scandal!" she snapped.

"Yes, but it seems the word's out you hired Grace for your wedding cake. Rumours are going around that Grace is having an affair with Guy." her assistant said shakily.

"What? How'd they find out?" she asked, taking her eyes away from her mobile.

"I did handle it. They must've spoken to one of the hens. It seems it's going to be big news and it'll take away attention from your wedding."

"Over my dead body. Tell them I'll give them the exclusive behind the cake and they can take pictures of the new cake. We'll show them how beautiful the new cake is instead of that *ghastly* thing

Libby sent. I'll sort the rumours regarding Libby, Grace, and Guy. I'll put them straight." Tamzin said icily. "Tell the kitchen, I'll be down to do an interview in front of the cake."

Few hours later, Tamzin appeared with Rumour Mill staff trailing behind her through the kitchen. Grace was applying gold colour sugar and edible gold marzipan leaves to layers of cake. She approached Grace and smiled broadly.

"Let me introduce you to my new baker, Grace Knowles of Delicious Bakery. As you see by the display before you, her talent supersedes that of Ms. Blackwell. " she introduced.

Tamzin's compliment took Grace back. She felt her cheeks blush with a deep scarlet colour.

"You can interview Ms. Knowles only on the subject of the cake. Nothing else and nothing more. If not I'll have my solicitor contact you regarding breach of contract." Tamzin commanded. The crew grumbled as they set up cameras and microphones.

At the other end of the kitchen, Trevor smirked whilst watching Grace. *She's flustered. She doesn't know what's coming to her.*

Tamzin left the Rumour Mill staff with Grace. Grace didn't want to do an interview. *What was she thinking placing me on the spot like this?* She looked to Trevor for help. Their eyes locked briefly. Instead he turned his attention to his sous-chef. *He's blanking me!*

Let her squirm and stew in her pot. She'll learn her lesson, Trevor thought, pushing a handful of leeks to his sous-chef.

♥

Early in the morning, Gemma crept back to her own suite. She sat on the edge of the porcelain tub pouring Acqua Di Parma bath gel into the hot water.

Slowly and painfully, she took off her clothing. She slipped in and brought a hot cloth to her aching body. Fat tears coursed down the tops of her cheeks. Mascara smudged around her eyes making her look like a raccoon. Through the soapy water she saw the bruises all over her thighs and arms. Her wrists had burns on them and her legs were covered with bites.

As Gemma ran the cloth over her body and drew it away, she saw blood on the white cloth. She bit her lip to muffle her cries.

What was I thinking? Why did I sleep with him? I'd call the police, but would they believe me given my reputation? Questions fell around Gemma like rain drops. She scowled and cried. *That bloody bastard raped me!*

When she took a cup of tea, she thought Trevor was being polite. She welcomed his affections as he cuddled next to her, assuring her that all will be fine. The storm increased its strength and she felt since she couldn't have Guy, at least she could have fun with him. But Gemma hadn't expected to feel woozy from tea. She tasted the brandy, but was unaware of the sedative added to it.

All it took was fifteen minutes and her body felt heavy. Her eyelids felt as though iron weights pressed down on them. Soon thereafter he managed to carry her into his bedroom. He stripped off her clothes, and began playing with her. In the beginning his touch felt soft to her. Then it turned to hard pinching, twists and slaps.

She watched as he brought out various sex toys that weren't sold in Ann Summers shops from a black briefcase. She pleaded with her eyes for him to stop as her voice was paralyzed. The words couldn't escape. She tried moving her arms and legs, but she was physically paralyzed. She watched as he mounted her and began his assault.

Gemma cringed and shuddered. Even now, she swore she could feel his clammy fingers gripping her neck as he tried suffocating her before climax. During his orgasm, Trevor hadn't bothered calling out her name. Instead he had shouted out *Grace* at the top of his lungs. It made her sick. Bile rose up her throat and she leaned over the tub edge to heave.

Grace...what does she have that I don't have? Why are men so interested in her? She looks plain and average to me?

Thinking about Grace receiving attention from Guy and Trevor sickened her. *It's not fair and something must be done!* She sat back in tub scowling. She decided as soon as she was done bathing she was going to have a word with Tamzin to settle the matter once and for all.

♥

In Ivy at The Bird in Hand Pub, Darren's anger slowly subsided as he watched his brother buy everyone a pint and a shot.

I can't keep doing this to Guy. He's right. I don't want to lose my only friend. He needed Guy to help keep his head straight. *I've got to apologise to him. I need him back.* It wasn't in his nature to apologise for his behaviour, but this time it was the right thing to do. Guy brought a pint and a shot to the table. He handed it off to Darren.

"Cheers mate." Darren said.

Guy nodded. He returned to his prior conversation with teammates. After thirty minutes of footie banter, Darren plucked up courage. *It's now or never. I can't lose my brother. I need him.* Darren tapped Guy on his shoulder. Guy turned around to come face to face with Darren.

"Can we talk, mate?" he asked.

"Now?" Guy questioned. Everyone looked at them in fear of another brawl breaking out between the two.

"Yes." Darren replied.

Guy shrugged his shoulders. He excused himself from the group and followed Darren out to the patio.

"What do you want?" Guy asked as soon as they're alone.

"Guy, I've been thinking a lot about what you said. I really don't want to lose you. You're my best mate and brother. I need you by my side. I know I haven't been a good friend to you. I'm sorry for all the trouble I've caused you. I don't want this conflict to ruin

Tamzin's wedding day." Darren said with sincerity in his voice. Guy's mouth went slack from gobsmack.

"Dog's bollocks!" Guy replied without thinking. *This isn't Darren! Darren doesn't apologise!*

"I know, I know! It sounds like dog's bollocks, but it isn't. Guy, I want to keep our relationship not tear it apart."

Guy felt his icy reserve slowly melting at a glacier's pace. *I can forgive, but can't forget.*

"What about your wedding? Are you sure you want to marry Tamzin? Are you truly deeply in love with her? Be honest." Guy asked.

"Love..." he chuckled. "Look, I'm marrying her for a reason. It may or may not be about love, but I don't turn back on my word. Let's leave it at that."

Guy felt his stomach flip in disgust. *There's nothing I can do. It's his fault when it all goes pear-shaped.*

"I'm sorry." Darren repeated, noticing the scowl on Guy's face. Darren knew how much Guy hated the cow.

"Apology accepted." Guy finally said. A smile broke across Darren's face. "Let's grab another pint." he added patting Darren on the back.

"It's my round." Darren replied happily. They walked back into the pub to join the others.

♥

The Savoury Plum was a madhouse. The steady stream of patrons made Cat and Corrie fluster about in stress. It caused much hair pulling by Olivia, as she was bearing the brunt of the twin's aggravations. Today was the worst of it. The call to Grace made Cat and Corrie sound like bats in a belfry with their assumptions and tirades.

"He tainted Grace! I can't believe Grace allowed Guy to... to... touch her! Rumour Mill said she's been caught being cheeky with him!" Cat howled.

Olivia rolled her eyes. It was only a small, brief paragraph five pages into the paper stating Guy and Grace been spotted walking to his car hand in hand. Nothing more.

"Grace should be flirting with Trevor! Not that crummy footie player. They're *all* bad news." Corrie chimed.

"Oh hush, you two! You sound just as bad as my Nan. They're only holding hands! That's nothing. By and by, steak and kidney pies are ready to go upstairs." Olivia huffed as she handed a pie to a server.

Although the twin's were her employers Olivia knew how to handle them. *Sometimes they need a swift kick up their arse!* The women looked at her as if she were insane. Her reaction prompted Corrie to grab two more pies and hurry up the stairs whilst Cat checked on a quiche baking in the oven.

Finally after the lunch service died down, Cat and Corrie decided to have their lunch at The Bird in Hand Pub. The Bird in Hand normally cooked meals that The Savoury Plum didn't use on their menu. It gave them a chance to eat something exotic and discuss Grace's downfall without Olivia's objection.

The ladies collected their light fall jackets and handbags to march over to the pub. When Cat and Corrie entered The Bird in Hand they were startled to see it fully packed with men upon men. Cat and Corrie pushed their way past through the throng of footballers, local and strangers alike to reach the bar.

As Corrie ordered two curries from the menu board and two shandies', Cat scoured the pub for a table. Her eyes blinked rapidly when she saw Guy Rowling sitting at a table watching *Sky Sports* with his teammates. She immediately recognised him from his dark hair and tanned skin. *There's no way I can forget a sexy devil like him!* Before Corrie noticed, she marched herself over to the table.

"You! Up! Now!" Cat ordered, pointing her finger directly at Guy. The lads all looked at each other and laughed.

"Who's this?" Darren asked.

"Mind your bloody pint!" Cat snapped, forcing Darren to cower in submission. *This woman is a hellcat!*

Guy put his hands up. He knew Cat wasn't going to give up until he went with her. He got up from the table and the lads let him out of his corner.

"What's this all about ladies?" he asked. Corrie joined Cat by her side.

"Where were you and Grace last night?" Cat demanded.

"What business is it to you?"He didn't mean to make it sound rude, but it wasn't their business. *Grace is a grown woman!*

"We all know your type. You use women like notches on a belt and when the fun is over you toss them aside. Grace isn't like other girls." Cat crowed.

In unison, they placed their hands on their hips. To Guy, they resembled angry prunes. He knew they were full of rage, so he tried his best not to laugh.

"Grace is a woman. She's not a little girl. She can take care of herself." he retorted. The twin's looked at one another angrily. Guy was getting underneath their skin.

"This morning I called Grace and she was whispering as if she didn't want someone to hear her conversation. I know you were in her suite. What were you doing there?" Cat asked calmly.

"Grace told you she was in the pantry." he let slip.

As soon as he said it, he quickly regretted it. Guy felt his blood run cold. They resembled two hulking she-wolves out for the kill.

"I knew it! You were with her! *You bastard!* If you harmed a *single* hair on our Grace, I'll crush your cock with a meat tenderizer!" Cat screamed.

The pub came to a full stop. Everyone watched Cat land a hard stinging slap on Guy's cheek. He brought his palm to his hot cheek and rubbed it. Corrie gasped in shock.

"How dare you! You're mad. I think you better leave." Guy warned.

"Let's go Cat. I think our tea is ready." Corrie said, pulling on Cats' arm.

Cat barged off and the pub went back to normal. Darren came over.

"What the bloody hell was that?" Darren asked.

"You don't want to know." Guy growled.

♥

The interview was over. Cameras and lights were being packed away. Grace let out a sigh of relief. Rumour Mill journalist, Zoe Goodall, stood behind as the others hurried out of the kitchen for their next interview with Tamzin. Zoe stood by Grace.

"Can I ask you a question?" Zoe asked.

Grace shook her head no. She had had enough of Zoe's questioning. She tried to explain she knew nothing of the scandal and continued on about the design, but they weren't interested. They wanted the dirt and they weren't getting it from Grace.

"Please. It's off the record. It's about your relationship with Guy Rowling." Zoe pleaded.

"What do you mean?"

"You have no idea then? This morning you were in our paper." Zoe replied, showing Grace the iPhone Rumour Mill app. On the screen was a picture of Guy and Grace holding hands beside his SUV.

"Is it true that you're having an affair?" Zoe asked.

Grace shook her head. She didn't know how to reply.

"No...no." she stammered. "I've got to get back to work." Zoe grinned cheekily.

"That's fine. I got my answer." she cooed, leaving Grace on her own.

Grace felt her Blackberry vibrate in her pocket. She fished her mobile out to see several text messages from Guy explaining the incident in the pub. She was mortified. Her heart skipped a beat. *Have they ruined my chances with Guy? What were they thinking?* She tried remaining cool, but she was frustrated at the thought of Cat slapping Guy in the pub.

She sent him a text apologizing for their behaviour. *Please Guy! Accept my apology.* Her stomach fluttered from nerves. *First the interview and now this drama!*

A few minutes later, a text arrived from Guy. He explained that he was fine and due to the rehearsal dinner he was unable to see her. He reassured her that he couldn't wait to see her in the morning.

It was a slight relief, but she was still worried. *I need to sort them out before they ruin the best thing that's happened to me.* She couldn't wait to hurry back to the cottage. She wanted a cup of PG tips and a hot bath. She desperately needed to relax.

"How did it go, Grace?" asked Trevor standing off to the side.

"Fine, Chef Hare." she replied, pulling her apron off.

"Can you spare a moment?" Trevor asked.

She didn't want to spare another minute with him. She turned to confront him. Trevor looked like a lost puppy.

"I want to apologise for my behaviour recently. I'm sorry for being forward. I assumed you were interested in me. But after you left in a panic, I became concerned. I couldn't run after you in the storm and I thought it best to wait until morning. Then when you didn't show, I had to check up on you." Trevor said quietly.

In sympathetic gesture, Trevor placed his hand on Grace. The touch unhinged her. She brought her hand back to put some utensils away.

"Thank you, Chef Hare. I apologise if I lead you to believe otherwise. Thank you for all of your help. Its' appreciated." she replied coolly.

"When you do move to London and you need any help or anything at all, please call on me. I'll always be available for you."

She shrugged her shoulders. She wanted to leave, but Trevor wasn't willing to let go without having a final word.

"I've got one final thing to say, just a word of advice. Not everything is all it seems, Grace. Guy Rowling is a footballer and they're notorious for their ways. He may have charmed you and promised you fame, but the only thing you'll end up with is a broken heart." he advised strongly. She looked directly into his eyes, and her aquamarine eyes didn't flinch.

"I think I can take care of myself, Chef Hare. But thank you for your advice."

Trevor flashed a smile as he moved to the side to let Grace leave the kitchen. His lips curved at the thought that he had planted a seed of doubt in her subconscious. *I only want Grace as much as Gemma wants Guy and we'll both get what we want.*

Exhausted and famished, Grace returned to her cottage. She went into the bedroom, and stripped off her clothes whilst running a hot bath.

Tonight it'll be me, the telly and a nice takeaway, she thought sitting on the bed to peel off her black trousers. As she did this she noticed that the clock on her nightstand was moved. She didn't recall moving it. An uneasy feeling settled over her and Grace tried to push it away.

Maybe my mind is playing tricks on me. Grace brushed the uneasy feeling away and hurried into the bath.

♥

ten

he wedding day finally arrived. A thick immense fog covered the grounds of the hall. It was much like the fog in Guy's head as he lifted himself up and swung his feet over the edge of his bed. His head was pounding and it hurt like hell.

Guy rubbed his eyes trying to focus. He recalled the pub crawl, Cat yelling at him and bits of the rehearsal, but thereafter everything became a blur. He knew he had a few drinks, but not that many to warrant a hangover this terrible. Yesterday evening he restrained himself because today he wanted to enjoy his time with Grace. It was to be their last day together before she went back to Ivy and he returned to London.

Grace! Guy thought. He looked at the clock, it was nearing ten. *She'll be here any minute.* He needed to shower and change into his morning suit. Guy turned his head and looked at the door to the loo. It was ajar.

Steam was flowing from the bathroom. *Someone's in my shower.* Guy felt his stomach drop to the pads of his feet. He had a feeling it wasn't Grace.

♥

Yesterday, late afternoon, Gemma went to Tamzin's suite to tell her what she witnessed between Guy and Grace. She found Clive busy gossiping to Tamzin. He informed Tamzin and Gemma that Guy had contacted him and that Grace was to attend the wedding as Guy's date. Whilst they waxed on about Grace, Tamzin sat in her chair with a painful expression on her face. *This isn't going to plan.*

"She must be stunning." Clive said. "Guy told me to choose only the best for her."

"She's not *that* stunning!" Tamzin and Gemma exclaimed in unison.

Tamzin got up from the chaise lounge she was resting on. Clive tinkered with the wedding rehearsal dress; whilst Gemma sat in a wingback chair, texting. Tamzin went into her bedroom suite and emerged a few minutes later.

"Clive, did you know Guy's been seeing Gemma for some time now?" she asked sweetly.

"No. No...I didn't know." Clive said looking to Gemma first and then to Tamzin. She knew he loved a bit of gossip and his chin could wag to the Yorkshire Dales.

"Before I tell you all, let me speak to Gemma. Please fetch the Christian Louboutins' for tonight. " Tamzin said. Clive nodded leaving the room. A few minutes later with shoes in hand Clive returned to Tamzin's suite. Gemma opened the door smiling. She was leaving.

"Aren't you staying?" Clive asked.

"No. Tamzin will tell you all. Laters." Gemma said.

When Clive entered, he saw Tamzin standing there with a wicked smile on her face.

"Come, sit. Let me tell you *all* about Guy." Tamzin enticed.

The following morning, Clive stood in front of the cottage door, his staff on hand with racks of clothing, shoe trunks and makeup kits. As Clive was about to knock again, the door swung open, and he came face to face with Grace. He was stunned. *She isn't anything like Tamzin described! She really is a beauty.*

Grace was dressed in a heavy terry cloth robe. Her wet hair was wrapped in a towel. *She's fresh faced and scrubbed.* She was a classic beauty, something rarely seen in Tamzin and Darren's social circle. Most of the girls Clive knew had Harley Street implants, teeth veneers and hair extensions.

"Helllllo darrrling!" Clive growled as he was led inside the cottage. "Were you up waiting for me, doll? Since the wee hours of the morning primping the hens for this grandiose wedding and now I'm ready for you."

"Thank you so much." she replied enthusiastically.

Grace liked Clive's demeanour. He was flamboyant and over the top. His skin was covered heavily with a fake-bake tan; his platinum blonde hair was gelled into spikes, and he wore a massive diamond earring on his left ear lobe.

He twirled on his feet showing off his light grey pinstripe Calvin Klein suit. Underneath the jacket, he wore a pink striped shirt from House of Fraser with a large white rose tucked in his lapel. Clive ordered his assistants to set up wherever they could.

"Darling, I'm going to transform you into a showstopper! Come along now. We don't have much time." Clive sang. Grace watched his assistants pulling out tongs, designer gowns and make-up kits. He grabbed her shoulders and pushed her down in a seat.

"Guy Rowling won't recognise you once I am through with you." he cackled.

She gulped hard. *I hope Guy likes this transformation!*

♥

Gemma sauntered around Guy's suite fully naked. Fresh from the shower, she was going to make sure Guy got a good look at what he was missing.

"*Get Out!*" Guy shouted for the umpteenth time.

"Last night you said otherwise. You dragged me here... when we did what we did in the elevator... you begged me to come here. Why the change of heart, Guy? You like me, Guy." she embroiled. "You kissed me, you told me you loved me and you even pleaded for us to make love."

Guy felt the vein in his temple throb. His jaw clenched and his fists were down to his sides. He didn't want to move. He was fearful of hurting her. He had never considered laying a finger on a woman, yet Gemma's accusations were tempting him.

She saw the look on his face. He was turning green. She wasn't going to back down. She had to stand her ground. Gemma was grateful of the cocktail of crushed drugs Tamzin had given her when Clive went to fetch Tamzin's shoes. *"They'll knock out a horse,"* Tamzin warned, *"and you'll have him to yourself."*

At the dinner, Gemma watched Guy as he ordered a drink from the waiter. When he had excused himself to the loo, she quickly slipped the drugs into his drink and stirred. It took only twenty minutes before Guy complained that he was feeling a bit ill and needed a lay down. Gemma insisted on taking him back to his suite, but Guy hadn't heard a word. He was far gone.

"We slept together, in this bed. You insisted not wearing a condom and you came inside me. It was wonderful. We had sex several times in the night." she continued.

Guy felt his stomach lurch. *There's no way I'd have sex with her! Not even when I'm drunk. I can barely get it up!* Guy wasn't going to tell her those things.

"If I'm pregnant because of you, I expect you to do right by us. You know, like take care of your responsibilities. I know we can make this work. I know we're perfect for one another."

As she sat on the bed Gemma leisurely pulled on her black lacy knickers. Unexpectedly, Guy rushed to her and grabbed her arm hard. He lifted her up with little strength but plenty of anger.

"*Nothing happened between us! Get out! Nothing happened. I don't want you, I don't like you and I never had sex with you!*" he roared.

Guy dragged her by her arm. He pinned Gemma to a wall and opened the door with his free hand. Gemma struggled in his grip and fought back by trying to scratch her way free.

There's no way in hell I'm having this slapper here when Grace arrives! She's not going to destroy the best thing that's happened to me!

"Guy!" Gemma cried out in pain. His grip was tight.

"I don't know what happened last night, but I know this, I never touched you, Gemma. I wouldn't touch you with a ten-foot pole. Every team in England worth their salt knows you're a *whore*. *Now get out!*" he growled.

He threw her out to the hallway. She was half-naked. She tried to get on her feet as Guy threw her clothes out to her.

"Stay away from us! Stay away from Grace!" he threatened before slamming the door.

Gemma scrambled around the floor collecting her clothes. Guests emerging from their rooms witnessed Gemma with her dress and shoes in hand. Embarrassment enraged her.

"You've not heard the last of me, Rowling!" she shrilled.

She stomped away, clutching her clothing. Secretly, Gemma hoped to be pregnant with Trevor's child to pass it off as Guy. *He'll learn his lesson and that nasty tart too!*

Guy leaned against the wall. His heart beat rapidly to the point that he thought he was having a heart attack. *I need to calm down before Grace arrives. Maybe, I can meet her at the cottage instead of having her come here. That's a better idea.* He knew there was time. He rushed to the shower to hurry to Grace.

♥

"How do you know the mister hot and fabulous Guy?" Clive asked rolling a piece of hair through curling iron. An assistant with a blush brush stroked rogue on the apples of Graces' cheeks whilst another looked over at the Chanel suit Clive had chosen for the ceremony.

"Guy was looking for a wedding cake." she chirped.

Her response sounded like a school girl in love with a first crush. Clive took this as an opportunity to inquire further.

"Hmm. I bet you were surprised to see him. Aren't you glad the cake was for Tamzin's wedding and not his? Although I hear in the near future there'll be wedding bells." he crooned.

"What do you mean?" Grace asked.

"Guy's moving up in the Premier league. He's joining the ranks of Rooney, Cole and Beckham. He's going to settle down after this wedding. Have you been seeing him? Have you shagged him yet? If you have, you better save it for a rainy day fund. You can sell your story to Rumour Mill." he replied, spraying Elnett and fluffing Graces' hair. She raised her eyebrows.

"Why would I do that?"

"Darling, you're aware that you're not his girl. You're just another bump on his road to stardom. He's using you as a way of getting back with his ex-bird, Gemma. You're just the catalyst in getting them back together, *you know*, to make her jealous. And I can see why she's jealous. You're totes hawt! I'm surprised that Guy won't be sticking with you." he revealed.

Grace felt her seat fell away. Her heart sank. *Did Guy really lie to me? And if so why would he go through all this to make some other woman jealous?* Her cheeks turned fiery red from anger. She sat straight up as Clive continued to fluff her hair.

"Did he tell you you're special? All men say that darling." he informed.

"I don't want to discuss this anymore. Please hurry." Grace replied bitterly. Clive looked at her through the mirror. He knew he had struck a nerve and planted a seed of doubt.

Her insides twisted and tore at the revelation. *I don't want to go to this wedding. I don't want to face him. But I've got to find out the truth!* Without another word spoken, Clive continued prepping as she fumed and mulled over Clive's callous words.

♥

Clive was leaving the cottage when Guy walked up the path. He winked and said hello to Guy before placing his belongings in the boot of his Mercedes.

The door was open and he stepped inside. Grace had her back to the door as she smoothed her Coco Chanel skirt down and fixed her fascinator. When she turned around, Guy sucked in his breath. *By God, she's the bee's knees! She looks smashing! If she looks this way now, I can only imagine tonight.*

She was startled by his presence and most of all, his looks. He stood before her, dressed in a bespoke Cad and the Dandy wedding morning suit. His sooty hair was freshly cut in the same style like David Beckham had at the Royal wedding and his face looked as though it was smooth like a baby's bottom. All the doubt planted seemed to fade away into the background.

His eyes were mesmerised by her beauty and didn't give away the worry of her finding out about Gemma. He toyed with telling her the truth, but kept his lips pursed as he was engrossed by Grace. The Coco Chanel grey suit fitted her curves perfect and Manolo Blahnik shoes were a lovely addition to the outfit. Guy wanted to pull off her fascinator and rip open her suit jacket in hungry needy passion, all whilst kissing her.

"You look gorgeous." Guy finally said as he held his top hat in his hands.

"You look handsome." she replied.

Guy considered telling her to forget all about the wedding. He wanted to ravish her and spend the rest of the day in bed with her. His cock twitched at the thought of her body against his, the taste and scent of her.

Grace, too, felt the same way. She wanted him to take her in the bedroom, push her skirt up and finger her until she screamed out his name. The clock in the lounge chimed. It was late and they needed to leave.

"Are you ready?" Guy asked.

"Yes." Grace said quickly fetching her clutch.

Guy took her by the arm, leading her out of the cottage.

It'll wait another day, Guy and Grace thought in unison, unbeknown to each other.

♥

The small stone-clad church was filled to the brim with guests. Footballers, glamour models, fashionistas, and celebrities alike were filling any available pew.

Media camped out near the entrance of the church and helicopters hovered above. Tamzin was running over an hour late, leaving the guests to chatter with one another.

Whilst waiting Guy introduced Grace to British Hollywood starlet, Amanda Priestly. She was gobsmacked and star-struck that he knew Amanda personally. Amanda's bubbly personality made her feel at ease. Suddenly, someone announced the bride's arrival and Guy left the women to sit in their pew.

Grace barely said a word to Amanda, who asked her many questions regarding her feelings about Guy. She was grateful that the orchestra began to play the wedding march. It meant they could no longer speak.

An hour later the ceremony was over with. Guy managed to find Grace through the throng of guests. He pulled her behind a stone pillar and gave her a long hard kiss. Throughout the ceremony all he thought about was kissing her and making love to her. Amazingly, his fantasies didn't force God to strike him dead for thinking such things in church.

"What was that for?" she asked breathless.

"You! I want you all to myself." he whispered against her ear. "I want to take you, right here right now, but we both know it's wrong." Her cheeks burned with sexual heat. She felt her knickers moisten.

"Guy!" called out one of the lads. "We got to take pictures." He turned around and waved. He turned his attention to Grace.

"Tonight, you're mine." he growled.

She weakly nodded as he planted a final kiss on her lips. He touched her cheek and left her.

♥

Grace looked at herself in the full length mirror one last time. *Phwoar! I don't look like the little village baker, I look different. I look beautiful. I can give Gemma a run for her money.* Grace watched as Gemma walked down the aisle. Not to boost her ego, but Grace thought that Gemma wasn't pretty. *Clive's right. Why would Guy give up on a girl like me?*

The first outfit was stunning, but the second one was sure to take Guy's breath away. She spun around in a silver Alexander McQueen gown that fit all her voluptuous curves. She evoked the late ghost of Hollywood starlets of the silver screen and felt as though she could take on Amanda herself. Clive gave her tips on how to fix her hair for this look and she was thankful that he gave her a pearl comb to create a side swept look. As she spun around in front of the mirror for a last look, Grace held her breath in anxious thought. *It's time to go and meet my prince.*

Grace entered Worthington Hall's ballroom. She saw the reception was in full party mode. She didn't have time to worry on whether or not she was late. Instead, she was in awe with the ballroom transformation. The room had been converted into a Greek pantheon.

The ballroom was peppered with marble statues of Zeus, Athena and various Greek Gods, Goddesses and creatures. Tall, massive columns covered in grape and ivy leaves were scattered along the edges of the ballroom. The ceiling, with a unique mural rumoured to have been done by someone who helped with the revitalisation of the Sistine chapel, was covered with billowing white cloth fabric to reflect camera images of a sunny outdoor day. Large, rotund dining room tables all held the finest white linens and silverware. The centrepieces with floral, fig and fruit bouquets were large, ornate and gaudy.

Adjacent to the dance floor was a long bar. It housed three large ice sculptures in the shape of the bride and groom and their initials. At the other end of the ballroom the stage was set with a piano, chairs and a DJ area for performances by Sir Elton John, The Royal London Orchestra, and Deadmau5, respectively.

She thought that the ballroom looked over the top for what should have been a romantic wedding. *There's no time to dwell on such things.* She scanned the ballroom for Guy. *It's an endless sea of celebrities, footballers, and friends.* She didn't see Guy standing a few feet away from her. To calm nerves, Grace helped herself to a glass of champagne that a waiter politely offered to her.

Guy's stomach fluttered as if he was on a roller coaster. At first, Guy didn't recognise Grace all dressed up. It wasn't till he saw the beauty in the silver dress had the same aquamarine eyes as Grace, that he realised it was her. The gown complemented her skin and fit her perfectly. Her hair in its side sweep style emulated that of Grace Kelly. She was demure and elegant. *She shines and stands out from all the other guests. She's like an angel. My angel!* Guy's footballer mates noticed Grace and let out a few cat-calls and whistles.

"Oi! Pack it in. Don't disrespect my lady." he snapped.

The lads straightened up and looked away to nurse their drinks. Guy walked away from them. Each step he took he felt his black Ralph Lauren bowtie choking him, but it was an instinctive reaction to her.

He walked around and came up behind Grace. He moved his arm around her waist and pulled her into his rising hard cock.

"You look fucking spectacular." he murmured in her ear. His breathe hot against her neck made her tingle.

She felt him clutch her tight against him. Guy drew his lips down onto the small heart-shape birthmark and kissed her there. Grace felt her knees buckling.

"Ta." she managed to reply. "I feel out of place here."

"There's nothing to worry about. I'll be by your side." he grinned. He pulled away to ease Grace in his arms to plant a kiss on her lips. "Come let me introduce you to a few people."

She gripped his hand tight whilst following him around the ballroom to meet and greet some of his friends.

Gemma watched them with raging envy. *They're acting as though they're the ones who got married. I'm not letting that slag get away with my blissful happiness.* Tamzin took notice and dragged Gemma into the loo.

"Stop looking that way. Tongues are wagging and I'm sure they won't be playing happy couple in a few hours. Stick to our plan and Guy will be yours." Tamzin coldly calculated.

"When are we going to do this?" Gemma asked.

"You'll approach Guy right before midnight as the cake is rolled out." Tamzin sneered as she checked her lipstick. Gemma nodded. She tasted vengeance on her tongue.

Guy and Grace danced, laughed, and chatted with other couples whilst stuffing themselves with the delicious meals Chef Hare prepared for the occasion. They drank tons of wine and snuck a few kisses here or there. They were like any other couple.

Trevor stood in a corner of the ballroom watching them. Guy twirled Grace around and pulled her in his arms for a kiss. Trevor shuddered with disgust before retreating to his domain.

Guy was over the moon. He had the girl of his dreams on his arm. He loved the way she eased into conversations and laughed at his silly jokes. She doted on him and he doted on her. People noticed how smitten he was with her. They wished them well and one person, joking, if he was the next man down the aisle.

"Hey, you never know." Guy said as he winked to Grace.

Time flew by quickly. It was now eleven and the wedding cake was rolled to the dance floor by staff. People walked over to look at the amazing cake that Grace had worked very hard on. They cooed over it and were impressed by the lavish and intricate art work.

Darren and Tamzin took plenty of photos with the cake. People asked about the baker and Tamzin bellowed her reply.

"Grace Knowles of Delicious created this gorgeous work of art." Tamzin walked over to where Grace was sitting.

"Please come up and take a few pictures with us. It's good for business." Tamzin said, pulling Grace up by her hand. She looked to Guy for support.

"Don't worry. All is OK. Go and shine." he assured.

Tamzin clutched Grace's hand as they walked back to the wedding cake. Rumour Mill photographers snapped pictures of the ladies standing next to the cake.

"Smile Ms. Knowles!" shouted photographers.

She gave a weak smile to the cameras. Tamzin put her arms around Graces' waist. She held on tight, refusing to let go.

"Grace, you may think Guy's in love with you, but *he isn't*. He doesn't have a thing for common girls like you. He's into Gemma. They've been trying to make amends since they broke up a year ago. But with parties, football and the wedding they haven't had the time." Tamzin whispered harshly in her ear.

She felt a lump rising in her throat. It was as though she was in the tight grip of a boa constrictor. The flash of the cameras made her dizzy. Grace searched for Guy among the crowd but the white glare from the flashing lights made it impossible.

"He's only using you because you're an easy target. You're just another *slag* to make Gemma jealous and it worked." Tamzin continued. Grace felt Tamzin's words cut through her body like a knife.

"Stop moving Ms. Knowles. We need lovely pictures." One Rumour Mill photographer ordered loudly.

At last, through the harsh lights, Grace saw him. Guy got up from the table to follow Gemma out of the ballroom.

"Here's your chance to make a name for yourself, Grace. Leave Guy alone and I promise you all the success you can ever ask for. If you continue seeing him, I'll make sure you'll regret it." Tamzin hissed.

When it was finally over with, Grace peeled herself away from Tamzin. She ran in the direction of Guy. Tamzin's lips curved upward.

"Mark my words Grace! Leave Guy alone or you'll regret it!" she cried out after Grace.

Grace shrugged it off. *I can't insult a bride on her wedding day,* she reasoned, *especially if I want my business to succeed.* She knew Tamzin tentacles could reach far and wide, but on further thought she threw Tamzin an icy glare to show she wasn't a woman to be reckoned with.

Outside of the ballroom, Grace stepped into the corridor. She spied them several feet away. They were walking hurriedly. She kept her distance as she followed them down the long hallway as Elton John's voice faded into the background.

They turned a corner, disappearing. Grace searched until she heard voices coming from an alcove. She reached a corner and hid behind a column.

"When are you going to tell that slag you slept with me?!" Gemma snapped. She stood close to Guy.

"I never slept with you Gemma! Stop your lies!" Guy spat. His voice was short and its tone filled with bitter heat.

"Last night meant something to me. Look at the pictures." Gemma said, pushing her iPhone into his hand.

Guy flicked through the pictures. It was a hard kick to his stomach. They were a harsh reality in colour. The pictures were of Guy and Gemma in his bed, in his suite. She was in her lacy black knickers straddling his waist and his eyes were half-shut. Clearly one would assume it was ecstasy and sex. He brought his palm up to his brow. Grace could tell Guy was upset at what he saw.

"It was one night?" he asked.

Gemma pulled in closer to Guy. She tossed her blonde hair over her shoulders and placed her arms around his neck.

"It was a *great* night. The best!" Gemma answered as she leaned in to kiss his neck.

Everyone's right! Guy's a no good footballer and he's seeing her!

"Blimey!" Grace gasped. They heard her. Guy turned to see Grace in all her anger, standing a few feet away from them.

He tried to jump back like a child touching fire. Grace felt anger rising from the bottom of her feet, travelling up her legs, into the pit of her stomach and heart.

"Grace, it's not what you think." he spurted nervously. He tried reaching out to her, but Gemma dug her nails into his skin.

"It is what it is, Guy! *You can sod off!*" she screamed.

Her rage exploded. Her words hit Guy hard like shrapnel. She wanted to pummel him and make him feel her pain. Instinct told her not to. Instead, Grace pivoted on her heels and bolted. Gemma grabbed his arm to prevent him from chasing her. Her nails pierced his wrist. He slapped her hand away.

"You sneaky bitch!" Guy snapped.

"Let her go! We're meant to be." Gemma implored.

"No! We never had anything! Tomorrow I'm contacting my solicitor. I'm getting a court order against you. You're mentally fucked in the head and those pictures are nothing but lies! I'll prove you wrong!" he roared.

Guy left Gemma in the hallway to wonder would happen next. He ran to the ballroom. Strobe lights, lasers, darkness and the crowd dancing made it difficult to find Grace.

Friends interrupted his search. They tried plying drinks to him and engaging him in conversation, but his focus was to find Grace and fast. His heart hammered away. His mouth felt dry and his stomach ached in worry. *I'm not losing the woman I love!*

After ten gruelling minutes, he finally escaped. He ran to the cottage to see if she was there. *Please God let her be there! Let her give me a chance to explain!* He reached the cottage to find the door ajar. Guy stepped inside.

It was cold, dark and empty. He reached for a light switch flicking it on. In the still of the empty living area the wall clock chimed midnight. His eyes focused on the coffee table. There sat a large dressing box filled with all the clothing Clive provided for her along with two pairs of shoes. She had magically dissipated from his life.

Fraught with worry, he drew his hands to his temples and ran them through his thick hair. *I can't lose her like this. I can't lose her due to Gemmas' lies!*

By the time Guy made it to the parking lot the sky opened up. Down tumbled icy rain. He jumped into his Range Rover and accelerated at high speed. He drove like a mad man to Ivy-upon-Wye. The torrential downpour wasn't a hindrance.

When he reached The Savoury Plum, Guy slammed on his brakes to bring the Range Rover to a screeching halt. He hopped out, running to the back door. He impatiently rang the doorbell several times whilst banging on the glass window of the door.

"*Grace! Grace!*" Guy repeatedly shouted.

A dog began to bark madly. Lights turned on from some of the homes surrounding The Savoury Plum. A few people opened windows to see the commotion.

"Oi! Quit yer hollering! It's late!" shouted a burly man.

"No!' he shouted back. "Grace…Grace!" he continued to scream.

"I'm calling the police!" A Welsh woman shouted.

Guy saw a light go on through the curtain covering the door window. Cat pulled back the net curtain to see who was pounding on their door.

Cat saw Guy standing dishevelled. He looked like a stray wet cat. His tie from his tuxedo hung from his collar and the first few buttons of his shirt were open. His dark hair was frizzed, curled and soaking wet. He was absolutely miserable. Cat opened the door halfway.

"Is Grace here?" he asked, panting out of breath. Cat shook her head no.

"She's here. She's got to be here." he insisted. "I've got to speak to her. It's urgent. I need to explain."

"Explain what exactly?" Cat asked roughly. She narrowed her beady eyes on him. "Where's Grace? And what's going on?"

"I thought she'd be here by now. Everything's gone pear-shaped." Guy lamented in confusion.

"What did you do to Grace? Where is she?" she demanded to know. Her voice was escalating in temper. It startled him. He took few steps back. He heard the faint sound of wailing police sirens.

"Oi Cat! The missus called the police. They'll be here in a minute!" shouted the burly man. Guy wasn't going to get into an argument with the police or Cat.

"Nothing, I did nothing." Guy said incensed. His head slung low as he walked to his SUV. Cat watched him as he walked away like a man dying of a broken heart.

As soon as he was gone, Cat closed the door. She walked up the stairs to the flat. She turned off the hallway light and entered the flat.

"There, there, petal." Corrie soothed. Grace was sobbing on her aunts' shoulder. They were seated in the dark lounge.

She felt her heart shattering into a million tiny pieces. *I'm an idiot to believe I could fall in love in four days! I thought he was the one.* Each tear rolling down her cheeks brought out a residual scent of Guy's Issy Miyake cologne. Corrie hugged her tight.

Grace felt foolish. *Here I am crying in front of my aunts, the ones who warned me that this would happen! What's wrong with me? Never again will I be naive. Never again will I allow a man like Guy Rowling to come into my life,* she silently vowed. Cat placed a cup of tea in front of her.

"All will be alright." Cat assured. Grace gave them a weak nod and picked up the hot cup to sip.

Never again! Guy taught me well, she repeated.

♥

eleven

A year and a half later, the sun scorched the London city skyline. In Covent Garden blistering heat from summer weather sent people looking for cool comfort in market shops. The colour of the sky was hazy shade of orange.

Delicious heaved with tourists, teenagers, and local workers trying to escape the frying temperature. They purchased iced coffees, frozen frappes and pastries to accompany their drinks. It was too hot for a big meal. People wanted light, quick and fresh meals to eat, and Grace was proud that Delicious was able to provide them.

It was a lovely old fashion glass front bakery that Grace had fitted out to emulate antique English coffee houses. Although the location wasn't in Covent Garden's piazza, it was right across from it, and it was perfect.

Delicious pulled in thousands of pounds in profit on a good day. The staff consisted of a general manager, two assistant managers, eight floor staff members, a pastry chef, savoury chef, catering chef and four junior chef apprentices who needed extra credit for the London Culinary Academy. They were all happy employees and were grateful to be working for a boss like Grace.

Grace emerged from the kitchen to oversee the floor and say hello to customers. She loved listening to their compliments. Since the wedding she changed from a shy butterfly to a prowling tiger. She had her uncle to thank for that.

Outside, she greeted a young couple polishing off a lemon tart. They raved on and on about how great the tart tasted and that they were going to recommend the bakery to family and friends. She thanked them and shook their hands.

Once she was done talking, Grace walked over to a vacant table with rubbish on it. On the table there were empty mugs, a coffee stain, and a copy of Rumour Mill topped with remnants of coffee crumb cake. The front-page was visible to her.

Her eyes focused their attention onto a shirtless, bronzed Guy. He was on a yacht with a petite brunette wearing a tiny red polka-dot bikini, her back was turned to the camera. They were off the coast of Saint Tropez. He looked as though he was having a great time. The headline glared at her.

Love Boat: Has Guy Rowling, our footie golden boy, found love with favourite British Hollywood It-Girl, Amanda Priestly?

She crumpled up the magazine and tossed the paper onto the tray. Ever since that night with Guy and when the shock had finally wore off, Grace poured her energy into achieving her goal of opening her business. Guy tried contacting her, but to no avail. She wasn't interested.

On three separate occasions Guy tried to visit her at The Savoury Plum, but her aunts thwarted him and his mission failed. The twins took it upon themselves to make sure Grace never heard from him ever again. All the gifts, flowers and letters he sent were returned unopened. She wanted nothing to do with him and the twins happily helped out.

Grace felt her stomach plummet as she recalled that night. She ran to the kitchen in a right state, clenching the skirt of her silver gown into her fists. Trevor came rushing to her aid, asking her what was wrong as he helped her to a nearby stool. Unable to speak she was feeling the effects of a full-blown panic attack; Trevor did his best to calm her down. He gave her a glass of water hoping to ease her.

Finally, she asked him to drive her to The Savoury Plum. He handed off his duties to another chef and watched her collected her belongings before driving her to Ivy-upon-Wye.

As he drove her back home, she didn't cry. She didn't want him to see her cry. She kept silent and watched icy rain tumble on the window. When they reached The Savoury Plum, Grace thanked

Trevor softly. He promised to ring the following morning to see if she was okay.

It was only when she closed the door to The Savoury Plum and climbed the stairs to the flat that Grace allowed tears to flow freely. Her heart was shattered and her mind confused.

She reminisced about their brief time together, the sensual lovemaking, and their private intimate moments that she thought only a couple in love would share. And then her anger boiled. *Did I seriously believe a man could fall in love with me in under four days?* The question seemed to haunt her forever.

The twins found her sitting on the landing crying. Cat swiftly ushered her inside, whilst Corrie rushed to the kitchen to put the kettle on the hob. It was evident that something had transpired between Guy and Grace.

Instead of questioning their niece they remained mum as gave her comfort. What they had not expected was for him to show up later that night acting like a belligerent fool. He had made a spectacle in trying to speak to her. Grace told Cat to make sure that he couldn't get in to talk to her. Cat obliged and went off to put a permanent end.

Days, nights, weeks and months went by. Grace began to believe that Guy was the typical footballer jerk. On a daily basis she scoured Rumour Mill. She searched for any article on their affair. Instead it was endless pages about Tamzin and Darren.

Four months later on the cover of Rumour Mill there was a picture of Guy exiting the London Lions stadium. He tried to shield his face from the cameras as he was escorted by security to his car. A blown up picture of Gemma was placed next to Guy's picture. Gemma looked horrible. Her face covered with mascara coloured tear streaks. The headline blared, **Gemma Loses Guy's Baby to Miscarriage. The Heartbreak, The Scandal, and The Denial!**

Gemma sold her story to Rumour Mill. Grief stricken, she told them that they had conceived their baby at Darren and Tamzin's wedding. Guy denied the scandalous claims. He called them false and nothing but lies.

Convincingly, Gemma waxed on about her heart ache over her miscarriage and their subsequent breakup. Gemma admitted that she was currently seeing another footballer, Rodney Taylor, from the Tottenham Heat and that they were looking to marry next year. The article had cemented Grace's thoughts and feelings about Guy; *he fed me a load of bollocks.*

But during the night, Guy crept in Grace's dreams. They were dreams of sexual nature. He would rain kisses down on her breasts and suckle at her puckering nipples whilst driving his hot velvet steel cock into her. He pounded her body, taking her every which way she wanted him to. These dreams were so vivid that she would awake, crying out in orgasm and reaching for him. Once reality sunk in that he wasn't there, she turned to clench her pillow sobbing. Her conscious was cruel to her, but during the day, Grace refocused her anger and pain on her goal.

After months of hard work and labour, the fit-out of the business was completed. Her uncle Alistair contacted Grace and told her that the renovations of her parent's Tooting Bec Victorian Home was nearing completion. The upper half of the home had been converted into Alistair's flat whilst the bottom half was converted into a garden flat for her. She couldn't wait to see it.

Moving day finally arrived. Bittersweet excitement filled the air. She was excited to be leaving Ivy-upon-Wye, but she also felt sad that she was leaving Cat and Corrie.

On the day of the move, the twins presented her with a fully-loaded, chilli-pepper red, Mini Cooper S convertible. She tried turning down their gift. She knew that London congestion charges were expensive and ludicrous, but Cat insisted that it was needed for her return visits. They took a firm stand knowing there was a garage tucked in the back of the house. At last, she relented and graciously accepted the gift.

Shortly after breakfast the movers arrived to pack up the contents of her bedroom. Other furniture for the flat was ordered via John Lewis, Marks and Spencer's, and Debenhams. Grace couldn't wait to lay her eyes on what was ordered and set up.

The moment came to say their goodbyes. Cat and Corrie cried hysterically. The movers looked at each other as they stifled their laughter. Grace kissed them both good-bye, before waving as she zipped off in her Mini down the cobble streets of Ivy-upon-Wye.

When she crossed the bridge by Three Trees, Grace knew it was a new dawn. She embraced it with open arms. She looked in her rear-view mirror to see Ivy, The Savoury Plum, and her non-existent life become smaller and smaller till it was no longer in view. Grace looked forward to living in the home that she should've grown up in. She assumed it would have been a different and more fulfilling life in comparison to the one now.

It was late afternoon when she finally arrived in Tooting Bec. Alistair greeted her with a strong bear hug whilst the movers carried her belongings into her flat. It had been many years since Grace last saw Alistair. She and many others thought that he bore a striking resemblance to boy-band singer, Robbie Williams. He was a few years older than Robbie and just as youthful looking.

Alistair's career as an abstract artist made him popular among the art scene. He created modern abstract paintings, sculptures, and metal artwork that appeared in galleries and small boutique hotels and bars.

Over the years Alistair kept busy. Frequently he travelled abroad with many of his boyfriends. He saw no future in settling down as he enjoyed his fancy-free life that London provided him. With travelling and nights out Alistair couldn't keep up with the house. When Grace contacted him about moving to Tooting Bec,

Alistair happily welcomed the idea. Thereafter Alistair hired an architect and contractor. Alistair's current boyfriend, Philippe, took the role as interior designer.

Philippe designed and decorated two posh modern flats with flair. Her flat was decorated with modern and vintage pieces, colours and textures that he thought a single, young, lady would adore, and Alistair's flat was fit for an artist.

She was thrilled when she set her eyes on her flat. Alistair gave her the grand tour. It was more than she had envisioned. In comparison to other flats in the area, the kitchen was huge. The cabinets fitted in modern flat acrylic red doors with a seamless white quartz countertop. The appliances were all stainless steel. *Perfect for a chef!*

The connected dining and living room were painted in soft grey and dark stained wood floors. The white ceiling retained its' original crown-moulding. Philippe had chosen a gorgeous white leather couch and modern rectangular crystal chandelier to hang above the dining room table. She loved all of it and even more so in knowing it was all hers.

The first few months of living in London was absorbed by working out the business kinks of the newly-opened and celebrated, *Delicious*. During that time Alistair was abroad in Thailand. On his return Alistair brought a bottle of wine down to Grace's flat. He then ordered a Chinese takeaway for two.

As they sat and ate he made a point of telling her that she needed to go out and socialise. She needed to explore the city and make friends. *'If not, you'll turn into a spinster.'* he warned. *'You have a point.'* She agreed.

From then on Grace accompanied Alistair to parties, events and social gatherings that were once off limits. Instantly she made friends and they took to her. Soon enough she was receiving her own invites, trips to the cinema and hosting dinner parties or Sunday brunches out at a new restaurant. A few men were keen on her, but after being burned by Guy she knew that she wasn't ready to date.

Even Trevor kept in contact with her. The day after the wedding as promised, he checked in on her. He sent the occasional email or would call. Over a year and a half he maintained contact. Trevor was even present at the opening of Delicious. She felt that he wasn't insistent in pursuing a sexual relationship and they were only friends.

But as busy as she was and her life fulfilled there was a flicker of a flame that still burned for Guy. Recently Rumour Mill was filled with Guy on the front cover. He was dubbed the U.K. golden-boy due to his recent winning goal for the London Lions at the English Premier. There was never a day that went by when he wasn't on the cover.

The crumpled Rumour Mill paper beckoned Grace to open it and read the article. Her curiosity nagged at her to take a peek and to see if he really was seeing Amanda. She shook her head. *It's silly!* She brought the tray inside. She dumped the contents into the garbage without wasting another thought on Guy.

♥

Exhausted and jetlagged from his Cyprus flight, Guy arrived at his Canary Wharf penthouse flat. He was looking forward to resting.

It had been a long football season and his hard work had paid off. His goal won the cup against the Tottenham Heat. With the media hounding him and the paparazzi following his every move, Guy had to get away. He couldn't wait to escape London.

After his win Amanda, his sister, had sent Guy an email. She praised Guy for his win and offered him a holiday on a Hollywood director's yacht. They would sail the Mediterranean Sea for ten days before going their separate ways when the boat docked in Cyprus. He took the opportunity to get out of town.

He knew that with her busy film schedule that it might be a very long time before they saw one another again. She was on her way to Greece to film *Helen of Troy* and when filming was complete, she was to return stateside. She wasn't interested in visiting England and preferred to avoid it. Only a handful of close people knew that the shy, meek, English rose, Amanda Rowling was also Hollywood minx, Amanda Priestley.

The ten days they spent together were wonderful. It kept his mind off of the game, Darren and on occasion, Grace. When the boat docked in Cyprus and he retreated to a villa, his thoughts returned to Grace. It started to get the best of him. After a few days, he was itching to return home to focus on the next Premier season. For Guy living without Grace in his life was sheer torture. He missed her like crazy and wanted her back. He would have done anything and given anything to have her in his life again.

Gemma ruined it all. Gemma and Tamzin, that sneaky bitch! He thought bitterly whilst placing his Louis Vuitton luggage in his bedroom.

He wanted to explain the truth to Grace that nothing had happened and it was all Gemma and her delusional lies. Yet Gemma got her way and her revenge. And she decided to dig her nails in deeper into him by nearly ruining his life with her fake pregnancy scandal.

Four months after the wedding, Gemma began to call him incessantly. When she didn't receive a response from him, Gemma contacted his solicitor with evidence of their so-called affair. She told his solicitor that she was pregnant with his child. She wanted him to pay an exorbitant amount of money to keep her silent. He refused.

When Gemma didn't get a pay out, she went to the nearest private clinic for an abortion, and sold her story to Rumour Mill. She told Rumour Mill that she miscarried the baby. He was in the dark regarding the truth until the paper was released the following day.

Shell-shocked by the scandal he insisted that he never laid a hand on Gemma, '*I know I never got her pregnant! I know I didn't sleep with her!*' He pleaded his version of events to his public relations agent, solicitors, teammates, captain and to the public. But it was too late for his image. The damage had been done.

A new football season began, Guy worked hard. He threw all of his rage and anger into exercising and focusing on his game on the pitch. Overnight he became a star player. In skills, he surpassed Darren and many others. People began buying the football shirt with his number. Football punters chanted his name during the games, praising him for each and every goal.

In his personal life, he didn't bother going out to clubs or socialising. When he was invited to parties, he would decline. When he played away games, he went back to his hotel alone. On his time off, he went to the gym or run laps. The only thing he wanted was Grace and he knew he couldn't have her.

Many nights passed by with Guy falling into restless sleep. He would descend into his dreams that were only about Grace. He dreamt of her beauty, her smile, her aqua eyes gleaming, the way her skin glistened during sex and taste, *oh god, her taste.*

The cruel part of it all was waking up to the cold empty space next to him. *It's where she should be!* He looked at his bed, which was well-made by his maid, Wendy. His heart longed for Grace to be sitting on the edge of the bed and smiling. He scowled in thought that it could never be, *at least not for now.*

Guy closed the door to his bedroom. He padded down the hall to his study. He rifled through the post left on his desk. He pressed voicemail button to his landline to listen to his messages.

The first few messages were from his accountants, and sport agents with multi-million trade contracts. There was a message from the drycleaners, one from Wendy leaving her schedule and one from his sports doctor requesting to see him. As he sat down in the leather chair to open his mail, the final message began to play. At first was the sound of heavy breathing. It was followed by a familiar voice filled with panic; it was Darren.

"Guy, it's me, Darren. I need your help. I'm in a world of shite and it's about to hit the fan. Call me at 02015556791. It's an emergency." The message ended. Dread and despair washed over him. Since the scandal they had stopped speaking to each other. It was for the best.

At Darren and Tamzin's' Kensington town home, Tamzin decided to hold crisis talks. She insisted that Guy make an honest woman out of Gemma by getting married and having the baby. He accused her of setting the whole thing up. He told her that he believed she was a conspirator with Gemma on the pregnancy and he wanted proof. Tamzin, not one to be called a liar, slapped him hard across the face.

It was in that moment he turned to Darren and told him, *'I'll never speak or see you again as long as you're married to that bitch!'* And he kept his word. It made his life easier not speaking to Darren. He had changed his Vodafone number, but kept his home number the same in case of an emergency.

This must be an emergency. Something horrible must've happened to Darren. A strange, uneasy feeling came over him. Icy shivers ran up and down his spine. Guy sensed his brother was in more trouble than he can handle.

♥

The day the London Lions won the English Premier was the day that Tamzin had put her plan in action. Out of all the teams to be pitted against one another it had to be the Lions and the Heat. It was truly a match for the ages and one that was to be spoken of for years to come.

After the team's shocking loss, Darren hung his head in shame and anger as he stalked off the field. He didn't want to face the cameras hanging outside of the stadium. He couldn't believe that he lost the game to his former teammate, best friend, and half-brother.

'Darren's a disgrace to football!' Sky sports correspondent commented. The loss was seen as a major failure for his career and the successful catapult of Guy's career. It was the winning goal that had secured Guy's position as new football golden-boy.

For Tamzin it was a horrible truth and it meant her worst nightmare was coming true. It meant the loss of all their major endorsements and their fan-base and telly reality show were on the brink of not being renewed for another season.

For the cameras she acted like a dutiful caring wife. She held Darren's hand as they were escorted to their car. She smiled and waved. She remained cool and composed. Once they were behind the polished black door of their town home, she unleashed hell. She called him all sorts of names, belittled his manhood and demanded a quick divorce. He sparred with his own choice of words and told her she was being a *tad* overly dramatic. He cracked open a bottle of Ketel One vodka to drink.

It annoyed her greatly. She threw a glass tumbler at his head. By sheer luck it missed him and it smashed on the kitchen cabinet behind him. He didn't flinch, so she stormed off to call her father.

A day later, Tamzin joined her father for lunch at Mayfair Bar. William wasn't in the mood for eating but he knew that he had to eat regardless if he had lost hundreds of thousands of pounds on the game. His princess sauntered into the Mayfair Bar dressed in a silk chiffon, bree printed, Diane Von Furstenberg dress. Her blonde hair was styled in a large bun. She wore Graff gold hoop earrings, and a pair of large oversize sunglasses. William rose from his chair and kissed her on the cheek.

Whilst they waited for their meals and discussed general matters, William insisted that Darren was no longer of use to her or himself for that matter. She agreed with her father. She spoke about alternatives and whether she'd receive a hefty settlement out of their divorce.

In the middle of lunch, William dug into his breast pocket to reveal a sleek, silver USB memory stick to Tamzin. It was the same memory stick that he had shown Tamzin right before the wedding. She looked up from her plate of nicoise salad with seared yellow fin tuna and quail eggs, surprised.

"What's on this memory stick?" she questioned.

"I told you on the big day that it's your insurance policy." he devilishly replied. She toyed with the stick in her hand. She looked at it in curiosity and wondered what was on the stick that would secure her financial well-being.

"Keep it safe, princess. It's your one-way ticket to the pot of gold at the end of a rainbow. I promise you, Darren won't be in the picture. Go and set your sights on another. Someone with clout and more money." William growled.

"There's no one else, daddy. Everyone's taken. Nobody earns the kind of money. "she whined, slipping the memory-stick in her clutch. She reached for her glass of pinot grigio.

"Yes, there is. There's only one man who's perfect for you. It's Guy Rowling." he answered sternly.

She choked on her wine and gulped hard. It stung her throat like a bee sting. *We hate each other like sworn enemies! Hell needs to freeze over in order for Guy to consider me as a potential wife, much less a girlfriend.* She listened intently to her father's plan. To her, the plan was far-fetched, but worth a shot.

Later that night whilst Darren slept off his hangover Tamzin with memory stick in hand snuck to the study. She slipped the stick into his iMac and moved the mouse over links. She came to a file and opened it. The screen went blank.

A video popped up on the iMac screen. She pressed play. Immediately she recognised the champagne room at Cherries. She saw Darren watching a black woman on the stripper pole. He pulled the woman down to his lap to kiss and fondle her.

She let out a small groan. She knew it wasn't grounds for divorce as it happened before the wedding. But what happened next was unexpected. The film showed him ripping off the woman's gold bikini bottom. They had rough, unprotected sex.

She thought that the woman was being raped, but quickly changed her mind. The woman was actually enjoying sex with him and kept begging for more. The sex acts between the two continued and more vulgar shots appeared, before the screen went blank.

Another video automatically played. This time the camera was hidden in a handbag. It was in an unknown pub. Darren and the woman from the prior video came into view. They greeted each other with a polite handshake. Darren sat down across from the woman.

"Darren, I'm sorry I brought you here. I thought it best to tell you as I've been keeping this secret for so long. A few months ago I gave birth to your son, Max." the woman said.

His reaction was one filled with shock, horror and denial. He didn't deny their encounter, but he did deny the child and insisted on a DNA test to prove the child was his. She agreed and the video concluded. Tamzin shook with rage.

A final video began to play and this time the scene was in an unknown flat. Darren was holding a six month old baby in his arms. He looked over the moon, but nervous.

"I'm sorry for you having to find out this way. I hope you can take care of Max." the woman said. Before it cut off, he promised the woman to take care of his son and the woman.

Tamzin had all the ammunition she needed in securing a full settlement divorce from him. Now all she needed was Guy Rowling as rich husband number two.

♥

<h1 style="text-align:center;font-style:italic;font-weight:normal;">twelve</h1>

On the Northern Line, an exhausted Grace emerged from Tooting Bec station. It was a long day. She felt achingly tired. The sweltering heat, humidity and sardine packed commute made her want time to fly by swiftly. She couldn't wait to get home for a shower, change and relax. Alistair was in tonight and he was barbequing a meal.

He reached her on her mobile whilst she was leaving Top Shop. He informed her not to worry about dinner as he was hosting an impromptu celebration in the garden. He told her that there was a surprise guest waiting for her at his flat. She begged Alistair to tell her who it was, but he kept mum.

She was looking forward to unwinding with good company, yummy food, and delicious wine. Walking home, she wondered who was waiting for her in Alistair's flat.

Along Tooting Bec High Street, she gingerly walked pass store fronts, a fish and chip shop, and the post office. She turned on Victoria Road, made a left onto Spencer Street and down to her Victorian home. She unlocked the front door and hurried inside.

After her cool refreshing shower she dressed in a new floral, summer maxi-dress. She tousled her long, caramel hair with fresh high-low lights, sprayed on some Escada perfume and applied a shimmery M.A.C lip-gloss.

Satisfied with her looks, Grace walked to her kitchen to make pitchers of Pimms and mojitos. She left the flat through her garden door with pitchers in hand. Alistair was firing up the grill and Philippe was setting up lawn chairs, tables and fairy lights.

"Grace! How was your day darling?" Alistair cooed. She placed the pitchers on a table that was a makeshift bar.

"It was good. Busy as usual." she replied, whilst air-kissing Alistair and Philippe.

"Love, you need a holiday abroad. Stop working so hard. You've got a great staff. Let them have control of the business. I know it's your life, but you need to live." he advised with a wink. "Ooo...look. Here comes your surprise now."

Walking down Alistair's patio spiral staircase was Trevor. He looked suntanned and well-rested. He held trays of marinated meats and kebabs. The sight of him caught her off guard. It was completely unexpected. She thought he was in Spain filming his new telly show.

"Hello Grace." Trevor greeted warmly. He handed Alistair the trays before kissing her. She turned her head to the side so he would miss her lips and grazed her cheek.

"I thought you were in Barcelona filming a new show?!" she exclaimed, stunned.

"I was in Barcelona, but I need a break from it all. I came back to London to unwind." he replied, smiling.

The truth was I need to get away from an incident with a prostitute. But Trevor didn't say what he was thinking. He came back to have his solicitors sort out the mess. He didn't want the prostitute pursuing charges. Spanish police were breathing down his neck. He wanted his solicitors to pay them off. He wanted them to retrieve all the incriminating photographs. *God forbid those get out! I will be ruined!* He decided that he was willing to pay any price to keep the scandal out of Rumour Mill and other media.

During the flight Trevor felt stress simmer in his stomach. He wanted to see Grace. He needed to see her. *She's such a tease! If Grace gave into me, I would've never done what I did.* Even that was a lie that he was telling himself. *My appetite is insatiable!*

As the plane taxied into Heathrow's and against aviation rules he called her. When he didn't receive an answer on her mobile, he tried reaching her at the bakery. Mark told him that she had left. Next was the flat. Surprisingly, Alistair answered the phone.

Alistair had a copy of her keys to the flat. He would collect her post and/or packages and bring them into her flat. He heard the phone ringing and answered it. He assumed it was Cat or Corrie, but instead it was Trevor.

Trevor explained that he had wanted to visit with Grace and wondered if it was alright to pop in for a visit. Alistair invited him to the barbeque on Trevor's request of keeping it a surprise.

"Welcome home and I hope you enjoy." she replied coolly.

Grace noticed some friends coming through garden gate. She politely excused herself and went off to greet them.

Although she was coming around to Trevor, she still felt uneasy. He was warm, friendly and attentive to her, but her gut told her something wasn't right. They would socialise in public settings such as food markets, restaurant openings and what not, but he never came to her home and she would rather not have him there. She was perturbed by it all. *I'm going to have a word with Alistair about it. Now's not the time.*

Drinks flowed freely and the meal of kebabs, steak and salad filled the bellies of all who attended the barbeque. Music by BBC One, Essential Selection by Pete Tong played from loud speakers. It was a party atmosphere that Grace enjoyed. She mingled with guests, laughed at jokes and conversed.

Trevor watched her closely. He noted how she flirted with other men and played coy with them, but not him. *It's driving me mad!* He joined Grace in a few conversations, but she acted aloof. Alistair tapped his wine glass with fork. Philippe lowered the music.

"Everyone hush, Alistair has an announcement." Philippe shouted over incessant chatter.

The crowd quieted down and turned their attention to the couple. As Grace looked over to Alistair and Philippe, she noticed Trevor drinking wine and staring at her. She looked away quickly. His stare made her edgy.

"Friends and family, Philippe and I want to thank you for today. We appreciate you coming and celebrating with us on a very special day. After years of travelling and never settling down, this morning I asked Philippe to marry me. He said yes! Finally I, a wild single fox, decided to take the plunge and marry. Philippe's my best friend, soul-mate and wonderful lover. I can't imagine life without Philippe." he announced. There was a loud round of applause and gasps of shock. Everyone knew Alistair wasn't one to settle, so this came as a pleasant surprise.

"Congratulations!" people cried running to the couple.

Grace was shocked by the sudden announcement. *Alistair never mentioned he was getting married. He probably thought it best to keep it a secret because he might not go through with it.* She weaved a way through the crowd to congratulate Alistair and Philippe on their engagement.

"Grace, can you get the bottles of bubbly I placed in the fridge?" Alistair asked after she congratulated them.

"Yes. I'll be back." she replied.

Trevor overheard them, swiftly jumping at the chance to be alone with Grace.

"I'll help you, champagne can be heavy." he offered.

On her heels, Trevor followed her into her flat. Grace opened the fridge door and pulled out the cold bottles of Veuve Clicquot to hand them off to Trevor. He placed them on the counter and turned his body to her. She closed the fridge. He was inching closer to her, too close to her personal space.

"It would be nice to see you get married." he murmured in a low and seductive tone. "But you've got to let a true man into your life."

She wanted to scurry away from Trevor. Rather she felt as though her back was a magnet pinned to the fridge. He looked down in her eyes. His gaze was deeply passionate. Trevor resembled a man possessed. He cupped her face to bring her lips to his. He kissed her. She felt his cold smoker's tongue which she detested. He pressed his body against hers with his hardness growing. Grace pushed him away.

"Trevor, not now, please. I've got to bring these bottles to Alistair." she whimpered.

"You can spare a few minutes with me. We've been at this for a year and a half. You continue to shut me out for no reason. Don't you like me?" he implored. His eyes searched hers.

She didn't know how to reply to his affection. Her mind screamed that she shouldn't have kissed him back. *It's not fair to him. I can't keep holding out. Maybe I should give him a chance.*

He saw that she was slowly relaxing her body and the tension he sensed was easing away. He decided to seize the moment. *I don't care what she wants! I just want her for sex. I want her screaming in torture and pain. I want her crying and begging for mercy.*

Once he had his way with her, he planned on breaking her heart. He wanted to scar every inch of her body and mind. A constant reminder of what a cock tease deserves when they didn't give into him. He took her hand drawing her into the lounge. He closed the door to ensure that there were no interruptions. When he was sure, he sat down on the couch, bringing her down to his lap.

He kissed her again. She tried responding warmly to his advances but her mind was on Guy smiling and standing in the River Wye. She tried to push it to the furthest recess of her mind, but they kept resurfacing.

He traced his fingers along the nape of her neck. He brought his fingers down to the top of her sleeveless sundress. He was going to have her. *It's my chance. Everyone's outside.*

Grace shifted her weight. Her heart skipped a beat. *This isn't right. I don't feel anything for Trevor.*

"Stop!" she insisted in a strong voice. She stood up. "I can't do this, Trevor. I'm sorry. I don't see us together."

Quickly Trevor rose to his feet. His rage exploded like an uncontrolled fire. Red flashed before his eyes. *This cock tease isn't going to get away with this any longer!* He couldn't recall meeting anyone as provocatively provoking like her. He swung his palm high up in the air, landing a stinging slap across her face. She tumbled backwards, falling over her coffee table. Her body crashed on the floor.

In excruciating pain she moved her palm to her cheek in hopes of soothing it. She tried fleeing by crawling backwards. Her voice was choked in panic. Horrified, she watched whilst he silently unbuckled his belt. She knew exactly what was next and she was gripped with fear that she couldn't scream.

If this bitch isn't going to let me have her, I'll just take her! Trevor angrily thought.

The kitchen door swung open. Alistair stood in threshold, shocked to find her on the floor and Trevor hovering above her with his trousers around his ankles.

"*Grace!*" he shouted, running over to her as Trevor rapidly dressed himself. "*What the fuck is going on?!*"

Baffled and embarrassed, Trevor didn't utter a word. He ran out of the flat slamming the door behind him.

Alistair lifted Grace into his arms. He placed her down on the couch. She sobbed when he moved her hand away to look at her face. A large red bruise made its appearance on her cheek.

"Oh my god! What happened here, Grace?" he asked.

"Trevor, he tried to kiss me. I tried to respond in the same way. But...but...I couldn't. I told him no. He became angry and he hit me across the face. It was unexpected. I think he wanted to rape me." she rambled through her sobs.

He held her in his arms. She was shaking like a leaf in wind with fear. *I trusted him! I looked up to him! That trust is violated.* Philippe appeared, unaware of the incident.

"Where's the bubbly?" Philippe asked. As soon as Philippe saw the look on Alistair's face and Grace in shambles he knew that something was terribly wrong.

"Go in the fridge. Grab me a bag of peas." Alistair ordered.

Philippe did as he was told. Quickly, he returned with bag of peas in hand. Alistair set the cold bag of peas on her cheek to ease the swelling.

"I'll sort out the guests. I'll ask them to leave. Besides, it's late." Philippe said staring at her with pity. He knew that whatever happened must have been severe. Alistair looked beyond rage.

"No...no...tonight's your night. I ruined it. Please don't tell the guests to leave on my behalf." she moaned.

"No. Grace, you did nothing wrong. You ruined nothing. Trevor ruined it. I'm calling the police." he said. He soothed Grace by rubbing her shoulders.

"Please don't. You'll make matters worse." she insisted.

Alistair wanted to hit Trevor like he hit Grace. He couldn't understand why Trevor wanted to take advantage of her. *Why did Trevor go after Grace?* The question tormented him.

When all the guests were gone, Philippe returned to the lounge with cups of milky tea and digestives. He joined them on the couch. She told him what happened. He was equally as outraged, startled and disgusted as Alistair.

Philippe and Alistair demanded for her to call the police. But after further pleading from her, Alistair reluctantly agreed as long as she promised to never speak or see him again. He firmly stated should he step foot in Delicious or come to see her at home that she was to dial 999 immediately.

For the sake of everyone's nerves she thought it best to visit Ivy-upon-Wye for the weekend. Besides she had the time off. She didn't know how she was going to explain the bruise to Cat and Corrie. They held high regard for Trevor. *This time honesty's the best policy. I need to knock Trevor off of that pedestal they placed him on.*

♥

Late Friday evening the intercom buzzed in Guy's flat. Reception announced Darren's arrival. The message had left him worried. He thought it best to contact Darren. When he finally reached him, Darren did not want to discuss it over phone. He insisted in meeting him at the flat. Guy faltered and told Darren to drop by.

Guy left the flat door open whilst he went to the kitchen to pour two gin and tonics. A few minutes later Darren appeared in the kitchen. He looked worse for wear. There were dark circles under his eyes from lack of sleep. He was curious.

"Where were you?" Darren asked. It wasn't a greeting, but it was expected of him. He took a seat on a barstool by the kitchen island.

"I was on holiday with Amanda. She had some time off in her schedule and thought of spending it with me on a yacht on the Med." he replied, handing over a tall glass to Darren.

"I've tried calling you, repeatedly. You disconnected your mobile. Thank God, you haven't changed your landline!"

Darren looked around the kitchen. He loved Guy's flat. It was open plan flat with a 180 degree unblocked view of Canary Wharf on the Thames. Tall curtains were pulled back from the floor to ceiling windows. It exposed the amber glittering lights of London.

Guy has everything I once had, a life with no commitments, no insane bitch of a wife, no mob father-in-law and an illegitimate child with a stripper no less. Now people are talking that I'll be traded to a less desirable team and less pay....what's Guy going to think?

If Darren could turn back time and make things right, he would have done the same. Instead he was stuck with life and a debt that was sucking his soul. He hoped Guy's sensible head would lead to sensible advice that he could use. He knocked back his drink and slammed the glass down on the cool black granite. Woefully he placed his head in his hands.

"You look rough mate. What's wrong? It's the team, isn't it?" Guy asked. The question was forward and honest considering that it was his goal damaged Darren's career.

"That's just the icing on cake." he murmured.

"Well, what is it then?" Guy questioned, topping up their drinks. Darren took a sip.

"Guy, I've got to apologise to you. You're right about everything, mate." he began. "I'm in a world of trouble."

Guy shook his head. He was growing impatient. *What is it now? I wish he wouldn't draw this out.*

"I'm in a lot of trouble. The week I got married, I got Alana that Cherries stripper pregnant. She's been raising my son." he confessed.

A look of shock befell Guy before he belted out a hearty, loud laugh. Guy thought it was all a joke, but when he took another look at his brother he knew that he was telling the truth. He took a long drink and sighed.

"That's not the only bad news I need to tell you..."

Guy pulled up a barstool. *It's going to be a long night.*

♥

thirteen

From her kitchen window, Grace watched two small birds eating seeds out of a birdfeeder. She took a sip of tea and nibbled on melba toast with marmalade. It was raining. It was a typical English shade of grey sky. The two birds were using the birdfeeder top as cover from the rain. *I wish I had someone to shelter me from the storm,* she thought. *'Someone like Guy?'* a little voice inside her asked. *I'm not going to answer that.*

She placed her mug and plate in the sink. Her eyes glanced over to the fridge. She shivered. Alistair offered her to spend the night upstairs and she had accepted the offer. Although she knew Trevor wouldn't return, Grace wanted to feel safe and Alistair's flat was the answer.

On second thought, she felt that she should have called the police but something told her *what good would it do? Harm his reputation? A celebrity chef's word against an upcoming pastry chef?*

That night she called Cat. She told her that she was coming to visit even though it was short notice. Cat and Corrie didn't mind at all. They were ecstatic for their niece to visit.

In the morning Grace drudged downstairs and went into her bedroom to pack her small travel suitcase. Whilst packing her clothes she considered calling Mark her manager. Although he was a great manager and didn't need supervision, Grace constantly worried about her business. She also knew Mark would tease her about her calling on her day off and she decided against it.

When she was done with washing up, dressing, packing and breakfast, she checked around the flat to make sure all the doors were locked and hob off. She went in the garage, and got in her Mini Cooper S to drive off in the opposite direction of the bakery towards the M4.

♥

Fresh from the shower and dressed in a white Pringle shirt and dark wash jeans, Guy emerged from his bedroom. He was exhausted from jetlag, and irritable about Darren's crisis. *Crisis is an understatement,* he thought walking into the kitchen. Wendy was spraying cleaner on his counter.

"Good morning! And welcome home, Mr. Rowling." Wendy greeted warmly. "Would you like a strong cup of coffee or tea?" She noticed the tired look across Guy's face.

"Good morning Wendy. It's good to see you again. I'd love a strong cup of coffee. By the way, Darren's sleeping in the guest bedroom. Don't disturb him." he said, plucking a banana from the fruit basket. She nodded whilst pushing a towel to dry the counter top.

"I'll only be a moment. Go in the lounge and I'll bring your drink in." she replied

Guy sauntered off into the lounge. He grabbed the remote and turned on the telly before plopping down onto leather couch. He ate the banana whilst flicking through the channels with his remote. He put on *Sky Sports*. There on the screen was Darren's team manager talking about the loss. Guy felt his stomach churn.

Last night, Darren confessed all to him. It knocked him off his feet. Darren's confession of having a child out of wedlock with a stripper was shocking enough, but Darren's other admission was bone-chilling. Darren owed his father-in-law, William, an exorbitant amount of money. Not only did he owe the money for a gambling debt, but he owed William for not participating in the Premier game fixing.

With tears in his eyes, Darren had completely broken down. He admitted that he felt horrible to cost the game for the team, but the loss wasn't on purpose. He was playing on the pitch as he normally played. It was just that Guy was better at the game than Darren.

Darren further disclosed that he was being hounded by banks regarding his mortgage payments for the Kensington town home and Hampshire estate. Tamzin had spent money to high-heaven with no consideration or regard for him. He had hoped for a renewal contract to their reality show, but he hadn't heard a peep from show's producers. Tamzin had eased up on glamour modelling and Rumour Mill was losing interest in her as she wasn't *it* this year.

The final straw came when William appeared at the home unannounced. Darren was lying down on his couch with a hangover and was unaware that William was in his home. It was the lit end of a cigarette branding into Darren's forehead that woke him. He had jumped off the couch, howling in pain.

"*What the fuck?!*" he howled, rubbing his forehead.

William puffed on his cigarette and stared at him with a mischievous glint in his eye.

"It got your arse up, you tosser! You owe me money and I want it now." his father-in-law had growled. William was flanked by several of his goons. One of them punched his fist into his open palm as a threat. It was to show him that William meant business.

He had explained to William that it was impossible to come up with that amount of money in such a short amount of time. But William disagreed and told him that he must work off the debt. He was to be a William's new supplier. It meant Darren was to supply drugs to his social circle. Guy lost it.

"You're telling me you are going to be a drug dealer?!" he shouted at Darren.

"That's what he wants!" Darren cried.

"Really? And you don't have the bollocks to go to Old Bill and tell them." he retorted.

"I can't Guy. I can't." Darren mumbled humbly.

"You know our past. You know what we've been through. Why are you allowing this man to do this to us? The solution is for you to go to Old Bill, confess all and divorce *that* tart!" Guy sternly advised. Darren's story and drinks had made Guy feel sick.

After hours of stern advice, and insisting for Darren to go to the police, he gave up. Besides, they had had one too many drinks to think coherently. He told Darren to spend the night. It was pointless sending him home.

Wendy appeared alongside the couch. She placed a plate and a hot coffee mug down on the table beside the couch. She picked up the banana peel to discard it.

"Thank you Wendy." he said as he picked up the muffin off the plate.

"That's a vanilla poppy seed muffin. I hope you enjoy." she replied. She went to clean the bathrooms and do laundry.

Guy drank his coffee and bit into the muffin. The muffin was delicious. It was fresh, moist, and full of flavour. The muffin had perfect texture. *I wonder if Grace can make a similar muffin like this one. I know she could,* he thought as he polished it off.

He decided to see if Wendy bought the muffin at a local bakery or if it was a new Marks and Spencer's item. He went off into the kitchen to find a mint blue pastry box sitting open on the island. He closed the lid. There was a pretty white label with Delicious written in hot pink cursive writing.

"*It's Grace's bakery!*" he shouted loudly.

Guy felt as if he had won the English Premier all over again. He jotted the address on a nearby notepad and grabbed the keys to his Range Rover. He barged into the bathroom that Wendy was cleaning.

"Wendy, I'm out the door. Please tell Darren that I'll call him later. Ta!" he rattled on, before running out the door and heading to Covent Garden.

♥

Delicious was more than what he had expected. Guy was amazed at the impressive English coffee house-bakery. He thought Grace might back out after *that* incident, but he was glad to see she hadn't.

Guy walked into the bakery undetected. He queued up on a line with several people. He searched among baristas and employees bringing out fresh sausage rolls and scones, hoping that he would catch a glimpse of Grace. Finally, it was his turn.

"Good morning. What can I get you, sir?" asked a young male barista.

"A tall cappuccino and a sausage roll." he replied. He was about to ask if Grace was available to speak, but before he could utter the words the barista was hyperventilating.

"*Bloody hell! It's...its Guy Rowling!*" shrieked the barista. Bakery patrons looked up from their meals. When they realised the barista was shrieking the truth, they retrieved their camera phones and paper and pen.

Guy rubbed his neck to ease his tension. He was swarmed by screaming fans. They snapped pictures whilst they shouted out for autographs. The young barista grabbed Guy around his shoulder and pulled him over the counter to take a picture on his iPhone.

Outside, people passing noticed. They entered the bakery out of curiosity and soon began participating in the uproar when they realised it was Guy. Mark emerged from the back of the store. His eyes bulged from their sockets. He rushed to the phone to call the police. It was a mad mob.

Rumour Mill paparazzi caught wind as their offices were only a stone's throw away. They came in, shouting at Guy for shots. He was overwhelmed by it all. People pulled at him in various directions for pictures and autographs. It was spiralling out of control. He searched aimlessly in the crowd for Grace. She was nowhere to be found.

♥

Grace's BlackBerry rang as she ready to leave the petrol station. She checked to see who was calling. It was Mark. She wanted to ignore it, but the temptation was too strong. Rarely, if ever, did Mark call her on her day off. It was only when he thought there was a serious problem but those were far and few between.

"Mark?" she answered. There was loud background noise. It was as if people were rioting in her store. Grace couldn't make out what they were shouting and chanting.

"Grace! I've been ringing you like mad! There's a mob! I rang the police. They're on their way!" he shouted down.

"A mob? I'll be right there!" she cried in panic. The line went dead. Grace started the Mini to rush to the bakery.

By the time she arrived in Covent Garden it was an hour later. Saturday morning traffic of red double-decker buses and black cabs weaving in and out, along with the addition of rain made it difficult for her to get there quick. She arrived to find two officers standing by the bakery doors. It was cordoned off.

"Identify yourself please." a bobby demanded.

"My name's Grace Knowles, I'm the owner." Grace replied handing the bobby her driver's licence. Once the bobby verified her as the owner, he opened the door and let her in.

As soon as she stepped foot inside, Mark came running to her side. He explained that police managed to contain the unruly crowd, but the damage was done. He had shut down the bakery to survey the damage.

"What happened?" she asked disheartened.

She surveyed the damage done. There were tables and chairs overturned. Broken dishes, cups, food and garbage were strewn about the floor. Her heart sunk. She was devastated. All her hard work was destroyed in an instant. Mark saw the look of despair on her face.

"He said he'll pay for it all." Mark assured her.

"Who? Who said that they will pay for the damage done?" she asked bitterly. She extended her arms to add emphasis to the damage surrounding them.

"He's right behind you." Mark answered nodding.

As if on cue, Guy emerged from the loo. Immediately, he saw her standing with Mark. *They're discussing matters.* His palms began to sweat and his mouth had gone dry. Nervously, he approached her as she turned around slowly.

Her mouth opened wide, her aquamarine eyes resembled large round saucers and her face went pale. Dazed, she lost all senses. *Guy Rowling did it! He did this! He has the Midas touch of a leper!*

On his approach, Guy's dark brooding cocoa eyes lit up. Each step he took her way made her feel as if the air was being sucked from her lungs. All the bittersweet memories of their time together came rushing back. His hard cock thrusting into her quivering, wet pussy as she called out his name. Guy whispering vulgar words in her ear with each thrilling pounding he gave her. Skin to skin contact, the taste, the smell, the need of release. There were other memories too…in the bath, the laughter, the talks. Grace shook her head. She felt faint. But another memory quickly resurfaced, one that gave her enough anger and rage to tell him to fuck off. It was Gemma's diabolical grin and admission of their affair. It rumbled from her stomach, coursed its way up her arms and face.

What annoyed her was how handsome Guy looked after all this time apart. His thick sooty hair tousled as if he just got out of bed. His body seemed bigger, more muscular, and tanned. She suppressed herself. She was ready for an attack.

Unassuming, he was ready to apologise. Taking one look at her, Guy was lost for words. She looked beautiful in all her anger. She wore navy skinny jeans with a long nautical stripped shirt and open vest. Her long hair was kissed with caramel high-low lights. Her cheeks were flushed and her lips, in clear gloss, puckered sourly.

Finally, Guy took his last few steps to come face to face with her. Before he uttered a single word, Grace splashed still lemonade on his face.

"Why did you do this to me?" she shrilled.

Everyone stopped in their tracks. The silence made her take a step back in defeat. An investigator came over to see if Guy needed help. He told him no and said all was fine. Mark gave him a tea towel to wipe his face.

"Grace, it wasn't my intention to come into your business and have a mob. I apologise for it all. I only wanted to see you. I wanted to talk to you." he said wiping the lemonade off his face.

"There's nothing to discuss. You should leave *now!*" she snapped. "You've done enough damage. Insurance will sort this out."

He held steadfast. He wasn't leaving, not when he had a chance to tell his side of the story. She didn't meet his eyes. She didn't want him to see her salty tears welling in the corners of her eyes. Emotion fluttered throughout her body. He sensed that she was fraught with mixed feelings.

"Grace...give me a chance to explain." he said softly.

"Ma'm we're done here." an investigator interrupted.

The investigator gave his report for Grace to file with her insurance adjusters. She handed it off to Mark to put in her office. He was too interested in the discussion between them to put the paperwork on her desk. She cleared her throat to make Mark realise he was intruding.

"Mark, please delegate staff on the clean up." she regimented.

Sullen, Mark nodded and went off to organise the staff. The police left the bakery. Soon they were standing alone in a corner.

"Grace, again, I apologise. I came here to see you. I hadn't expected a mob of fans." he said.

"Are you done here? I've got to repair the damage you've done." she replied frostily. She crouched down to pick up chards of glass.

I wish he'd leave! Doesn't he realise all the damage he's done! She wanted to shout her thoughts at him, but her heart convinced herself not to. He bent down to her level and touched her hand to stop her from picking up the broken glass. It was a soft touch. It made her tremble.

"Leave it be." he muttered. He noticed a dark bruise covered in make-up on her cheek. It looked as though someone had smacked her hard. "Grace, what happened to your face?"

"Nothing that concerns you." she replied. Her voice was cross from his inquiry.

Briefly their eyes met. He scowled. He was in a rage. *She's hiding her attacker! Why is she hiding him?*

"Grace tell me who did this to you?" he asked.

"No. Do you think that you can walk into my life a year and a half later expecting me to open up to you?" she retorted. She wasn't a fool. *I'm not going to open my heart to him again!*

"I know you think I slept with Gemma, but it's not true. I didn't sleep with her. That night was a blur. I drank a lot and I believe I passed out. Grace, I was set up. You have to believe me!" he insisted. She got up on her feet to place the broken glass onto a tray. She ignored him.

"Grace, all this time I thought about you. I missed you and I want you back. I know... you think its infatuation and lust but it's not. I'm in love with you Grace. *In love.*" he poured out his heart. He was honest in his feelings about her.

"What about the baby, the miscarriage, and the scandal in Rumour Mill? How can you explain *that*?" she asked, slamming a chair upright. She wasn't going to let any small detail slip by.

"The baby wasn't mine. I swear to you, Grace. I'll prove to you! I was never with that whore!" he cried. "Stop making this hard, Grace. We had something great, even if it was short lived. I haven't stopped thinking about you. I miss you so much."

"I want *you* to go now. You've done enough. Please leave." she whispered. She looked around, trying to avoid his eyes. Grace bit her lip and placed her hands on her hips.

"Why are you making this bloody difficult? I contacted the contractors. They will be here soon. I said I'll pay for it all." he throatily growled. His reaction startled her. He sounded angry with her as she wasn't relenting or forgiving him. He judged her reaction. He took a step back.

"I'm sorry." he mumbled, swallowing hard. "Let's go out to dinner tonight, after the contractors come and sort out a quote."

She didn't say a word. Her face unchanged.

"Please, Grace."

She knew he wasn't the type of man to beg for a date. *But here he is pleading.* He stood in front of her like a lost puppy with his head hung in shame.

"I'll think about it, but not tonight." she surrendered.

"I'll stay and help out. I'll introduce you to the contractor. I still want to know what happened to your face."

She nodded. They began to collect pieces of broken glass. Secretly and simultaneously, they both hoped they were picking up the pieces of their broken hearts.

♥

Tamzin stood outside of Delicious watching Guy and Grace. The crowd around her didn't recognise her as she was incognito. She wore a straw fedora with her hair tucked underneath it. To shield her eyes, she wore a pair of vintage Ray-Ban sunglasses. She clutched a Marc Jacobs bag underneath her arm. She watched as they collected broken plates and cups.

Uugh! It's that damn baker! What's with these footballers and bakers? They've got Nigella fever! Tamzin sneered in disgust. *Here she is again, just when I need to seduce Guy!*

Tamzin was visiting with her publicist who was in the same building as Rumour Mill. She had given her publicist a copy of her husband's indiscretion. They discussed Tamzin's bleak future when her mobile vibrated on the desk. It was news that Guy was in nearby Covent Garden causing fan frenzy.

"You're father's right. Seek Guy out. He's the U.K.'s darling. I can get you on many covers of Rumour Mill right after Darren's scandal." her publicist advised.

She hurried off to rescue Guy from the horde of fans, but upon arriving the Bobbies refused to admit her. *It seems Guy has other plans that don't include me.* A finger tapped her on her shoulder. She turned around to see who tapped her shoulder. She saw a large bouquet of flowers. They hid a stranger's face.

"Excuse me miss. What's happened here?" a familiar voice ask. The bouquet slowly came down to reveal the stranger's face. Surprisingly, it was Trevor. She grinned wickedly.

"Trevor! I'm surprised to see you! What brings you here, stranger?" she asked.

He came to apologise to Grace for his behaviour. He saw the police and was told by an officer that no one was allowed inside. It was then that he had decided to ask a stranger, who looked as if they were watching the upheaval for ages, for further details. He hadn't expected to find Tamzin in disguise.

"It seems Guy drop in and caused fan-fever. It turned into a melee. The horde destroyed the place." she purred.

Trevor shook his head. He couldn't believe he was talking to Tamzin, his nightmare in the flesh returned.

"Who are these flowers for?" she asked sweetly.

"Grace. She designed your cake." he replied.

"Yes I know darling. Are you dating her?" she inquired.

"No." he answered quickly. He didn't like how Tamzin directed the conversation. *It's none of her bloody business!*

"Why don't we get a glass of wine? I know a local pub that has a private room so we can talk." she offered.

She was fully aware of his sadistic dalliances. Gemma had told her everything. She knew that he liked sweet girls like Grace and that he wanted her. *He'll be a great ally. He's perfect! He'll be what I need to get rid of Grace!*

Trevor wasn't too sure about having wine with her. He didn't want to get caught in her flytrap. He looked back at the window. He saw Grace walking to back of the bakery with Guy in tow. *That bastard! Guy wasn't even there for her like I've been!* Tamzin knew by the look on Trevor's face that he'd be game.

"I can help you with her. After all Guy is moving in on your bird." she mewled. "Now, how about that drink?"

"Lead the way." he snorted as he took Tamzin's' arm.

She escorted him in the opposite direction of the bakery. *Now this plan may just work!* Tamzin thought cheerfully.

♥

Worried, Cat rang Grace's mobile several times. The calls went unanswered or straight to voicemail. Frustrated by lack of response, she placed the receiver in its cradle.

Corrie walked down the steps with dirty dishes. She saw Cat wringing her hands. Her cheeks were puffy and red and her silvery hair was out of place. She knew her twin was more than worried.

"Still no answer?" she asked. "By now she would've rang."

"I know!" Cat grumbled in annoyance.

Once Grace reached the mid-way point on the M4, she always contacted them at a rest stop. The call never came. They were growing concerned for her well being.

"I pray she wasn't in an accident." Corrie muttered under her breath.

Cat shot her sister a look. She didn't want to hear it. Corrie shrugged her shoulders as she continued to load the dishwasher. Cat took her black phonebook down from the shelf that held recipe books. She flipped through the pages and found Alistair's mobile. Cat grabbed the phone. She quickly dialled it.

"Allo!" greeted Alistair on the third ring.

He was busy browsing Selfridge's racks with Philippe and his best-friend, Sharon.

"Allo Alistair! Have you heard from Grace? She hasn't rung us and we are worried." Cat said as a matter of fact.

"No. No, I haven't. I'm sure she should've been there now. Have you tried her mobile?" he asked.

Philippe and Sharon were several feet away from him. He pressed a Prada white shirt to his chest, admiring himself in a mirror whilst Sharon was reading Rumour Mill on her iPhone.

"Of course I've called her mobile!" Cat snapped.

"Bugger me!" Sharon gasped whilst looking at her screen. "Alistair...Alistair!" she tried interrupting Alistair. He walked away from her to continue his conversation with Cat.

She showed the phone to Philippe. Philippe was amazed by what he saw there were pictures of Guy and Grace standing in the bakery. They looked as if they were in heated conversation. Then there was the final picture of Grace dousing a liquid onto the hot footballer.

"Alistair! Alistair! Are you there?" Cat cried out.

"I'm still here Cat." Alistair bellowed.

"I've tried the restaurant and the flat. Are you sure Grace left?" she asked.

"Yes I'm sure. I bet there was a problem at the bakery that she needed to resolve and most likely she forgot to call. I'll go to Delicious to see if she is there. I'll contact you when I've spoken directly to her. Is that fine?" he asked.

He was annoyed. *Why can't they leave Grace alone? She's a bloody, grown woman who can do as she pleases!* It was on the tip of his tongue to say it, but Alistair knew she was a hellion. He didn't dare to deal with her wrath. Cat ignored his attitude.

"Yes please! Call me right away! Speak to you soon. Ta!" she replied.

She ended the conversation, leaving Alistair staring at his phone. He pushed his mobile into his trouser pocket to continue shopping. Sharon and Philippe rushed over.

"I was on the phone. What's so important that you two felt a need to interrupt?" he asked hotly. The conversation with Cat had bothered him.

"This!" cried Sharon. She pressed her mobile into his palm.

"You won't believe it!" gasped Philippe.

Alistair looked at the iPhone. Startled he gasped out. There in colour photos, Grace stood in a ruined Delicious arguing with the hottest Premier footballer around!

♥

fourteen

ight fell over London. The bakery was at last in relative order. Staff, who had remained behind to help, finally left. Grace and Guy were alone in the shop. She looked over the quote the contractor had given her. She was satisfied that the work would only be a few days. There wasn't any major damage done.

Earlier whilst the contractor had surveyed the damage, Guy picked up a mop and bucket. He washed down floors, and lifted tables and chairs to place them in appropriate places and cleaned. Not once did he moan about the hard work. Grace would glance over to Guy a few times. He'd catch her eye, grin and whistle happily.

When it was over and the damage was quoted, Guy insisted on paying for the repairs. The contractor kept his word and told her that he had no intention on charging her. The bill went directly to

Guy. She relented. After all, she was losing a few days of profit. The bakery would remain closed until Tuesday morning.

She dimmed the lights to the bakery before pulling out a bottle of spring water from the fridge. She brought it over to Guy sitting at a table.

"You really attract crowds." murmured Grace. She opened the cold bottle pouring the water into a glass for Guy.

"Ta!" he replied lifting it to his lips. Thirstily, he drank it.

"I wish you had attracted the crowd for a right reason. Instead, I'm losing three days of profits." she said.

"I can if you wish. You can name a power-bar muffin after me. I'll endorse it for free." he replied seriously. She looked at him as if he was joking.

"Yes. It'll be filled with nothing, but bran and fluff!" Grace teased. They laughed.

It feels good laughing with Guy, Grace thought. *It feels good to see him too.* She noticed how his smile curved upwards and his lush lips had droplets of cool water on them. Her mind began to wander.

A fantasy weaved its way in her mind. She wanted him to pour ice water on her flesh, then lap it slowly. She wanted his dark eyes staring at her with every lap of his tongue against her tummy. She felt herself begin to moisten and contract.

"Grace? Grace, are you OK?" he asked, breaking the silence between them.

"I'm fine." she mumbled. "I'm thinking about this work."

"Don't worry. I'll take care of it." he replied whilst she got up from the table.

Grace shook her hair with her hand as if trying to shake the thought. She was unaware that her makeup on her face had worn away and her hair pushed back exposing the dark bruise. He leapt up. He grabbed her free hand. He pulled her to his body and placed his palm on her cheek.

"Who did this to you?" he asked in low growl. She felt her spine tingle.

"Nobody. I don't want to talk about it." she lied.

"Grace... I'm sorry for the past, but please don't let it affect our future. I want you Grace, I've always wanted you. Please tell me who did this to you." he murmured. He tucked a piece of her hair behind her ear.

Guy cupped her face. Her heart was pulsing hard. His lips grazed hers. Their foreheads pressed against one another.

"If you give me a chance, Grace, I promise you to keep you safe from harm." His words were strong and reassuring. It made her shudder.

She felt her heart begging her to forgive him, but her mind told her no. A loud knock interrupted them. She pulled away to see three shadowy figures at the door.

"Who's there?" he barked. *Who the hell has the cheek to interrupt my time with Grace?*

Grace peered closely. She assessed that the shadowy figures were Alistair, Philippe and Sharon.

"It's my family." she replied, squirming out of his arms and walking over to the door to open it.

Loud with chatter, Alistair, Philippe and Sharon came into the bakery. She locked the door behind them. They all turned to look at Guy standing in the middle of the room.

"Hello." Alistair said, walking closer to inspect him. Guy blinked twice. "I'm Grace's uncle, Alistair." he introduced.

"Bloody hell! I thought you were Robbie Williams." he admitted. Everyone laughed.

"I'm older than Robbie and twice as handsome." Alistair cheekily replied. He was used to the mistaken identity quips.

"This is Philippe, Alistair's fiancé and Sharon, their best-friend." Grace continued on Alistair's behalf.

Politely, Guy shook their hands. He said hello to them all. Alistair eyed Guy up and down. He couldn't believe that this famous footballer was in Grace's business in the near-dark. Alistair turned to Grace.

"How did you know I was here?" she asked.

"Cat called me. They're worried to death. You hadn't rung so I told them I'd come by here. Philippe and Sharon showed me Rumour Mill and then I knew it all." he countered.

Grace shifted her body in discomfort. She didn't want Guy thinking she was still living under her aunts' thumbs. He smiled at her and pulled her hand into his. It brought her body closer to his side. Alistair didn't miss a thing. *They're close...very close.*

"I'll call them in a bit. All this fiasco and business took up all of my time." she replied softly. Alistair looked at the damage needing repair.

"All because of a hot footballer!" Sharon joked. Everyone chuckled.

"I must be going, Grace." Guy murmured. "Make a promise to me that we'll go to dinner this week."

"She promises to have dinner." Alistair answered for her. She felt her face growing hot and flush. The trio stared at them with curious eyes waiting for their next move.

"Well, dinner with him is better than dinner with Trevor." Philippe said bashful. "Guy's handsome!"

Inquisitively, Guy looked at her. "Are you dating Trevor?" he asked.

"No! No I'm not!" she replied sharply.

He took her cue. *She's uncomfortable and it's time for me to go.*

"We'll discuss it on a later date. I'll call you. It's a pleasure to meet you all." Guy said turning to everyone.

"The pleasure's most likely ours." Sharon retorted eagerly.

Guy gave Grace a kiss on both cheeks. He smiled at her and winked.

"Good night!" The trio choired.

Once he was gone everyone exploded in loud chatter.

"Oh my god! He's bloody gorgeous!" Sharon cried.

"Too bad he's straight!" Philippe chimed.

"Why? So we can fight over him like cats?" Alistair joked.

Grace laughed as she straightened out a chair.

"We've got a minx here, Alistair." Philippe said, coming from around the other side of the table.

"Ms. Minx Grace." Alistair teased.

"How do you know him?" queried Philippe.

"Why don't we go home and I'll tell all." she said.

Exhausted, she was ready to go home and to the comfort of her bed. Her original intention of leaving London was out of the window. She gathered her things and turned off the lights.

The group walked out into the street and followed Grace to the car park. They climbed in her Mini to go to Tooting Bec to find out what really went down between Guy and Grace.

♥

The sound of an ambulance heading to a nearby hospital woke Tamzin from her slumber. She had fallen asleep in Trevor's arms. She reached over his cold body for a pack of Silk Cut resting on the nightstand. Trevor grumbled as he woke. He took the box from her hand, fished out a fag, and lit a cigarette. In silence and in their own deep thoughts they smoked.

"What time is it?" she asked.

Trevor stubbed his cigarette out in an ashtray by the bed. He looked at the clock.

"Gone nine." he replied as Tamzin handed her cigarette off to him.

Briefly she wondered about shacking up with Trevor. *Trevor's a celebrity chef with loads of money. What can be better than that? I can be the first WAG's of celebrity chefs. Or did Ollie's wife hold title?* She circled her fingers on his stomach. Unlike Darren's taut abs, his stomach felt like soft pudding. The thought of shacking with Trevor vanished.

"What does Grace have that I don't have?" she asked.

He sat up on the bed. He swung his feet over the edge and stood up, lifting his jeans over his legs and hips.

"Simply put, she is not *you*." he said.

"I know she's not me! But what is it about her that makes men drool?" Tamzin snapped. She wanted to learn what she was up against.

Trevor drew his shirt over his head. He walked over to the wash basin and looked in the cracked mirror.

"Grace is everything that you're not. She isn't conniving or greedy. You're always plotting, deceiving, and backstabbing. Your work as a glamour model is drying up. If what you're saying's true, then your sham of a marriage is failing too. You need men to provide a lavish lifestyle for you. I'm not that man. You're hard, rough, defiant, and cold. Grace is the girl I want. She'll submit to me, and she'll break down unlike you." Trevor divulged brutally.

He turned around to see her getting up from the bed. She reached down to the floor to retrieve her knickers.

"You're all fur coat, no knickers, Tamzin. That's the type of woman you are." he snorted.

"I see. Well then, let's get this plan into action." she replied scooping up her clothes.

"I'll be in the shower. When I get out I expect you gone." he growled.

He felt disgusted in making a deal with Tamzin, the she-devil, when he preferred to be the devil himself.

"Remember our agreement." she sniffed.

"I will. You want Guy and I want Grace. We both get what we want if we do what we say. Enough chatter." he hissed before walking to the shower.

Tamzin dressed and left the hotel. She looked around her to ensure there were no paparazzi. *Thank heavens Trevor chose a seedy hotel in Kings Cross rather than a posh place.*

♥

Shattered, Darren left Guy's flat late evening. He took a lift to the parking garage and walked over to his red Lotus Elise S. He hoped no paparazzi were around. One thing he appreciated about Guy was that the media wasn't interested in Guy unless a major story broke. Since Guy's fame had surged overnight, and Darren wasn't too sure if the media was waiting for Guy or him.

Even with Guy's prior scandal with Gemma, Guy managed to go unscathed. It became a small blip on the radar screen of Guy's life, whereas his blips were all big shocking scandals. Last night, he thought about confessing the truth to Guy in regards to Gemma.

The last time he saw Guy he had overheard Tamzin and Gemma talking. Gemma claimed the baby she conceived was by another man and not Guy. He didn't hear other man's name, and he preferred not to know. *Besides*, he thought, *I need Guy more than he needs me. Last night wasn't the night to tell Guy.* Darren drove off satisfied in the thought.

As the parking gate slid open and Darren turned right, he was unaware of the black BMW moving out of its' parking-space to follow him.

♥

Alistair, Sharon and Philippe sat in the lounge drinking glasses of chardonnay whilst she called Cat from the privacy of her bedroom. Dutifully Grace apologised for not calling sooner.

She explained about the mob damage to the business, but didn't tell them that it was Guy's presence that brought it on. Cat wasn't pleased to hear the news. Corrie was disappointed. They told her that they were willing to come and help her with repairs. She declined. She ended their call with a promise to visit them after the repairs have been made.

As Alistair poured another round of chardonnay she returned to the lounge. She sat next to Sharon and picked up a wine glass.

"Now you've returned, please tell us all how you know the handsome, Guy Rowling." Philippe implored.

The trio waited in baited breath to hear the story of how they met. She smiled half-heartedly. She drank some wine to gain Dutch courage.

Slowly Grace told her tale of the wedding. She said how Guy came to The Savoury Plum looking for a wedding cake. She explained how he rented a cottage on the grounds of the hall and visited her whilst she baked. She even told them about the picnic Guy had planned for them and the quality time they spent, but she left out all of the intimate details.

Then there was the heartbreak. She told them about his terrible betrayal. When she spoke she choked back on her tears. She held steadfast by refusing to let them roll down her cheeks.

They all sat glued in their seats and in awe. The group was even more surprised when Grace explained Guy's apologies, gifts and desire to rekindle their 'relationship'. By the way she spoke, Alistair saw Grace as a woman in love with Guy Rowling, but she wasn't sure if she trusted him.

"Guy disappointed me." she admitted with a sigh.

"Guy disappointed you? I believe the only person you're disappointing is yourself." Alistair said pointedly.

"Why do you say that?" she asked.

"Grace, you believed Gemma over Guy. Do you know how often glamour girls lie to get the man that they want? It could be a strong possibility, if not fact, that Gemma lied about their so-called relationship. Those pictures can be photo-shopped and manipulated. Rumours are spread through gossip mongers. As Guy's popularity increases, so will the scandals." Alistair replied, placing his wineglass down.

"It might be possible that he's telling you the truth." Philippe added. "He loves you. He sent you flowers, letters and gifts to win your affection. He apologised profusely and he wants you back. You should've given him a chance."

"Blimey, Guy didn't keep his eyes off of you!" cried Sharon.

"I can't believe you believed coked-up conniving glamour model Gemma over him." he retorted. "And if you read Rumour Mill its' quite obvious she's moved on. Guy's set his sight on you."

For a half an hour she listened intently to their theories. *One thing's certain they all believe that he loves me.* The thought gave her confidence and chills up her spine.

"I do hope he calls you." Alistair chimed. "I'm fairly certain he will. Tomorrow let's go to Harvey Nichols and pick out a new dress for dinner."

"I'm perfectly capable of choosing a dress from my own wardrobe." she moaned tiredly as she collected wineglasses off of her coffee table. She was exhausted and she wanted to go to bed, but first she was bringing the glasses into the kitchen.

They looked at each other. They got up from their seats to help clear the mess. Grace said goodbye to Sharon before Alistair and Philippe retreated to their upstairs flat.

After a hot shower and changing into her pyjamas, Grace lay in bed staring at the ceiling in deep thought. *I hope they are right. If he loves me and wants me back, it's going to be on my terms and conditions. I don't want to be in the spotlight. I just pray that the ghosts of Worthington Hall don't resurrect themselves. I don't need Tamzin or Gemma in my life.*

Shortly after midnight she finally closed her eyes dreaming of Guy whispering *'I love you'* in her ear.

fifteen

efore sunrise Guy escaped to the London Lions stadium to exercise. He felt the stadium was like a second home. He enjoyed the comfort and quietness of it all especially in the early hours of morning.

On the pitch he repeatedly kicked a football around. He fine-tuned his football skills before taking a jog around the pitch. As he jogged he listened to music on his iPhone and lost himself in the thought of Grace. *I need to impress Grace. I want to win her heart and never lose her again.* His heart pounded hard against his breastplate. *Grace makes me feel things I've never felt before. She's a woman I can marry.*

He dreamt of her walking down the aisle of St. Paul's Cathedral dressed in a billowing white gown and her hair tousled in curls. *I want this date perfect. I need Grace to believe she is the one for me.* His iPhone vibrated mid-jog. He stopped to look at it. It was a call from security at the gate.

"Yes?" he growled.

"Mr. Rowling, Mrs. Tamzin Dowling's here to see you." Aaron, the security guard said.

Mystified he didn't reply. Yesterday when he returned to his flat he saw that Darren left without leaving notice. He tried to ring Darren's mobile to see if he was okay, but there was no answer.

"Mr. Rowling, Rumour Mill paps and media paparazzi are surrounding the gates. The police have been called and we need additional security guards. Are you seeing her?" Aaron asked.

"Fine, I'll see her. Send her to the clubhouse." he replied.

I'm not going to rush to Tamzin. She can wait until after my jog and shower to see me.

♥

Patiently, Tamzin waited for Guy in the London Lions clubhouse. She went behind the bar. She got a cold bottle of J2O, opened it and poured it into a glass. No one was about except for her, Guy and security. She was glad they were keeping the media at bay. *Good! Now they'll have pictures of me leaving with Guy!*

When Tamzin had left King's Cross, she called her father, asking him to put surveillance on Guy. She wanted to know his whereabouts at all times. She was determined to get *her* man. *A man that's better than Darren any day of the week. What an embarrassment he is!*

Shortly after returning to their home Darren arrived in a drunken stupor. She watched from their window as he climbed the steps. The media swarmed around him. He brushed past Rumour Mill paparazzi as they shouted their questions whilst taking pictures. As he tripped up the steps, Darren garbled 'Fuck off!' before opening the front door and waving two fingers at the paparazzi.

When he entered the lounge, he didn't greet her. He didn't notice that she was standing by the window. Instead he plopped himself on the couch to fall asleep. She refused to wake him. *What was the point? It's not going to change my view.*

Early in the morning, Tamzin checked her mobile for text messages. There was one from the man tailing Guy. He informed her that Guy was at the London Lions stadium.

Quickly she hopped out of bed. She dressed in a pair of dark- wash skinny jeans, a white t-shirt and leopard print ballet flats. She pulled her hair up into a messy ponytail. She hadn't bothered to plaster on her make-up as she was going for the scorned wife look.

Even though the sun had yet to make a dent in the sky, she wore a pair of L'Wren Scott oversized sunglasses to cover her eyes. She wanted Rumour Mill to think she spent all night crying from her husband's terrible betrayal.

As soon as the front door crept open and she stepped out on to the steps sleep-eyed paparazzi came to life. They ran to her shouting questions.

"Did you know about the baby?"

"Did you know about the affair?"

"Do you know the stripper who worked for your father?"

Without uttering a single word she bypassed them all. She waved them off. She slipped into the silver Mercedes GLK 350 that waited for her. As the car careened through dark silent streets, Tamzin felt like Princess Diana being chased. She was grateful to arrive at the stadium in one piece.

In the still of the room, she drank and wondered how she was going to entice Guy to date her. *This time I can't play baby games with Guy. I'm going in for the kill. What's taking him so long?*

Tamzin looked over to the double doors. He appeared. She slipped the sunglasses down over the bridge of her nose to take a peek at him. For the first time, she noticed how hot Guy truly was. *Flipping Nora! He's incredibly sexy!* She bit her lip and smiled wryly.

She noticed his charcoal hair was wet and slick from the shower. His face was shaven and the smell of his Issey Miyake cologne wafted to her nose. He was dressed in a Ralph Lauren polo shirt and dark denim shorts. She tried not to show her smile or pleasure in his appearance.

"Hello Tamzin." he greeted.

"Hello Guy." she replied weakly.

He strolled over to the bar to make himself a coffee.

"Guy, did you know about the baby?" she asked.

"No...No. What baby?" he asked placing a Nescafe capsule into the Nescafe coffee machine.

Tamzin shoved fresh print copies of Rumour Mill and the Sun to Guy. His eyes settled on the front pages. In black and white ink there were pictures of Darren with Alana at Cherries gracing the pages. The headlines screamed *'Doomed Darren the Drunk!' "What will the Smythe syndicate do to Darren? Tamzin betrayed.' 'Affair with Cherries stripper leaves Darren red in the face!'*

She pulled off her shades, tossing them in her Christian Dior handbag. He looked at her with a twinge of sympathy. Her eyes were swollen, puffy and red.

"Guy, you would've told me right?" she asked. It was a soft grieving voice.

He didn't know what to say to her. He wasn't going to tell her that the night before Darren stayed at his and told him all. He couldn't stand Tamzin and yet she stood before him as lost little girl seeking help.

"Coffee?" he offered. Tamzin shook her head no.

"I thought he loved me. I knew that Darren was a player, but I thought he would put it all behind him once we married. I didn't even think Darren was capable of having a baby out of wedlock." she wailed. "But a baby with a stripper?! And no less someone who works for my father. My father's angry about this, Guy. I don't know what to do."

As he stirred in his sugar, he silently recalled every detail of his conversation with Darren. He felt the bile rising in the back of his throat. *She isn't a victim.*

"Tamzin, stop playing all innocent here. William had to know about Darren's indiscretion. It was at his club for God's sake. How can William, the all seeing, all knowing gangster, not know? Presently, Darren owes him a great deal of money and I'm sure it was your father who leaked this to the press to push him to pay his debts by working for him." he spat at her. He wasn't going to hold his tongue. He felt the need to defend his brother.

"It's possible my father knew, but I didn't know! It's the honest truth. I didn't know Darren cheated on me like that. I surely didn't have a clue about the baby!" she howled. She slammed her hands onto the granite slab.

"What do you want from me Tamzin? I've got nothing to say on this matter. This is between you and your husband. Why don't you go home to him and sort it out?" he said strongly.

"Ever since he lost the Premier Darren arrives home drunk. He drinks like there is an endless supply of vodka. He's been like this for quite some time. I'm scared of him. Once, he raised his hands at me in anger. He wanted to hit me because I made a comment on how horrible he did on the pitch! I can't stay married. He betrayed me and he betrayed our relationship. I'm filing for a divorce." she sobbed. Tears streamed down her face. She pushed the back of her palm to her cheek to wipe her tears away woefully. She wanted him to pity and feel sorry for her. Most of all, she wanted him to wrap his strong muscular arms around her body and comfort her. *Then I'll have him...*

"All I want...all I need is a friend." she added mournfully.

He staggered. *This is Tamzin's finest performance, BAFTA worthy.* He saw right through Tamzin. *She's transparent like a jellyfish and just as deadly.*

"You've got friends. Gemma's your friend. Why don't you visit her and dump your problems on her?" he asked.

"Gemma isn't interested. We fell out regarding you getting her pregnant. She's not happy that I didn't succeed as a friend in helping achieve her goal of marrying you." she lied.

"I never got her pregnant and I believe that you had a lot to do with Gemma and *that* scandal." he retorted.

Tamzin realised she poured salt on a freshly open wound. His face turned beet red in anger. *I need to get him back before I lose him.*

"It's in past." she said, stepping forward. She slimily inched herself towards him, placing her hand down over his. He flinched. He grabbed his cup of coffee and walked over to a leather couch to take a seat.

"Let's be friends, Guy. Please. I need a friend who's strong and has a good head on their shoulders. Are you willing to help me through this crisis?" she moaned.

"I've never been on the best of terms with you. It'll most likely stay that way. You always get what you want, but being friends with me is highly unlikely. If divorce is what you want then seek the advice of a solicitor, not me."

Frustrated by his lack of emotion, she stormed forward, pushing his legs open with her own to stand in between him and look down. He sat coolly drinking his coffee, unmoved. Tamzin reached out to run her fingers through his hair.

"Darren's your best friend, Guy. Don't you want to see us happy?" she cooed. He reached up to her and pulled her hands off of him. He threw a frosty glare at her.

"I can't answer for Darren, but I can answer for myself. I don't give a sod's arse whether or not you two stay together. If anything, I'm delightfully ecstatic that this has all come to light. Finally he'll grow up and learn his lesson that this was a mistake from the beginning!" he countered ferociously.

There's no way of garnering sympathy from this bastard! It's not working! I'm going to pull out all the military tactics.

"You're gloating, aren't you? I can't believe it. I thought you were sensitive, the one with a heart of gold." she cried out.

He lifted himself from the seat and pushed Tamzin back. She moved into him again, this time pushing her index finger into his chest.

"I thought I'd lean on you for support. I guess I was wrong. Now that you're a top footballer, the fame and fortune's gone to your head just as it did Darren. I'll never forget my roots like you and Darren." she snickered as her talon dug into his chest.

Guy blinked at her. The comment struck his nerve. Before he could reply, Tamzin twirled on her heels to exit the clubhouse.

♥

Early morning Grace unlocked the front doors to Delicious for the construction workers. She was staying for the first half of the day and Mark was to arrive in the afternoon to supervise. She made herself a cappuccino to wake herself up and grabbed a muffin for breakfast. She took her belongings into her office where she sat to eat breakfast and read the morning papers.

She opened her Rumour Mill paper. She bypassed front-page headlines. Instead she went straight to page six which had a headline that interested her. It was a small article followed with a picture of Amanda Priestly and hot Hollywood heartthrob, Jake Reiss. Underneath that picture was another picture of Guy and Grace standing close together in Delicious.

Rumour Has It: Amanda Priestly leans on Hollywood Hottie, Jake Reiss, after breakup with Guy Rowling.

It seems after yesterday's fiasco in Covent Garden bakery, Delicious, in which Guy Rowling sudden appearance caused a fan mob to erupt, Amanda Priestly has called it quits with Guy. It was rumoured Amanda and Guy were dating and she has had enough of the English golden-boy charming way.

Sources say that Amanda is deeply upset upon hearing that Guy was seen comforting baker of the stars, Grace Knowles and assuring her that any damages to her business would be paid for by the footballer.

Currently Amanda is filming a Helen of Troy remake on the island of Cyprus with Jake Reiss. Amanda and Jake were seen leaving a small, quaint restaurant, holding hands. This doesn't bode well for Jake's wife, Abrielle Vaughn, who is in the Philippines adopting their twelfth child.

Sources close to Amanda say that Jake is tired of changing nappies and is interested in women who are dangerously seductive like Amanda. We'll keep you update on this developing Rumour Mill.

Unaware of her office door ajar, she didn't look up to see Guy slowly opening the door watching her. He knocked softly so not to startle her. She looked up in surprise and smiled. *He's jaw droppingly sexy today.* But her smile quickly turned to a frown when she thought about the article she just read.

"Oh. I wasn't expecting to see you here." she murmured, folding the paper and pushing it under some invoices. She didn't want Guy catching her reading it.

"I came to see if the workers had arrived on time." he replied. She was blushing. He had caught her looking at Rumour Mill before he knocked. He knew she was embarrassed by it.

"Why do you read that trash?" he asked, propping himself on the edge of her desk.

"It seems to be more honest than you." she replied, her voice barely above a whisper. Grace didn't hide her annoyance about the article. She grimaced.

"What did you read that you believe is even credible?" he questioned, rubbing his chin.

When she didn't reply, Guy picked up the paper to see for himself. He, too, didn't bother looking at the first pages as he already knew what they were about. Flippantly, he searched the pages until he found the article. He began to laugh.

"Why are you laughing?" she crowed.

"Because you believe this nonsense. Do you want to know the truth or are you that gullible that you couldn't be bothered to ask about Amanda?" he said tossing the paper in a nearby trash bin.

"Well, what's going on between you and Amanda?" Grace asked crossing her arms beneath her bosom. She pouted.

Guy loved the way she pouted. He wanted to toss her over his shoulder and take her to a hotel. He'd rip her knickers off to lick every inch of her quivering, sopping pussy until she unleashed every last drop of sweet cream whilst she was still in a strop.

"Amanda's my sister." he admitted with a heavy sigh. He shifted his weight to avoid showing his pronounced erection.

"Your sister? And I'm to believe *that*." she laughed haughty.

"Yes, she's my sister. My biological sister. No one knows about our family relationship and we prefer it that way. Amanda, Darren and I go to great lengths to keep our past a secret from the media. We know we can get further on our own without our family history involved." he said sternly. She shook her head in disbelief.

"Amanda leads a separate life. It is one built by her publicist, management and others. When I went off to train with the London Lions, I left Amanda and our young sister, Scarlet behind with our parents. I shouldn't have done it. I should've stayed, but I didn't. Later on, Amanda ran away. She came to London and befriended people in television. They took her in and she became Amanda Priestly. Scarlet followed suit a few years later. She was to meet with Amanda before she flew to Los Angeles, but never showed up. We know that Scarlet is alive and well as she sends us letters from places abroad and in London, but she never tells us who she is staying with. She tells us she has a wonderful job as a personal assistant to a wealthy couple and that's it." Guy said, hopping off the desk.

Grace rose from her chair and came up beside him. She put her hand on his shoulder and looked in his eyes, they had lost their shine. He felt miserable when he spoke of them. It was as though he regretted not being a better man to them.

"Rumour Mill's a rag and that's all. Next time, ask." he said.

"Yes I will." she replied with a weak smile.

"Tonight I'm going to Scotland to film an advert for a pair of trainers. I'll be back before Saturday for our date." he said with a wry smile.

"Did I say yes?" she snickered.

"No, but I got permission from your look-a-like uncle, which is a yes to me." he retorted with a twinkle in his eye.

Guy walked to the door to leave. She walked a few steps behind him. He turned to her and moved close into her body. The smell of his cologne, the brisk touch of his arms near hers made her shiver. Suddenly, she felt panic. The room seemed to close in on her. She was afraid, but not because of Guy. Unconsciously, she pressed her palm to the bruise that Trevor gave her. He put his hand on top of hers.

"Who did this to you?" he asked, staring directly in her eyes. He wanted the truth and to hurt the bastard that had done the damage. "Grace, please tell me. You never answered my question yesterday, but I expect an answer now."

"Guy it's over with, I promise you. It doesn't matter now." she said. She didn't dare bring herself to look at him in the eye. She knew that he might go insane if he knew it was Trevor. Someone cleared their throat. She looked over Guy's shoulder to see it was Mark.

"Grace, you won't believe what has arrived! Flowers by Samantha are delivering dozens upon dozens of rose bouquets. They're all for you! Here's the card!" Mark squealed as he handed her the card. Grace looked at Guy. Guy shook his head in denial that he had sent her the roses. Carefully she opened the ecru envelop. She pulled out a handwritten note.

It was from Trevor. Guy watched her reaction. Her face turned ashen and pale. He took the letter from her shaking hand and read it.

Now I got my answer! Trevor slapped Grace. Trevor did the damage and now he's going to pay for it! His demeanour changed. He looked like a hulking lion on the hunt with his prey in sight. Grace reached out to him.

"Please Guy, its' over." she promised, touching his cheek.

"I'm sorry, Grace, but Trevor needs to pay for what he did to you." he growled. His jaw clenched to the point that his teeth might shatter and his fist held tightly to his sides.

"Ahem! Those roses are disturbing our work, missus!" A worker said standing behind Mark.

Guy ran out of the office. He rushed into the store and saw the roses coming in by droves. The workers stood in their places, scratching their heads because of their inability to work. Mark and Grace tried stopping the delivery, but the drivers insisted since it was all bought and paid for, it had to remain with Grace. They had other deliveries to do instead of carting around over twenty-four dozen of roses back to the shop. He scowled and swore under his breath.

Quickly, Guy said his goodbye to Grace and promised to call her later. Her body shook in nervousness. *I hope Guy doesn't do any harm.* It was a far-fetched wish on her part.

♥

When Guy arrived at The Rabbit and Hare it was closed for service, but the front door was open. Guy walked in just as a photographer brought in equipment for a photo shoot for *U.K. Culinary* magazine.

Staff walked about, setting tables with crisp white linen, fine crystal goblets and polished silverware. Trevor stood in the middle of the restaurant with his back to Guy as he talked to the journalist. Trevor felt a hand grab his shoulder, and spun him around.

A hard knuckled fist came crashing down onto Trevor's face, knocking him in tables around him. Bewildered, Trevor regained his composure as his eye began to swell rapidly and a cut appeared just under it. He blinked to see Guy raving mad and hulking over him, to land another hit.

"Crikey!" cried the reporter, jumping out of their way to save herself from getting hurt in the brawl.

"What the hell did you hit me for?!" Trevor shouted.

"That's for Grace! You stay away from her, you hear me! Far, far away from her! You ever come near her again I'll beat you to a pulp and I'll have you arrested!" Guy roared.

"I should have you arrested for assault!" Trevor snarled.

"It's a bruise! It's exactly like the one you gave Grace!" Guy snorted before walking off.

Trevor stormed off to the kitchen. He snatched ice from the fridge, throwing it on a teacloth and placing it over his eye. Puzzled, everyone stood around wondering what just unfolded.

♥

In Ivy-upon-Wye, Cat and Corrie went to The Bird in Hand Pub for afternoon tea. Simultaneously, they doused their fish and chips with malt vinegar, whilst they chatted about their work and random bits of gossip. Ms. Penny came to their table to join them for lunch.

"I've heard about your niece's business." Ms. Penny said, placing three shandies down onto the table.

As Corrie bit into her chip, she looked up to see Ms. Penny sitting down with a Rumour Mill paper tucked under her arm.

"How did you know about Grace's business?" Cat asked, cutting through her cod.

Lately, The Savoury Plum was overwhelmed with tourists from all over. They hadn't had much of chance to sit down with their local friends to talk about life in general. This was a first in a long time to sit in a pub, have lunch and drink with a good friend.

"It was in the paper this morning." Ms. Penny replied.

The twins looked at each other quizzically. Last night Grace explained it was nothing and the ruckus was between two customers fighting on the queue. Ms. Penny gave the paper to Cat. She had taken the liberty of highlighting the headline and creasing the page so Cat could find it quickly.

Cat read the article as Ms. Penny and Corrie continued to eat her meal. She felt as though the bottom of her feet were on flaming hot coals and the fire worked its way up her body. She looked like a pressure cooker ready to explode.

"Are you alright Cat?" asked Corrie.

"No...I'm not alright. That bloody bastard's returned!" Cat snapped viciously.

"Who?" Corrie asked.

"Guy...Guy Rowling!" Cat yelled.

♥

Over late afternoon brunch and hair of the dog, Darren settled down to read the papers. It was the first bit of peace he had since his arrival last night. The endless doorbell ringing by the paparazzi had finally ceased after he acquired security services.

He read all the articles in the papers about his relationship with Tamzin, the baby with Alana, and what-not thoroughly. He digested the fact that Tamzin knew all about his affair and he felt a bit relieved. He tried contacting her, but she refused to answer his texts or voicemails. His publicist reached out to him and insisted that the scandal was ruining his reputation faster than bonfire flames.

"Darren, there are rumours flying about London. Some I can control, some I can't control. You've sunken to a new low. You're drinking excessively. Everyone thinks you need a stint at the Priory." his publicist warned.

Shortly after that call, his manager of the Tottenham Heat rang. He ripped into Darren.

"You need to take your lumps like a real bloke! Sort it out! Go to Gran Canarias for a bit of holiday and come back when you are ready." His manager had shouted down the phone.

Darren declined on taking a private jet to Gran Canarias. He had better things to do, like sorting out his debt with William. As much as he had wanted to run away from it all, he knew it was better to deal with it.

Appetite diminished, he flipped the pages of the paper. He didn't want to read about his problems. He wanted to read about someone else's problems. His eyes rested on Guy's and Amanda's headline.

At first, he was amused by the article. *Boy, do the papers get it wrong.* He laughed. Then he saw her face, it was the baker from his wedding. It was Grace. *I'm not going to let a woman ruin Guy's career like I allowed Tamzin to do*, Darren vowed silently.

♥

$$sixteen$$

uy nibbled on Grace's earlobe as he pumped his cock in and out of her dripping, wet sex in rhythmic motion. He held her tightly under her arms, his hands cupping her head and pushing it to the side so he could lick her neck there. The wet sand pressed into her body and the ocean sprayed against them. A massive wave barrelled down on their bodies.

She awoke with a jolt. Her heart was pounding madly and she was nearing orgasm, but was quickly disappointed when he didn't materialise. She picked up the television remote to turn off the telly. She had fallen asleep on the couch watching *From Here to Eternity*. She glanced at the clock. *It's not even midnight and it's still Friday,* Grace thought sourly. She was excited that her date was only one sleep away.

As Guy had promised, he called her whilst he was filming his advert in Scotland.

"Grace, can you hear me?" he asked loudly.

It was a windy day in the Scottish highlands. A storm was brewing making mobile reception terrible. It was unseasonably cool, damp and stormy.

"Barely." she replied.

In a tent pitched for protecting equipment, he shivered from the cold, damp wind blowing. Crew ran about gathering all the supplies to head back into town.

"I'll pick you up at 6.30 on Saturday. I've got a wonderful evening planned for us. I'm looking forward to seeing you." he shouted down his mobile. He jogged in place to keep warm.

"I'm looking forward to it." she replied aloud.

After his visit to the bakery, she was desperate to spend her time alone with him. She knew he meant well and was genuinely concerned for her. Most of all she wanted to rekindle what they once had. *Maybe it'll be even better than before,* she hoped.

"I can't wait to see you Grace. I miss you terribly. I wish you were here with me." he said, his tone glum. She knew his words spoke the truth. She held back before she answered.

"I miss you too." she whispered.

But the connection was lost. He didn't hear a word. Guy wasn't able to ring back as there wasn't reception on his iPhone. The crew had packed up their equipment into transit vans and hightailed into town to find a bed and breakfast for the night.

When they settled at the B & B, Guy was told the landlines were out of order due to flooding. There was still no reception on his mobile. Frustrated, he went to bed. The next morning the skies had cleared and there was a concerned text from Grace. He replied that they were all fine and he was finishing the advert today.

Guy returned to hot, steamy London the following day. In a string of unfortunate events, he came down with a cold and fever. The miserable spring-like conditions of Scotland had made him ill. He wound up losing his voice and texting Grace to tell her all. He swore he'd be fine for dinner the following Saturday as long as he had a few days to recover.

Grace understood completely. When Delicious reopened for business, she delivered a thermos of warm chicken soup, hot buttery rolls and freshly squeezed orange juice to his flat. He told her not to do it, but she couldn't resist as he was helpless. She promised not to deliver the goods herself as he told her that he didn't want her to get sick.

As he recovered Grace kept her focus on the reopening of the business. Since it was in the papers that Guy had visited the shop, there was a new influx of customers. They were celebrity spotters and watchers. They were desperate to spot the celebrity and Delicious was touted as the place to be seen for celebrities.

All sorts of celebrities drifted in. Some faces were familiar to her because she had seen them at the wedding, but there were many that weren't so familiar.

WAG's, footballers, actors and actresses alike came to drink cappuccinos, eat treats and order luxurious catering from the store. They'd find spots outside or nearest to the windows to be seen as they tweet on their android mobiles.

Tourists and paparazzi maintained distance when they took pictures. On occasion some would approach their favourite celeb for an autograph, but it wasn't near the hysteria that Guy's prior visit produced.

Much to her delight profit had quadrupled. She discussed the possibility of opening a second shop with Mark. It excited them. *Guy re-entering my life wasn't as bad as I thought it would be. I just wish my aunts thought the same way.* But she felt twinges of guilt. Cat called her following their lunch with Ms. Penny.

'I hope you're not giving him another chance! After all he did.' she snapped at Grace.

She tried to convince them it wasn't what they thought, but it didn't work. Cat was even more upset at the fact that she had lied. She explained that it was *that* unreasonable reaction forced her to lie. She apologised, but Cat didn't listen. Cat told her that they would speak on another day when things 'settled'.

To ease the stress from work, her aunts, and Saturday's date, Alistair took her shopping at Harvey Nichols. They scoured the racks until he set his sights on a gorgeous black asymmetrical Lanvin wrap dress. The dress was paired with gold Michael Kors open-toe booties and Ios Sellani gold and black fringe earrings. Alistair insisted that Guy was going to take her somewhere posh so Grace must look divine. She was satisfied with her goodies. She couldn't wait to go on the date.

Grace collected her plate resting on a side table next to the couch. *Just another night to go and soon I'll be alone with Guy.* She padded across her lounge into the kitchen. When she entered the kitchen she froze in her tracks. She dropped her plate, forcing it to break into many pieces on the floor.

The garden door was wide open. She knew she had locked it as she'd been out all day. *There's no way I left it open! I know I closed it.* She hadn't opened the garden door at least a day before yesterday. She went to the door to inspect it. Clearly the lock been picked. With the telly on loud, she hadn't heard a thing and fallen asleep.

She ran back to the lounge to fetch her Blackberry to dial 999.

♥

"Sixteen weeks! Sixteen bloody weeks for a divorce!" Tamzin shrieked on top of lungs, pacing back and forth in her solicitor's office.

It was Friday afternoon and if she could show anger with a facial expression she would've. But a visit to Harley Street for Botox injections deterred her from making facial expressions. It was on this occasion that sparked her unexpected visit to the solicitors. When the appointment with her plastic surgeon came to an end, she went to the receptionist to make a payment. She learned that her credit cards had been declined.

The receptionist took pity on Tamzin by not announcing her demise to the other patients waiting in area. She told Tamzin to call someone else to settle the bill as payment was due at the time of service. *Thankfully Daddy came to my rescue.* After the surgeon was paid she went over to her solicitors' office, Cuthbert and Withers, to demand they speed up the process for divorce.

"There isn't much we can do, Mrs. Dowling. Sixteen weeks is the norm and we must abide by it. You're lucky, others have to wait at least two years for a divorce." Barrister Cuthbert said. "By the way, how do you intend to pay us?"

She threw a fireball of a glare his way. If she could spit venom his way she would have done it. She knew exactly what her solicitor was getting at. It was in Rumour Mill that she might have to file bankruptcy due to being married to a useless pariah. *There's no money.* All of it was tied in assets. The only person she could rely on was her father, but William told her that she must sink her claws into Guy.

"I intend to pay you as soon as the divorce is settled." she answered coolly.

"You're in dire financial straits, Mrs. Dowling. You should consider bankruptcy. This morning it was reported that the bank intends on foreclosing on your manor." Barrister Cuthbert said. He plucked a piece of imaginary lint from his grey Anderson and Sheppard suit. "I wouldn't be surprised if your Kensington town home is next. You should visit your accountant."

She looked as though she was going to blow a smoke stack. Instead, she forced herself to remain cool and collective. Once the meeting was over with and no resolution, she got into a black cab. Sitting back, she called Guy's agent to schedule a date. Instead, his agent told her that she needed to connect through to Guy's personal assistant or visit him at his office.

He has a personal assistant and an office? What's this world coming to? Tamzin gave the cab driver the address. It was located in a building a few blocks away from the London Lion stadium.

She sauntered through the doors of Guy's office. Behind a sleek white desk sat a young, spotty man who didn't blink when Tamzin walked in.

"May I help you?" asked the chap.

"Yes, I'm looking for Guy Rowling. Tell him his favourite glamour girl, Tam, is here to see him." she mewled.

Gary wasn't impressed. He continued to focus on his work on his iMac.

"He isn't here, but I will relay the message to him that you came for a visit." he replied.

"Can you give me his address?" she queried hotly.

"No!" he snapped.

"I would love to set up a date with him and I need direct contact with Guy." she crowed.

"No. I'll pass the message on. Please leave I've got work to do." he sternly replied. Guy made it clear that Gary would lose his job if mentioned his whereabouts or information to anyone especially Tamzin.

She snapped back and straightened up. Seething, she stormed from Guy's office. She was keen on getting any valuable information and then she realised her way to Guy was through Darren.

By the time Tamzin arrived home, she searched the house for Darren. He wasn't around. She found a note in the kitchen from him. It stated that he went on holiday to think things through. She crushed the note in her palm.

She called his mobile only to be greeted by a tone that said it had been disconnected. In her anger, she threw her iPhone on the floor and kicked it. After a few minutes of panicking, she picked up the phone and dialled William. *Darren needs to be put down like the no good racehorse! And maybe Daddy can get rid of that bloody baker too. I'm sure she'll be good on the sex trade market!* She thought wickedly.

♥

"Alistair! Thank god, you're here!" she cried. Alistair walked in the flat surprised by the police presence in front of the house.

"What happened now?" He saw two officers investigating the broken garden door in her kitchen.

She explained to Alistair that the flat was broken into whilst she was asleep. The telly must have frightened the burglar away. He hugged her tightly. The night wore on. The police questioned her and Alistair. Finally the officers' concluded the break-in must've been done by yobs (youth offending boys) local to area, looking to burglarise a flat. Their assessment didn't ease her. Since Trevor had hit her, she was already on edge and now this break in added to her fears. Alistair advised her to stay in his flat until he got the locksmith out to change the locks.

As she slept in the guest bedroom, Grace contemplated on texting Guy. She knew he'd come to her rescue. He would whisk her to a hotel, but she thought better of it. *Tomorrow's another day and will be a better day. It's all just a bad coincidence.*

♥

Saturday morning Darren hid behind the trees on his estate. He watched as bailiffs' entered his home, repossessing all tangible assets for outstanding debts. Tamzin stood in the driveway, crying. Her father held her in his arms.

Magda, the housekeeper, watched as priceless works of art, expensive furniture, and a massive flat-screen telly came out of the front door. Mounted onto tow-trucks were Darren's favourite Ferrari and Lamborghini. The scene crushed a blow to Darren's greedy ego. The repossession of personal possessions signalled the end of their former lifestyle and marriage.

All week William had sent a slew of text messages to Darren. All of them had went unanswered. William was at the end of his tether and he wanted his son-in-law dead and buried. He even coerced Alana to contact Darren on the basis that a cheque bounced. She left him a voicemail message pleading with him to meet with her in a seedy part of London so that he could give her cash.

He knew it was a set-up. Sources told him that Alana was shopping her story around. The highest bidder so far was from Rumour Mill. There was no need for money. Besides he had checked his account and the cheque that she claimed bounced had cleared. The money came from a private, offshore account. It was an account Tamzin didn't have access to. He didn't trust her. Darren chose to get rid his mobile and went into hiding at a bed and breakfast.

Earlier in the week he had sought Guy's advice. Guy finally recovered from his cold and his voice had returned. He answered Darren's call.

"Darren you need to sort your own life out. Stop dragging me into it." Guy coughed after listening to him.

"What? Now you're too big to help your brother out?" he snidely remarked.

"No. It's not that and it's got nothing to do with us being brothers. I told you to go to the police, divorce Tamzin, and seek legal counsel, but you haven't done a thing. Darren, grow a set of balls and be a man about this." Guy replied.

"You know something, Guy? I think the fame, the game, the money and that bird have gone to your head!" he snapped.

Guy didn't reply. He was tired of being Darren's crutch. He barely had any energy to argue.

"Leave her out of this. Frankly you're out of line." Guy said calmly. "I must be going. I need my rest." He didn't wait for Darren's reply. The call disconnected.

Darren recounted the conversation. *Guy's right, I need to own up to my responsibilities. I need to sort this out.* It wasn't what he wanted to do, but he had to do it.

♥

Fully recovered and shaking with fear, Guy stood in his bedroom admiring himself at the mirror. He was grateful that the zinc tablets, vitamins and freshly-squeezed orange juice had worked like a charm. He looked like his old self again.

Guy would've hated to cancel the date after all of Gary's hard work on helping prepare for it. Several times Gary had contacted the Waterside Inn to ensure that the private cottage was prepared for dinner and the yacht was ready for dessert.

He had also arranged security for them. Guy's agent insisted on getting security for him as the paparazzi were increasing their presence and trying to catch images of him. There was a soft knock on the bedroom door.

"Come in." Guy called out. Wendy entered the room.

"The Bentley's arrived." she announced. "Is there anything you need before I leave for the evening?"

"No, you're done for the evening. Which tie should I wear?" he asked, holding up a grey tie and a red tie to go with his dark grey pin stripe Armani suit.

"The red one." she replied. "Feel free to contact me should you need any help." she added, watching him adjust his tie in the full length mirror.

"Thank you for your help, Wendy. You're a treasure." he complimented as she took over in adjusting his tie.

He kissed her on the cheek. Leaving he realised that he had forgotten the Graff gift box on the mahogany dresser. Wendy had it in her hand and held it out to him.

"She must be special." she quipped.

"She is special." he replied taking the box.

He winked and smiled before leaving on his date. *Grace is beyond special.*

♥

seventeen

listair and Sharon twitched the window curtains like a pair of old nosy biddies'. In anticipation of Guy's arrival they looked longingly out the window. When the sleek onyx Bentley Mulsanne parked in front of the house they shrieked like school girls.

"He's here Grace!" Alistair shouted out.

She emerged from her bedroom applying an earring to her left earlobe. They turned to her and were stunned by the vision of beauty standing before them.

"*Phwoar!* You look totes hawt!" Sharon said. Alistair was lost for words.

"Absolutely beautiful." he finally piped.

She was a woman on fire. Her hair styled in a messy side-swept bun. Her eyelids were heavily made in smoky grey colour, cheeks bronzed with Nars blush and lips glossed with M.A.C. lip glass. The Lanvin dress Alistair chosen hugged her curves perfectly and the gold booties added emphasis to her height. The feeling of being dolled up made her stomach churn in excitement.

The front door bell chimed. Sharon forced Grace back into her bedroom whilst Alistair went to the door. Guy stood at the door with a hulking bodyguard next to him.

"Hello, Mr. Rowling! It's so nice to see you again!" Alistair greeted excitedly.

"Thank you. It's nice seeing you again as well. You can call me, Guy." he replied.

"Come in. Grace is nearly ready." Alistair beckoned.

Nervous, he stepped inside. He motioned to his guard to wait outside. He didn't want Grace to be put off by the security presence. He followed behind Alistair to the flat. He looked around the flat grinning from ear to ear. *The flat is perfectly Grace and decorated to her taste.*

"Would you like some wine?" Alistair offered holding out a wine glass to him. He took it and thanked Alistair.

He needed that drink. His mouth was dry at the thought of the date going awful. A few minutes later Grace emerged from her bedroom with Sharon in tow. His cock had a mind of its' own. It twitched at the sight of her.

He couldn't believe how dazzling Grace looked. It was as though the girl he had met earlier was emerging from her cocoon like a mature butterfly. *She was beautiful to begin with; smashing at the wedding and this look...it's beyond words!*

Alistair and Sharon watched his expression. They grinned and giggled like plotting hyenas.

Grace, too, didn't believe what she saw. His handsome presence shocked her. *He's standing in my flat!* She was stunned by his look. He didn't look like the man she had first met at The Savoury Plum. He was well-dressed and kempt before and looked great for the wedding, but the look he wore tonight was as though Guy taken fashion advice from David Beckham.

Even Guy's fresh hair cut was something to behold. His jet black hair slick back whilst his sides were trimmed short. His suit looked as if it was sewn onto him. His cocoa eyes glistened with mischief, a mischief that she was familiar with.

"Grace...you're breathtaking." He knew dinner was going to be a struggle as his thoughts wandered in shagging her.

"Thank you. You look handsome."

"Are you ready?"

"Yes, I am." she replied, looking for her clutch. Alistair gave her the clutch and kissed her on the cheek.

"Have fun. We won't be waiting up for you." Alistair sang as they walked out of the flat together.

She looked back at Alistair. She threw him a knowing look. Guy took her hand and the driver opened the Bentley door to let her in.

♥

With the hour drive to Bray ahead of them, it gave Guy and Grace an opportunity to talk. He asked her about the business. She told him that she was pleased with the repair results. She asked him if he knew the contractor who did the work. He said yes and that the contractor was an old family friend. She went on to tell him that his impromptu visit had increased revenue for the business. She was extremely happy for the increase and for that she was grateful.

"I told you I'm good for something." he chuckled.

She laughed. Impulsively he rested his palm on her bare knee. Goose pimples erupted along her legs and arms. Her insides were twisting with elated excitement.

They arrived at the Inn. She immediately recognised the restaurant. The Waterside Inn was a restaurant that she always wanted to visit for dinner, due to its' prestigious Michelin rating and recommendation. They were greeted by their own private butler. He led them down the path to a private cottage that Gary arranged for them.

Inside, she was taken by the cottage's decor and opulence. It was decorated in the richest velvets, silk drapes, and beautiful antique furniture. It housed expensive Lalique crystal and fine works of art.

In the centre of the room there was a table set for two with the best china, candles and flowers.

Once they were seated, their butler poured sweet wine. It was a top of the line vintage 1981 Chateau D'Yquem Sauternes. The butler left the cottage to check on their meal.

"A toast to you, Grace." Guy said, lifting his glass.

"Why, Guy?" she asked.

"For giving me another chance." he replied with a smile.

"Am I giving you, or us a second chance?" Grace cooed.

"Well, then why are you here?" he answered the question with a question.

She thought for a moment. *I know exactly why I'm here. I want to be with Guy. Alistair is right. What man would go to great lengths to try and win me back, even if it was just a shag?*

"A toast to us, Guy! To letting go of the past and moving forward to the future, wherever it may take us!" she cheered. She lifted her glass. Their glasses touched and they drank smiling.

The meal was superb. It was two courses, consisting of the finest sea scallops and Angus beef made to perfection. It barely wet his appetite because his hunger was only for Grace. He watched her eat, savouring each and every bite.

"Did you like your dinner?" she asked, noticing that Guy had barely touched his plate.

"Yes I did. It's all delicious." he replied.

She couldn't believe her taste buds. The Waterside Inn chef had outdone themselves. She wondered if her parent's had made food this tasty.

"Why are you quiet?" he asked.

"I wonder if my father and mother cooked like this, it's an art and it's ever so delicious." she said.

"We'll never know, Grace. But, what I do know is that they would've been proud of you. You've truly made a success of yourself and business." he replied. "Speaking of family, how are your aunts?" He wiped his mouth with a napkin.

"They're fine. They are happy for me. They're happy with Delicious. I don't think they'll be too happy to know I'm seeing you." she replied. She didn't bother to mention that they were very angry about his visit to Delicious. She knew it might ruin a perfect evening.

"Who cares what anyone else thinks! Come. We have to go." he exclaimed, getting up from his chair.

"Where are we going?" she asked.

He didn't answer her. Instead Guy extended his hand for her to take. She followed him out of the cottage, down a small path to a dock on the Thames river. A cruising yacht decorated in fairy lights awaited them.

"Are we getting on this?" she asked excitedly.

"Yes we are. I want you all to myself. No interruptions." he replied. "This yacht belongs to my agent who loaned it to me for tonight."

He helped her aboard the yacht. The captain greeted them and directed them to a seating area at the back of the yacht. It was set for dessert. A large silver dome rested on a tray next to some cordials. Grace took a seat as Guy took two cordials for them. He handed a cordial to Grace and sat down next to her.

As the yacht cruised up the Thames towards London they sat in silence drinking cordials. She eased herself into his strong arms. A light breeze picked up, caressing her hair and making her feel slightly cold. She shivered. He rubbed her arms and cuddled with her as she rested her head on his chest. *I can get use to this,* Grace thought as she stretched her legs out on the seat.

He lightly kissed her on her crown. His fingertips grazed her bare shoulder. The soft gentle touch aroused her. It was as if they had never parted. He lifted her chin to bring her lips to his.

Softly he planted a kiss. He tasted the sweet wine they drank during dinner. Her mouth relaxed as his tongue swirled around hers. The intensity soon increased. She pulled herself up in his arms to get more of Guy, but he abruptly stopped.

"Grace, lift the dome." he whispered in her ear. Puzzled, she lifted it.

Among chocolate truffles, chocolate covered strawberries and profiteroles, there was a dark blue jewellery box from Graff.

"Guy!" she cried. "I hope you're not asking to marry me." Grace looked at Guy as if he was crazy. He laughed loudly.

"I do want to marry you, but no, this isn't a proposal. I'd be rushing things if I proposed." he said.

Relief washed over her. As lovely it was and suitable for a proposal, she felt it was presumptuous of him. In her opinion to get married soon after reuniting wouldn't resolve their past and wouldn't bode well for their future.

"Open the box." he whispered.

She delicately picked up the box in her hands and opened it slowly to reveal its' contents. Inside was a stunning diamond on diamond necklace. A necklace designed in the finest white gold with links of sparkly diamonds. There was a hanging locket of white gold with two entwined letter G in pave diamonds.

"Guy, I can't accept this. As beautiful as it is, it's too expensive. I don't deserve such a gift!" she exclaimed, touching the sparkling diamonds lightly with her fingers.

"You can accept it. All this time I've thought of you, dreamt of you, and physically craved you. I never thought of anyone else, but you. I've waited patiently for you to come to your senses whilst I focused my game." he throatily murmured. He lifted the necklace, clasping it around her neck.

"Why are you doing this, Guy?" she implored.

'Because ever since I saw you at The Savoury Plum, I knew I had to have you. You were flushed from a hard day of work. Your demeanour, innocence and naivety made me want you. I knew you'd be hard work. I want to impress you, take care of you, and love you like no other man has loved you before. There's no woman like you, Grace." he said. She threw her arms around his neck. She kissed him hard against the lips. *He loves me! He really does love me!*

Each kiss melded into another, and another, and another. His cock stiffened as their kisses became carnal and erotic. Grace threw her hair back as he released his lips from hers. He dragged his lips down along her jaw to her neck. There, he nibbled as he inhaled the sweet scent of Grace. He pulled Grace into his lap. She obliged. She began to pant as his fingertips ran on the top of her thighs. Her clit pulsed. *I want him to make love to me now!*

♥

As if Guy read her mind, he lifted Grace into his arms to carry her below deck. Initially, he planned for them to take in the sights of London, but the idea veered off course. He brought Grace into the bedroom. He placed her on the bed before locking the door. He came over to the edge of the bed where she lay in front of him.

He lifted each one of her legs to pull off her booties. He massaged the pads of her feet. She moaned softly. His strong fingers wrapped around her calves to pull her to the edge of the bed. He took off his jacket and tie tossing them aimlessly on the floor. She looked up at him coyly. *This time I'm not going to be an innocent victim. This time I'm ready.*

She lifted herself up his body. She brought her fingers to the buttons on his shirt. She ripped them off without a care of their expense. The buttons popped off like tearing open a box of chocolate Smarties. She hungrily kissed Guy's throat and neck. She followed her hands down his chest to his nipples where she gently tugged them. He throatily growled. He was stunned by her eagerness.

"Aren't we the eager one?" he joked. She pulled away.

"Guy, if you're making assumptions that I've been with other men, I haven't. I haven't been with anyone else except you." she snapped. He noticed the look on her face. He hadn't mean to offend her.

"I know you haven't Grace. I know you want to please me, I just don't want to rush it." he assured.

When he kissed her again, she responded in great arousal. A little hiccup was not going to divert their attention away. He unzipped her dress. He pulled the dress down over her body and tossed it. Achingly slow and pulse-pounding, he removed her knickers and bra, throwing it down on a growing pile of clothing. He added his trousers to the pile as well.

Fully naked, Grace trembled in anticipation. He stared at her. His look was one that told her that she was his and his forever. He wanted to burn the image of her beauty into his mind. *I don't ever want to forget how Grace looks tonight. She's more beautiful than any model or celebrity around.* Tonight he was going to savour every minute with her.

Grace turned her eyes up at Guy. His body had changed. His chest seemed bigger, muscular, and more built. His abs were taut. She saw he was tan. Her eyes travelled down to his boxers. He hooked his thumbs into the elastic band pulling them down. His cock sprung forth like a thick, meaty, baton. *Is it me or is it longer and thicker than before?* She curiously thought.

She felt her pussy dampen. The familiar pulse beating in her clit was now fluttering madly. He wedged his knee between her open and kneeling legs. He grabbed her supple arse in his rough palms to bring her down on the bed. She placed her delicate fingers in his hair to help brace her fall. He continued to biting and sucking at her neck with his hot, velvet, cock pressing against her barren sex.

"I've waited so long for you." he murmured with his hand reaching between them.

His fingers found the sweet nub of her pussy. He played with her clit, feeling her get wetter and buck up to him. She felt his hand pull apart her lips and rub there. Grace pushed forward and upward. Her pussy begged for his fingers or cock to provide reprieve.

"Please, Guy." she mewled.

He gave in by sliding one of his long fingers in her creamy tightness. He nearly came when he felt her contract her womb and release around his finger. His thumb held onto her clit, rubbing it slowly as she liked it.

He moved his lips down her body. He reached her breasts, taking one nipple between his lips and suckling gently. Whilst he kissed her there, he fingered her pussy teasingly slow, just the way he knew she liked it. His actions brought Grace to exhilarating heights.

Panting, moaning, and squirming her body against the bed, she felt as though she'd never come down from this sexual high. She increased her movements against his hand. Guy felt she was reaching peak. Creamy, dripping, wetness gushed between her thighs. He wanted her to orgasm all over his hand.

She felt the sparks of orgasm coursing through her body like an electrical current. Her toes curled and her fingers gripped the duvet cover tightly. Her womb quaked with sexual delight.

Guy looked down at his hand. It was wet with pleasure. He brought his thumb to her lips.

'Taste...tastes the nectar I made from you." he murmured grittily.

His thumb ran along the edge of her lip. Slowly, she parted her glossed mouth, easing her tongue out to lick salty creamy goodness. She took his thumb in her mouth and sucked. Through half-shut eyes, he watched his innocent, precious, she suckled. The vein on his throat twitched impatiently. He wanted to taste her pussy. *But it must wait for now...my cock can't take this anymore.*

He lifted her legs onto his shoulders. Her arse lifted off the bed. He hovered over her body. He pushed his engorged bulbous angry head into her trembling pussy. Grace didn't expect the move. She tightened her grip around his head. *It feels like a massive...*the thought left her as he pushed his cock in further. He held tight on her legs. He growled and gruffed at her tight, sopping, wetness. She felt as though her body was being stretch beyond her limit. She swore to herself that she could feel his cock pressing against her belly button. *I don't think I'll survive.*

"You'll survive." he huffed. Grace didn't realise she had said it aloud.

Before she could utter a reply, Guy no longer could take the cock-teasing. He impaled his cock in her. No longer was he going to be nice or gentle about it. She cried out loud. Tears trickled from the corners of her eyes. Wildly he pumped his cock in and out of her. The sensations that she experienced made her cry out with pleasure. The length and girth of his cock rubbed against her trembling walls, ensuring that every inch was touched by him.

All Guy could hear was a variety of *oohs, ahhs, yes, please, more, harder,* from Grace. His balls slapped loudly against her dripping arse and his cock wanted to go deeper and further than before. To appease this want, he pulled his cock out, holding it for a brief second and rubbing it all over her clit. He'd then push his cock into Grace to the hilt. His head rubbed the back of her womb.

When he did this move she pleaded and cried mercy. She clawed at him, trying to get him to fill her pussy again. The teasing, aromatic smell of sex and his hulking body kept her wanting more. Guy gritted his teeth as he picked up tempo.

Like bullets shot from a gun, Grace felt small explosions ricocheting through her womb. Her pussy clenched around him, demanding to milk every drop. The feeling forced him to bear down and fuck her hard. She arched her hips up to him to get more of his cock.

"Oh god, I'm coming!" she cried loudly. It was without a care if the yacht captain heard.

"I love you, Grace." he roared. The words brought her over the edge. Her womb convulsed and her body shook hard.

No longer attempting to hold back, Guy dug his cock deep into her. His white hot seed spilled into her, coating every inch of her womb. Gleaming in sweat with his cock still pulsing inside her, he fell forward, kissing her all her over body. She collapsed beneath him and responded with her own kisses.

Grace held Guy's face in her hands. She stared into his glossy chocolate eyes filled with lust, amour and love. He kissed her hard against her lips.

"Did I hurt you?" he asked.

"No. You'll never hurt me." she replied. He rolled off of her to give her air to breath. She toyed with the necklace around her neck which remained unscathed through the frenzy.

"Guy, I have to tell you something." Grace said as she lay in his arms face to face. He groaned.

"You can't be a virgin." he joked.

"No...It's not that." she said with a crooked smile.

"Guy, I don't want to tell you if you didn't mean what you said when you came." she added.

"What? That I love you Grace? Because I am...I'm in love with you, Grace...absolutely, insanely, in love with you." he replied, kissing her shoulder.

"I love you too, Guy. I didn't want to tell you because I'm afraid of you breaking my heart. All this time apart, I never forgot you, and I didn't want anyone else like I want you."

"Good." he said. "I was starting to feel like this was all a bit one-sided. Come, we should be in London soon. I'm starving for dessert." he added. He noticed the yacht had slowed down to a creep and the river waves splashing against the boat had grown softer. She agreed. They rose from the bed and dressed alongside each other. Guy and Grace returned to deck hand in hand.

As they basked in the glow of the city lights of London they ate profiteroles, handmade truffles, and strawberries. Happily they drank champagne, laughed at jokes, and talked about the lovemaking they experienced. He teased her by saying it must've been the diamonds. For her it was the whole night that made her desire him.

The yacht cruised along the Thames. They were coming up to the Houses of Parliament and the London Eye. They stood next to the yacht railing taking in the sights.

"This is the way I always envisioned showing you London." he murmured in her ear. "After tonight, I plan on showing you the world. You'll have to be patient and realise that I'm a footballer. People will take photographs, ask for autographs and there'll always be paparazzi. Some people will spread malicious rumours to see us part. But I promise to always protect you."

She held tight onto the railing. He took her hand to bring her back to the seating area. There, he took out a blue bag and pulled a large scrapbook out.

"Look through this." he said.

With delicate fingers, she turned pages of his scrapbook. It was filled with chubby baby faced pictures of Guy, alongside toddler and young boy pictures. There were pictures of his siblings, but one picture captured Grace's attention, an old shoddy colour photograph. On a school football pitch Guy, Darren, Gareth, Amanda and Scarlet, linked arm and arm. They were smiling for the camera. She instantly recognised Amanda Priestly.

"She really is your sister." she stated in more of an answer than a question.

"That picture was taken many years ago, before it all went horribly wrong. I'll never lie to you, Grace, and I assure you I've never lied in the past. I'll prove it."

"You can stop proving yourself to me Guy. I don't need proof. I only need your love." she whispered. *He truly loves me. I need to stop pretending that I don't feel the same way about him because I do.*

Suddenly the skies opened up, unleashing a burst of heavy rain. Grace squealed as Guy picked up the scrapbook.

"Let's get in the cabin!" he exclaimed.

She followed him to the cabin wondering if it was an omen to worry about.

♥

eighteen

Eight glorious weeks later, Guy rolled over spooning Grace from behind. His alarm went off at 5 AM. Guy groaned at the thought of taking a flight to Tokyo. He had to film a commercial for a Japanese sports drink. He inhaled the fragrant scent of her as she stirred in slumber. She didn't want to wake, but she had to get ready for Delicious.

It still amazed them how much their lives had changed in the last eight weeks. For Guy, the love of his life was in his bed, *where she needs to be always,* he cheekily grinned. They spent all available time together as the Premier season was closing in on them, and if they couldn't see each other, they spoke on a daily basis.

The tabloids quickly picked up the story. They became front page fodder, knocking out Tamzin and Darren as the 'it' couple. Rumour Mill reported on them daily. She was adjusting to the constant picture taking outside of her business or outside of Guy's flat. On a few occasions paparazzi had followed her home, but she managed to avoid it by speaking to the police regarding her safety. A solicitor's notice on Grace's behalf was sent to Rumour Mill asking for them to stop hounding her at home.

As Guy nuzzled his face in her caramel ombre tresses he reflected on their first date. His cock stiffened in arousal.

The rain didn't dampen their night, it only enhanced it. In the cover of the interior cabin, they kissed passionately up against the wall. Her legs were wrapped around his waist as he grinded his hard cock up against her. When they separated for air, she brought her feet down to the floor. This time, she pushed him hard on the bed. He fell backwards landing on the plush mattress.

"I'm in charge now." she purred, moving like a seductive minx.

Excited, he watched her perform a sexy striptease. When she was finally naked, she crawled over to his body. She put her hands on the top of his trousers, unbuttoning them, pulling them off and shucking them aside.

She climbed over him and brought the tip of her tongue down to his lips to tease him. He tried completing their kiss, but she pulled back from him. Grace teasingly wagged her finger at him. She continued kissing him down and over his throat, neck, shoulders, chest and abs. She followed his happy trail, down to his cock which was standing at attention like a proud male salute. Her hot breath against him made his cock pulsed and begged to be pleased.

Guy had fantasised about her mouth exploring further. He knew there was a strong possibility she might not, but then again her actions surprised him. Regardless of his thought, he wanted her on *his* mouth. As he was about to move her body over his face, Grace took hold of his manhood.

"Grace, what are you doing?" he asked.

"Nothing, nothing at all." she teased.

She held the velvety, steel, rod in between her forefinger and thumb. She rubbed its' head, stroking gently. He groaned as his head hit the pillow. She bent her head over his cock. A soft flick of her tantalising tongue against it had him grinning from ear to ear. She licked the rim of his head and the outer edges, teasing it with no mercy. His cock produced small, tempting beads of semen for her to taste. She savoured the salty taste of his secretions. She followed her tongue down to his heavy testicles. There, she lapped delicately. His breathing was shallow, jerkier and short.

"Good god, girl! You're so good at this. Please, Grace go further." he groaned.

Guy buried his palms in Grace's hair. He loved the feeling of her soft hair wrapped in his fingertips, it made him wickedly horny. With big aquamarine eyes, she looked up from his groin. She wondered if his cock would fit in her mouth. Her lips wet from licking and exploring, pursed in thought. He looked at her, his eyes pleading for her to continue. It was all she needed.

She led her mouth to the top of his cock to swallow him whole. Guy's abs flexed, his thighs tightened. His mind enveloped in a haze of pure ecstasy. She bobbed her head up and down, licking, sucking, and savouring every moment.

"Oh Grace! You're my girl. No one else." he growled.

A few times the tip of Guy's cock hit the back of her throat. It made her gag, but Grace wanted him deeper.

"Keep going baby. I love what you're doing."

She increased her speed as his cock pulsed against her tongue. He was at his brink. Each suckle brought him closer to coming and he'd be damned if Grace didn't let him come in her mouth. Each bob downward caused saliva to drip to his testicles. Each bob upward Grace would run her tongue around the head whilst pumping it with her fist. He clenched her hair. He needed release.

"Fuck! Grace!" Guy cried in ecstasy. He exploded ribbons of hot, milky come deep within her warm mouth.

She felt him rupture along her pink tongue. Grace inhaled deeply, forcing her to swallow every drop of his come. His hard body convulsed. A bewildered look fell over her face. Guy chuckled as she sat up.

"I wasn't expecting that." she said.

"I was." he panted.

She's a tease! An innocent tease at that! Does she know how she pleases me? Does she know how much I need her? I'm going to teach her things she has never done before.

Guy rubbed his head. He reached out for Grace. He pulled her into his arms. They were exhausted.

"Let's lie down together." She tiredly agreed. She curled her naked body to his and soon they both drifted off to sweet, pleasant dreams.

♥

The following morning the yacht docked in Canary Wharf. A thick blanket of fog came in. The fog created zero visibility. Guy stood on deck. He couldn't see the landing, the Bentley or the people walking along the bank.

Grace awakened. Sleepily, she lifted her head and reached out for Guy. *He isn't here.* In fear, she rose from the bed, grabbing his white dress shirt and placing it on to search for him. She found him on deck, half-dressed. She walked up behind him, wrapping her arms tightly around his waist.

He turned half-way to smile down at her as she played with the thick, jet-black, wet curls on the nape of his neck. The fog had curled Guy's hair. *He looks so sexy.*

"Did you have a good night's rest?" he asked.

"Yes I did." she replied looking up at him.

Her hair was dishevelled and loose around her face. Her makeup had since worn off, allowing her natural beauty to shine through. Guy became aroused. It was the fact that she had laid with him all night and looked sexually messy that piqued his arousal. It was wishes come true.

He led her to the settee. He pulled her onto his lap. She felt his hard cock pressing against her bare arse.

"Guy, not now. Someone might see us." she insisted.

"How's that? The fog is like a thick cloak." he nipped.

Guy pushed her hair aside to kiss the back of her neck. His hands ran over the tops of her thighs, slowly pushing them apart. Surprisingly, she obliged. She allowed her legs to drift apart as he caressed the inside of her thighs. She felt weak. Her head fell back to rest against his chest. She moved against him, her pussy damp and aching.

He dragged his fingers along to her pussy. He parted the swollen flesh to gain access to her sweet rosy clit. She stifled her moans as his finger rubbed at her sensitive bud with diabolical pleasure. She pushed herself back on his cock, resting her bare arse against it. As he increased his touch, she moved her body against him. He slipped one long hard finger into her dripping sex. It made her cry out. He grabbed her face with his free hand, pulling her to him and kissing her carnally. Her mouth was open as their tongues duelled in erotic rapture. She pumped her body on his palm. Grace was desperate to be filled with his cock.

Guy pulled his shirt apart from her skin. He grabbed a hard pink nipple, tweaking it between his forefinger and thumb. She felt herself become incredibly wet. Her walls quivered.

"I want you, Guy. I want you now." she purred.

"You've got to wait." he replied throatily.

She rubbed herself madly. She was nearing orgasm.

In a sudden turn of events, he stopped teasing her. He lifted her up to sit her arse down on the table before them. The damp air and cold wetness of the table made her wince.

"What are you doing?" she asked her eyes wide.

"Nothing. Nothing at all." he repeated the same sentence as she had said the night before.

Guy pushed her legs open. He brought his head down to her legs and licked the inside of her thighs. She suppressed her moans of delight, but cried out a massive OOOO when his mouth found her clit. He wrapped his lips around her swollen syrupy bud. He sucked as he fingered her with his other hand. Grace felt her body falling back on the table allowing him access to the rest of her musky sex. His tongue swirled, dipped, and dived into her dripping wetness.

The shirt fell away from her plum breasts. Her stiff cherry nipples now exposed to the elements and Guy's wandering hand. *I can't believe he's devouring me here on a table, on a yacht in fog. I'll never look at London fog the same way again!* She tilted her head back, moaning in ecstasy and dying in pleasure.

Grace felt her body tremble, her mind explode and her senses heighten to levels unknown, as Guy ran his tongue all over her pussy and down to her arsehole. She moaned as he licked her there and she moved her body, debating on whether or not to allow it to continue. Instead, she chose to enjoy.

No longer able to contain himself, Guy unleashed his cock from the confines of his trouser. He drew the throbbing head to her creaminess, holding it there, briefly. He used her legs like scissors, closing her legs to create tightness. Guy impaled his angry, engorged member into her deep crevice.

"Guy! Guy!" she cried out.

Her womb contracted, unleashing a tidal wave of come onto his cock. He released her legs, allowing her to wrap them around his buttocks. He leaned over her body, taking a nipple between his teeth to suckle on as he pumped. He lifted her in his arms whilst thrusting his rigid swollen member deep within the confines of her warm womb. She pumped her body up and down against him. Her breasts smashed against his chest. She felt the prickle of his short chest hair rubbing against her breast.

"Grace you're so wet. You're so tight. I love you baby." Guy hissed in her ear. "I want to fuck you from behind. I need to come all over that pretty arse of yours." The words turned her on even more. She pressed herself down on his cock.

"Do whatever you like." she managed to pant.

Guy turned her on her stomach. Her breasts slid on the damp table as he laid her down. He slapped both of his palms on her round supple arse cheeks, separating them to get a view of his cock entering her swollen, scarlet, pussy from behind. As he looked down he got a view of all the cream that was resting in her puckering hole. Guy eased his cock into her as he gripped her waist. *Bloody hell! He feels bloody massive from this angle!*

He slowly pumped his cock into her, her clit rubbing against the wet table, creating sensations that she knew she couldn't repeat with her hands. He continued his thrusting. He threw his head back, basking in sex. He wanted the feeling to last forever. Guy felt Grace quaking as she writhed beneath him. He moved his hands up her smooth back to the base of her neck. He took a fistful of hair and tugged gently. She thought she was going to melt into the table and vanish in the fog.

His grunting and her moans became louder. The sound of skin to skin contact was audible to any passing stranger in the fog. The sun pierced its way through the clouds and the fog clearing. He knew he had to hurry as he didn't want anyone to catch them in the act, but she was too bewildered to notice. She tightened her pussy against his cock. She exploded against him like fireworks on bonfire night. He thrusted his cock a final time, pulsating his hot, white molten semen into her.

Grace felt her legs go weak as she screamed out his name. He tightened his grip on her hair as he fell forward pushing his cock into her, ensuring that every last drop of his seed coated her walls. They were panting heavily and gasping for air. They were trying to recover from the mind blowing sex.

The fog dissipated. A Yorkshire terrier barked towards the yacht. An old woman, walking the small dog, appeared in the lifting mist. Quickly, he grabbed Grace and threw the shirt over her naked flesh. In one swoop Guy lifted his trousers. The terrier continued to bark at them, but the old woman seemed not to care. Unbeknownst to the couple, the woman was as blind as a bat.

"Hush, Mr. Tiddlywinks. It's only pigeons." the old woman crooned as she walked pass.

He held Grace in his arms. In anticipation of the woman's reaction, she held her breath. The woman and the barking dog continued on their way with no further notice.

"I don't believe she saw us." he said. They both laughed.

♥

Reminiscing about the incident made him laugh now. Grace rolled her body over to bury herself into his chest. She felt his raging hard on pressing against her thigh. He wanted to make love to her, but there was little to no time.

"Do you really have to go to Tokyo?" she murmured.

"I do. I wish you would come with me." he said, into the crown of her hair.

Although, she did want to join him the last weeks of the summer season were the busiest for Delicious. Her catering chef had come down with a flu-like illness, which left her to pick up the slack. She didn't mind at all, after all, it was her business. She also had two celebrity weddings, and three celebrity baby-showers to cater. Baby-showers were becoming increasingly common in the British celebrity circuit.

"I can't wait for our holiday together." she said, resting her arms on his muscular chest. She peeked up at him with her sleepy aquamarine eyes.

During Christmas and New Years, Guy arranged for them to holiday in the Maldives. He had a tough Premier season ahead and knew that they would spend little time together. His agent made it clear that he was extremely bank now that he was the U.K.'s golden boy. *But I'm determined to make it work between Grace and I. I want to keep her.* He silently thought.

She kissed his chest. He lifted her up his body and kissed her hard on the lips.

"I've got to get ready. You relax before you go to work." he said, getting out of the bed naked. She pouted whilst watching him pull black Calvin Klein underwear over his arse.

"I don't want you to leave." she whined, playful. He looked back at her with a warm smile.

"Neither do I, love." he replied, bending over the bed to kiss her again.

She fell back on the plush pillows as Guy went off to the loo to shower. *If only people understood how much I love him. It's hard when people who supposedly love you don't think it's going to work. It has to work between us.*

Her thoughts were her worst fears. Ever since their first date, she'd been on the cover of Rumour Mill. Paparazzi snapped a picture of her getting into the Bentley. They followed them to Tooting Bec. Rumour Mill published front page pictures of Grace escorted by Guy and security into her flat. It was that front cover caused a maelstrom to ensue from Cat and Corrie.

At home, the twins choked on their tea and scones whilst they read the article and looked at the accompanying photos. Cat angrily punched Grace's mobile number into the phone. Grace barely had a chance to say hello before she screamed at her.

"Grace Ann Knowles, how dare you get back together with *that* man! Do you think your parents would've been proud seeing you walk through the front door of their home dressed like a street-walker!?" Cat howled.

"Aunt Cat, please! You're making a mountain out of mole-hills." her voice stern. She was in her office looking an order over when the call came.

"I'm disappointed in you." Corrie wept loudly behind Cat. "You're like your mum, always chasing unattainable men."

"What do you mean?" she questioned. Cat and Corrie had Grace's undivided attention.

"Your father took your mother away from us. If she hadn't run off to London to attend culinary school Jane would be alive today. Leave Guy before it's too late for you Grace." Cat warned.

"My parents died in a car accident, what haven't you told me?" she asked with concern.

"Yes, they died in a horrific car accident, but it could've been prevented if Jane didn't marry your father." The twins said in unison.

"We know it was a drunk driver, are you saying my father had something to do with the accident?" she inquired.

"No...No. It's just your mother could've chosen better. She chose your father." Cat said coolly.

She didn't like this conversation. She had enough from her aunt. She didn't like the fact that they had dragged her mum into it. They were using her death as a warning for love.

"I must be going. I've got work to do." she sighed.

"When do you plan on visiting us? We must discuss this further." Cat said.

"I don't know. Perhaps, sometime soon." she alluded.

They said their goodbyes. She put her Blackberry down on her desk. Over the weeks that followed she spoke to Cat and Corrie briefly. She sensed their residual anger from their initial conversation and the media's intense scrutiny didn't help.

Alistair, too, noticed a change in Grace. Rarely was she at home, but when she was, she was always busy talking to Guy.

"Take it easy. Take it slow, love. You have all the time in the world with Guy." he advised. "Besides, we need to focus on my wedding." She knew he had a point. She did need to focus on helping Alistair and Philippe prepare for their fall wedding.

He kissed her on the lips, startling her from her dream. She batted her eyelashes. He was fully dressed and ready for his flight.

"I must be going." he murmured.

Grace got up from the bed. She stretched and dressed in Guy's London Lions football t-shirt. He came from behind her, twirled Grace on her feet and kissed her hard.

"I'm going to miss you. I want you to know that if you need anything, anything at all call on my assistant, Gary. Security is at your beck and call. Don't feel you have to go home alone on the tube. And if you want to get away from it all, come to my flat." Guy said as he folded a key to his flat in Grace's palm.

He was aware that her flat been broken into. Even though nothing been stolen and police assured her it was yob's, he was concerned. He pleaded to have his security by her side twenty-four seven, but Grace declined. She didn't want to be like members of the Royal family.

"Guy, you'll be gone for a week."

"I know, but it feels like a lifetime apart. I hate spending time away from you."

She nodded and knew the feeling. There were knots in her stomach. She watched Guy as he grabbed his luggage. She followed him out into the kitchen. The intercom buzzed. They looked at each other knowingly. It was his driver ready to take Guy to Heathrow airport. They said their goodbyes and final I love you's with promises to talk.

Sadly, she closed the door behind him. As she turned to walk back to his bedroom, Grace noticed the pictures on his wall. One was crooked. It was a picture of Guy at the Dowling wedding. Tamzin was standing a few feet away from where the picture was taken. She had the look of a sourpuss.

She realised that she was the one who had taken the picture. She straightened the picture without giving it a further thought. She had to hurry for work.

♥

For Tamzin, the past eight weeks were hell for her. Her father had managed to save their Kensington town home and retrieved most of their repossessed items from their Hampshire estate.

She was briefly relieved, but it still didn't bring Darren out of hiding. She wanted her husband's head on a platter and Grace permanently out of the picture. Tamzin would show up at all of Darren's local spots to see if he would show. She, too, followed Guy around, making sure that he saw her at any event that he was invited to. Tamzin cringed when Guy ignored her and walked past her with Grace on his arm.

Several times a day, she left messages at Guy's office. She wanted to know where her husband was and if Guy had any idea. Not a single call was returned, leaving her fuming. One evening her iPhone rang. It was an unknown number. It was Darren.

"My husband falls off the face of the Earth and he doesn't bother to check up on me!" Tamzin snapped when she heard his voice.

"You're fine Tamzin. I see you in the papers all the time. I didn't call to check up on you. I want to know what your father wants from me." he said.

"*His money, Darren!*" she shrieked. "It was arranged for you to win the Premier. Instead you lost him money!"

"You knew I wasn't a willing participant. I told you many times Tamzin. I'm in it for the game, not to make someone else rich and definitely not to be blackmailed in winning." he snarled.

"Think what you like, but Daddy has done plenty for us. All you needed to do was to win and bring in the money." she crowed.

"Think what I like? I want to know how those videos of Alana and I got in the hands of Rumour Mill employees. Only your dad and Alana could've done such a thing, but I believe you play a bigger role in all of this. Every day you were on the front page until Guy's relationship with Grace took to the tabloids. Are you missing your throne?" he accused.

"I've got nothing more to say to you. If anything, you need to put in a good word for me with Guy. After all, he's the one that I want, and the one I have always wanted! He has more money in his little toe than you have in a lifetime. He and I will be walking down the aisle, as soon as I can secure a divorce from you. Tell me, where you are hiding?" she asked.

"First off, Guy wants nothing to do with you. He's in love with Grace. He wants her, not some two-bit money grubbing slag like you. Second, I have no intention on telling you where I am. I know you and Daddy are dying to get rid of me!" Darren spat. She stood silent, before letting out a heavy sigh, whilst admiring her newly polished fingernails.

"Grace won't be a problem in a few weeks, and neither will you, as soon as my daddy finds out where you are hiding!" she hissed, her tone dripping with venom.

He turned to see two Scotland Yard detectives giving him the thumbs up. They were recording the call.

"And how do you plan on getting rid of us?" he asked.

"That's for me to know and for you to find out soon." she sneered before ending the call.

Darren put the mobile down and turned to the detectives. "Did you get it all, DI Jones?" he asked.

"Yes, but we don't know if it'll be enough." DI Jones said.

He hoped it would put her in prison before someone ended up dead.

♥

nineteen

ome things are just hard to come by." Trevor said as he rolled off of Tamzin's body. It was their third sexual tryst in eight weeks. They were both fairly bored of one another.

I want Grace so badly, I can taste it. Why must I settle for tripe when I can have beef? For now, he had to satisfy his desires by using Tamzin as his personal plaything. Every time he fucked Tamzin, he thought of Grace. It made him come, but it didn't make him orgasm as he would've like. *Tamzin isn't the real thing!*

Trevor dreamt of Grace tied to his bed, begging for mercy as he thrusted one of his special vibrators into her. He wanted to leave welts along her bottom for betraying him for sleeping with Guy. He thought about how he'd clean her up, paint her nails, dress her in tight leather corsets and a dog collar to make her his own once he was through abusing her. He'd be her master and she his servant. *I'd never have to settle for others who disappoint me.*

The closest he had came to having Grace on his own, was when he broke into her flat. She was sleeping soundly on the couch. The telly was on too loud. He was about to touch her face when she stirred. In her sleep, she had mumbled Guy's name. Fearing Grace's screams might bring her uncle to her flat, Trevor bolted. *I want to pummel that bastard, Guy Rowling. He deserves to be in a grave!* He silently groaned.

Tamzin, too, groaned. She was anxious to have Guy all to herself. Finally, there was a break. Gary had gossiped to another personal assistant about Guy. The personal assistant was a friend of a friend of Tamzin's who gladly dished away Guy's schedule. It gave her an upper hand advantage.

She was at every public and social event that he attended. Every time she thought she would have a chance to talk to him, Tamzin realised he was there with Grace. She learnt that he was off to Japan to film an advert. It gave her the opportunity to get rid of Grace for good and bring Darren out into the open.

"Don't worry, Trevor. It'll work out for us. I'll get Guy and you'll get Grace and Darren's out of the picture. I promise you." she said. She got out of bed naked and threw a Mandarin Oriental Hotel terry-cloth robe on her body. Tamzin lifted her long blonde hair, placing it in a ponytail. She sauntered over to the desk to retrieve a pack of Silk Cut that was in her handbag. She lit a cigarette and took a puff. She walked over to the window to take a look at the afternoon skyline.

"What do you plan on doing with Grace? Raping her?" she asked, jokingly and inhaling cigarette fumes.

"That's a crude joke. It's not funny." he snorted.

He sat with his back against the bed's upholstered headboard. She sat down, handing him her Silk Cut.

"Tell me, what do you like, Trevor? Tell me, what gets your jollies off? What would you do to Grace?" she asked.

He knew what she meant by her questioning. She wanted to know what made him hard. *It definitely isn't you love. A woman who gets her tits out for Page 3 and Rumour Mill isn't my type.* Trevor wanted to say, but chose to bite his tongue instead. After a bit of thought, Trevor decided to tell a little to Tamzin.

"First, I'll force Grace to stand naked with her arms above her head. I'll tie her wrists to my bed post with heavy rope. I'll have her bend over with her arse in the air and I'll whip her hard with my riding crop. I'll keep her like that until Grace apologises for wasting my time and dating Guy. Then when I'm through with her, I'll fuck her until she passes out. I'll bring out my toys and play with her." he said. Tamzin smirked.

"A riding crop! I thought you are worse than that! Gemma told me that you're bad." she replied laughing. He exhaled a cloud of smoke towards Tamzin.

"I am. I bet Gemma only told you a smidgen of what was done to her." he said coolly.

"I fucked Gemma with my tools. I've got dildos with studs on them that bled her out. I'll do the same to you, if you keep on with your stupid questioning."

She was lost for words. Gemma didn't tell her all that had happened and this was all new news to her. She knew he was a sadistic bastard, but Tamzin was curious as to how much a sadist.

"I plan on doing the same to Grace. I plan on making her plead, cry, and beg until she becomes a willing victim. Once I get what I deserve, I plan on tossing her to the side until she crawls back to me and lick my boots, begging me to marry her." he continued leaning to her. He was aroused by the thought.

"What do you want me to do to you?" Trevor breathed in Tamzin's ear, dropping hot ash on the exposed flesh of her thigh. She didn't flinch as it painfully seared her skin.

"I think you've done enough." she replied. "I may procure your services later."

"Are we on for next Saturday? I made my arrangements. I hope you keep to your end of the bargain." he said.

She rubbed her chin in thought. *Maybe I need Trevor now.*

"Yes we are. As a matter of fact, I need your services now. It's the only way to get Darren out from wherever he is hiding." she said. Trevor smirked. *With pleasure, Tamzin. With pleasure.*

♥

British Airways Flight 153 landed safely in Tokyo. Wearily, Guy disembarked from the plane. He was fatigued from jet lag and his long journey. The time difference made it Sunday afternoon for Guy whilst Grace was most likely asleep.

As soon as the plane landed and taxied to the gate, he sent her a text message to say that he had arrived safely and missed her terribly. *I hope she's using my security services and not taking chances on her own. I wish she wasn't so bloody independent.* He knew Grace to be stubborn and headstrong.

Guy and his agent, Frederick went to customs. When they finished with customs officials, they emerged into the airport to throngs of screaming Japanese school girls and boys, beseeching autographs and pictures. Fully awake, he didn't realise how big his celebrity status was in Asia. It took him by surprise.

Airport security and Japanese police escorted them out to awaiting white Lexus IS. They clambered into the car whilst police pushed eccentric fans away whilst their driver put luggage into the boot. Frederick checked his voicemail messages as Guy waved at fans.

"Mr. Frederick Asante, this is DI Martin Jones. I'm calling in regards to a case with your former player, Darren Dowling. We believe..." DI Jones said, but Frederick didn't bother listening to the message. He quickly deleted it. He wasn't interested in Darren's problems, as Darren had left him for another team. Guy was his only concern.

"All OK?" Guy asked.

The driver pulled away from the kerb. Japanese police cars led an escort for them out of the airport.

"Everything's fine and on schedule. I want you to focus on completing the advert and practicing for the first Premier game." Frederick replied, tucking his iPhone away, unaware of the events about to unfold.

♥

Alistair and Philippe were out in the garden enjoying the last day of warm glorious summer weather. They poured over fabrics for their fabulous fall wedding. A Yorkie puppy was lying on the grass ripping a wedding magazine to shreds.

Grace came into the garden with a bottle of wine in hand. She was finally home after another long hard day at Delicious. They didn't notice her arrival until she placed the bottle down on the table.

"What do you think?"Alistair asked. He lifted two pieces of linen to show her. One was a piece in the colour of rich burgundy and the other in classic cream.

"Cream." she answered as she uncorked the bottle.

"Grace, we've been debating on the wedding cake. Alistair insists on a traditional fruit cake, but I'd love a devil's food cake." Philippe said as he scoured some wedding cake books.

Earlier in the month, she gave them books to look through. They still couldn't make up their mind.

"It's a wedding. I've always felt a traditional sophisticated look is better than one that's over the top. Just because we're the pink pound doesn't mean we have to go over the top." he chided.

"Yes, but that's not what guests are expecting of you both. You and Philippe set trends. Your artwork and Philippe's interior design speaks volumes. You both chose the Tate Modern for your ceremony and reception. Your wedding can be traditional and glamorous." she said. The Yorkie pup nipped at her bare feet. It took her by surprise.

"Who is this? Did you two get a puppy?" she asked. She bent forward to pick up the golden tea coloured pup.

"Us a dog? No way. We can barely plan a wedding. Much less take care of a dog." Philippe retorted with laughter.

"Look at the tag." he said distracted, engrossing himself in another wedding book.

Around the puppy's neck was a large pink bowtie with a massive white gift tag. She pulled it off the pup. She left the pup on her lap to lick her paws. The tag read:

Mrs. Tiddlywinks
Security Yorkie to Protect and Serve.
She'll keep you company until my return.

Love, Guy

Grace smiled. She loved Mrs. Tiddlywinks. Alistair rubbed Mrs. Tiddlywinks ears.

"The pet store delivered her early this morning. A dirty little scallywag that Mrs. Tiddlywinks, but I assume she's not much of a guard dog." Alistair said playfully.

Mrs. Tiddlywinks barked at Alistair as if she was annoyed by his comment. Grace picked her up and cuddled her.

"She's doing her job, just fine." she replied amused.

They continued on with their conversation regarding the wedding. After they settled on the wedding cake; Alistair, Grace and Philippe enter Grace's flat for dinner with Mrs. Tiddlywinks happily trailing behind them.

♥

Monday morning turned out to be one of the worst mornings at Delicious. Not only was Grace's catering chef ill, but her pastry chef was as well. She knew she could call on Cat and Corrie to help out since Olivia was fully capable of managing The Savoury Plum, but she hesitated. She mulled over the idea of calling whilst she reviewed orders. *There's no choice. I need their help.* At tea time she decided to ring The Savoury Plum.

"Allo! Savoury Plum!" Cat answered on the first ring.

"Hello Aunt Cat. How are you?" Grace chirped.

"Well and you?" Cat asked with her tone distant and aloof. Immediately Grace could tell Cat was still holding a grudge.

"I'm well." she said, silently praying that Cat would not bring up the topic of Guy.

"I've been reading Rumour Mill..." her aunt began. Grace braced herself for what she believed to be a bollocking regarding an article Cat had read about her. "Darren Dowling went and beat that poor glamour model to a pulp!"

"Really? I don't read the papers anymore." she replied, grateful it wasn't about her and hoped her answer would end this part of the conversation.

"I can't believe you baked their wedding cake and now their marriage is ending! The Old Bill's searching for Darren. He's been in hiding ever since the scandal about the stripper's baby. It's been all over the news, not just the tabloids. This is what happens when foolish young girls fall for the wrong guy." Cat said icily.

The sharp sting of her aunt's comment stung her. *I need to ignore it. I need their help,* she assured herself.

"Aunt Cat, I need to ask a favour of you." she said changing the subject before their conversation ended in argument. "Amy, my catering chef and Thomas, my pastry chef are both very ill. This week we've got two celebrity weddings and three baby showers to cater. I was wondering if you or Corrie would be able to provide me with help."

The other end of the call became silent. She knew that Cat was still there as she heard kitchen staff running about.

"Aunt Cat?" she questioned.

"Unfortunately, we can't help you Grace. We're busy. On Saturday we're hosting an event for Ivy-upon-Wye's women's league. It's for charity, a good cause, children with leukaemia." Cat replied. *I wish I could help her, but she chose her life. She needs to learn her lesson.*

"That's fine. No worries. I must be going. Lots to do here." she murmured softly.

"Bye Grace. Love you."

She didn't say goodbye. She cradled the phone receiver. She was angry by her aunt's cool response. Desperate, Grace wanted to hear Guy's voice. Her Blackberry mobile phone rang. She checked her caller ID. It was Guy. It was an answer to her prayers. She answered it.

"Hello Guy! It's so good to hear your voice! I miss you." she greeted, instantly in a better mood.

"I miss you too." he replied.

He was standing outside a sushi bar. He wanted fresh air after drinking too much sake. Frederick stood inside entertaining advertising executives. "Did you receive my text messages?"

"I received one text message regarding saying you landed safely." she replied.

"I've sent numerous text messages since then. I guess they got lost in text message space. I've tried calling too, but the calls must have dropped or not go through. I barely got through now."

"I'm glad you called."

He noticed a quiver in her voice. Although she was in a better mood, he thought she had sounded a bit downtrodden. He implored her to discuss her feelings. She told him about her business problems and the twin's reluctance to help her out. He assured her that she'd be able to handle it on her own. He told her that he would be home soon enough.

"Next week will be the London Lion's first game. I want to have ample time with you beforehand and I hope you can make to the game, Grace. I'd love to see you in the stadium rooting for us."

"I'll try to see you on Sunday. It all depends on my staff." she replied.

"I've got to go, Frederick's calling me. I hope everything sorts out soon. I love you." he said.

"Love you too." she murmured. The line disconnected. She rose from her chair to hurry to the kitchen. *The wedding cakes and other delectable aren't going to bake themselves.*

♥

The jingle of Rumour Mill Today coming on air gained Darren's attention. He stopped brushing his teeth, gargled and went over to the telly which sat on a chest of draws. His eyes narrowed on Louise Grimshaw discussing the latest news on Tamzin's claims. He felt sick to his stomach. *This bitch is claiming I abused her! I burnt her with cigarettes! I haven't even seen her!*

He scowled. He hated being holed up in a tatty bed and breakfast in Hampshire. *I can't defend myself. She's crying to the media. She wants a quickie divorce to get to Guy, not because I supposedly did harm to her.*

After the media clip, Darren contacted DI Jones of London Metropolitan Police at Scotland Yard, questioning the detective on whether the media were reporting facts that there was an appeal for his arrest. DI Jones insisted that they had no intention on arresting him as they knew he wasn't with Tamzin. But they couldn't ensure his safety from William. He insisted for Darren to stay put.

"What about Guy and Grace? Are they safe? Can't you arrest Tamzin on the fact that she threatened them?" he asked.

"We've tried contacting Guy's agent, Mr. Frederick Asante. He hasn't responded to our message." DI Jones said, looking at his computer screen.

DI Jones received an email from an officer investigating the burglary. The fingerprints taken didn't have a match. The detective in the burglary division stated that Grace wasn't in danger then or any foreseeable danger now.

"Why didn't you contact him directly?" Darren impatiently growled. *Scotland Yard isn't taking my accusations seriously. The police know Tamzin's a live-wire and William's blackmailing me. They've got all the evidence for an arrest!*

"We feel your accusations don't stand ground. Instead you come off as a jilted husband who wants blood, rather than arrest. If Mr. Dowling and Ms. Knowles are in danger we would've seen some evidence by now." DI Jones replied deadpan. "I can't discuss this case any further, unless there is proof of your situation with Mr. Smythe."

DI Jones swivelled around in his chair. He stood on his feet, grabbing his jacket to head out for lunch.

"Accusations? Tamzin's threats aren't accusations. Tamzin will get her way and will do harm to them. Something must be done. Can you, at least, arrest her?!" he cried.

"Threats aren't good enough. Tamzin's feeding you a load of bollocks. Why don't you stop worrying about Mr. Rowling and Ms. Knowles? Focus all your energy onto resuming your career." DI Jones advised irritably. DI Jones's workmates signalled to him to get off the phone. They wanted to hurry to the pub.

He slammed the phone down without regards to DI Jones. DI Jones looked at the receiver, shrugged whilst placing it in the cradle and hurried out the door.

I've got to do something about this before someone gets hurt. This is the final straw! Darren thought to himself whilst getting dressed.

♥

It was nearly midnight by the time Grace finished with the cakes. A few of her staff that had stayed to work late were long gone. She turned the kitchen lights off and went to her office to collect her handbag.

She toyed with the idea of calling Guy's driver to collect her to take her home, but she thought it was possible to catch the last tube train home. She rubbed her neck trying to ease the tension. An overwhelming feeling of exhaustion befell her. She wanted a hot bath and her own bed, *with Guy in it of course*. She wanted his strong arms around her and Guy's kisses as he told her some silly story or talked about life in general.

After Grace filed some documents away, she grabbed her handbag and keys to lock the bakery up. Unexpectedly, she was stricken with a severe bout of nausea. She dropped her keys and bag on the desk to run to the loo. She fell to her hands and knees by the toilet to heave. *Oh god! I can't have the flu now! The possibility is highly likely.*

When she finished, she rose to her feet. *I don't feel sick like it's the flu, I just feel tired.* Grace shook the feeling away. She grabbed her belongings to hurry out the door. *I can't miss the last tube train!*

As she walked to Covent Garden tube station another feeling replaced her exhaustion. The cool air and sounds of people in nearby pubs heightened her senses, but it wasn't one of calm. She felt as though someone was watching her or following her. She clutched her handbag tight whilst looking over her shoulder. She took out her Blackberry in case she had to dial 999. Finally she reached the station and banged on the gates. It was closed.

"Shite!" she swore under her breath.

"Grace, Grace Knowles." A familiar masculine voice said.

Grace turned to her left. She saw a man in dark jeans and a grey hooded sweatshirt standing several feet away from her. She couldn't see his face as the hood hid and created shadows. She didn't recognise him.

"Grace you're in trouble. You need to come with me now!" the stranger demanded. People walking past stared at them.

"I don't know you, but you need to leave me alone." she said firmly. "I'll call the police."

She walked away, but the man followed her. He picked up his stride as she created distance. She felt icy fear coursing through her body, her pulse racing rapidly. She entered a pub for safety. The stranger stood outside watching her get lost in the crowd of patrons.

She dialled Billy, Guy's security guard. He answered her call, and finally she felt some relief. He promised to be at The Nag's Head within fifteen minutes. Whilst waiting she ordered a drink at the bar. *I need something to calm my nerves.*

Fifteen minutes later, as promised, Billy entered the pub. He found Grace pinned to the wall looking at her Blackberry.

"Are you OK? Is the stranger here?" Billy asked, looking around. He reminded her of a buff Vinnie Jones.

"No. No, he didn't come inside. I was worried he might be waiting for me outside. I think he's gone." she replied, setting her empty glass on a nearby table.

"Do you think you know the stranger? Did his voice sound familiar to you?" Billy questioned.

"No, I don't believe I know him. Oddly his voice did sound familiar to me. I just want to go home. I'm not feeling well." she replied. He understood. By the look on her face it was clear that she had quite a fright.

"Let's get you home then. You had a scare." Billy said.

Billy placed the palm of his hand on the small of her back to escort Grace out of the pub. He looked around once more to see if someone was following them.

He opened the Range Rover door and Grace climbed in. She leaned into the plush leather seat, inhaling the scent of Guy. It was the closest she would have of him till she reached Tooting Bec. She fell asleep.

♥

twenty

Corrie was bushed from her long drive to London from Ivy-upon-Wye, and couldn't wait for a hot cup of tea. Despite the protest from Cat, she snuck out and left in the wee hours of the morning. She was disappointed in Cat for speaking in her turn. Corrie told her sister that when their niece needs them that they should heed the call regardless of what they thought of her boyfriend.

But Cat insisted the charity event was more important than Grace's dilemma. At dinner they argued their points endlessly and leaving their meals untouched. It left Cat annoyed and Corrie went off to bed to get her rest for her early start. Corrie left a note on the kitchen counter stating she'd be back by Saturday.

She turned the key in the lock to Grace's flat. An unexpected yapping Yorkie pup greeted her. As she moved around the flat, she noticed Grace was at home and not at work. Slowly, she opened the door to Grace's bedroom. She saw Grace sleeping soundly under her duvet cover.

"Grace? Grace?" Corrie whispered. "It's 8 AM."

Grace turned around. Groggily, she saw Corrie standing at her bedroom door.

"When did you get in?" she asked, rubbing her eyes.

"A few minutes ago. I'll put the kettle on and let this dog out. It seems to have piddled on your floor." she replied.

Grace nodded. She watched as Corrie walk away with Mrs. Tiddlywinks scampering behind her. She got up. Sluggishly she went to the loo for a quick shower and change in fresh pyjamas. She threw her robe over and headed out into the lounge. *I must have the flu. I have never slept in like this before. Luckily, Mark called me early this morning to say Amy's much better and will be at work today.*

"Good morning, Grace. Whose dog is this?" Corrie asked, handing Grace a mug of hot milky tea.

"Good morning, Aunt Corrie. She's my dog. Her name is Mrs. Tiddlywinks. Guy bought her for me." she replied as she curled up on her couch. She blew the steam off the top of her cup. "What brings you to London? Aunt Cat said you were unable to help." she added before taking a sip of her tea.

"Cat spoke for herself. I understand that you need my help and so I came to help." Corrie said patting Grace's hand. "You look a bit under the weather. Are you feeling ill?"

She noticed that Grace looked awful. *Her skin's pale and grey.*

"I think I've got the flu like my chefs, Amy and Thomas had. I just need my rest." she groaned.

"I'm here now. After my tea, I'll go to the bakery to pick up the slack. Don't you worry a thing."

"Thank you so much, Aunt Corrie. Is Aunt Cat still angry with me in regards to dating Guy?" she asked, desperate to know the truth.

"Catherine's still angry. She wants you to be with a man who's good for you and I, too, want what's best for you. It seems some footballers are out to break girl's hearts. You read it in the paper all the time. Look at Darren and Tamzin. You were at their wedding. Their marriage has gone up in flames faster than the great fire of London. At one point, you wanted nothing to do with Guy. Now you're in London dating him. You never told us why."

Corrie laid her cards out for Grace. Grace shook her head.

"He's not what I'd imagined him to be. Guy's really great, Aunt Corrie. He loves me and I love him. Plus, I'm not a child." Grace said. "Why did you mention my father? What did my father do to my mother for you both to hate him?"

Corrie looked down at her tea cup as if she was searching for the right answer.

"Nothing. Your father did nothing at all except loving Jane. We felt Gordon took a piece of us away when he married Jane. At the time, with Jane living in London and getting married to Gordon, it was like she had moved to the moon. She was so far away from us. I think Cat and I envied her." Corrie admitted. "Grace, you resemble your mum so much. After your parents died, when we came to collect you, Cat and I made a vow to never let you go. We believed had we gotten a piece of Jane back. It's hard to let you go and even harder to view you as an adult when all we see is Jane."

"I understand, Aunt Corrie but it's time for you and Cat to let me go. I'm my own person with a great business. I think I can make the right decisions on my own. It's something I wish and hope you both will accept." she replied, pausing to put her mug down. "I wish Cat wasn't disappointed in me."

"Cat isn't disappointed in you. She's very proud of you and so am I." Corrie admitted, getting up from the sofa.

"Thank you for coming to my rescue." she said.

Corrie leaned over Grace to hug her tight.

"That's what family's for. No matter how old you get, I'll always be here to help you. I must be going. I'm sure Mark is pulling at his hair. You get the rest you need and I'll sort the business out." Corrie replied. She collected the cups and brought them into the kitchen.

Corrie let Mrs. Tiddlywinks in from the garden. She went to the loo, spruced up and returned to the lounge. She said goodbye and promised to make a nice dinner when she returned.

Grace scooped Mrs. Tiddlywinks in her arms, grabbed the remote and turned on the telly to watch *Jeremy Kyle*.

♥

Things aren't going as planned. It wasn't supposed to happen like this. Trevor grimaced at the thought that the Spanish police had decided to pursue all the charges against him. The charges were statutory rape and physical assault of a prostitute. It didn't help that the prostitute was an underage young girl. His solicitors visited him at The Rabbit and Hare to tell Trevor the bad news.

"Unless you go on your own accord, you'll be extradited to Spain. It's been leaked to the media and it's making news as we speak. Your public relations agent dropped you and it's up to us to make a statement. We will claim your innocence, but you must go to Barcelona and answer to these charges." his chubby faced solicitor said whilst watching Trevor cutting into lamb.

"Take this, James." he said pushing the lamb away. James didn't move fast enough for him.

"*I said take this now!*" screamed Trevor at the top of his lungs. He threw a knife at the shaking boy, a junior chef. It just missed James by a sliver. Everyone in the kitchen jumped at his violent reaction.

"Yes Chef." James meekly replied, grabbing the lamb and dart away.

He slammed his hands down onto the stainless steel counter. His nostrils flared angrily like a bull. His eyes filled with rage.

"Alfie, you told me this would be sorted. You said you would get them to drop the charges. I thought you paid them off! I thought you paid the police and that whore as well! That whore wanted me to fuck her and I did fuck her! Now she's crying rape because she doesn't like a bit of rough foreplay? *She's a whore!* This isn't my fault!" Trevor snarled. His scarlet eyes narrowed on Barrister Alfred Whitaker.

"I won't discuss details of the case. We should do this in a private setting." Alfie replied, moving his hands around. He knew that Trevor's angry reaction wasn't to be done in public.

"Private setting? You came to my business with this news. You sought me out! You should've arranged a private setting, you dimwit fuck! Here, I'm paying you! *Get out!*" Trevor roared. "*Get out!*"

When Alfie didn't budge, he slammed his fist into the shelf above his head that held plates of china. The force of the punch cause several plates to fall and shatter.

"*Get out now!*"

"Trevor, if you don't comply, Scotland Yard and Interpol will be collecting you. We assured them it wasn't necessary and that you're willing to go back to Barcelona on your own, if they can keep this out of the media till tonight. Trevor, please think about going to Barcelona without police assistance."

He clenched his French knife. He readied himself to throw it at Alfie. Alfie placed his hands up and walked out of the kitchen, praying that Trevor would come to his senses.

♥

Tamzin sat in her lounge with Rumour Mill staff for an exclusive interview regarding the abuse she endured during her marriage to Darren. It was arranged for a flat fee of £30,000. *Trevor's done me well,* she thought cheekily. He had punched her hard on her right cheek and gave her Chinese burns along her arms.

From the threshold, her father watched his princess described the horrors of abuse she had falsely endured by Darren to a reporter. A photographer snapped pictures of her at every angle looking sad and glum. Tamzin explained how Darren's loss at the Premier game and the shock of a baby with a stripper who he presumably raped had gutted her.

A thin wry smile cracked along William's lips. *My Princess, the story teller. This has to get Darren into the open. As soon as the bastard makes his appearance, the quicker he'll be killed. Tamzin will make pretty pence coins on his insurance cheque.*

His henchmen were doing their job by staking and sniffing out every spot Darren was known to frequent. *Finally the Premier season is about to begin. Hopefully he'll show up for his first game. Darren's obligated to play.*

Darren's solicitors contacted Tamzin to tell her that they planned on discrediting her stories in court. They knew that all the allegations were false. Darren didn't need to come out of hiding as long as he had his high-priced barristers as advocates.

I've got to get Alana to sell her story! She needs to stick with the plan and if she screws up now, I'll kill her too! William frowned at the thought. He liked Alana. *She's a good fuck, but loose ends need to be severed.* He recalled last night's conversation.

'You can't do this to him. He's a good father to Max. He's a better father than you and more than you'll ever be. You know he's never laid a finger on Tamzin. Darren maybe an arse and a player, but a domestic abuser and a rapist? No one will believe it.' Alana said.

'Alana, you'll tell the press and police that Darren raped you.' he insisted as he exhaled smoke. *He sat at the dining room table waiting for the maid to bring him spotted dick pudding.*

'You know, I went with Darren only 'cause you paid me. You knew it was to blackmail him. When I didn't get pregnant, you knocked me up. You changed the DNA report. I went along with it for the money, but now I can't, I've got Max to worry about.' she cried. *He sat in stony silence, listening to Alana, whilst dipping his spoon in his pudding.*

'Please William. Don't make me do this.' she begged him. *He heard the tears. He ended the call.*

William knew what he had to do. All he had to figure out was what to do with Max, his bastard child was about to become an orphan.

The interview was interrupted by a mobile phone vibrating loudly. It was the reporters.

"Pardon me for a sec." she said.

Tamzin nodded. She continued to pose, pout and look sad for the photographer as he continued to take photos.

"Sorry, Mrs. Dowling, I need to end this interview now. A major story's breaking and I have to cover it." the reporter said rising from her chair. She motioned to the photographer to pack up.

"What's more important than me?" Tamzin asked getting up from the sofa to follow them out.

"Celebrity chef, Trevor Hare is being flown to Barcelona to answer criminal charges of statutory rape and assault. It seems men are going mad with abuse lately, eh." the reporter replied, brushing by William. "I need to get to his solicitor's office before the BBC does."

The slamming of the front door echoed through the home. Perplexed, Tamzin looked at William for an answer. She bit her bottom lip in tart disappointment. Suddenly her mobile rang. She went to collect it from the side table in the lounge as William went to fetch an apple in the kitchen.

"What have you done?" she murmured sternly. *"Where the bloody hell are you?"*

"I've got to leave London tonight. I'm not going to jail over some whore!" Trevor whispered into his mobile as he entered a black cab. He was rushing to his flat to pack his belongings.

"You promised that we're in this together. You were going to get rid of Grace for me. What are you doing about it? Are you leaving without her? Are you not keeping your end of the deal?" she snapped, folding her arm beneath her bosom whilst holding her mobile with her other free hand to her ear.

"I'm not leaving without Grace. Meet me at this address..." Trevor said before rattling off an unknown address to Tamzin.

"Be there in a hour." he demanded, ending the call.

"Who is it, Tam?" William asked as he approached Tamzin from behind.

"Umm, it was Gemma. I must go meet her at Regents Park for coffee. Are you fine on your own?" she asked, watching her dad take a bite from the juicy red apple.

William nodded. He knew his princess was up to no good. *I'm not going to question her about it.*

Tamzin kissed her father on the cheek before hurrying off to meet Trevor at the disclosed location.

♥

Early Tuesday morning in Japan, Guy finished his interview with a Japanese sports magazine when his iPhone rang. He thanked them profusely for their time and they thanked him for his. Frederick led the reporters out of the suite as he went to answer his phone.

He was surprised to see it was Darren ringing, late Monday night, Greenwich median time.

"Hello Darren." he answered.

"I've got to speak to you. Did I wake you?" Darren asked hurriedly.

"No. I'm in Tokyo shooting a commercial and interviews. Are you alright, mate?" he asked, pouring himself orange juice.

"I don't know how to tell you this, but Grace is in danger. Tamzin's planning something horrible. I don't know when or how, but it must be soon. I tried telling Grace when she left work, but she got spooked by me. She ran in The Nag's Head where she waited for your security to drive her home." Darren revealed.

"Why were you following Grace? She probably didn't even know it was you. The last time she saw you was at the wedding." he snapped concerned and annoyed at Darren.

"I did it because Tamzin's plotting to do harm to Grace. She said she wants you Guy, and she plans on destroying anyone who gets in her way. Now that things have gone sour, Tamzin's making her moves on you, and Grace is in her way. I've gone to the police regarding Tamzin's threats and they won't do anything to protect you or Grace. They say it's an empty threat. But she has gone to Rumour Mill and police saying I've assaulted her. Tamzin's poison, Guy, don't let Grace out of your sight. You need to keep Grace safe." Guy heard the seriousness in his tone. His brother was stern about the potential harm that Tamzin would do to them.

"Darren, don't worry, I'm on it!" he growled. Suddenly Guy's iPhone lost reception. The call dropped. Frederick returned to find Guy sitting at a desk, opening his laptop.

"What are you doing? We have the store opening to do." Frederick said looking over his shoulder.

"I can't. There's an emergency in London. I have to leave now." he said, pulling up British Airways flight information.

"No! You can't leave. You must finish here first." Frederick reprimanded.

"Frederick, my fiancé is in danger. It's imperative I return to her right now!" he snapped.

Flabbergasted, Frederick looked at Guy. *When did Guy pop the question to some bird and who is she?*

♥

The nausea remained with Grace all day. It frustrated her. She finally decided it was time to phone her GP to arrange for an afternoon appointment. She called Corrie and told her that she was stepping out to run a few errands. Corrie insisted that the errands could wait, but she was adamant. She didn't want Corrie to worry if she told her she was going to surgery.

She showered, dressed, fed Mrs. Tiddlywinks and then checked her messages. There was one from Guy written on Monday saying that he loved her and missed Grace deeply. He described some of his visit to her. Grace sent a message back to Guy, hoping it got to him. As Grace wrote the text, Alistair popped his head into the lounge.

"Grace, in case you're wondering where I am later, I'll be at Philippe's flat. We are sorting out the invites for the wedding and popping them in the post tomorrow." Alistair said holding the door open.

"Okay. Aunt Corrie's here. She's helping me out with work. I think I caught Amy's flu bug." she replied, looking up from her mobile.

"Oh, I'll stay away then. Give my love to Corrie. I hope you feel better soon. Cheerio!" Alistair said closing the door,

"Bye!" she shouted.

Grace put her mobile on vibrate, placing it in her light brown suede River Island duffle and grabbed her keys. She went in the garage and got in her Mini to drive to her GP.

♥

In the first class lounge of British Airways, Guy waited patiently for his afternoon flight back to London. He sent a text message to

Grace, telling her to stay put until a member from his security team arrived. He typed out his flight details and told her he would be in London by three o'clock local time. His phone came back with Grace's reply to a previous text message.

Shit! I hope Grace is getting my messages! They seem to be arriving at will!, he grimaced. He hoped his security detail would reach her in time to prevent any harm from happening to her.

♥

twenty one

*I*n a crowded waiting room of her GP's surgery, Grace sat patiently. She waited for her name to be called by a nurse for appointment. She checked on her Blackberry for messages from Guy. Nothing. To pass the time she read the Rumour Mill news ticker on her app. Shock, horror and disgust enveloped Grace.

Celebrity Chef Trevor Hare in Sex Scandal! Must answer to charges brought by Spanish Police of statutory rape and assault of a minor!

As she read the accompanying article to the headline, she felt her nausea turn into horrible retching. She threw her hand over her mouth to suppress her vomit. A nurse appeared in the waiting room.

"Ms. Knowles, Grace Knowles." The nurse announced to the waiting area. "Dr. Mills is ready to see you."

She regained composure, grabbing her handbag to follow the nurse down the hallway. As they walked Grace wondered if she should've called the police as Alistair had suggested on the night of the engagement party. She wondered if it was Trevor who had followed her to The Nag's Head.

A million thoughts raced through her mind before they reached the doctor's office. The nurse knocked on Dr. Mill's office door. When the nurse heard the prompt 'Enter', she opened the door for Grace. Graciously, the nurse pulled out a chair for Grace. She thanked the sweet nurse whilst feeling as if her knees might buckle from the horrid discovery that Trevor was an insane man.

"You look rather peak." Dr. Mills said looking up from her computer screen. "Would you like some water?"

"Yes, please." she replied.

Dr. Mills got up from her desk, retrieved a cup from the water cooler and drew Grace a cool cup of water. Dr. Mills gave her the cup. She drank it slowly.

"I have some news for you, Grace." Dr. Mills began once she saw that Grace was a bit better. "I hope it doesn't take you by surprise."

She peeked up at Dr. Mills, anxiously holding her breath for bad news. *What's wrong with me?*

"Rest assure, you don't have the flu. But, we did a dipstick analysis on your urine sample that you provided when the nurse did your vitals. And it came back with an answer to your illness." Dr. Mills stated. "You're pregnant." The words fell on Grace like World War II air raid bombs. *Pregnant! P.R.E.G.N.A.N.T.*

For eight weeks she was having unprotected sex with Guy. Not once did either them think of using a condom or the fact that unprotected sex would naturally lead to pregnancy. Any thoughts of Trevor vanished into thin air. Judging by her reaction, Dr. Mills saw it was a shock to Grace.

"It seems that this pregnancy wasn't planned. You're clearly stunned by the news. I'm sorry this comes as such a shock to you. The symptoms you described and urine results all lead to pregnancy. Morning sickness can strike at any time of the day, and so can extreme bouts of exhaustion. You need to slow down and rest. Your position at work, does it allow you to rest?" Dr. Mills inquired.

"I'm a business owner. I own a bakery. I think I can sort some time out." she rambled with her eyes wide. "Can there be a mistake or false positive?"

"No. When was your last period, Grace?" Dr. Mills asked.

She had to think back. *It was two months ago, right before Guy re-entered my life! Why didn't I keep track of my period?!* She was fairly regular and felt ashamed in having to admit she not kept up with the matter.

"Are you and the father in a fairly stable relationship? Do you want this child? Do you think he wants this child?" Dr. Mills pressed. She noticed Grace's face flushed red in embarrassment.

"I...don't...know." she stammered. *What's Guy going to say when I tell him? Does he want this baby?* She was flustered.

"I see. Here is a prescription for some prenatal vitamins. On this paper I've included the number to our in-house midwife. You'll need to contact her so she can see you. Your midwife will contact St. George's hospital for your ultrasound appointment and to listen to the baby's heartbeat. This is done between your eighth and twelfth week." Dr. Mills said getting up from her chair. She walked over to her file cabinet and pulled out a nappy bag. It was filled with information for new mothers.

Grace felt her hands shake as she took the bag.

"Here's a kit I give all my patients. It's filled with tons of helpful information and resources. Look through it." Grace shook her head in disbelief. Her mouth went dry. *I'm pregnant.*

"Will you be fine, Grace?" Dr. Mills asked.

"Yes, I think so." she murmured, rising and clutching the nappy bag tight to her chest.

"Congratulations, Grace. Good luck." Dr. Mills said holding the door for Grace.

"Ta." Grace replied before she exited the surgery.

♥

Trevor left his flat in the nick of time. The paparazzi and media were at his solicitor's office for a press conference. It gave him more than a few minutes to get his backpack, his passport and some money together. He was cutting it close. His persistence on getting to the location on time hurried him along. He didn't want to leave Tamzin waiting.

He walked the streets of London in a hooded parka and dark sunglasses, even though it was grey and raining. *I've got to get on the tube! I need to get lost in the crowd. Once I'm done with this part, Grace will be mine.*

♥

Tamzin was lost. *I should've taken a cab or had my driver take me!* she scowled. Trevor insisted that she take the bus or the tube to the location. She hated the cold, damp weather, the crowds and being in an area that was beneath her.

It was getting late, and the rain was now falling heavily. Tamzin was grateful to have put on her fedora before she left her house. It protected her precious hair from the rain. She hid her eyes behind Dolce and Gabbana sunglasses. She wore black yoga pants and a black jumper. Strangers walking in the streets didn't recognise her nor did they care. She was just another face lost in the crowd.

Tamzin looked around. She decided to go into Boots to see if someone could guide her to the address Trevor had given her. A security guard was kind enough to answer her questions. She thanked him and turned to leave. As she opened the door to walk right out of Boots a woman walked in.

"Excuse me. Thank you." the woman replied politely.

It's Grace! Tamzin knew she had the right directions.

♥

"It's a slight wait." the chemist said, taking the forms from Grace. "Thank you for completing your forms and you'll be pleased to know that all your prescriptions during maternity are free."

She thanked the chemist and went off to pick up a Boots blue hand basket. *I might as well shop whilst I wait.*

Gingerly, Grace walked the aisles. She felt a strong need to browse in the baby aisle. She picked up baby powder, opened it, sniffing the sweet magical scent. She felt her stomach flutter from nerves.

Oh god, I hope Guy wants this baby. I hope he wants and loves this baby as much as I do. The realisation that Grace wanted this baby hit her like a lorry. All doubts of not keeping their baby washed away. Another thought hit her, *what will Aunt Cat and Corrie think?*

She decided to leave the baby aisle. She needed to focus on the present. She walked over to the shampoo aisle to look for shampoo.

Stealthily Tamzin followed Grace all around the shop. She blinked in amusement when Grace picked up the baby powder to sniff. Her stomach flipped when she saw that Grace was touching a soft baby blanket. *She can't be pregnant! She isn't pregnant!*

Grace returned to the pharmacy area to pay for her things and collect her vitamins. She didn't realise that a stranger stood behind her in a grey hooded sweatshirt. As she turned to leave, she bumped right into the stranger's chest, dropping her wallet. He bent down to pick it up, coming eye to eye with her. She immediately recognised the face. It was Darren.

"Grace, don't say a word. Don't say my name and act calm. I'm here on behalf of Guy. You're in danger. Tamzin wants to do you harm. We need to go back to your flat and stay there until security arrives." he said handing Grace her wallet.

"What do you mean I'm in danger?" she asked.

"Let's not talk here. I don't know if you're being followed. Let's get you home." he replied. Grace nodded, looking around.

"Come. I parked my car around back." she replied. Darren took her arm. They walked out of Boots.

Tamzin watched as they walked out. The stranger turned his head to see if anyone was following them. She saw her husband's face, *Darren! That bloody bastard's with her!* Her mobile rang. It was Trevor.

"Where are you?" Trevor growled.

"I'm on my way." Tamzin hissed.

♥

It was the longest twelve hour flight of his life. Guy did manage to sleep, albeit, a restless one. He dreamt that Grace was in danger. He saw her screaming for help and begging for mercy.

As the plane banked over the London Eye on its descent into Heathrow, Guy felt a slight sense of relief. He wanted to be on the ground to see Grace safe. He had sent an email to security, but didn't hear a word from them. Frederick looked over to Guy looking out the window.

"I hope she's worth it." Frederick chortled, putting down the Financial Times.

"She is Fred. I love her with all my heart. I can't imagine life without her." Guy countered, rubbing his face. He was trying to rub out the exhaustion. His face was no longer clean shaven and was creased from worry. Dark stubble hugged his tight jaw line. His temple throbbed. *I want Grace to be safe.* He couldn't close his eyes without seeing Grace.

"I hope she doesn't take away from the game. You need to focus on the pitch. I can't lose money on you after I lost money on Darren." Frederick retorted.

"Fred, Grace and I've been through a lot. Not once have I lost it over a girl. Money doesn't mean a bloody damn thing, if I don't have someone I love to share my wealth and happiness. I played a great last season and my goal won the Barclay Premier cup, so Fred, *fuck off!*" Guy said angrily. He got up and pushed pass Fred's legs to go to the loo.

♥

Grace and Darren sat in her Mini Cooper. She drove towards her flat, unaware of her mobile vibrating profusely. All of Guy's text messages had appeared on her phone.

"What makes you think Tamzin is after me? I think you're paranoid." she said as she manoeuvred her Mini through the streets.

"I'm not paranoid. Far from it. I know Tamzin very well. Three years I've been with her. She doesn't want you in her way, Grace. She wants Guy. Tamzin's a crazy, greedy, bunny-boiling bitch. If you are in her way, she'll do anything to get rid of you. She may try to kill you. She's like her father, William."

"How do you know?"she asked clutching the steering wheel tight as she turned down a street. She was trying to focus on the road before her but Darren's bone chilling confession made it difficult.

"She said it during a phone tap. Old Bill's investigating Tamzin and William." he replied.

"Why aren't the police here to help?" she queried, shaking her head. It was too much to process.

"The police think it's an empty threat. I know it's not an empty threat. Tamzin's angry with me about my son, Max and my losing the Premier. She and her father are hell bent on revenge. They want me dead. They want you gone, so Tamzin can marry Guy. I've been in hiding. I'm unable to practice football or go about my business. Everything's done through my solicitors. When we did the tap we only found out about you because Tamzin wanted me to put in a good word to Guy. She made her threat when I told her that Guy only wants you." he replied.

She scrutinized his face. He was rubbing his chin. He was thinking deeply and Grace saw he was serious.

"Does Guy know?"she asked.

"Yes he does. I called him, right after I followed you to The Nag's Head. Sorry that I startled you. I didn't know how to get in touch. I've been following you ever since, and today I followed you to your GP and Boots." he admitted. "I don't want any harm to come to you or my brother. None of this is your fault. It's my doing. I'm sorry for the way I treated Guy, and I'm sorry I allowed Tamzin to do all the cruel things she has done."

"What do you mean?" she inquired.

"Gemma never slept with Guy. The baby she carried had belonged to someone else. One night I overheard a conversation between Tamzin and Gemma. Gemma was upset that their plan on getting Guy to marry her backfired." Darren revealed. "Now, Tamzin wants to sink her teeth in Guy."

Oh my god! It's true. Gemma never slept with Guy! Grace felt her heart leaping in joy. She couldn't wait to see Guy and apologise for doubting him.

Grace parked the Mini in her garage. She turned off the ignition. They got out and walked to the garden door. Instantly, Darren noticed it was open. Mrs. Tiddlywinks appeared at the door and barked loudly.

"Do you think someone's inside?" she whispered.

"I don't know. There's no broken glass and the lock looks fine." he whispered back. "Let me look around."

He entered her flat. Everything seemed in order. Nothing stolen or damaged. He checked Grace's bedroom and loo in case a burglar hidden them self. *Nothing*, he thought returning.

"Everything looks fine." he huffed.

"I must've left the door unlocked when I left to my GP and the wind blew it open." she said. She placed Mrs. Tiddlywinks down on the kitchen floor.

This day is turning out to be full of pear-shaped surprises! First Trevor, then the news that I'm pregnant, now Tamzin and Darren, what next? It was arduously overwhelming for her.

Darren noticed Grace looking pale. *She needs to lay down.*

"Are you sick?" he asked as she dropped her duffle on the kitchen counter.

There's no way I'm confessing my pregnancy to Darren, she thought.

"Flu." she replied.

"Go lay down. I'll make us a cuppa. Tell me where the tea and cups are." he offered. Grace pointed to the cupboard.

"Thank you." she said.

The door bell rang loudly, sending Mrs. Tiddlywinks into a mad barking spree. She looked at her watch. It's coming up to three. *It's the Royal Mail delivering my online shopping from Oasis.*

"I'll get it." she called out.

Darren placed two tea bags into cups. He turned on the electric kettle and looked out to the living room. A sixth sense screamed at him to tell her not to answer the door. In a rush to stop her from answering the door, he knocked over her handbag spilling its contents next to the pup's water bowl.

He ran in the lounge and saw Grace standing there with her mouth open. Her eyes were large as saucers and her hand was at the base of her neck. Trevor was in front of her with a gun in his hand. Tamzin took off her fedora and sunglasses, shaking beside Trevor.

♥

Fear and reality sank into Tamzin. She had given him her father's Glock thinking he was only going to use it to scare Grace. Instead, Trevor turned the gun on her.

"It's too late, Tamzin. I'm tired of bitches like you." Trevor growled in her ear pushing the gun into her rib. *Now here we are, in Grace's flat. This isn't real. He's going to kill us all!*

"You're insane! You can't do this to us!" she shouted.

"Shut your gob before I kill you!" he threatened.

Grace terrified, stood frozen in fear. Darren stood behind her wondering what Trevor's next move was.

♥

"You won't believe this, Jones!" exclaimed DI Frey, approaching DI Jones desk. DI Jones furrowed his brow. He was knee deep in paperwork and didn't want to be bothered. DI Frey threw the manila file on the desk.

"It seems Trevor Hare's case is bigger than Spain. Women have come forward, telling us that they've been abused by Mr. Hare, sexually and physically. We've got dozens of calls from Newcastle, London and Cardiff. Some of the women are former employees of his, some are prostitutes and others are just normal women. They said he bought their silence." DI Frey elaborated.

DI Jones flipped through the papers.

"Now here is the kicker. Grace Knowles, a business owner in Covent Garden, contacted us because someone broke into her flat in Tooting Bec. The finger prints collected from her garden door didn't result in a perpetrator match. Spanish police sent their report regarding Mr. Hare. His fingerprints match. He's insane. Why would he break into her flat?"

"Where's the connection?" DI Jones asked.

"Ms. Knowles was the pastry chef at the Dowling wedding. Ms. Knowles worked along Mr. Hare. From what I've gathered, Mr.

Hare has seen Ms. Knowles since the Dowling's marriage and her arrival in London. But they aren't dating. She's dating Guy Rowling, football star." DI Frey pulled up a chair and sat down.

DI Jones read a few paragraphs of the investigation.

"This is too strange. Mr. Dowling had contacted me to say that he felt Ms. Knowles and Mr. Rowling are in danger. But he thought it was his wife, Mrs. Dowling, not Mr. Hare that's to do them harm. I wonder if Mrs. Dowling has a connection with Mr. Hare aside from the wedding." DI Jones said.

"Well, it's Christmas in July. You know, Alana Croxley, the stripper claiming she has a baby with Darren Dowling? She came in to report that she's being threatened by William Smythe. Ms. Croxley admitted she's involved in the blackmail of Mr. Dowling. She's reported that Mrs. Dowling and Mr. Smythe are all behind it all. It's alleged that they had planned this way before the Dowling nuptials." DI Frey replied.

"I want to speak to Mrs. Dowling as soon as possible." DI Jones said. "Make sure you have police on standby and a tail on Smythe. Has Mr. Hare left the country yet?"

"No, Mr. Hare hasn't left. He has till five to turn himself in. It's three thirty. His solicitor's insisting that Mr. Hare is coming on his own accord. I've already taken the liberty of submitting forms to Magistrates Court for a warrant for Mrs. Dowling and Mr. Smythe arrest." DI Frey said.

"Good. I hope we catch them before someone gets killed." DI Jones retorted.

♥

twenty two

uy left Frederick and his luggage at Heathrow airport. He jumped in the first black cab available. He decided not to take any chances. He told the cabbie the address. As the cabbie pulled away from the kerb, Guy called his security. They told him they never received his email. He angrily ended the call. He dialled Grace's mobile number. There was an answer, but it wasn't hello. He heard shouting, screaming and crying.

"Please don't do this to me! You killed them!" she wailed. A panic like no other settled in his chest.

"Grace! Grace!" he shouted down the phone.

There were inaudible voices in the background. Guy tried to make out the voices, but couldn't hear due to the radio.

"Please, can you turn down the radio? It's an emergency!" he cried.

"Anything for you Rowling." The cabbie replied.

"*Where are you taking me? Why are you doing this?*" Grace screamed, sobbing hysterically.

It was clear to him that Grace didn't have her mobile in hand. He felt hot tears welling in his eyes. His heart hammered away at his chest. He swore the cabbie heard it. In his entire life he never felt more frightened as he did now. Suddenly there was a commotion. Guy heard the sound of keys jangling.

"*Trevor, please don't do this. You've done enough harm.*"

"*I'm doing this for me.* You've done enough with your cock teasing. You're mine and you will do as told. We must go, now!" he snapped.

Grace continued crying. "*Shut up!*" A sharp piercing scream, followed by silence barrelled down the mobile.

"*I'm going to kill you Trevor! You're dead!*" he roared. The cabbie looked back at Guy concerned. His fist tightly clenched his iPhone. He listened to fumbling in the background, then he heard breathing and the sound of licking. A small bark answered his question. Mrs. Tiddlywinks ended the call with her tongue.

"*Driver, get me to Tooting Bec fast!*" he screamed.

The cabbie nodded. Guy dialled 999 hoping the police would get to Grace before he did.

♥

Corrie got off at Tooting Bec tube stop. She opened her brolly to shield her from the pouring rain. Whilst walking, she had noticed police helicopters flying above, and traffic was at a standstill on the High street. She didn't think much of it. It wasn't her concern.

Corrie reached Grace's street, a lump rose in her throat. The street was cordoned off by Bobbies. Slews of police cars, crime investigation unit vans, and ambulances blocked the road. Corrie knew something was wrong. Panic rushed to her chest. She sprinted towards the house. A police officer stopped her in her tracks from running through the front gate.

"Ma'am, are you the owner of this home?" questioned the bobby.

"No, I'm not. My niece, Grace Knowles, is the owner. I'm her next of kin. Is she OK? Where is she?" she asked, watching in disbelief as a man she didn't recognise was brought out on a gurney to an ambulance.

"I'm not in a position to discuss information with you. You must wait here for DI Jones. He'll brief you when he's available. " the bobby replied.

"*Please! Please tell me my niece is ok!*" she begged. Distraught, Corrie brought her hand to her chest.

"Mrs. Fielding?" a voice spoke from behind. She turned around to see Guy standing before her.

"Guy, what's happening here? Where's Grace? Did you do something to her?" she fired off.

"No, I'd never harm Grace. Officer please let DI Jones that Guy Rowling is here to see him." he said. The bobby nodded and hurried off to find DI Jones.

"What do you know, Guy? Is Grace fine?" she demanded to know. *Cat's right, ever since he arrived at The Savoury Plum he has been a curse!*

"Calm down. I've only arrived myself. I know that Trevor's kidnapped Grace." he admitted sourly.

"Trevor? Trevor Hare? What does he have to do with this? He wouldn't harm a hair on Grace. He's a good man to her!" cried Corrie.

Guy shook his head. He didn't know how to answer Corrie. It was all he knew. In the cab he contacted 999. Upon hearing the story the dispatcher placed the call to DI Jones. DI Jones told Guy to meet him at the flat. When he arrived in Tooting Bec, Guy noticed traffic was blocked. He paid the cabbie and ran the rest of the way to Grace's flat, still unaware of what happened.

They watched from outside of the Victorian bay windows, investigators snapping pictures and moving in the flat. After twenty minutes DI Jones emerged.

"Mr. Rowling, my apologies for the wait. It's crucial for us to gather all evidence as soon as possible. I was speaking with another detective regarding the arrest of Mr. William Smythe." DI Jones said. "Who is this?"

"I'm Corrie Fielding, Grace's aunt. I'm her next of kin. Is she ok? Did Trevor take her?" she fired off hysterically.

"Come with me." DI Jones deflected. They followed him to a white police transit van and climbed in.

"Mr. Rowling, what's your connection to Ms. Knowles and Mr. Hare?" DI Jones questioned.

"Eighteen months ago I had met Grace in Ivy-upon-Wye. I procured Grace's services as a pastry chef to bake a replacement wedding cake for my half-brother, Darren's wedding. Trevor was hired as the chef. Grace worked alongside Trevor. Recently we reunited. She's my girlfriend. I love her. I learnt that Trevor has an unnatural affinity towards Grace." he admitted.

"You're aware that Mr. Hare is a dangerous man. In Spain, Mr. Hare is charged with statutory rape and assault. This evening he's to return to Spain to answer to these charges. Instead, Mr. Hare and Mrs. Dowling came to see Ms. Knowles. Mr. Hare shot Mrs. Dowling and Mr. Dowling. He then kidnapped Ms. Knowles." DI Jones revealed.

"*Bloody Nora!*" Corrie wailed. She held her hands together. Her legs shook nervously. She fell into Guy's arms. He held her tight against his chest.

"How did Darren get into Grace's flat? I'm confused. Is he ok?" Guy asked the worry in his voice increasing.

"CCTV collected footage from local businesses came up with a timeline. It seems Mr. Dowling met Ms. Knowles at Boots. We're waiting to see other footage from CCTV in hopes it gives us clues as to where Mr. Hare has taken Ms. Knowles." DI Jones replied.

"Is Darren dead?" he asked.

"Mr. Dowling's in critical care at St. George's Hospital. He was brought there about a half an hour ago. But before you leave we need to connect the dots on this case. Please disclose any information you may find beneficial into solving this crime. It's important in finding Ms. Knowles alive." DI Jones said firmly.

Guy pressed his palms together. *Grace is alive and when I get my hands on that bloody nutter, I'm killing him!*

DI Jones scribbled notes as Guy told him everything from the wedding up to now. DI Jones listened intently. Corrie softly sobbed in her handkerchief that she pulled from her handbag. *Please lord, let Grace be alright! Please! What will I tell Cat?*

"Do you have a place to stay tonight, Ms. Fielding?" asked DI Jones, once he completed taking Guy's statement.

"No. No. I don't." she replied with a hiccup.

"There's also the matter of a small dog and tenant above Ms. Knowles flat." DI Jones said. Guy looked to Corrie, then to DI Jones.

"Corrie and the dog will be at my flat tonight. It's secure." he said.

"What about Alistair? I'll contact him, but I don't know if he has a place to stay." she asked.

"He, too, can stay if he wishes." he replied, patting Corrie's hand. His touch eased her.

"Good. Thank you both for your cooperation. I assure you that we'll find Ms. Knowles and bring her home safely." DI Jones stated as a matter of fact.

They exited the van. DI Jones went off to collect the dog. Once Ms. Tiddlywinks was in Corrie's arms, Guy walked Corrie to the other end of the block where Billy was waiting. He wanted to avoid media camping out at the beginning of the street. He was grateful for the police vehicles blocking access to the street. He helped Corrie in the backseat of his Range Rover. Her body shook as if someone was shaking her like a salt from a shaker.

"Guy, find Grace. Bring her home alive." she croaked.

"I promise you I'll bring her back to you." The window rolled up and SUV slipped away.

A bobby on his way to the hospital to deal with increasing media scrutiny offered Guy a lift. As they drove in the police car with sirens blaring, his focus was to speak to Darren. He wanted any valuable information that his brother may have before police interrogated him.

♥

St. George's Hospital was mayhem. The media circus was larger than on Victoria Street. Another group of police officers escorted Guy into the hospital. He ignored the screaming questions from media personnel. He raised his hand to shield his eyes from light flashing.

The police and Guy rushed through the A&E department. Curious patients, along with their concerned loved ones, looked on as Guy made his way to Darren's private room. A few cheekily tried asking for a photograph or autograph, but police deflected them. They reached the door to the private room. They met a tall lanky Indian doctor.

"Mr. Rowling, I'm Dr. Khan. I'm the doctor in care of Mr. Dowling. I'm aware you're his half-brother, is that correct?" Dr. Khan asked.

"Yes, I'm Darren's half-brother." he replied.

"Good. Darren's given me his permission to disclose all information regarding him and his wife, Tamzin to you solely." Dr. Khan said. "Darren's in stable condition. We'll be prepping him for surgery shortly. He suffered one gunshot wound to his abdomen in what I assume was a struggle. The bullet missed vital organs, but he's lost much blood. Overall Darren's healthy. I believe he'll make a speedy recovery.".

"Thank you Dr. Khan." He felt some nervous relief.

"But I do have terrible news that Darren's unaware of. I was waiting for your arrival to discuss it with you. Unfortunately, shortly after their arrival Tamzin Dowling passed away. The severities of her wounds were too great. She suffered a shot to her face and abdomen. The shot to her face likely killed her. It's tragic." Dr Khan informed. "Darren hasn't been informed yet of his wife's passing. We thought it best that a member of the family was here to be by his side. Will you be able to confirm Tamzin's body?"

"Yes." he replied, shaking his head. "Can I see Darren?"

"Yes, you may." They walked in the room. Two officers stood by Darren's bedside, whilst a nurse hovered over, checking his tubes. His eyes were closed. Darren looked peaceful and still, lying on the hospital bed. Intravenous tubes jutted from his arms including one for blood. The image startled him.

"May I have privacy please?" he asked. Dr. Khan nodded. Everyone left the room, leaving him alone to be with Darren. He went to Darren's side and softly reached out to touch his hand.

"Darren, are you awake?" he asked.

Groggily, Darren opened his eyes, cocking a thin smile to Guy. He was happy to see his brother standing at his side.

"I'm glad you're here. I knew you'd come." Darren replied with cough. He winced in pain.

"I left shortly after you rang." He squeezed Darren's hand tight. "Can you tell me what happened?"

"After placing the call to you, I stood outside of Grace's flat in a Peugeot I hired. I watched Grace go in her flat. I spent the night in the car until the following morning when she left to her GP and then Boots. I approached her in Boots and told her that she wasn't safe. I insisted on us going back to her flat to wait it out for security. Grace was fine with it, but not feeling well. She said that she had the flu.

Once we were in her flat, I offered to make a cup of tea. As I prepared tea, the doorbell rang. She went to answer it. When Grace opened the door she was surprised by Trevor and Tamzin. Trevor was holding a gun at us. He ordered the women into the lounge. I came up behind Grace.

Trevor started screaming how we all ruined his life; we're the bane of his existence. His life was better before the wedding. He waved the gun about wildly before directing his rage to Tamzin. He told Tamzin that it was all her fault. Women like her need to be beaten into submission. She's too demanding and thinks the world revolves around her. She needs to learn her place." Darren whispered. His eyes were wet and full of emotion from the pains of his wound. He needed extra morphine.

"I tried, Guy, really tried. I lied to Trevor by telling him I understood his point of view. That it was ok. I told him to put the gun down. There's no need to scare us to get his point across. He told me to fuck off and shut up. He said men like me had no balls to stand up to women like Tamzin. If I had a pair, I'd still be on top of the game. I lost it. That's when I lunged at him. Tamzin and Grace screamed. Suddenly the gun went off. I was shot in the stomach. I felt myself fall back on the floor. He didn't react. Instead he turned to Tamzin. He shot Tamzin in the stomach then in her face. Grace was screaming."

Guy's heart stopped as arctic shivers danced along his spine.

"Trevor turned to Grace. He told her that she was the only good thing that had happened to him. It was shame that she had chosen you over him. He told her 'Look Guy isn't here to protect you. I'm taking you now.' He told her he was taking her to where they first met. He's taking her to Worthington Hall. Grace pleaded no, but it fell on deaf ears." Darren continued, coughing.

"Did you tell this to the police?" he asked.

"No. I didn't. I wanted you to know so you can find the bloody bastard yourself. I want you to get your hands on him first. I've got no plans on telling them till after the surgery. I'll stay mum till then." Darren replied. He was getting sleepy.

"Darren, I have terrible news about Tamzin..." he began softly.

"I know. She's dead. I overheard a conversation between ambulance personnel. There's no way she could've survived those shots. As much as a bitch she was, she was always fragile. Have her parents been informed?" he asked.

"Not that I'm aware of. Earlier the police arrested William due to blackmailing you and the game fixing." Guy replied. He watched Darren closing his eyes. He was falling asleep.

"Darren, do you still have the keys to the Peugeot?"

"Yes, over there. It's parked by Boots." Darren groaned.

Guy looked over to the table that Darren motioned to.

"I'm sorry for being a bloody bastard to you, Guy. Good luck mate. Thank you."

"No apologies necessary. You're my brother." he replied.

There was a knock. The door opened it was Dr. Khan.

"We must prep for surgery." Dr. Khan announced.

Guy said goodbye to Darren before grabbing the keys and viewing Tamzin's body.

♥

Trevor was smart. He avoided all major motorways by sticking to A or country roads. Grace was in the passenger seat unconscious. He punched her when she refused to hand him her fallen keys on the floor. *It was necessary. I don't feel sorry about it. She deserved it. Tamzin and Darren are gone. Now I have my prize, my Grace.*

There was something about Grace that he preferred over the others. In his mind he had built an imaginary relationship. It was an unconventional relationship not built on tradition or romance. It was fear, submission and dominance all rolled into one. It was a relationship that he craved deeply to have with her.

After four hours of driving he arrived at the edge of the hall. He knew that if he went through the main gate he'd be recognised immediately by the other guests. He knew police were searching for them. He was familiar with the grounds of the estate and knew of a way to get in undetected.

During the wedding, Trevor had explored the grounds and discovered that the cottages led back to a steep valley creek that came off the River Wye. There were makeshift steps made by hikers long ago, but it had overgrown with foliage since then. It was easy to get into the estate since there wasn't a physical barrier. He was aware that security patrolled the entire grounds when celebrities stayed at the hall, but they typically stayed close to the hall and parking area if there were no celebrity guests.

He parked in a lay-by that was adjacent to a cobblestone bridge. It was dark and night. He searched the Mini for a torch, and quickly found it in the small boot. He lifted Grace out of her seat and tossed her over his shoulder like a sack of rice. He found his way through the creek, climbed the steps and came to the cottage. He placed her down on the ground and searched the windows of the cottage to determine whether or not it was empty. Trevor found an unlocked window. He climbed through, opened the door and brought Grace inside.

In the bedroom, he laid Grace down, and stared longingly. *I want to see the fear in her face when I finally wrap my fingers around her soft delicate neck.*

Trevor reached into his backpack, pulling out silver duct tape. He bounded her hand and feet together. *I hope she wakes up soon, so I can have her all to myself.*

♥

twenty three

race stood at the oversized window, admiring Canary Wharf on a sunny Thursday morning. It was her first sleep over at his flat. She was taken by the views, the cleanliness and its decor. It was spectacular.

The night before they went to a movie premiere at Leicester Square. When the star-studded premiere concluded they went to an after party, but his mind was on getting her back to his flat to make love to her. It was the only time they would have together before she returned to work and he was off to an event in Bedfordshire.

Guy found her standing there, staring out the window. She was half-dressed in his London Lions jersey. Her hair was damp from her shower. He came from behind, brushing her hair aside and gave her a kiss on her neck. She fell back in his arms. She let out a low moan as she felt his hard cock press into her arse.

"Good morning, love. Did you enjoy last night?" he asked holding her close to his chest.

"It was wonderful. I enjoyed myself." she replied excitedly. "I can't believe you live here. This place is massive!"

"I bought it for the views. I like how when the city lights turn on they remind me of the stars in the night sky. But most of all, I love you the view of you standing here, being here with me." he whispered breathily.

"I like being right here too." she said. "Did you enjoy the movie?"

"I did, but I'm a fan of older movies like spaghetti western and old romances like *From Here to Eternity*."

"Funny you should mention it. I watched that movie the night before our date." she replied.

"What's your favourite movie?" he questioned

"*The Wizard of Oz*. It's one of my favourites. There is something magical about Dorothy finding herself and her way back home whilst being surrounded by those who love her. It makes me feel you can conquer all your fears and hardships if you continue on your path." she admitted, turning around in his arm.

"Interesting perspective." He pushed her back against the window and leaned into her for a hard kiss. The kiss which began slow, turned carnal, erotic, and sensual. They couldn't get enough of each other.

She felt herself dampen. Her clit ached, her breast heavy and needy, desperate for his mouth. She wanted and needed him inside her. He pulled away. He knew how much he excited Grace. He looked at her, his expression was intense. It was as if he could see right through her. The love and lust he had for her at times felt unbearable and unrelenting. He pulled her in his arms. She placed her head on his shoulder and inhaled his musky Prada cologne, before peeking up at him, smiling.

"I'm making breakfast." she said taking his hand, dragging him off to the kitchen.

He sat at the kitchen island, watching her, his intense dark chocolate eyes following her whilst she spun around on her feet. She poured him coffee, buttered his toast and cracked some eggs in a bowl. *Fucking eh! She's sexy. She's giving me a hard on just by being herself!*

"What?" she asked, noticing Guy's wicked grin.

"Nothing. I love you wearing my shirt. I love you cooking a meal. I love when you sleep next to me. I love when you wake next to me. I love you when you're just being you, Grace. I love you Grace," he said with deep emotion. "And I want to make love to you, now."

Her chest heaved and her cheeks were flush and felt hot. In excited anticipation, she bit her bottom lip as he walked over to the hob to turn it off. She looked at the scrambled eggs resting in the pan.

"What am I going to do with all this food?" she asked.

"Forget it. You're mine." Guy murmured moving to her. He pressed her body up against the cool black granite of the kitchen island. Guy wedged himself between her legs cupping her face to kiss her. His tongue prodded her mouth ever so sensual. The kiss awakened all their senses. She felt as though stars were exploding from the crown of her head to the soles of her feet. Her hands explored his rippled tight back as Guy cupped her naked arse.

"Naked...mmm. Just the way I like you." he growled.

Grace shyly nodded. Coy, she bit the tip of her finger. Guy cocked his head smiling. He kissed her, whilst his hands lifted his shirt over her body until she was fully naked. His mouth trailed kisses down her chin, throat, and shoulders. He ran his tongue over her puckering nipples, and sweet softness of her stomach until his mouth hover over her pussy. She felt his hot breath there. She looked down at Guy's face and smiled.

Guy lifted Grace up onto the granite counter. He saw some ingredients on the counter. One of the ingredients was a bowl of Cadbury chocolate chips and a jar of chocolate sauce. She was going to make him delicious chocolate chip pancakes. He recalled his first fantasy about her, *floured hands and chocolate sauce. It's time to make it a reality.*

Brazen, he dipped his fingers in dark chocolate sauce. He ran one finger down the middle of her body to the top of her clit. He stopped short.

"Oh my..."she moaned.

His tongue followed the syrupy trail. He laid Grace down on the counter. He took the rest of the chocolate sauce, pouring it over her pussy. She couldn't believe it. *He's making breakfast out of me!*

She gulped hard as Guy ran his tongue up and down her creamy chocolate clit. He licked every delicious inch of her. He threw her legs onto his shoulders to help brace her from falling off the counter. She writhed her body, arching her back to meet his tongue. She felt her orgasm building and her body began to shudder. When he felt that she was too wound up by his tongue, he stopped. He wanted to be inside her. He kissed her hard.

"Grace...Grace..." he chanted repeatedly. His cock prodded her sopping, creamy, chocolate goodness. Her clit protruded for his hand. He eased his way in whilst rubbing her sweet salty clit. Grace's eyes were half-shut in drunken ecstasy.

"Grace...Grace...open your eyes....look at me." She opened them to look up at Guy; instead she saw Trevor's face.

Her heart sank. Her dream was turning into a nightmare.

♥

Grace's eyes shot open. Her head throbbed from the pain of the initial blow that rendered her unconscious. Her ears rang loudly. She tried screaming, but her mouth was sealed with duct tape. She blinked rapidly, trying to focus on the fixtures of the room. She was desperate to find out where she was. It was too dark.

She tried to shift her body. She wanted to see if there was a window behind her, but her hands were tied behind her back. Her legs were bound as well. Her body ached from being in the same position. It told her that she'd been in the same position for quite some time. The only thing she knew was that she was in a bed with nightstand next to it. The room seemed familiar to her, but she was unable to gather thoughts. She couldn't remember. There was no time. All she knew was that she was trapped and had to escape. *I need to escape before he comes in! I need to get out of here. He's going to kill me!*

The bedroom door creaked open. Light poured in creating a silhouette of his figure. She closed her eyes tight. She didn't want him to know that she was awake. He walked over to the bed and sat down, the weight of him made the bed squeak.

"Grace, are you awake?" he murmured, his hands moving over her jeans. "When you wake I'm going to do things I've only dreamt of doing to you." he was caressing the hair off her face.

Trevor patted her knee. He rose from the bed to leave the room. Once gone, Grace opened her eyes. There were tears in the corners that she had tried hard to suppress. *I've got to get out of here. Oh god, please let me survive this.*

♥

Guy drove to Ivy-upon-Wye without stopping. He was driving on pure adrenaline by drinking copious amounts of Red Bull. His exhaustion was seemingly gone.

Before the journey, he called Corrie to make sure she was fine and safe at his flat. She informed him that she had spoken to Alistair and Philippe. They were on their way to Canary Wharf. She asked why he was in Ivy. He told her that he had a hunch that Trevor was in Ivy, but he wasn't sure where. She assured him if he should need any help that Cat was available. He thanked her.

Now as he drove along the motorways at high speeds, Guy thought back to the eight weeks he spent with Grace. He recalled that she was adamant about staying in one night. She didn't want dinner at a fancy restaurant where they would be under the watchful lens of Rumour Mill paparazzi.

Instead, they ordered dinner from Pizza Express, a classic Italian antipasti and large padana leggera pizza. Guy rented some films, purchased a large bag of sweets, kettle corn popcorn, and bottles of Red Stripe. It was the perfect night in.

As they sat on her couch, Guy played with her hair as she lay on his lap. It was then and there that Guy knew he wanted to marry her. He wasn't able to focus on the film before him as he was busy thinking whether he should propose on their trip to the Maldives or sooner.

That night they went to her bedroom, and they didn't rush into making love. Instead, he held her in his arms as he sat back against her headboard. They talked about life. Grace expressed her wishes of her aunts' approval on their relationship and how much her family meant to her. He was slightly envious of the relationship she had with her family. It was nothing like his relationship with his so-called parents. He decided to make his intentions clear.

'Grace I want a future with you. I want a family, a home and happiness. I only see it with you.'

Her heart had leapt for joy. She showered him with kisses and held him. To Guy it was the best feeling in the world.

Now there was an uncertainty, a growing uncertainty that Guy hated with every passing minute. He swallowed the last of his drink hard and crumpled the can in anger. *That bastard's going to pay! Trevor's answering to me!* A horrible thought flashed in Guy's mind, *Is he touching her? Is he trying to rape her? She'll fight him off!* He pushed his foot down on the pedal, accelerating his speed. *I'm determined to find him and see the tosser suffer.*

♥

William sat in the interrogation room. He held his head in hands. He was mad as hell. His solicitors couldn't get him out of this one. The Old Bill arrested him outside of Tamzin's home. The police searched the home from top to bottom looking for her. There was no evidence of her being there nor was this team of officers aware of the events unfolding in Tooting Bec.

Several hours later DI Frey entered the interrogation room, holding a thick manila folder and a cup of tea. He looked up at DI Frey and threw him a look of murderous rage. DI Frey took a seat opposite, drinking his tea and smiling at an angry William.

"What do you want with my daughter, Tamzin?" William snarled.

"We'll talk about it, but first let's discuss your charges." DI Frey said, opening the manila folder. He looked over the accusations and charges.

William grumbled under his breath, calling him a wanker, which DI Frey chose to ignore. DI Frey firmly told him and his solicitors of the charges, ranging from blackmail to game-fixing and murder. He retorted that they were trumped up charges but was baffled by murder.

"Murder? Who've I murdered?" William laughed.

"We'll get to that. Let's talk about Alana Croxley." DI Frey said. William folded his arms and sat back cross.

"Alana? She isn't dead, is she? I'm an outstanding citizen and a well-respected business man. I wouldn't do harm to poor Alana." he chortled.

"No, Alana isn't dead, but you've threatened to kill her if she told us the truth."

"Threatening to kill someone and murdering a person are two different matters, DI Frey." his solicitor stated.

"Yes, but where's your gun Mr. Smythe?" DI Frey asked.

"My gun, what gun?" he denied.

"Your gun. The illegal Glock you've acquired. I'm not going to pussy foot around the subject, the Glock you gave to Trevor Hare." DI Frey said as a matter of fact.

William looked at his solicitors and shrugged. *I have no clue what this copper is talking about and where is my gun?*

DI Frey saw the look on William's face. *He has no clue.*

"Mr. Hare used your gun tonight at a murder scene. You're aware owning an unregistered firearm is illegal, and by law you're responsible for your daughter's death, Tamzin Dowling." DI Frey said coldly.

William felt his heat pound wildly, his chin hurt and arm in pain. *What is he talking about? Tamzin is dead?*

"Tamzin isn't dead. She went to Regents Park to visit with a friend, Gemma." he supplied with fire in his voice.

"Mr. Smythe, this evening your daughter was killed by your gun. The shot fired was by Trevor Hare. Did you supply him the gun?"

William reached over the table, grabbing DI Frey's throat. The poor detective was in William's grip, struggling as he applied pressure. He wanted to snap DI Frey's neck. His solicitors jumped up to defuse the explosive situation. William's eyes bulged from their socket; his face went red with sweat on his brow. He began to gasp for air. A sharp pain shot across his chest. He released DI Frey from his villainous like grip and dropped him down onto the chair. William was foaming at the mouth before shouting his last word, 'Tamzin!' and collapsed on the table.

"Someone call a medic!" shouted DI Frey.

♥

I can't believe it! I'm in Guy's flat, thought Alistair placing a kettle on the hob to make tea for Corrie. Philippe retrieved some Marks and Spencer's cream biscuits. He placed them on a plate. Alistair looked around. *Not only I'm here, but I'm here because Trevor's kidnapped Grace! I hope she's found soon.*

At the time the news broke they were placing stamps on wedding invites. He was shocked when he saw a Rumour Mill correspondent on the telly describing the crime and Grace's kidnapping. It was his intention to rush home, but Corrie caught him in the nick of time. She told him to meet her at Guy's flat. Corrie told him everything that the media didn't disclose.

Corrie wasn't comfortable in Guy's flat. She was grateful that Alistair had come to her aide. Philippe joined them as well. Wendy emerged from the guest bedroom. She had turned down the duvet for Corrie. It was clear to Wendy that she was emotionally exhausted and frail. Corrie was fixated on the telly screen hoping for any news regarding Grace. They returned with cups of tea and biscuits on a tray. Alistair gave Corrie a sleeping pill and a glass of water.

"Drink it. It will help you sleep." Alistair said.

"Thank you Alistair." Corrie replied, taking the glass and pill in her hand. She struggled to gulp the pill down.

"You've got to calm down. You need your rest. Grace will be fine." Philippe said as he stirred milk into Corrie's tea cup.

It brought a fresh round a sobs from Corrie. Alistair shot him a fiery glance. Wendy noticed.

"Ms. Fielding, why don't we take this cuppa and biscuits in the bedroom? There you can rest easy and watch telly." Wendy offered softly.

Corrie nodded. They helped her up from the sofa. Alistair followed Wendy to the guest bedroom. He watched Wendy help Corrie into bed before exploring the rest of the flat.

Alistair went to Guy's bedroom, looking over the designer furniture from Dwell and other high end shops. He walked over to a mahogany dresser. On the dresser, he noticed a Tiffany silver picture frame. He picked up the frame and saw it was a picture of Grace and Guy on the yacht. *They're clearly smitten with each other. He loves her,* he judged by the photo.

"What are you doing in here?" asked Philippe, coming to Alistair side.

"Nothing. I'm curious. Everywhere in this flat I have found pictures of Grace. Guy's in love with her. I hope that he finds her." his voice wavered.

Philippe saw through his lovers' strong facade. It crumbled a little with each passing minute.

♥

Cat paced back and forth in her lounge. She wrung her hands in prayer. Religion wasn't in her vocabulary, but Grace's kidnapping was worthy of praying to God. *Please God let Grace be alright! As soon as she's home with me, I'll sort everything out! Guy is a curse to us! If only Grace hadn't baked that wedding cake! If only she had stayed away from him! And Trevor didn't do what the police are accusing him of, he's a good man!*

Disbelief and shock rattled Cat. All she wanted was for her niece to be returned to her safely. The phone rang. It was Corrie.

"Any news?" she asked.

"No. Guy said he thinks she was taken to Ivy. He'll be there shortly." Cat replied.

"Fine." she huffed.

They continued their conversation a few minutes more, before ending. Cat decided she wasn't going to wait around for Guy to find her. *I have to do something now!*

♥

twenty four

fraid that Trevor would hear the bed squeak and creak, Grace carefully rolled herself onto her back. She slid off the bed onto the floor, hoping that the nightstand edge would help her cut through the duct tape. She scooted towards the nightstand, but accidently butted the table with her head. The lamp moved making a noise.

Trevor looked up from what he was doing. *Good! She's awake.* He finished placing down the last of the plastic sheets. *I'm going to make her bleed and feel pain like she's never felt before. Grace deserves it for all the pain she's put me through.* He stalked off to the bedroom, opening the door to find her lying on the floor. Grace's eyes went wide in fear and terror. She struggled in her binds.

"You're up. I've been patiently waiting for you. Now I can prepare you to do all the things I want to do to you." he gleamed. He marched over to her.

She closed her eyes, squeezing tiny tears out. The vision of Trevor before her was repulsive. He was half-naked and hulking over her. He wore tight black leather pants. His chest was visible. He had two nipple piercings and a belly button piercing, it made her quiver in fright. *He's puffy, pasty, and creepy.* Trevor brought his face close to hers.

"I'm going to remove the binds, Grace. If you scream or try to run, I'll make life very difficult for you. If you obey, you'll be treated *fairly.*" he chuckled at the word fairly. He lifted her up, tossing her on the bed.

"I'm going to remove the tape from your mouth. If you scream I'll stuff it with a rag."

If she was going to escape from his clutches, Grace felt it was best to comply with his demand. He ripped off the tape from her mouth. Although painful she didn't scream out, instead she scowled in disgust.

"Good. When I command you to do things Grace, you are to reply yes chef. Is that clear?" he ordered.

"Yes Chef." she answered sourly. The words tasted like spoilt milk. She hated him deeply.

Trevor noticed her pinched face. *I'm going to make you grovel!*

♥

Guy arrived at the gates of Worthington Hall. As he drove under the arches and up the gravel driveway, he felt fury channel his body. The hall wasn't the same as when he first arrived for Darren's wedding. It was subdued, quiet, and sleepy.

When he drove the car around to the valet, the valet asked if he had any luggage. He shook his head no and entered the reception area. It wasn't a beehive of activity as it was during the wedding nor guests running to and fro. It was a civilised hotel.

A few guests lurked about in a soft lull. At one point, he swore that he heard Tamzin's high heels clicking behind him. It was an elderly woman walking with a cane. He went to the desk.

"How may I be of assistance?" asked the receptionist.

"I need to speak to your manager." he replied.

The receptionist nodded and went off to fetch a manager.

♥

Trevor cut off the tape on her wrists first with a sharp knife. She sat still, calculating. *I should smash the lamp over his bloody head!* She decided against it. She needed him to cut the tape off her feet.

"Lift your arms." he ordered.

"Yes Chef." she replied.

She lifted her arms above her head. She winced as they ached from being bound behind her back. He tugged her long jersey knit shirt over her head.

His eyes roamed over her body, taking in every delicious inch. *Her breasts are plump and swollen as if the bra she's wearing is too small.*

Her period! She must be getting her period! Trevor grinned wickedly at the thought. *Even better!*

He ran a sharp knife down the centre of Grace's body. She swallowed hard, felt sick to her stomach, and was desperate to escape from his sadistic clutches. She waited for him to cut the tape. He peered into her eyes. She remained emotionless.

"You can't stay like this forever." he devilishly whispered.

"Yes Chef." she mumbled, growing impatient.

He dragged his knife down to her ankles. He cut the silver tape off. As soon as it was severed, Grace swung her feet upwards kicking him in his gut. The sharp blow sent him reeling backwards. She clambered over the bed to escape.

"*You bitch!*" he snarled.

Filled with fear and fright, Grace ran into lounge unaware of the plastic sheets spread out on the floor. She skidded across a sheet. Quickly he recovered and gained on her. She made it to the door. As soon as her hand landed on the door knob to twist it, he threw himself on the door to prevent her from escaping. He pulled her hair, throwing her across the room and forcing her to topple over herself. She fell on plastic sheets.

"You're not getting away so easily, Grace!" he hissed. "I've patiently waited, and waited, now the waits over! No one's going to help you Grace. *No one!*"

Trevor's eyes, filled with diabolical rage, said it all. Grace felt the icy hand of death grip her. *He's not going to shoot me. He's going to torture me! Please let the police or Guy find me. Anyone find me! Please! This isn't the way I thought I'd go. This is the way Trevor planned for me to go.*

He pinned her body down with his own. He held a roll of electrical tape to bind her with. She fought back by clawing at him. She ripped off one of his piercings. It made him bleed and howl out in pain, but it didn't stop his attempt. Her attack made him intensely virile and strong. He managed to get Grace out of her jeans as she tried to crawl away screaming for help.

She sobbed whilst he bound her hands and feet again. Her whimpering made his arousal rocket through his body. He was *beyond* turned on. With a kiss he tried prying her lips open. She refused by turning her face away from him. He squeezed her cheeks forcing her mouth open and violated her with his tongue. Instead she bit his tongue, making him wince then smile as he smacked her hard against the face.

"You like to fight don't you?" It was a rhetorical question, one that needed no answer. Grace was fighting for her survival, not for the pleasure of a fight, if there was such a thing.

Trevor ran his hands down between them. He pushed his hands into her knickers and stuck a finger inside her. It made her scream out in pain.

"Please don't do this! I'm pregnant!" she cried, hoping her confession stopped him in his tracks.

The words didn't fall on deaf ears. The news enraged him. His body turned red from rage. He hulked over her. *Guy's done his worse! He's impregnated her! And she allowed it to happen! Grace is going to pay dearly for it!*

♥

Cat sat in Ivy-upon-Wye's police station. It was small and no bigger than the size of The Savoury Plum dining area. The reception desk was behind a glass partition wall.

"They're going to be awhile." receptionist said in Welsh whilst flipping the pages of her Rumour Mill magazine.

"Fine by me. I can wait." she replied in Welsh.

She was desperate to talk to the police to see if they knew anything about Grace's whereabouts. She had to wait patiently as the police were called to a nearby farm, whose sheep escaped from their pen. The sheep were taking a late night stroll on dark country roads. The police and farmer needed to round them and returned the sheep to their proper pens.

♥

Guy arrived at the cottage. The lights were on. He had convinced the manager to allow him to come to the cottage without alerting security. He wanted to confront the bloody bastard.

"I didn't rent this cottage." the manager said, shaking his head.

"He's in there with her. He's armed and dangerous. Go back and call the police." he ordered.

"What about you?" the manager asked, handing over the key to the cottage. Guy insisted that if the police didn't arrive in time, he needed to go in and save her.

"I'll wait here." he lied with no intention on waiting for the police. *I'm going in and saving Grace.* The manager nodded before running back to the hall.

He crept around the cottage and looked in the bedroom window. It was vacant. Instinct told him that Trevor was in the lounge with Grace. He checked the window to see if it was open. It was locked. A shrill scream pierced the silence. He knew it was her. *I can't let this go on! I'm going in!* Guy lifted a fallen tree branch and smashed the window. He opened it.

Trevor heard a noise. He looked up, loosening his grip on Grace's throat. It was glass shattering. *Someone's trying to get in!* He left her crying on the floor as he went to inspect the bedroom. Trevor opened the bedroom door slowly. He checked behind the door in case the intruder hid there. He walked to the window and saw pieces of glass on the floor. There was no one in the bedroom. Trevor stormed in the bathroom and pulled back the shower curtain. *No one!*

Trevor ran back to the lounge, only to discover that she was gone! The front door was left wide open.

"*Grace! Grace!*" he screamed.

She heard Trevor shouting out. She ran barefoot through the woods. Branches, leaves, and rocks all snapped and crunched beneath her feet. They became imbedded on her. *I can't let this bother me! I've got to get help!* Guy told her to run to the hall but stay off the path in case Trevor made a run for her.

"*Grace!*" Trevor ran from the cottage to search for her.

Unexpectedly, he fell down by a swift hard punch. Guy had hid on the side of the cottage and as soon as he saw Trevor running he made a dash for him. He brought his fist down on Trevor's face. Trevor recovered quickly. He threw a punch to Guy that missed, but the second blow landed on his jaw. Enraged Guy lunged for Trevor.

Grace made it to the lawn. Her face was scratched, bloody and bruised, and her legs ached. She clawed at grass breaking a few nails as she tried to make it up a small hill. The manager and security guards saw her. They ran to her.

"Are you okay, miss?" asked the hotel manager throwing his jacket over her naked body. Grace fell in his arms, clearly exhausted and shaking. "The police are on their way."

She looked back to see security running in the direction in which she came.

"Why did you kidnap her?! Why are you trying to kill her?!" Guy shouted during each blow.

He didn't expect an answer. Instead, Trevor bellowed a deep guttural laugh.

"You think you can swan here and save Grace. She doesn't love you. She doesn't need you. I'll always be in her life. I have something you'll never have with her." he replied smugly, wiping blood off his lips.

"Mr. Rowling! Mr. Rowling!" They heard men shouting. Trevor looked at Guy before running off into the woods.

Guy ran, following close behind. He was grateful for his strenuous workout, running and playing on the pitch. It made him an incredibly fast runner. He was able to dodge branches and leap over fallen trees after Trevor. He darted in and out of the brush with only the moonlight to guide him. He was closing in on him.

Unaware of his surroundings, Trevor made it to a steep cliff jutting out over a ravine. He heard Guy coming through the thick overgrown brush and saw glimpses of torches shining through the trees. *There's nowhere to run! I'm trapped! It's over!*

"Come away from there!" Guy shouted. "Come away from the edge. Answer to your crimes like a man! You've done enough damage!"

Trevor held his hands up. He stepped backwards towards the rocky edge. The glare of the torches made him blink rapidly. *My life's over.* It was his final thought before taking another step back, falling over the cliff and his body landing on jagged rocks. Guy ran to the edge. He looked over, stunned. Trevor was dead.

♥

The police returned from their sheep outing. They bypassed Cat and headed straight for the receptionist. Seconds later the switchboard lit up like Christmas lights on a tree. Several calls came in regarding Worthington Hall. The officers tried to run out to their cars, but Cat jumped up stopping them.

"It's Grace isn't it?!" she demanded to know.

"We'll speak when we return. An incident has happened at the hall, that's all we know." one officer stated.

They pushed past her. Quick on her heels, Cat went to her car to follow them to the hall.

♥

Swarms of police from Ivy-upon-Wye, Hereford and Clyro, along with helicopters, approached Worthington Hall. Grace was curled in a foetal position on the bed. A maid placed a damp cool cloth on her head. Her body shook with fear.

A woman police officer came into the room to see her. The officer asked questions which Grace answered, but she desperately wanted to leave. She wanted to go home and be left alone. She didn't want to see anyone but family. Ambulance personnel came into the room to take her vitals before moving her to the hospital.

There was a short heavy knock on the door. The officer opened it. Cat pushed past without disclosing who she was.

"Grace!" Cat cried taking Grace in her arms.

The officer was about to ask about the strange woman.

"I'm her aunt! *She's my niece!*" Cat croaked. "I thought I lost you."

Grace began to choke on her tears. The taste of salt on her lips made her appreciative to be alive. An attendant came over to move her on a gurney.

"Will she be fine?" Cat asked.

"We will let the doctors determine if she'll be fine." he replied securing Grace on the gurney.

They moved her out of the room into the reception area to bring her to the ambulance. Guy came running in, but it was late.

"Grace!" he cried out as they placed her in ambulance.

"Leave her be! She doesn't want to know you! You've done enough damage to her!" Cat snapped. "You've ruined her off of men for good!"

Guy ran to ambulance doors.

"Grace is it true?" he asked pitifully.

"Leave me be." Grace answered stoic.

Cat climbed in the ambulance. The attendant closed the doors, blaring sirens for the journey to hospital. Guy stood in the gravel driveway feeling his heart break for the second time.

twenty five

fortnight passed as Grace, shocked by the shooting and kidnapping, made herself a recluse in Ivy-upon-Wye. It didn't help she was nearly seven weeks pregnant. She needed to recover physically and emotionally from the damage that Trevor had done. It made her scared of everyone and anything.

Paparazzi camped out in front of her home in Tooting Bec and Delicious. Grace stood in Ivy-upon-Wye to avoid them, but they had their way of finding her. Rumour Mill called on a daily basis to The Savoury Plum regarding Grace. Cat firmly told them to sod off.

The night of the rescue, something clicked in her. An inner voice spoke to her, telling her that her relationship with Guy was cursed. She didn't want their love to be cursed. Grace worried for their baby and their lives. She knew they'd never have a 'normal' relationship without the constant scrutiny and spotlight. *There's always something, someone, media, and football. We will never be left to our own devices to let our love grow. It's the truth of our future,* she wasn't sure she should settle for and the baby.

Corrie remained in London to oversee Delicious and flat. She stayed at Guy's until the police investigation was over. Once it was over with, Corrie returned to the house. She stayed with Alistair whilst professional cleaners came to restore Grace's flat. Grace was thankful for her aunt. Corrie promised to return to Ivy when Grace was ready to return home.

♥

Guy tried contacting Grace. It was exactly like before. Cat refused to let him speak to Grace. He tried Grace on her mobile, but his calls went straight to voicemail. He left endless messages begging her to return his call. She never did. One night during a hospital visit, Guy talked it through with Darren.

"Give it time mate. She's been through the wars." Darren said as he ate his orange gelatine.

"You're right. Grace needs space and time." he admitted.

In a matter of eight weeks, their lives were turned upside down. Guy watched as their relationship crumbled due to the actions of a greedy glamour model, a mobster and a psychotic chef. Rumour Mill had a field day.

Tamzin's death brought on spotlight for the brothers. The shooting and death garnered a status of celebrity sainthood. Her funeral was a week away and lines of celebrities, footballers, and models offered their deepest condolences to Darren. His room was filled with balloons, cards and flowers ranging from get well soon to sympathy.

To Guy's surprise, he appeared subdued. Deep within, he knew that Darren was grieving for the woman he thought to believe he married, not a bitch who wanted Darren dead for his money.

Earlier, Darren's solicitor's popped by the hospital for a visit. They came with great news. Her death was a windfall for Darren. Her insurance paid off all their debts, leaving him scot-free from those responsibilities. He owned their town home and their manor outright. Strangely enough, her last will and testament stated Darren was to inherit everything including anything inherited by her in the event of her father's untimely death. It meant since William was dead, Darren collected his life insurance policy as well.

In a surreal twist of fate, William had suffered a massive heart attack the day of Tamzin's death and died the next day whilst undergoing heart surgery. DI Frey was upset. He thought he was going to lose his job over it, but it was determined that the news of Tamzin's death didn't kill William. It was his diet and smoking.

Thereafter Alana came to visit with Darren. She had Max in her arms and was glad Darren had allowed the visit.

"Hello Alana." he said.

"Thank you for seeing me. I thought you'd never want to hear from me again." she replied timidly.

"I didn't. I realise you were just as much as a victim in this." He touched Max's hand.

"I'm aware Max isn't my child. I want to assure you he'll always be taken care of. That's the least I can do for him. I'd hate for Max to grow without a father." he added, smiling and taking Max in his arms. Max held a Postman Pat toy out to Darren.

"Thank you. I'm so sorry for everything I have done to you." Alana replied. Fat tears rolled down on her cheeks.

"Apology accepted. I'm sorry too. I should've never done what I did to you, it was foolish. These actions were careless and thoughtless." he patted her hand to let her know that he was genuine in his forgiveness and apology.

A few days later he was released from hospital. His mother collected him and brought him back to the town home. With the help of his mum, Darren recuperated. They oversaw the sale of the town home so he could move on with his life.

♥

Grace couldn't bring herself to tell Cat that she was pregnant. She stood in the bedroom that was once hers, contemplating how she was going to tell her. Corrie approached Grace the day before her return to London.

"You don't have to go if you don't want to." Corrie said as she watched Grace pack her suitcase with her belongings.

"I've got to get back. As they say, keep calm and carry on."

"Yes, but not in your condition." Corrie replied picking up a jumper and folding it. She caught Grace's gaze.

"Grace, I know you're pregnant. I came across your GP's pregnancy information kit. It took me by surprise. Normally I'd tell Cat, but I couldn't bring myself to tell her. I believe that's your story to tell."

"I'll tell Cat before I leave to London. I just needed time to think about what I was going to do. I don't know if I can raise a child on my own or with Guy. I do know I don't want to raise a child in the crazy environment I've been living in the past few weeks." she sadly sighed.

"It's not where you're living. It's who you're associating yourself with. I'm not going to lie and say that I'm jumping for joy regarding all that's happened. At the end of it all, I know Guy truly does love you. I've never seen a man love a woman as much as you. The exception of your own father, of course. He loves you Grace. Now that Tamzin and Trevor are not in your life, maybe this baby's the opportunity for you two to start afresh." Corrie replied sitting on the bed. "Do you really want to stay in Ivy forever? Do you want to give up your business and your true love to raise this baby here?"

She shrugged. The questions were ones she thought about daily. She couldn't keep this baby from him, but Grace was afraid for their future, terrified in fact. *Was this kidnapping and murder the tip of the iceberg?*

Prior to meeting Guy, she read all the Rumour Mill articles regarding blackmail attempts, and kidnapping plots. She had never thought that it would happen to her. Yet it did and she didn't want anything like this to happen to her and their baby.

"No." she replied.

"This wasn't your fault or his, as much as I'd love to blame him for it. Don't keep Guy away from his child, Grace and don't be afraid of the future. I think you've been through enough and your bad luck's at an end." Corrie said confidently.

Corrie was sure. *There's no way Grace could undergo another round of craziness in her life time and surely God didn't do things in jest!*

Grace nodded. She felt uncomfortable. Her jeans were too snug around her waist. She wanted to release her jean zipper for some room. Corrie smiled.

"You can't hide the baby for long." Corrie added, getting up whilst Grace popped a button to her jeans. *It's true. I've got to tell Cat, but tonight it can wait a little whilst longer.*

♥

At the funeral paparazzi descended on the crematorium in full-force. They aimed their camera lenses on Guy. He detested every single second of it.

Now a hero, it made Guy desirable to all the tabloids. They were desperate for an exclusive interview regarding the whole ordeal. They wanted Guy's version of the tale. There wasn't a minute that went by in the news that didn't have some story related to Trevor, Tamzin, Guy or Darren. Finally he put a stop to all the press calls by having Frederick issue statements asking for privacy at this time. On the day of the funeral Rumour Mill paps took the opportunity to hound Guy as it was a private event in a public setting.

During the procession Guy walked alongside Darren. He noticed that Darren was strong, yet distant. Darren broke down emotionally when Tamzin's coffin was lowered for cremation. The chains of her greediness and her father's grip were released, and he cried for the woman he wished Tamzin to be. After the services, he approached Guy.

"I'm leaving England for awhile, mate." Darren announced as Guy turned to him before he got into the Bentley.

"When are you leaving? You've got a season to play with Tottenham Heat and a contract to live up to?" Guy asked.

"Tottenham allowed compassionate leave and besides they're investigating the blackmail and game fixing scandal. I've already booked my ticket. I'm leaving soon." he replied, putting his hand on Guy's shoulder.

"Where are you going to?"Guy wondered, his brother leaving England temporarily was probably a good idea.

"Brazil. I need to clear my mind and think about things for a bit."

"Good for you. It's for the best." Guy was sincere. He knew Darren needed rest.

"Guy, don't let Grace go for one more minute. I know she needs her time to think. She's a great girl. Call her in a few days." Darren advised.

"I will. I must be going Darren." he replied, looking at his watch. He did not want to stay any longer than he did. He knew the paparazzi were chomping at the bit to get more photographs of them together.

The brothers hugged tightly before saying last goodbyes. Guy knew it'd be some time before he heard from Darren.

♥

Grace kept in daily contact with Mark at Delicious. All was going well and profits were up. She was grateful for her reliable staff and the fact that they all maintained sanity. Now it was time to return and she felt uneasy. The thought of going back to her own flat sickened Grace. Images of Trevor pulling the trigger to shoot them were embedded in her mind.

At night, Trevor crept into her dreams. She'd see his enraged face, and naked body hovering above hers. She'd feel his dirty hands running over her breasts and sex, forcing her to wake up screaming. Cat would run in to assure her that he wasn't there and all was ok. *It's hard to get away from nightmares. It's as though even in death Trevor's still reaching out to me.* Her last night before her return was even more difficult.

Grace woke up with a jolt clutching her pillow. She turned to grab a glass of water on her nightstand. She put her feet on the ground of her old bedroom and looked around. She missed the old look of her bedroom and realised she didn't belong here. She needed Guy. He was the one who made her feel safe.

He had kept his promise that he would always be there no matter what. He made the long journey back from Tokyo without knowing what was going to happen, he did it because he loved her. Grace knew what to do next. She drank her water and placed the glass down.

She went to her handbag to fish out her Blackberry. It was late, but she wanted to hear his deep voice. The phone rang a few times before Grace heard his throaty growl.

"Grace?" he whispered, sitting up in bed. "Are you alright, love? Do you need me to come get you from where you are?"

"Guy, he haunts my dreams. He's always there and I want him gone. I want you here and I want to be in your arms." she wept.

"I've got so much to tell you. I don't want to stay here, but I'm afraid and don't want to live in fear."

"You don't have to live in fear Grace. He's dead and gone along with Tamzin. I made promises that I'll always protect you. I came for you and I was there. I'll always be regardless of what others may think." He ran his fingers through his dark silky hair.

"I don't want to go back to my flat." she admitted.

"And you don't have to. I gave you my key. You can come here and stay with me forever if you wish." he replied.

She stood silent for a moment. The offer sounded so good to her. She was still unsure how he would react to the pregnancy.

"When are you returning to London?" he asked.

"Tomorrow. Alistair's collecting me." she replied softly.

"Why don't you come to my flat? I'll be in practice all day and I've got a game in the early evening. I can be home sharp. Are you fine with that?" he asked.

"Yes." She looked around her bedroom once more. The talk comforted her, but she felt out of place. She wanted to be at his flat, in his bed, in his arms.

"Good. Get what you can from your flat and I'll see you tomorrow evening then."

"Thank you Guy."

"Don't thank me. I love you." he responded warmly.

Those three little words made Grace feel as though a soft warm cashmere blanket been thrown over her body. She knew he meant those words and she cherished it.

"I love you, Guy. I can't wait to see you tomorrow."

They ended the conversation with a simple goodbye and another round of I love you's. She went to bed and he fell back on his fluffy pillow. The two both fell asleep peacefully that night dreaming of tomorrow.

♥

twenty six

he following morning Grace went downstairs to The Savoury Plum. When she entered, she saw Cat pulling down chairs in preparation for the business day.

"Good morning, Grace." Cat greeted. "Alistair's here. He arrived early. He's down at the chicken farmer getting fresh eggs. It seems our delivery was missing at least a few dozen eggs."

Grace went around the serving counter to make herself a pot of tea for them. There were some fresh chocolate stuffed croissants that Olivia made and she placed a few on a plate. She brought the plate and the pot of tea to where Cat sat, reading the papers.

"Are you ready to go back? You know you're more than welcome to stay here. We can hire more people for Delicious and it can run by itself." Cat said pouring the tea into her cup.

"No. I'm ready. I'm looking forward to going back. It's my business. I need to be there instead of here." she replied, biting in a croissant.

"I don't understand the rush in going back. Is it because of Guy? Rumour Mill this morning said how Guy was at the Dowling funeral flirting with some girlfriends." Cat chortled, narrowing her eyes.

"It's all lies, Aunt Cat. I don't understand why you believe everything that is printed in *that* gossip rag." She wasn't in the mood for this.

"I don't want you running back into the arms of trouble. He's been nothing, but a nuisance since stepping foot in here. I bet if it wasn't for him, you would've never opened the business." Cat replied aware that she wouldn't like her opinion.

Grace wasn't amused by her aunt's accusations. It was one thing to say she didn't want her running back to Guy. It was another to assume she didn't have willpower to move and open up her own business.

"Aunt Cat, I opened my business because it's my dream and my goal. It has nothing to do with Guy and it'll stay that way. As for Guy, he'll always be a part of my life." she said firmly.

Cat didn't like her tone and grimaced in displeasure.

"What do you mean he'll always be part of your life? Why can't you leave him alone? He's a footballer for God's sake." Cat questioned shrilly.

"What difference does it make? You idolised Trevor and look what happened. You'd rather have me marry a psycho than one who loves me. Career has nothing to do with who Guy is as a person. I can't believe you've learned nothing about us or me." Grace was now snappy. She looked to the entryway hoping to see Alistair pull up. She wanted to hurry back to London as soon as possible.

"Grace..." she sniffed. She fumbled for the right words. Cat didn't want to get into an argument with Grace that would lead to them not speaking.

"Aunt Cat, Guy will always be a part of my life because I'm pregnant. We're having a baby." Grace blurted out. She couldn't hold back her secret any longer and felt the quicker she told Cat, the quicker the pain would be over with.

Cat was stunned, and shook her head in disbelief.

"Leave now." she ordered, avoiding looking directly at Grace. Tears were in her eyes. She didn't want Grace to see her cry. "Go back to London and to *him*. You'll never be happy." Cat predicted.

"See, that's where the problem lies. No one wants us to be happy. Nobody's happy for us. We're in love. Yet nosy-bodied people like Trevor, Tamzin, William, and you, try to determine our fate!

Nobody can leave good alone. Be miserable and alone then! I never want to speak or hear from you again." she snapped with a frosty air.

Shocked Cat wasn't familiar with this side of her niece. Grace got up throwing her napkin on the plate.

Alistair pulled up and parked right in front of The Savoury Plum. He walked in with three dozen eggs in hand. Grace took them from him and placed it on the counter. He looked over to Cat to see her crying.

"What happened?" he asked.

"Nothing. Let's go." she replied, without directing another word to her aunt.

♥

The drive back to London took longer than expected. During the ride she told Alistair all. He sat in silence from shock. He knew how much Cat meant to Grace. For Grace to say she'd never speak to her again was hard to comprehend. Alistair saw her frustration, and he decided it was best to change the subject.

"Your car was delivered. Yesterday, DI Jones drove it to the house in hopes of speaking with you. He wanted to see how you're doing. He said the case is officially closed. You're no longer in danger. Trevor's death was deemed a suicide."

"I'm going to trade the Mini in. I need something bigger." she said. She wanted to avoid the subject of Trevor.

Grace didn't want to think of *him* any further. Doctors told her that should the nightmares get out of hand she should seek a therapist. She quickly shot down the idea. She felt hat if she could have time with Guy it would be better. *The nightmares will go away. They must go away.*

"Bigger? We live in London, anything bigger it's going to cost you a few bob." he replied as a matter of fact.

"I know. I need it. I don't plan on staying in Tooting Bec. I'm thinking about letting the flat out." she said, looking out the window as they drove along the M4.

Alistair arched his eyebrows. *She really doesn't want to go back to the flat*, he thought, *and who could blame her?*

"I was thinking of letting it out to Sharon." she added.

She knew Sharon lived with a flatmate and it was a tad on the expensive side. Sharon could afford the flat if Grace let it out for a reasonable rate.

"When are you planning on leaving?" he asked, signalling to their exit.

"I don't know yet. I'm meeting Guy tonight to discuss. We've got to talk about things and we'll figure something out." she replied softly.

They arrived at the house. She felt her lungs tightening. Panic settled in. Alistair patted her hand as he drove the rental on the driveway and parked right behind the Mini.

"No one's here except for us." he reassured.

They emerged from the Volkswagen. He left her bags in the car as she instructed. She had no intention of spending the night. He opened the garden door and stepped foot inside.

"Where's Mrs. Tiddlywinks?" she asked. She expected a bark from the small Yorkie.

"Guy kept her." he answered.

They walked into the kitchen. She looked around. The memories came back in full force; Trevor with his sinister eyes, screaming at her about the whore she was for sleeping with Guy.

She entered the lounge. *There's no evidence of the shooting. Everything's immaculate and in order.* It was as if she went on holiday and returned to a clean, sparkling home. She shut her eyes to close her mind to the memory. Instead, she saw Tamzin standing in front of her, Darren standing by her side, and Trevor waving the gun at their direction.

"Grace?" Alistair asked. "Do you want to go up to my flat?" He recognised it was too soon for her to come back to the flat.

"No. I want to get out of here. I'm going to see Guy." she replied, turning away from the lounge.

He saw the discomfort in her face and body. She held her arms over her shoulders trying to protect herself. He saw she had no intention of staying in the flat. *She's better off at Guy's flat.*

"Call him and see if you can go there now." Alistair said.

Grace decided to call and miraculously, he answered. He was just getting dressed for the game.

"Guy, I'm on my way to your flat. Is it OK with you?" she asked.

"Of course. Unless you'd feel more comfortable attending the game." he said. "I can get you into box seats and you'll have nothing to worry about. We can go home together right after the game. Would you like that?"

"Yes." she replied.

"I'll have my driver collect you now."

She thanked him and they hung up. She went to gather her things. It was then that Grace realised it would probably the last time she would be in her flat. She smiled at the thought. *I'm going to start a new life with Guy as long as he wants this baby.* Alistair helped her pack the things that she would need and told her not to worry about anything else. He told her to figure it out with Guy, and then make any decisions later. He gave Grace his blessing.

"You'll be at my wedding right?" he asked, walking Grace outside to the SUV. Guy's security driver arrived.

"Of course! As much as I hate weddings I wouldn't miss yours for the world." she said with a smile.

She kissed him on the cheek and told him to give Philippe her love. Alistair watched Grace getting into the SUV and pull away.

He waved after her knowing it was the end to her living in Tooting Bec.

♥

Rumour Mill paparazzi bombarded the vehicle as it approached the player's entrance. They wondered who was inside the SUV as Guy was already inside preparing for the game. Billy told Grace "Don't worry. Ignore them and don't roll down the window."

She had no intention of rolling down the window and drawing attention to herself. Billy made sure that he parked as close as he could to the player's entrance to get her inside and up to the clubhouse to watch the game.

Guy stood on the line with this other teammates. It was their second match of the Premier season. It was against Manchester City. He watched the box intensely to see if Grace would show, and just as *God Save the Queen* came over the speaker, she appeared in the window. He smiled up to her.

When the anthem was over, he blew a kiss to her, which she noticed and waved back. It brought a wide happy grin. The pundits were wondering what it was all about and if it would affect Guy's game.

It was the first time she watched him play. There were other WAG's, decked in their designer duds, seated nearby, gossiping and pretending to watch the game. They whispered to each other knowing full well who Grace was. She thought they all looked like cast members and extras from *The Only Way is Essex*. It was hard for her to ignore them especially since they were staring right at her. Midway through the game, one of the wives, rose from their seat and came over to her.

"You're Grace Knowles, right? Guy's bird?" the petite framed brunette asked.

The brunette wore a pair of red Helmut Lang skinny jeans with tight fit team t-shirt that accentuated her oversize silicone breasts. She eased into the leather seat next to Grace. The woman motioned to a waiter to bring over whatever Grace was drinking and a champagne for herself.

"Yes, I am." Grace replied "And you are?"

"My name's Minnie, Minnie Collins. I'm married to Owen Collins, the captain of the team. He's retiring this year. We have met before at Darren's wedding." she said, extending her hand to shake Grace's.

Grace shook her hand. She didn't recall meeting Minnie at the wedding. The waiter returned with drinks. Minnie gave Grace a glass of J2O.

"I came over to welcome you to the team and to say we're thankful for you. As much as we understand all the trauma and tragedy you've suffered, we're thankful Tamzin's officially out of our hair." Minnie said.

"You 're welcome here and we love someone who is down to earth, respectable and goal-oriented. Tamzin was never those things. She gave us all a reputation that's hard to shake." Minnie looked over to the other two ladies and smiled. They, too, nodded their head in agreement.

"Wow. I really don't know what to say. It was neither my intention to replace Tamzin nor wish ill on her." Grace retorted. "Frankly, it's a position that I believe nobody would want to be in including yourselves."

Her tone was as sharp as Minnie's tactic, it was a clear point made. Minnie agreed half-hearted, pulling a business card with her details on it from her purse. Delicately, she handed the embossed card over to Grace.

"Welcome to our group. Please feel free to contact me for brunch, shopping, spa or pub outing anytime. As a group we do many things together and love having you on our team." Minnie drank her champagne and placed the glass on the table beside her.

Minnie got up, smoothing down her top. She checked her hot pink lip-gloss in a mirror adjacent to Grace's chair. Grace watched her saunter back to her seat and the other ladies waved to her as a welcoming. Grace sat in disbelief. *These women think I did them a favour. How odd?*

The game ended with the London Lions losing 2-1. Minnie laughed it off.

"It's you! Usually when the first time the love of a player's life comes to visit, they can't focus on the game. Come, let me show you where you'll meet Guy." Minnie teased, taking her arm.

Minnie led the way to through the double doors to larger part of the clubhouse where all the wives and girlfriends along with agents waited to greet the team.

A small buffet was set up for the team and the guests. The smell of roast beef made Grace carnivorous. She quickly filled a plate with meats and vegetables, along with hot rolls. Minnie watched inquisitively. She told Grace to pace herself if she didn't want to lose her figure over it.

"I'm hungry. I haven't eaten for days." she rushed. It felt like years since her last fitting meal and the chocolate croissant was long since gone.

"I think you're more than hungry." she replied. She knew the tell-tale signs of pregnancy when she saw one. Minnie smiled at her, deciding it best to let her be.

Guy was the first player to enter the room to a round of hisses and boo's. *It's okay, my favourite faithful fan is standing here!* When he walked pass he watched Grace with her deep aquamarine eyes, staring at him in amazement.

His hair was wet from the shower. He was dressed in dark blue jeans, a London Lions jersey and crisp white trainers. It made her feel meagre. He approached Grace, forcing her to put her plate down. The twinkle in his eyes showed her how he was happy to see her. He swept her into his arms, kissing her.

The kiss made the room, sounds of people whistling, and overall noise fall away. It was as if it was just the two of them in one confined space. She didn't want to let go and this time she refused to let go. It was her chance to prove to the world that Guy was her man and hers alone. *No other woman is going to take my place.* Guy pulled away to give Grace some air. She blushed at the cheers.

"Let's go home." he whispered in her ear.

♥

twenty seven

*I*n the door the key clicked and knob twisted. With his foot Guy pushed it open. He carried her into the flat like newlywed bride. Mrs. Tiddlywinks barked at their feet.

"Let me down!" Grace cried playfully.

"No. I want to take you into the bedroom and make love to you." he said.

Her face fell. She wasn't ready for sex. She had to tell Guy the truth about everything that had happened and the baby.

"Guy, I'm not ready. We need to talk." She walked into the lounge, picking up Tiddlywinks in her arms. She rubbed the small dog's ears as she sat down on Guy's couch. Guy sat beside her.

"I understand everything you've went through, Grace. If you need to speak to me about it, you can. I'll always listen. Are you afraid of me?" he questioned.

"No...I'm not afraid of you. I know Trevor's dead and gone. I know he won't be able to hurt me. I'm afraid someone else may come along and do further damage." she replied, uneasy.

He completely understood and placed his hand on Grace's shoulder to look directly in her eyes.

"As long as we stick together no one will do us harm. I've hired the best security team to look after us. I assure you they'll always be by your side." he said robustly.

"I still have nightmares about the ordeal. His hands on me and things that must've went through his mind. It's all so fresh and frightening. I never would have thought he was psychotic. I mean... the day he lashed out at me...yes he hit me, but to kidnap me and do me harm?" She toyed with her fingers nervously. Tiddlywinks jumped off her lap to find a chew toy to gnaw at.

"Grace, I'll do anything to help you through this." He meant every single word. If he had to pay for therapy he'd do it and no one would have to know.

"Are you afraid to go back to Delicious? Are you afraid to leave this flat on your own?" he asked. Grace shook her head no.

"I've to tell you something else, Guy." she said.

He felt his stomach churning in revolt. He didn't want to know if she'd been raped by Trevor. The notion of that bastard doing something so ghastly to her was his own personal nightmare. He tried his damndest not to focus on it.

"Guy, please don't be upset with me." she pleaded.

"I'll never be upset with you. Tell me, my love." he replied, wrapping his arm around her to try and comfort her in telling him what was distressing her.

"I..am...pregnant." she confessed at a snail's pace.

Guy looked at her for a moment. His expression was one of scepticism gradually turned into ecstatic excitement.

"Are you sure?" he gulped.

"Yes...I found out the day of the kidnapping. I was five weeks pregnant then. I'm eight weeks now." she admitted. "If you don't want me now that I'm pregnant, please let me know. I can stay with Alistair until I sort out my flat and move elsewhere." She scanned his face for any clue that he was disturbed by the news.

Guy leapt up and looked down at Grace. *It's incredulous for her to think I wouldn't want our baby.* Random thoughts raced in his mind. The penthouse flat boasted three bedrooms. Enough room to raise a child.

But to him a penthouse flat in Canary Wharf wasn't an ideal place to raise his future child. *Also, what child is raised with parents who weren't married?* He was aware that many parents weren't married and raised their children happily, but Guy didn't want *his* baby to be born out of wedlock. It was an old-fashioned way of thinking, *I want a life for us and our baby. A proper family life.* They needed to marry immediately.

"Guy?" Grace questioned as she watched him in thought.

"Grace, let's get married!" he exclaimed.

She was perplexed by his rushed proposal. The last thing she wanted was a wedding. *Marriage yes, wedding no.*

"Guy, I said I'm pregnant. I'm not forcing you down the aisle or asking for hand in marriage. My family won't approve. They don't approve of this baby and they mean the world to me. We're no longer on speaking terms." she said, rising up on her feet and pulling his hands towards her.

"Yes, but I'm asking you. Grace Ann Knowles, will you marry me? Will you and the baby spend the rest of your life with me? Share our lives together for infinite time being and grow old together?"

He looked at her, eyes full of intense, raw, emotional, love and intentions. She was lost for words and unable to reply except that her heart screamed yes.

"We don't have to have a big wedding reception. In fact we don't have to have a wedding at all. It can be just the two of us. We have the trip to the Maldives planned. We can marry there on the beach. You and me! No one else. No wedding party or cake just an officiator and a sunset dinner for two." he elaborated.

The more he relished on the idea of marriage, the more she was certain of her answer. She knew her old life was over with. She wanted her life with him and to accept it was to help put the past to rest. It'd be just the two of them and baby.

"*Yes! Yes!*" Grace shrieked back throwing her arms around him. Guy kissed her hard holding her tight.

"I'll never ever let you go again. Anywhere I go, you go and so will our baby. Tomorrow I'm calling Portland Hospital. I want only the best for my wee one and you." Guy said rubbing his palm over her tummy.

She was barely showing, but expanding. She decided to wear stretch leggings because her size ten jeans no longer fit.

"And if you're having trouble with memories and feelings Grace, we'll get you help. Sometimes you may need someone to talk to, to help us through the rough patches. Anything you need is at your disposal." he added.

She rubbed her face in the crook of his neck. *Here's where I want to be, always.* He lifted her into his arms to carry her into his bedroom. He placed Grace on the bed. Guy peeled her clothes away making Grace tremble with fear.

"Don't think I'll hurt you. I don't have to make love to you to prove how much I want or love you. I just want to feel you, caress you and show you what truly love is. I want to take away all those horrible feelings you're harbouring. Please realise that I'm not Trevor or any other man. I'm the man who's about to be your husband." Guy said as he stood before Grace who sat on the bed with her legs curled behind her.

"You're in charge." Guy added. She humbly nodded.

"Take off your shirt." she ordered softly.

Grace needed to see him with his shirt off. The image of Trevor was ingrained in her mind, and she wanted it out. She wanted to see Guy in all his muscular glory with his tight six pack abs and ripped biceps. She loved when he pulled the shirt over his head how it ruffled his jet black hair. She reached up to touch him.

"All I want to do is lay down with you." she whispered. "I want you to hold me and tell me we're going to be alright."

"I can do that." she said kissing on her forehead. She fell backward, and they lay side by side curled up, facing each other.

She caressed his face softly. He pulled her close, kissing her delicately against her lips.

"Mrs. Grace Ann Rowling." he whispered. "Can you handle that?"

"I've come this far. I think I can handle a change." They were true survivors of the scandalous storm and the prospect of marriage and baby didn't seem daunting at all. Their future looked better and brighter than ever before.

Grace leaned over to kiss Guy. She wanted to go further. She wanted to wash away the traces of Trevor's lips on her body by making love to Guy. The kiss was sweet, romantic and endearing. It wasn't the rush of two lost lovers needing each other after time had separated them for so long. It was tender, saccharine and proper, like a love that spanned the ages of time and endured the weathered fringes of life.

She dragged herself up on top of Guy's body. *I'm in charge.* He clutched her hair softly behind her neck as she came forward to continue their kissing. Her silky caramel hair weaved through his fingers. She moved to lay her head over his beating heart.

"Do you hear that Grace?" he asked whilst she listened to the slow thumping beat of his heart. She nodded against his chest.

"It only beats for you." Guy replied softly.

Grace placed her chin on his chest and grinned.

"Always..." she added drawing herself back up to kiss him again.

He reached up to touch the blades of her shoulders. He slowly pulled down the straps of her bra watching her face for any change to say that she did not want this. Grace relented. He tossed her bra to the floor. She threw her head back and moaned low as the tips of his fingers traced their way down the tops of her breast over the peaks of her nipples.

Her breasts were large and swollen. Her nipples took on a scarlet flush that wasn't her normal rosy glow. He ran his thumb against them. The touch made her body gyrate against his jeans.

Guy took one of her nipples into his mouth. He gradually licked the harden bud suckling Grace to the point she could feel the walls of her womb tightening. She was wet, gloriously wet.

Only Guy can make me wet, not some crazy man. The more he suckled, the more she moved against him. She wanted him inside her, to reach the state of ecstasy that she knew was filled with cosmic sexual explosions and the promise of tranquillity.

"Please Guy." she purred.

He continued suckling and caressing her extremely sensitive breasts. He knew that if he went on she'd most likely orgasm before having his fill of her. She started pleading and he felt dampness between them. He pulled her away to look up at her.

"Are you sure you want to do this?" he asked. "Is it safe for the baby?" He searched her face for the answers.

Grace bit her lip and nodded shyly. Goose pimples ran up and down the length of her body at the thought of mind blowing sex with Guy. She rolled off of Guy as he got up to take his jeans off. He looked back at her. She was staring at him as his soft black cotton Jasper Conran boxer briefs came off. He turned around, his cock pompously protruding through the darkness of his pubic hair. She gasped.

Looking at him is like seeing David by Michelangelo for the first time; spellbinding! She was still in awe of him even after the many times they spent together in bed.

"Lay down, Grace." he delicately demanded.

She did as she was told and he brought his fingers to the fine waistband of her underwear. Leisurely, he rolled them off over her legs, down around her ankles and off her feet dropping them on his pile of clothing.

"I don't want to be on top. I want you in charge. I want you to be sure you want to do this." he said, taking his place beside her.

He caressed her soft skin and tummy again, still reeling from the surprise of a baby. He didn't want to hurt her and he surely didn't want to do anything that would hurt the baby. Grace saw he was uneasy, and she assured him it was ok. She mounted him again, leaning in for a kiss with her sweet swollen pussy inches away from his bulbous head.

He felt her wetness so close to him, he gritted his teeth in anticipation. Just the thought of pushing inside of her musky creamy lips with his pre-cum wet cock was thrilling.

She kissed and licked at his neck. She brought her mouth down to his nipples, licking them with pleasure. These weren't the ghastly white pierced ones like Trevor, Guy was tan and untouched. His body warm and inviting. He sucked in his breath and hissed.

"You don't know what you do to me." he managed to say as she looked down at him starry eyed.

Unaware of her own actions, Grace moved her dripping, sex against him. His cock nuzzled at her tight entrance. *Good grief! She's so wet and excited,* he thought. He felt the wetness on his groin and abs as she rubbed her clit against his skin to create friction as she continued tasting him.

"Grace...Grace..." he chanted as if he was in prayer.

Grace felt the pressure mounting between them and his cock searching his way into her. She arched her back and pressed her clit down against him to help ease his way into her. Guy ran the palm of his hands down to her arse spreading her cheeks to gain easy access. Her breathing went ragged from the way he held her. It took one move by Grace to allow Guy to enter her. She could feel his cock making its way up her moist canal filling her to the brim making her full and achy. She let out a long Ooo as if she was relieved to finally have him inside her.

She moved upward and brought herself down for a first deep thrust of his cock. She moved her body gradually up and down with a downward thrust. She gyrated her hips like a belly dancer. He placed his hands on her waist to hold her as Grace moved. He threw his head back on the pillow. The molten wet feeling of her pussy intensified. It detonated millions of tiny explosions of stimulation run throughout his body.

Grace moaned his name several times each increasing loudly in volume. The louder she said Guy's name the more liberated she felt. She rocked her womb along his cock and Guy ran his thumb along her bottom lip taking it into her mouth. He nearly shot his hot load when she did this, and he held on for dear life. He wanted her to tighten her syrupy pussy around his cock and feel her pulsing orgasm.

Guy drew himself up Grace's body to suckle her breasts as she continued to pump herself on him. He grabbed onto her arse and she wrapped her arms around his head her fingers clutching the thick jet black hair, making her gasp loudly. Their intense lovemaking sucked the air from their bodies and their need for release barrelling down upon them.

The rubbing of her clit against his groin and the licking of her sensitive nipple made her womb contract tightly around his cock to release her orgasm. She cried out loudly. Tears squeezed out from the corners of her eyes overwhelmed by the power of it all.

He didn't hold back. Semen flooded every inch of her vivacious pussy that clenched around his cock, milking each last drop. He shuddered against her whilst still holding her tight.

The couple fell backward, panting heavily, and trying to recover. When she dismounted and placed herself right beside him, her legs were still shaking. Guy swept her sweaty hair away from her face kissing her lips tenderly.

"If I didn't know any better I could've gotten you pregnant again." he joked.

She grinned. *I'm truly at home with the man I love.*

♥

The next morning whilst she recuperated in bed from the few times of lovemaking throughout the night, Guy returned with a tray filled with an English breakfast for two. It didn't bode well for her.

"Oh God!" she groaned clutching her mouth as she ran to the loo. She slammed the door behind her. Pregnancy had given her aversion to eggs.

"What! What did I do wrong?" he asked, knocking on the door not thinking it was the food.

"Nothing." Grace managed to say after brushing her teeth.

She explained to him what had happened and how she appreciated his kind gesture. He wolfed down the eggs and let her eat the buttered toast. He apologised saying the pregnancy thing was new to him. She understood.

Guy spent most of the morning arranging appointments at Portland Hospital whilst she went back to work at Delicious. Mark was surprised to see her back in relatively good form.

Grace held a meeting with the staff to tell them the news. She had decided since Delicious ran fairly well without her being there that she was hiring a few more staff members. She was going to promote one of the chefs already employed and put them in charge. She announced that she was going to manage from a far, whilst looking for space to open a brand new location.

"Are you sure you want to do this?" Mark asked, looking up from some reports she handed him.

"It's probably for the best in the long run, honestly. Whilst you were gone we had some fanatics in here inquiring whether or not they could get your autograph. I believe some people think you have an oddly glamorous life because you're dating Guy Rowling, your saviour from *that* lunatic." he commented, clicking his pen.

"That's why I'm finding it hard to come back. Guy and I discussed it. We'll be looking for a home in the countryside and eloping after Christmas." she announced.

"Good for you! Congratulations!" Mark cried.

Mark placed the reports down on the desk and leaned over to hug her. He kissed her on both cheeks. *She deserves all the happiness,* he thought to himself.

Her Blackberry beeped. Mark backed away, returning to his seat next to her desk. It was a text message from Corrie.

As she read the message from Corrie her face fell. It said that Cat wasn't attending Alistair and Philippe's wedding if she was attending with Guy. Corrie apologised regarding the matter and wished her well.

"Excuse me, Mark. I've got to call my family." Grace said, reaching for the phone and dialling the number to The Savoury Plum.

Mark nodded. He left to the shop front to man the register.

"Allo." Cat said on the third ring.

"Aunt Cat, we need to talk." she said.

"We have nothing further to discuss. As long as you're with *that* man, I'll no longer be speaking to you." Cat replied.

"This has nothing to do with..." she was cut short by a dial tone.

♥

Guy was about to leave his flat to the London Lions Club when the intercom buzzer rang. Concierge announced the arrival of DI Martin Jones wanting a brief word with him.

"Yes, that's fine." he said, placing his keys to his newly acquired Aston Martin in his pocket.

He was curious. He thought the case regarding Trevor was closed, and that he had been exonerated from any wrong doing by saving Grace. He waited with the door open to watch DI Jones emerge from the elevator and waved him in. DI Jones shook his brolly, wet from the rain and placed it at the side of the front door to Guy's flat.

"Thank you for taking time to see me." DI Jones greeted.

"Can I take your jacket? Would you like a drink?" he offered, closing the door behind them and showing him the way into the flat.

"No, thank you. I'll only be a moment. I've got only a few questions to ask." DI Jones said looking around the flat.

It amazed DI Jones when he visited swanky places and Guy's flat wasn't an exception. DI Jones found himself a tad bit envious. He made pittance on a copper's salary and lived in a flat in Bethnal Green because that was all he could afford.

"Is this regarding Trevor?" he asked entering the lounge. He motioned to the couch for DI Jones to take a seat which he did. Guy prayed that this wouldn't take long.

"No. The case has been formally closed. I'm inquiring on the Dowling's. We never recovered the bullets from Ms. Knowles home or the Worthington Hall cottage. We managed to retrieve bullet casings in the flat. What mystifies us is that we recovered a bullet from Darren's injury, but we haven't recovered any from Tamzin." DI Jones said rubbing his chin.

"What do you mean? Isn't that done during autopsy?" Guy replied, taking his seat across from the detective. DI Jones looked at him sternly and frowned.

"When you went to view Mrs. Dowling's body, were you positive it was her?" DI Jones asked.

"Yes. I'm sure. Given she was shot in the face, but I could recognise her blond hair and her hands." he answered.

"In confidence, I have to admit to you something rather serious. Somehow an autopsy on Tamzin's body was bypassed. A mistake was made in the paperwork. We never had an autopsy done. It was never done. When we learned of the cremation, we waited at the crematory for the possibility of bullets or remnants. There were none when the ashes were excavated. We assumed the heat had melted them, but something tells us otherwise. Her family want to learn the truth on whether the gun that killed her actually belonged to William. Do you know of your brother's whereabouts?" DI Jones questioned.

Guy sat stiff in his seat, wondering as to where this mini interrogation was going.

"Darren went to Brazil. He was given compassionate leave from his team." he replied. "What are you trying to conclude here, DI Jones?"

"Are you sure? Other sources say Argentina. We're trying to be certain that all the i's have been dotted and the t's crossed. That's all." DI Jones said getting up. Guy shrugged as he stood up.

"He didn't tell me Argentina. Darren told me Brazil unless he changed his mind in the last minute. I'm sorry I can't be much help to you." They politely shook hands and Guy lead the way out.

"By the way how is Ms. Knowles?" DI Jones asked.

"Fine. We're getting married this winter and expecting a baby." he supplied happily.

"Congratulations and good luck. If you hear from Darren please contact me immediately. I'd like to have a word with him." DI Jones said.

He nodded. He said farewell to DI Jones. He watched and waited for him to get on the elevator before he left himself.

♥

twenty eight

eeks flew by swiftly. Grace moved in the penthouse flat with Guy. She let her flat out to Sharon along with furnishings. Sharon was grateful for it all. Alistair was elated that his best friend was going to be living downstairs from him. After their wedding, Philippe would move into Alistair's flat. Grace couldn't bring herself to tell Alistair what Cat had said. She felt if Cat wanted to decline her invitation then she should tell Alistair herself instead of using Grace as an excuse.

As her pregnancy progressed, Grace expanded. No longer was she able to fit in High Street designer clothing. She started shopping for her maternity wear at Mothercare. She looked positively radiantly beautiful. She felt great. Guy loved it all. He wanted to get Grace an engagement ring to go with the fact that they were now engaged and starting a family. She protested. She was going to swell and she didn't want to have the ring refitted. It would wait until after the baby is born.

Guy managed to get her an appointment with one of the best midwives at Portland Hospital. Since she passed her eight week mark for her ultrasound, she went in at twelve weeks. He arranged it around their hectic schedule. She had another several weeks to go before handover. The day of the ultrasound appointment, Guy paced nervously in the room whilst they waited for the technician to arrive.

"I can only imagine how you'll react when baby is born!" she teased.

As soon as the technician arrived, she prepared Grace and dimmed the lights to the room, Guy held her hand firmly as the technician rolled the wand over her belly. An image popped up on the screen and the technician explained all she saw. There in black and white images a tiny bean with a small beating heart took their breath away.

"You're due in late April." the technician said happily.

Once they finished the technician gave them copies of the scan and lead the way to the midwife's office to continue their appointment.

They left Portland Hospital grinning from cheek to cheek. Rumour Mill paparazzi waited for the couple to take pictures and threw questions to them, which they ignored. They got into the

Range Rover with Billy and drove off discussing the next scan that would tell them the sex of the child.

"We need to buy a bigger place." Guy suggested "Somewhere in the country perhaps. Alderly Edge? What do you think?"

"I want a place that's private and hard to get onto the property. I'd like to be near a market town so I can open up another *Delicious*." she replied, looking down at the scan. She knew Alderly Edge would give them notoriety with the paps.

"I'll leave it entirely up to you then. I don't mind a place that needs work. We can always hire out people to fix it up to our tastes. Remember, my schedule is a bit daunting. I can manage to see a place on my day off." he responded.

"What about the penthouse?" she asked.

"We'll keep it for when I'm playing local or we have to go abroad. We will use it as a pied-et-terre."

It was a great idea. When she returned to Delicious, she quickly made a few phone calls to estate agents that dealt with countryside properties.

♥

The last crimson, citrine and tangerine leaves of Regents Park fell softly to the ground when the wedding of Alistair and Philippe was upon them.

Guy, unfortunately, couldn't make it. He was in Newcastle playing an away game. He truly wanted to be there to help in a way he could and to be supportive.

Although, Cat declined her invitation, Alistair gave Cat a ring at home and spoke with her directly. He assured her that Guy wasn't going to be at the wedding, but Grace would be and it wasn't fair that their argument was dissuading Cat not to come. They had known each other for so many years and why would she let a tiff destroy their own relationship.

Alistair did come to Grace's defence. He told Cat that Grace was a grown woman. Her decision to be with Guy was her choice. She should have the support and love of family, instead of judgment and prejudice. Cat didn't agree with what he had to say, but gave in by saying she would attend the wedding on behalf of their friendship.

The Tate Gallery 9 was decorated to perfection for the civil ceremony wedding of Alistair Knowles to his fiancé, Philippe Geoffrey. The backdrop of romantic art works from the likes of Turner, Martin and Danby was something to behold creating the dramatic atmosphere Alistair and Philippe wanted with tradition behind it. Large vases held autumn and winter mix floral around the gallery. Rows of sparkling gold Kartell Louis ghost chairs provided seating for their two hundred closest family and friends.

Alistair and Philippe were dressed in black Ralph Lauren tuxedos with traditional white cummerbunds and bowties. They both wore large dark blood red poppies on their lapels. Sharon, the maid-of- honour wore a red long gown with beautiful ruffles from Marchesa, whilst Grace wore the exact same one in black altered to fit her budding bump. Grace and Sharon had their hair and makeup prepared by celebrity makeup artist, Nicola Wayne. She wore her Graff diamond necklace that Guy given her. She was comforted by wearing it. It was the closest she'd get to Guy being there with her. Alistair was a nervous wreck. He paced nervously as he waited to go down the aisle to Philippe.

"You'll be fine." Grace assured watching him down a glass of Cristal champagne.

In the back of Grace's mind she wished she could do the same. She peeked from behind the long red velvet curtains to see all the guests being escorted to their seats whilst a string quartet played the *Queen of Sheba*. She held her breath over the arrival of her aunts. Grace took the glass and stuck her finger in it to grasp the last drop of champagne. She licked her finger to taste pure heavenly, liquid relaxation.

"Ease up love. I'm the nervous one." Alistair chuckled.

The string quartet began to play their rendition of Moby's *God Moving over the Face of Waters* as the grand entrance for the groom. Grace walked down the aisle first clutching her bouquet filled with blood red, dark royal purple, mustard yellow flowers. Flashes from photos being taken blocked her view of the guests as she smiled for cameras.

She reached Philippe, who was holding his own breath, tears streaming down his face from the strong emotion of love. Sharon followed behind taking place beside Grace. At long last Alistair came down the aisle like a man in love and when he arrived the officiator asked them all to be seated.

Grace couldn't pay attention to the guests. She focused on the marriage ceremony. As they exchanged their vows, she thought of Guy. In over a month's time they'd be in the Maldives exchanging their own vows without their family or friends to share their joy. The thought made her tremble inside. She wanted this, her family and friends, and a simple wedding, but the two people who mattered certainly didn't approve, nor were they talking to her. It made her heart break. She truly hoped that Cat was among the guests. She wanted to talk to Cat to convince her that everything was okay.

"I now pronounce you married. Guests please stand up to receive them. Mr and Mr. Philippe Alistair Knowles-Geoffrey." the officiator announced.

The crowd clapped their hands into loud applause. *Cosmic Love* by Florence and the Machine sang from loudspeakers as they kissed. Grace and Sharon were the first to receive them. They congratulated them over and over again. They all walked up the aisle together laughing, kissing and waving at guests as they entered Sackler Octagon for the reception.

♥

Throughout dinner, Grace thought of ways to approach her aunts. They sat at a table, barely socialising with other guests. Cat and Corrie were both dressed in a champagne colour suit. They wore beautiful gold feather fascinators in their curled hair and their faces were made up in makeup which Grace wasn't use to seeing.

She sat at her own table and ate a piece of dark devil's food cake with red fondant made by her staff at Delicious. Alistair excused himself from the dance floor, dancing his way to her.

"Grace, speak to them. I can't have you moping about at my wedding. The photographers complained about the pregnant moping lady in gorgeous Marchesa gown." Alistair admonished.

She gave a faint grin, wiping off cake crumbs from her lips with her tongue.

"I can't help it. Every time I build the courage, I discourage myself." she said frowning.

"Don't! Catherine's the problem. Face Cat and make her see your side. Guy's wonderful and you're in love. Don't let her feelings get in the way of your true happiness." he advised.

Alistair grabbed her arm, picking her up from the chair to bring her over to the table. He poked her hard in the ribs to greet her aunts. Suddenly, Alistair was pulled by Philippe to say goodbye to a few friends.

"Hello, Aunt Corrie, Aunt Cat!" Grace exclaimed loudly with false jubilation. The twins looked up from their plates and Corrie smiled.

"Oh, there you are Grace. I'm so happy to see you." Corrie said. She rose from her chair to greet her niece with a kiss.

Cat blinked her eyes rapidly getting up too.

"I'm going to the loo." Cat announced, ignoring Grace. She looked at Grace up and down pausing at the bump to only turn to walk away.

"Don't!" Grace snapped. "Don't you walk away from me." Astound by her reaction, Cat turned to her to confront her.

"How dare you tell me I can't walk away!" she barked back. It caught the attention of the other guests at the table.

"Aunt Catherine, I just wanted to say 'hello' that's all and wish you well. You could have the courtesy to do the same." she replied, bringing her tone back down to something more cordial.

Grace felt fingers intertwine with hers. She looked over her shoulder to see Guy standing there dressed in a tuxedo.

"Hello, Ms. Fielding and Ms. Fielding." he greeted. "Come Grace, how about a dance?" he added not waiting for a reply.

She was speechless when he twirled her away from her aunt's disdain and uncouth reaction.

"How did you get here so fast? Why are you here?" she asked, swaying with him.

"I knew you needed me. It was a late afternoon game. I managed to get a helicopter ride in by a mate from the other team. I wasn't going to come back down by car. Too long of a drive. I need to be here for you and the bump." he said staring at her.

"Thank you." she said meekly.

"For what? The dance?" he questioned.

"For rescuing me yet again." she replied, placing her head on his shoulder.

"You really need to stop thanking me, Grace. I'll always rescue you." he kissed the top of her head whilst Cat watched from a distance with antagonism.

"You need to stop." Corrie said with irritation in her voice. "Grace isn't just a niece to us. We raised her like a daughter and you should be so proud! You're reacting the same way when Jane ran to London. She has her mother's streak and yet you continue to act like a fool."

"And you approve of this?!" Cat snapped, waving her hand in a rolling fashion directed at them dancing.

"Why not? They're young, in love, and expecting a baby. What did you expect would happen? He saved her life and for that we should be grateful!" Corrie pointed out. "Yet you continue to alienate her for being in love. You should've learnt a few things from

Jane prior to her death and you should've learnt something from raising Grace, who's like a *daughter* to me."

Corrie dropped her napkin on the plate and excused herself from the table to join Alistair, Philippe, Grace and Guy on the dance floor with other guests. Cat sat back cross. She wasn't going to let this go.

♥

Big Ben tolled its bell twelve times, letting all of London know that it was midnight. The first snow began to fall from the night sky as they left the Tate to get into the Bentley and head home. Grace felt emotionally drained by Cat's reaction and told Guy on the way home how hurt she was by the whole thing. He listened and nodded respectfully. He clutched her hand, whilst rubbing her protruding pregnancy belly over layers of Marchesa fabric.

"All I want for Christmas is my family back. My aunts are like a mum to me. I never got to truly know my own mum and I lost her at a young age. Now I'm losing them when we should be all excited for the newest member arriving in our family." she moaned.

"You'll get them back. I'll make good on my promise." he said, secretly vowing to charm Cat before it was too late.

She rolled her eyes, turning her vision to the streets coated in glistening white snow. She knew trying to get them to come around was like Guy trying to chip ice off a massive glacier with a toothpick.

"Stop it! You can't fix it!" she snapped. "The only ways I can fix this is by not marrying you and raise our baby on my own."

The words cut him like a sharp knife. He didn't like how the conversation turned. She was throwing a tantrum over something she had no control over. He didn't like when she got like this.

"Look at me, Grace." he demanded. Grace bought her fist to her mouth. She didn't want to turn around to face him as her tears made her makeup run.

"Look at me!" he ordered again firmly. She turned. He saw that she was crying.

"Grace, you can't control what anyone thinks! Running away and raising this baby on your own is not going to get them to approve of what has happened. Understand?" He brought his hand up to her cheek to wipe the tears away.

As a response to her reaction, the baby kicked hard against Guy's hand. It was the first kick. Guy was taken back and Grace too.

"See the baby doesn't approve of you being sad." he joked. "I think we've got a tiny footballer in training."

"Or ballerina." she offered.

He kissed her and rubbed his forehead against Grace's.

"I love you." he whispered. The baby kicked again. "And yes I love you too." he added, patting the bump.

♥

twenty nine

Across town on Harley Street, a black Sapphire BMW 5 Series drove slowly through the snow covered street. It parked in front of an immaculate Georgian town home. The driver stopped the car. He got out and opened the door for his backseat passenger.

Her Rupert Sanderson high-heeled boot hit the ground and a blast of cold air made her shiver as she stepped out. Dressed in a short brown rabbit fur coat with matching hat, the woman extended her leather-glove hand to her driver to help her out. She looked like a brunette Russian doll and thanked her driver.

"You're welcome, Mrs. Collins." the driver replied.

He didn't understand why Minnie needed to come to Harley Street in the dead of night. *She must be desperate for a Botox injection,* he thought wryly as he got back into the driver's seat.

The door to the town home opened and there waiting was a nurse in the vestibule. Minnie made her way up the stairs and shook the older woman's hand.

"Is she alright?" asked Minnie as the nurse took her coat.

"Yes. All day she's been waiting. She refuses to take off her bandages until she sees you." the nurse replied.

"I hope she understands. I've got the paparazzi breathing down my neck. Everything must be done in secrecy." Minnie replied following the nurse up a flight of stairs.

They entered the hospital-like bedroom. It was fitted out with all of the features of a clinical setting and the comforts of a very expensive, five star, London hotel room. Large bouquets of flowers adorned the nightstand. Diptyque candles and Molton Brown toiletries graced the six drawer dresser.

Minnie sat down next to the hospital bed. She placed her hand over the woman wrapped in bandages. To Minnie the woman looked like an Egyptian mummy with exception of her eyes, nose, mouth and ears. They were left open to see, breath, drink and hear.

"I'm here." Minnie said in her sing-song voice.

The woman opened her eyes. Her deep emerald green eyes lit up when she saw Minnie. Minnie noticed.

"Your eyes are green!" she cried out.

"It's the contacts." the woman retorted.

Minnie sat back in her chair. She thought the doctor to be the world's best plastic surgeon by surgically changing the colour of one's eyes!

"How do you feel?" she asked.

"Fine. The drugs they give me for the pain works a treat." the woman said hoarsely.

"I can't believe you've managed to pull this off!"

The mystery woman would've nodded in agreement, but she couldn't. Instead she grunted. There was a knock on the door and Minnie said come in. Dr. Burton entered the room greeting Minnie and his patient.

"Are you ready to take off your bandages, Ms. Townsend?" asked Dr. Burton directing the question to the woman on the bed.

"Yes, I'm ready." the woman replied cheerfully. She'd been waiting a full three months to see her face and body free from the scars of extreme plastic surgery.

Minnie moved for Dr. Burton to help the woman out of her bed. They walked over to a large wall mirror. The nurse helped the woman out of her dressing gown whilst Dr. Burton pulled out the medical scissors.

Delicately unhurried, Dr. Burton removed every bandage that held the woman in place. The patient kept her eyes close until the last bandage was removed. When she opened her eyes, she gasped with satisfaction. Minnie nearly swooned off her feet.

Gone were the long blond extensions on her friend's head. In its place was a choppy mocha bob with cafe-au-lait highlights and lowlights. Her friend was no longer large breasted. Instead, she opted for small perky boobs that looked natural and not as noticeable to men. The nose tip that had been naturally hooked was straightened. Her former jagged teeth with old veneers were replaced with newer, smaller pearly white veneers.

"Do you think Darren will recognise me?" she asked, turning to Minnie.

Minnie shook her head no. She didn't recognise her own friend before her.

"He will never recognise you. You don't look like the same person I met years ago." Minnie replied.

The woman clapped her hands in glee. She walked over to the dresser to open the draw. She took out a tattered photograph of Tamzin Smythe standing with her family on her wedding day. She went back to the mirror. The woman moved her body to side profile. *Surely, I don't look the same.* She smiled devilishly.

"Where's that bastard hiding?" the woman asked.

"Guy says Brazil but my sources say Argentina. To think, Darren got a fat cheque from the insurance adjusters for nearly £100 million pounds! He has sold the townhouse. He's on compassionate leave from his team." Minnie elaborated.

"Dr. Burton, when will I be ready for travel?" the woman turned to Dr. Burton. He was placing bandages in the garbage.

"Whenever you're ready, Ms. Townsend." Dr. Burton replied. "I'll leave you two now." he added, washing his hands in a nearby sink.

Dr. Burton said goodbye to Minnie and told Ms. Townsend he'd check on her in the morning at a more reasonable hour.

"Rebecca, are you sure you want to go through with this plan? You've got a new body and face; why not use it to your advantage? Find yourself a new target." Minnie asked, standing next to Rebecca who was still admiring her newly created body. *It's like Frankenstein's bride, but beautiful and appealing to the eye*, thought Minnie. "And what about Guy?" she added.

"Guy is too wrapped up in Grace. Besides, revenge is a dish best served hot, not cold like death. Darren Dowling's going to pay for everything he's ever done to me." Rebecca grinned. She spun on her heels one more time in her nakedness.

"Let's celebrate." Rebecca said putting on her silk robe.

Minnie watched Rebecca sauntering over to an ice bucket filled with ice and Krug champagne chilling. Minnie grabbed two flutes. Rebecca popped open the bottle and the women squealed with joy. They held their filled champagne flutes ready to toast.

"To Tamzin." Rebecca said.

"Tamzin." Minnie replied, clinking the two glasses together and drinking happily.

♥

Halfway around the world the sun was setting over Buenos Aires. In a dirty bar, Darren rolled two bullets in his palms. They were Tamzin's. He had paid Dr. Khan a handsome sum of money to retrieve the metal remains and not hand them over to the police. He managed to smuggle them out of the country and he wasn't going to let go of the only reminder he had of that bitch's death. He swirled the last of his rum and coke in a small glass. He drank and thought about her.

It was the look Tamzin gave before Trevor shot her. It was a taunting look, like *'Do it! Do it now!'* Even though Darren was on the floor bleeding to death, he noticed that she was egging Trevor on, berating him as if Trevor wasn't man enough to pull the trigger. He wondered if she was the one who had planned it all. *Why did she allow this to happen? I hope she is watching from her seat in hell, grimacing that she died instead of me and I walked away with all the loot.*

Darren knew deep down that if her soul was truly looking on she'd be seething at what he'd done to her ashes. He thought a proper disposal of Tamzin's ashes were to be in a bin. So he quietly dumped them in a bin, behind a pub in Manor House, which he felt was a better send off and what she deserved.

On his way to Buenos Aires in duty free shopping Darren managed to buy a green shirt in Spanish that said *Karma's a Bitch*. He chuckled in silence at the shirt now. He wore it once on the fly and never wore it again.

As he continued to roll the spent rivets in his hand he did feel slightly awful in lying to Guy that he was going to Rio. *It isn't far off from the truth*, he thought. He knew that the media was hounding him and that Scotland Yard was watching him like a hawk. He didn't want Guy to let it slip or tell them of his whereabouts. He wanted peace and quiet, away from brooding eyes and wagging tongues. Buenos Aires provided it all as the perfect getaway.

A tan hand came down on the table, placing a bill. Darren looked up to see a young girl standing there, retracting her hand back on her hip and another holding on to her black serving tray.

"Will that be all?" she asked in Spanish. "We're closing in a few minutes for a private party." she added.

"Yes. I'd love to have your name and number. I want to take you back to my room to fuck you." he replied in English.

The girl shook her head, unable to understand and thankfully she didn't. It was his luck. He immediately regretted saying the words. His brother's voice echoed in his ears 'You need to change.' He needed to live his life without women and recover from his vices even though £100 million pounds was sitting in his bank account waiting to burn.

"Si, si." Darren replied in Spanish. He placed his glass on the table. He left an ample tip for her and tipped his hat to her as he got up to leave.

♥

thirty

It was the right place and just perfect. Grace had finally found the home they wanted to buy just a fortnight shy of their wedding date. It wasn't where they thought of looking. Guy persisted, even though it was quite far from London.

He assured her that they still had the penthouse flat and that her second shop would do exceptionally well here. She was still unsure as she meandered through the twenty rooms of the small manor. She stopped by the kitchen window and took a long look at the breathtaking views of snow covered mountains knowing full well that just beyond those hills is Ivy-upon-Wye.

The estate agent was beside herself as she showed Grace the manor outside of another small village, Hay-on-Wye. She had read all about the couple in Rumour Mill. She couldn't believe her luck when she got the call from Grace saying that she was interested in Swan Manor.

It was a rundown manor home that a wealthy elderly couple needed to get rid of in order to pay for their new home in Jersey. There were no children or close relatives to leave the property to and the expense of inheritance tax had made them leery.

"They'll entertain all offers." the estate agent said. "A bit of Farrow and Ball paint here and there, some wallpaper there and new classic furniture. A woman's touch will bring this estate back to its glory day." she added, making the home alluring.

The floral wallpaper was peeling, the floorboards creaked and there was a smell of musty dampness. Guy looked through cupboards and turned on the taps checking the plumbing.

"What do you think?" he asked her.

It does need a lot of work, she thought. She did love the place. It was on thirty acres of land with a small pond that had an inlet to the River Wye. The estate agent explained to them that the pond attracted many swans, christening the estate its name. They were informed of a three-bedroom groundskeeper cottage on the ground that came with the price of the manor and land.

"Will it be ready by the baby's birth?" she asked.

"My mate said that he'll have a majority of it done before we move in. Some rooms must be left to chance. The electrical and plumbing will definitely be updated." he assured.

"Okay! Let's do it." she said happily.

The estate agent looked bug eyed. She couldn't believe it. The manor house had spent a year on the market and not a single bite from prospects. She was even more flummoxed when Guy said he would pay the full asking price in cash and wanted to close within a fortnight. She managed to get the couple on the telephone. They gladly accepted the offer whilst Grace and Guy continued to wander through the house. Once she was done with the couple, another call came through regarding a commercial property that Grace was interested in for her second shop.

"Ms. Knowles, I've got the owner of the small shop in Hereford available to show you the property for Delicious on the mobile. Would you like to see this property today as well?" the estate agent asked, holding her hand over her Nokia.

"Yes, please." she said. "Is this fine?" Grace turned to Guy.

"Go! I'll see you in Hereford in a bit. I have some work to do first. I want to look around the estate and jot some notes." he lied.

He hated lying to her, but he had to for her sake and sanity. He had no intentions on jotting down notes about the repairs needed and design ideas in his mind. He knew how close he was to Ivy and Guy's only interest was meeting with Cat for conversation.

She kissed him goodbye and got in the agents silver Audi A3. She waved him off. Guy hurried back inside to retrieve his hat and keys to his new Land Rover.

♥

Ivy-upon-Wye looked like a storybook winter wonderland as Guy drove over the stone bridge through the narrow cobbled streets towards The Savoury Plum. The town square evergreen tree was decorated as a Christmas tree and the large clock tower had a bright red bow around it. The village was filled with tourists and folk alike all shopping at the Saturday outdoor market, buying anything ranging from Christmas trinkets or gifts to freshly killed fat goose for Christmas dinner.

Guy didn't think he'd find a parking spot. As if by miracle a spot in front of the restaurant was available. He drew his breath. Guy was worried that he would be kicked out of the Plum before he had an opportunity to plead that the stalemate between Grace and Cat must end.

The Savoury Plum was filled with customers. They were enjoying scrumptious mugs of hot frothy chocolate topped with peppermint whip crème. Corrie didn't recognise Guy when he ordered his mug of chocolate. She gasped in surprise when Guy handed her coins. He wore a cap, a thick cable knit cardigan style sweater and a large knotted over plaid scarf.

"Is Grace here?" she asked, not saying his name. Corrie was aware that if she did mention his name it might start a riot as his previous appearance had done. This season, he played better than his last, and his fan base increased ten-fold.

"No. She's in Hereford looking at some shops." he replied, taking his mug of chocolate.

"Why are you here? Is she OK?" she asked, motioning him to the side. "Laura, please take over for me." She took off her apron and handing it to the young counter girl.

"I came on my own. I came to see Cat."

Her stance changed. She took on the demeanour of a stressed person. Corrie twisted her hands in nervousness.

"Please, I have to see her." he begged.

"Cat's ill. She has the flu and is resting upstairs in the flat." she lied. He could tell that she was lying. He threw her a fireball of a look that told Corrie he didn't believe her.

"Okay, she's not sick, but she will be if this thing between them continues. I don't know what you'll tell her to convince Cat that you're the man for Grace. I hope whatever you've planned will work in the long run. Cat's been crying for days knowing that Christmas is approaching and Grace will soon be married to you. She's heartbroken and devastated that she's allowed it to get this bad." she admitted glumly.

"Let me see her. I have something I would like to give you both." he said, holding out a manila envelope.

"Come along now. I can't be responsible if the woman stabs you with a butcher knife." she joked. He blanched as he was aware of the story regarding Ian and the rifle.

Corrie opened the door that led to the stairs of the flat. Each step he took to the flat made Guy feel as if he was walking towards the guillotine. They walked into the flat and up another set of steps into the large living area where Cat sat on the couch, red eyed and unkempt. She was watching the Saturday afternoon movie.

"What are you doing here?" she asked, looking up and in annoyance. "Get out!"

"I'm not leaving." he said. His feet were planted firmly to the ground like roots on a tree. "We have a matter to discuss and that matter is Grace." His voice was strong and his back went rigid.

Corrie took the mug from his hand. Cat sat straight up, not moving her position from the couch.

"Is Grace well?" she grumbled.

"She's fine, and the baby is fine. We're all doing well." he replied.

"Then what do you want? You've already stolen her from us." she spat vehemently.

"I didn't do such a thing, Ms. Fielding. I came here because Grace only asked for one thing for Christmas and that was her family back. Her family means you and Corrie. She loves you to bits and she loves me as well. We love each other dearly and if I didn't, then I would've stopped pursuing her as soon as the wedding ended. Cat, you can't ask someone you consider as a daughter to make sacrifices for the sake of your own love and respect. It's selfish to her and to you." he stated. Cat looked away shamefully.

"I came here to extend my apologies. I apologise for putting Grace in danger, and I apologise for all that's happened. I know you blame me, and blame me if you must. It's not going to stop Grace and me from marrying or having this child. She really would love to have you both at her wedding. It's a very simple beach wedding in the Maldives. The only witness will be my sister, Amanda Priestly. Alistair and Philippe told Grace they're unable to attend the wedding but they'll be there as a surprise. Grace considers you both as mums. It'd truly be a shame and your loss if you weren't to attend. I'll leave the matter in your hands." he said.

Cat held back her tears. She vowed that she wasn't going to cry. She watched Guy give Corrie the manila envelope he held under his arm.

"By the way, today we purchased a manor several miles away. Grace wanted the baby to grow up near family. She didn't want you to miss out on this baby's life." he added.

Cat nodded. She watched Guy turn around. He muttered Happy Christmas to them before leaving their flat. Guy didn't expect a reply from them. Once he was gone, Corrie opened the envelope, pulling out some papers along with Christmas paper-wrapped gift. She gave the gift to Cat whilst she looked at the papers. She gasped in shock and brought her hand to her mouth. It was two reserved seats on a private jet to the Maldives for Grace's wedding.

"What is it Corrie?" Cat questioned.

"An all expenses paid roundtrip to the Maldives including meals!" she exclaimed, reaching further into the envelope and pulling out twenty fifty pound notes. "Spending money too!"

Cat unwrapped the gift. She withdrew a closed silver picture frame. She opened it. Inside were two pictures one of Cat and the other of Corrie, both with Grace age three years old in their laps shortly after she had arrived in Ivy. It was inscribed with *My Two Mums*. She realised that Grace had bought this gift and didn't know whether or not she should give it to them. Guy took it upon himself to deliver it.

"What are you going to do Cat?" Corrie asked, shaking her head. She was excited. Regardless of what Cat thought Corrie was going on this trip and leaving Cat's grumpy arse behind if she could not find it in her heart to move forward.

"I...don't...know." Cat stammered, shrinking back into the couch.

♥

Guy drove to Hereford. He met Grace at the commercial property. Grace negotiated the terms and conditions of the commercial lease with the property owner. The owner was willing to oblige many of Grace's requests as long as she leased for five years.

Finally negotiations were agreed upon between Grace and the owner. The contract signed by Grace allowed her to take over the location as soon as possible. The fit out of this new location was to be completed within twelve weeks. She hoped for a grand opening for spring. Guy told her of his concerns as the baby was due in April, but Grace assured him that she had a chef and manager in mind who was looking to relocate to Hereford as it was their home town.

"As long as you're happy." he replied.

"Everything OK with the house?"she asked.

"I have lots to do and a growing list tall as the hills." Guy replied kissing her. He prayed that he had gotten through to Cat and Corrie.

♥

epilogue

ew Year's morning, they laid in bed overlooking a white sandy beach that ran the perimeter of their Four Seasons Kuda Huraa bungalow. Grace's body glistened in post sex glow. She was wrapped in light white Egyptian sheets as Guy sat naked massaging Grace's feet. They stared at the crystal clear ocean literally inches away from their patio door.

"Are you enjoying all of this, Grace?" Guy asked rubbing her feet delicately.

"MMMM..." Grace replied, her eyes half-open. "I love it. I could stay here forever."

They wished they could stay like this forever. Everything they both ever wanted was here. Guy got the woman he truly loved and Grace got her man. In addition to each other, she received her wish on her wedding, and recalling the day, she smiled.

Yesterday, she couldn't believe how soft beach sand felt between her toes. It was the texture of confectioner's sugar and almost as white. It was a beautiful glorious day, not a single cloud for hundreds of miles around. The sky and the sea were the same colour of cerulean, and one couldn't tell where they met.

Grace wore a long flowing white maxi halter sun dress. Her hair was done in beach combed tresses; the only makeup she wore was Nars crème blush and lip-gloss. She clutched a small bouquet of fresh tropical flowers with glee. Then she heard the melodic sounds of the band playing a sonnet of *Four Seasons* by Vivaldi.

As she turned a corner to make her way down the aisle towards the arch of native flowers to where Guy waited, dressed in his pale blue seersucker suit, she gasped in stunned happiness. There stood Alistair and Philippe alongside Amanda Priestly and Guy. *Alistair and Philippe said they wouldn't be able to attend. It seems they changed their minds.* Suddenly she heard two voices shouting and the band stopped playing.

"Don't start the wedding without us!" She turned her body to look behind her, and there was Cat trying to run in heels in the sand. It wasn't working. Cat was hopping on one foot trying to get the other shoe off.

"I told you not to wear heels!" Corrie screamed.

Grace heard laughter coming from Guy and the small group of family, watching the scene unfolding before them. The twins reached Grace panting and holding their knees.

"Grace..." Cat said trying to catch her breath. "I'm sorry for all that I've done. It was foolish of me to think you'd stay young forever and never marry. I realise how selfish I was."

"Thank you." she replied, hugging Cat. She didn't want to cry and ruin her makeup.

"Are we going to start?" Guy shouted out.

The women near tears all nodded. Corrie dragged Cat out of Grace's arms, and made their way down to the waiting others. The band strummed up again and Grace made her way down the sandy aisle.

The ceremony was quick, but very personal. It brought tears of joy to everyone's eyes as Guy revealed his undying love for Grace. Grace spoke of how Guy was her rock, her everything and through the face of adversity, her hero, and for that she loved him.

As they were about to exchange rings, Guy knew Grace had wanted to wait until after the baby was born for her to wear her wedding ring. Instead, Guy pulled a gorgeous white gold bracelet with pave diamonds and two letters G entwined out from a Graff box. It matched her necklace. He clasped it around her wrist.

Grace gave him a gorgeous Rolex white gold Sky-dweller watch with the inscription: *We have all the time in the world, love*

Grace. They sealed their vows with a single kiss. The group all clapped happily receiving the couple.

For the reception on the beach, they ate a late afternoon dinner of goat cheese and duck prosciutto, pumpkin tortelli; shallot baked white snapper followed by espresso and prosecco granite. Instead of wedding cake for dessert, they insisted on the Chef's take of English trifle filled with layers of different fruit mousses, Victoria sponge cake doused with top-shelf Sherry, and finished with whipped cream.

Everyone licked their lips in delight and marvelled at the whole occasion. They laughed over childhood stories of the couple and talked about the impending arrival of the baby.

"Do you know the sex of the baby?" Amanda chirped.

"Yes we do." Guy answered. "It's a girl."

The group went wild and they all congratulated them on their baby girl. They couldn't wait till spring for the arrival of Poppy Jane Rowling.

The knock on their bungalow door brought Grace out of her trance. Guy rose from the bed. He dressed in his terry cloth robe. Guy answered the door. It was a member of staff carrying a FedEx package for Guy and Grace. Guy was baffled. He tipped the staff member for delivering the box and closing the door behind him.

"Who's it from?" Grace asked, sitting up in the four post bed.

"I don't know." Guy replied, tearing it open.

Guy pulled out its contents and saw a small cake box with a note attached to it. He sat on the bed next to her and read the note aloud. *To Grace and Guy, here is a small token of your love. It's the cake that started it all.'*

He opened the box. Inside was a slice of the red velvet cake Grace made for the Dowling-Smythe wedding. It was a piece of cake traditionally reserved for the first wedding anniversary.

"What an odd gift and no name included on the note!" Guy said scratching his head.

"Throw it away." Grace replied, leaning up to kiss him.

Pregnancy made her horny, and she cared less about the cake that started it all. She wanted Guy and she wanted him now.

He tossed the cake on the floor and went in to kiss Grace, their tongues touching as they fell back. She tasted so sweet from the fresh fruit juice that she just drank.

"I love you, Guy." Grace mewled as his hands began to roam her naked body.

"I love you, Grace... always and forever. Nothing will ever tear us apart." Guy replied in her ear as he nibbled her shoulders.

To Grace, the words he spoke were *delicious*.

♥